ABIGAIL'S NEW HOPE

MARY ELLIS

HARVEST HOUSE PUBLISHERS

EUGENE, OREGON

Scripture verses are taken from the *Holy Bible,* New Living Translation, copyright © 1996, 2004. Used by permission of Tyndale House Publishers, Inc., Wheaton, IL 60189 USA. All rights reserved.

Cover by Garborg Design Works, Savage, Minnesota

Cover photos © Chris Garborg

ABIGAIL'S NEW HOPE
Copyright © 2011 by Mary Ellis
Published by Harvest House Publishers
Eugene, Oregon 97402

ISBN 978-1-61129-671-6

Printed in the United States of America

*To the dedicated women who serve as midwives
to the Amish and Mennonite communities.*

May all your deliveries run smooth as silk.

Acknowledgments

Thanks to Carol Lee Shevlin, who introduced me to the New Bedford Care Center in Fresno, Ohio, a nonprofit birthing center owned and operated by local Mennonite and Amish communities.

A special thank-you to the fine officers of the Wayne County Sheriff's Office, for answering my endless questions about department procedures and their jail facility.

Thanks also to Mrs. Sue Jarvis and the other dedicated men and women working with Jail Ministries, who bring hope, faith, and the Word of God to those incarcerated.

Thanks to Patricia Daly Marconi for her wonderful inspiration.

Thanks to my agent, Mary Sue Seymour, who had faith in me from the beginning, and to my lovely proofreader, Mrs. Joycelyn Sullivan.

Finally, thanks to my editor, Kim Moore, and the wonderful staff at Harvest House Publishers.

And thanks be to God—all things in this world are by His hand.

One

June

Come help us, *mamm*!" The excited voice of six-year-old Laura floated across the lawn. Abby grinned, watching her daughter and four-year-old son, Jake, chase lightning bugs through the grass with jelly jars in hand. Despite the industrious efforts of the *kinner*, the fireflies successfully evaded capture to blink and glow another night.

"Why are you two off the porch? You both were already washed for bed." Abby walked back from the barn with her palms perched on her hips.

She glanced up as a squeak from the screen door signaled the arrival of the final Graber family member, her *ehemann* of ten years. "I thought you were reading them a story," she said with a sly smile.

Daniel slicked a hand through his thick hair, his hat nowhere in sight. Then he braced calloused palms against the porch rail. "Relax, wife. That grass looks pretty clean from where I'm standing. You won't have to start from scratch. Didn't it rain just the other day?" His smile deepened the lines around his eyes. With the setting sun glinting off his sun-burnished nose, he looked as mischievous as one of their children.

Abby watched the warm summer night unfold around her family with no desire to scold. The young ones would have the rest of their lives to have perfectly clean feet, but the summers of childhood were numbered. Besides, it was too nice an evening for anyone to go to bed on time. Walking up the porch steps, she stepped easily into Daniel's strong arms and rested her head against his shoulder. Within his embrace, and with her two healthy offspring darting about like honeybees in spring clover, she savored the almost-longest day of the year.

Swifts and swallows made their final canvass above the meadow before settling for the night in barn rafter nests or in the hollows of dead trees. Upon their exit from the sky, bats would take their place, swooping and soaring on wind currents, gobbling pesky mosquitoes. The breeze, scented with the last of the lilacs and the first of the honeysuckle, felt cool on her overheated skin.

"Everything all charged up for the night?" he asked close to her ear.

Daniel's question, the same one he asked nearly every night since she'd become a midwife, broke the idyllic trance she had wandered into—the all's-well-with-the-world feeling one gets after a satisfying day. "*Jah,*" she murmured. "I ran the generator long enough to charge my battery packs. And I put a fresh battery in my cell phone for tonight, but I don't expect any middle-of-the-night calls. After yesterday's delivery, no babies are expected for several weeks."

"Hmm," he concluded, nuzzling the top of her head. "We both know how well babies stick to doctors' timetables. I'm fixing a cup of tea and heading upstairs. Yours will be cooling on the table for whenever you're ready." He brushed his lips across the top of her *kapp* before going inside, the screen door slamming behind him.

The nice thing about being married for ten years is that a person gets to know someone very well. Daniel Graber knew she enjoyed her beverages at room temperature—not too hot and not too cold. And she knew he needed to take mental inventory before going to bed to make sure the family's ducks were all in a row. So she didn't mind being asked about her cell phone charger each evening.

After all, a midwife, even an Amish midwife, needed to be accessible twenty-four hours a day. The *Ordnung,* or rules that governed their Old Order district, didn't stipulate how Amish wives had their babies. A woman could have an obstetrician deliver at an English hospital, or she could go to a birthing center where a specially trained, certified nurse-midwife would bring her baby into the world. But many Old Order Amish preferred to have their babies at home, the center of their rural lives. Unlike their English counterparts, they usually continued to work during labor—washing dishes, picking beans in the garden, even giving the porch rocker a fresh coat of paint—until the baby made its grand entrance.

At thirty, Abigail Graber was an experienced midwife, having assisted the local physician or nurse-midwife in hundreds of deliveries. She'd received training and apprenticed with a nurse-midwife for several years, but she'd never set foot in college because she was Amish like her patients. And though her time-honored vocation allowed Abigail to witness the miracle of creation firsthand, even without advanced education she understood how quickly things could go wrong for either mother or child.

Ohio and Pennsylvania, the two states with the highest population of Amish families, didn't license midwives who weren't registered nurses under current guidelines. Therefore, Abby's duties generally involved preparing the mother—and the father—for the baby's arrival. She would give the women back massages to loosen tight muscles or have them soak in warm tubs to speed the delivery. Because their rural doctor refused to sit around people's kitchens waiting for babies to be born, Abigail would monitor the mother's contractions to keep him informed. Abby loved the waiting time while fathers debated possible names and mothers crocheted last-minute socks. Dr. Weller would usually arrive just in time to deliver the infant, and then he returned to his office patients or his own warm bed. Abby would remain to wash the new mother, bathe the infant in the kitchen sink, and finish the paperwork at the table. She never left a home until the newborn was comfortably nursing at the mother's breast.

Home births were solely for healthy women with low-risk pregnancies and not for women with diabetes, high blood pressure, heart disease, or if a previous birth had been difficult. Patients were to receive regular prenatal care in the doctor's office to monitor their medical condition and the baby's development. For that reason, Abby knew none of the doctor's patients was due any time soon. But, as Daniel aptly pointed out, babies didn't listen very well.

And God often had other plans when a woman grew too comfortable, too placid in the sheer flawlessness of her life. On that June evening, as her own two healthy children scrambled up the steps to bed, their feet surprisingly clean, Abby almost felt smug in her contentment. She rocked in the porch swing, sipping tea and contemplating the planet Venus as it sat low and bright on the horizon.

The ring of her cell phone jarred her senses. "Hello. Graber residence."

"Abigail Graber?" asked an unfamiliar voice. "This is Nathan Fisher. Ruth and I rented the Levi Yoder place here in Shreve after the elder Mr. Yoder passed on. I'm calling you from the neighbor's house."

Silence ensued as Abby wracked her brain. Fisher was a very common name, but she didn't recall meeting someone named Ruth Fisher in Dr. Weller's office. "What can I do for you, Mr. Fisher?" She finished her tea in one long swallow.

"My wife wants you to come see her. She said that I should call you and nobody else. She got your number from one of the gals in our district."

Abby frowned, feeling annoyance take hold. Her Plain brethren maintained the old-fashioned habit of never referring to a pregnancy directly, as though babies arrived under blessed but unknown circumstances. "I take it your wife is expecting a *boppli*? She needs to contact the doctor's office for an appointment and then be examined by him before—"

"No, you need to come over right now. She's crying out and is in a lot of pain."

Abby's annoyance changed to fear. "Are you saying your wife is in labor right *now*?" She tried unsuccessfully to keep her voice calm as she paced the porch. No sense in waking the rest of the family. Her *kinner* had probably just fallen asleep.

"*Jah,* she is." His three succinct words conveyed none of the same apprehension that tightened her stomach into a knot.

"Who has she been seeing? Who is her doctor?"

"Nobody. She saw a lady doctor back in Indiana, but then we moved here so I could find work. She heard at preaching service that the doctor who makes house calls in these parts was a man." Nathan Fisher stated these facts conversationally.

Abby's knuckles went white from gripping the porch rail. "There are plenty of *lady* doctors at the clinic in Wooster, plus they have a van that would pick your wife up and bring her home afterward for a nominal charge." Daniel slipped out the door behind her and put a reassuring arm around her shoulders.

"I'll debate what my wife should or shouldn't have done with you another day, Mrs. Graber, but right now she is having a baby."

Despite the joyous connotation those last five words usually contained, Abby's gut clenched with dread. "I want you to call an ambulance, Mr. Fisher. Or, if you prefer, I'd be happy to call one for you."

"My wife said she won't go to a hospital, so don't call any ambulance." His tone brooked no further discussion on the matter. "If you don't want to help us, then don't come. But you have no right telling us our business."

Abby breathed in and out several times as though she were in labor, but it took her no time whatsoever to make up her mind. "Give me your address and specific directions on how to find your house." She stumbled back inside the kitchen for pencil and paper. Despite having lived in Wayne County her entire life, she didn't know the whereabouts of the Levi Yoder farm.

Nathan spoke slowly while Abby scribbled notes on the pad. He recited a complete description of road landmarks to find his farm. "So you'll come?"

"*Jah*, I'll be there as soon as possible. Go back and tend to your wife. Do everything she tells you to do, and don't be afraid."

"I'm not afraid, Mrs. Graber." Nathan's voice lifted with renewed excitement. "Even though this will be our first baby. *Danki* very much." He hung up without another word.

Her first pregnancy, and she's probably had no prenatal care, Abby thought. She sent up a silent prayer.

"I'll hitch up your buggy while you gather your supplies." Daniel had followed her back into the kitchen and leaned against the sink with his arms crossed over his chest. "Don't worry, Abby. It's probably not as bad as it sounds. You know how green most first-timers are, especially if the woman doesn't have her *mamm* and sisters living nearby to give advice."

"It sounds as though they just moved here from Indiana." Abby covered her face with her hands and rubbed away her sleepiness, and then she headed to the sink to wash. She would scrub her hands, arms, and under her nails for five minutes, even though she would do it again once she arrived at the Fisher home.

"Do you want me to come with you?" Daniel asked. "We could take Laura and Jake along and they can sleep in the back of the buggy."

His question took her by surprise as she collected supplies and checked the first aid kit for things she might need. Daniel never offered to accompany her. If there was one job he considered "woman's work," this was it.

She emerged from the bathroom and found him where she'd left him, looking even more exhausted. He had been cutting hay that day from sunup until sundown. "Oh, no," she said. "You go up to bed after I leave. Make sure our two little ones are under the covers and not still playing. Tomorrow morning you'll have to get up with the chickens, but I'll be able to sleep in."

He flashed her a smile, and then he loped out the door to hitch up their fastest standardbred horse and attach several battery-powered lights on her open buggy. Abby changed clothes and carried out a case of bottled water along with her medical supplies.

After she climbed into the buggy, Daniel gave her a quick good night kiss and then sent her off with his usual jest. "Let's hope it's either a girl or a boy this time." He slapped the mare's hindquarter to get her moving.

Abby waved before tightening her grip on the reins. It was a silly thing to say, but Daniel's joke never failed to bring a smile to her face.

It would be the last happy expression she would wear that night... or for many nights to come.

During the four-mile drive, she punched in the doctor's speed dial button on her phone. Typically at ten o'clock at night his answering service would pick up. This time was no exception. "Doctor Gerald Weller's answering service," came a perfunctory voice after the third ring.

"Janice? This is Abigail Graber over in Shreve. I'm on my way to the Nathan Fisher residence. Mrs. Fisher is in labor. I don't think she's a patient of the doctor's. At least I know I've never met her. She might not be a patient of anyone." Just voicing those words sent a chill up the midwife's back. Most of the things that can go wrong during delivery could be avoided if the medical history of the woman was known and the baby's development had been tracked. "Apparently, they just moved here from out of state. Please ask Dr. Weller to meet me there. Tell him I'm sorry to get him up if he's already gone to bed—"

The woman on the other end cut her short. "He's not home, Abby. He was called down to Ashland. There was a multicar pileup on the interstate. Fortunately, no fatalities have been reported, but a tanker of chemicals overturned and dumped its contents. Ashland asked for all medical personnel in the surrounding area to treat possible respiratory distress from toxic exposure. He will be tied up in that mess at the emergency room all night. You'll have to call the paramedics for Mrs. Fisher."

"That's what I plan to do." Despite the cool evening breeze, Abby's back began to perspire. "Their farm is in sight. Let me give you the address and directions of where I'll be in case something changes with Dr. Weller." She recited the exact description Nathan had provided as her mare trotted up the loose-stoned driveway.

The Levi Yoder farmstead was one of the few that didn't conform to the usual standard of Amish orderliness, but probably not from lack of trying on the part of the young couple. After a certain number of years, paint and caulk cannot repair old, dry-rotted wood or crumbling foundations. However, she wasn't here to take photographs for *Country Living* magazine. She had a job to do.

As the buggy rolled to a stop and she set the brake, Nathan Fisher came running from the house. He bounded down the sagging steps and grabbed her horse's bridle. "Please go on inside. I'll tend to your horse. My wife's hurting real bad."

Even before she heard the ominous words his blanched complexion terrified Abby. "Just turn my mare out into your paddock and don't fuss with her because I might need you. And bring in the case of bottled water when you come." She hefted her bag of supplies out of the buggy and ran to the house.

Abby set the bag on the table and punched 9-1-1 into her cell phone. When the dispatcher came on the line, she identified herself, gave the address and explicit directions, and stated that a woman in labor needed an ambulance. Her hands shook as she held the phone next to her ear. If the situation beyond the closed door turned out to be anything less than an emergency, she would take the blame for the call. The dispatcher repeated the information, stated that an ambulance was on the way, and, blessedly, allowed her to hang up instead of keeping her tied up with unnecessary details. The dispatcher offered no approximation of the estimated time of arrival. Next, Abby scrubbed her hands and arms at the sink as quickly and thoroughly as possible.

Drying her hands on a paper towel, she glanced around the Fisher kitchen. Vandals wreaking mischief or a storybook cyclone usually caused such havoc. Cupboards stood open, water had been spilled between the sink and the stove, soiled linens lay in a heap near the steps to the cellar, and someone had knocked over a box of Cheerios across the counter. Never had she seen spilled food in an Amish home that hadn't immediately been cleaned up.

For a moment her eyes locked on the cereal with bizarre fascination. Then the piercing wail of a woman broke her paralysis, and she grabbed her bag and ran in the direction of the sobs. Inside the bedroom she found a woman in advanced stages of labor. Sweat ran down the woman's nose and cheeks like spring rain. The room, hot and airless, held the coppery sweet scent of blood.

"I'm the midwife, Abigail Graber. What's your given name, Mrs. Fisher?" she asked, trying to engage the woman in conversation.

The woman's complexion was the color of skim milk, her *kapp* was on the floor, and her damp hair clung to her scalp like a helmet. "Ruth," she managed to say between clenched teeth.

"I called the doctor, but he's at an emergency in Ashland, so then I called the paramedics—no arguments. I'm not licensed to deliver babies by my lonesome." While Abby rattled on, she pulled off the quilts and sheets that were covering Mrs. Fisher, as though keeping her warm was of chief importance. Once Abby had stripped off the layers down to the woman's nightgown, her words and breath froze in her throat.

There was a lot of blood—too much. It pooled on the sodden sheet, trapped by the protective plastic sheeting Ruth probably placed atop the mattress cover when her labor first began.

Ruth dug her fingernails into the bed with the next contraction, while Abby sped back to the kitchen, pressing the redial button on her cell phone.

Nathan Fisher was just walking into the kitchen carrying the bottled water. She thrust the phone toward him. "When they answer, tell them we need that ambulance *right now.* Give them the address again and tell them that your wife is hemorrhaging. Then bring the phone back into the bedroom."

"Will do," he said with a shaky voice. All color drained from his face. He dropped the case on the counter and grabbed for her phone.

Abby ran back to the bedroom. Ruth lay back against the pillows.

Her dark eyes seemed to have sunk lower in her pale face. "I'm going to examine you now," Abby said, forcing a pleasant smile. "We need to deliver this baby sooner rather than later." She went about her routine—one used hundreds of times—and tried to maintain professional control. Panicking this woman further would serve no purpose.

Despite the feigned attempt at reassurance, Ruth Fisher had not been fooled. After Abby checked to make sure the baby wasn't in a breech position, Ruth grabbed her arm. "Save my baby. Don't worry about me." Her words were little more than a hoarse whisper. "This was my choice and I have no regrets. But save my baby so it wasn't all for naught."

This was no time to decipher cryptic messages. If the placenta tore away from the uterine wall in just the right place at just the right time, a woman could lose enough blood within fifteen minutes to die. Abby believed that was what was happening. Anxiety constricted her chest so that her breathing was almost as difficult as Ruth's. "This baby must come now, Ruth, so I want you to push with all your might."

She did as she was told, somehow mustering enough energy to send the infant into the world. Abby caught the baby and lifted him away from the sodden sheets. Miraculously, he breathed on his own and squalled with strong lungs the moment she cleaned the mucus from his nose and mouth. "A healthy baby boy, Ruth. You have a son."

Abby held the boy where Ruth could see, and for a fleeting moment a smile flickered across the woman's face. Then her complexion blanched to the color of ash, and she lapsed into unconsciousness. There was no request to cradle her son or comments about his size or boisterous cries. Ruth's breathing grew thin and raspy while her blood continued to pool.

Wrapping a receiving blanket around the infant, she passed him to Nathan, who stood helplessly in the doorway. "Will my wife be all right?" he gasped.

Abby couldn't meet his gaze. "I'm going to stay with her. You make sure the baby keeps warm. Watch for the ambulance at the front window and holler when you see them pull into the driveway." He hurried away, carrying the baby like a fragile porcelain ornament while Abby returned to Ruth's side.

Without hesitation she pulled out a prefilled syringe from her bag and injected Ruth with a powerful drug to stop hemorrhaging...a drug she wasn't supposed to have. But if anything could save this thin, dark-haired woman's life, it would be the medicine in the syringe, entrusted to her by the retiring nurse-midwife. And then she prayed. She prayed God would save this young woman with every ounce of faith she possessed.

Abby tried everything she could to stem the tide, but God had His own plans for Ruth Fisher and her son—and for Abigail Graber, for that matter. By the time the paramedics arrived ten minutes later, she could no longer discern a pulse or even a wisp of breath. They flew into the room and went to work with clamps, defibrillators, and powerful drugs. One of the paramedics came to the kitchen to check the baby's lungs, heart rate, and airways and pronounced him sound. Then Abby bathed the infant at the kitchen sink and wrapped him in a clean blanket, while Nathan stood by helplessly as the medical personnel exhausted every heroic avenue to save his wife. Finally, a paramedic exited the bedroom with an expression that required few words. "We're sorry, Mr. Fisher. We did everything we could, but she's gone. We're going to call the sheriff's department now."

Nathan looked almost as pale as his wife. "May I sit with her?"

After a moment's hesitation, the paramedic nodded. "Of course. Go on in, sir. We're very sorry for your loss."

Later, Abby sat at the scarred oak table with the new father and filled out the birth certificate. Ruth had selected the name Rachel for a girl and Andrew for a boy, but Nathan said he favored Abraham—the patriarch of the Jewish people. "It is a strong name, and a boy without a *mamm* will need to be strong, so it is fitting," he declared.

Someone from the sheriff's department and the coroner arrived to ask questions and to fill out more paperwork. Abby provided what information she knew about the Fisher situation, which was a hair more than nothing. Nathan, in stupefied shock, answered the deputy's questions using one- or two-word responses. They had to ask him twice if he wished to ride to the hospital with his wife—his late wife—to have the baby examined. At first he refused, but then it occurred to him that the midwife would soon leave, and he would be left alone in the house with a hungry infant. In the end he agreed to ride to the hospital and allow his son to be admitted for observation. Before he left, he wrote down the name and address of his aunt, his closest relative in their new community, and handed it to Abby. She assured him she would explain to her what had happened, and also inform the bishop of his district, because the Fisher farm lay just beyond the boundary line in a different district from hers. Nathan would need help during the coming days and weeks with both his home and with young Abraham.

Abby couldn't have agreed more with his name selection. The seven-pound boy had fought his way into the world with a strong heart and good set of lungs. He might have been born with poor color, showing little enthusiasm to breathe, but Abraham Fisher hadn't needed the paramedic's bag of oxygen. His face had scrunched up and released a howl at birth, and he wailed while being prepared for transport to the hospital. She had expected Nathan to fawn and pat and utter soothing baby talk while the EMTs were hooking up monitors, but he did none of that. The man was in shock, pure and simple. He'd changed from a proud, expectant father to a widower and sole parent within a of couple hours.

Abby washed up, changed into the clean dress she always kept with her supplies, and wrapped her soiled smock to throw on the burn pile back home. Before leaving she swept up the spilled Cheerios so they wouldn't draw ants in Nathan's absence. On legs turned to rubber, she found her horse in the paddock and hitched her to the buggy. Then she drove to visit Nathan's aunt.

Iris Fisher turned out to be a kindly soul—a widow with several grown and married sons. Without hesitation the woman said she would pack a bag and move to Nathan's home to prepare for the baby's return from the hospital. She assured Abby she would stay as long as needed.

"That might be quite some time," Abby said impulsively.

"*Jah,* I suppose so, but he has no one else in the area for family. My sons live with their wives on my farm. They can manage without me while I care for Nathan and his son."

"*Danki,*" said Abby, for lack of something better.

The aunt offered a weak smile. "Thank you, Abigail." Iris walked Abby to the door but caught her arm before she could leave. "Do you know what? I never met Nathan's wife. They moved here several months ago, but she never seemed to be home when I stopped by to visit. Or, at least, that's what he told me. I couldn't attend their wedding in Indiana, so if I ever do meet Ruth Fisher, it will be in the hereafter."

Abby stood in the doorway and blinked twice. She couldn't remember a member of the Plain community ever doubting a person's truthfulness, but she was too tired to consider the matter. She was too tired to think about anything. With a nod and mumbled, "*Gut nacht,*" she left the woman's farm and headed home. It would soon be dawn...the beginning of a new day. For Abraham Fisher, it would be his first day as a child of God, and as a child without a mother. Abby stared mindlessly at the road ahead, praying during the entire drive while her horse found the way on her own. She prayed for the baby and his distraught father and for Iris Fisher. As she prayed, tears filled her eyes and ran unchecked down her cheeks.

Trust in the LORD with all your heart; do not depend on your own understanding. Seek his will in all you do, and he will show you which path to take. As her favorite passage from the book of Proverbs filled her mind, Abby wondered if that's what she had done or if she'd acted on her own.

Save my baby. Don't worry about me. This was my choice and I have no regrets. Ruth's words had etched themselves into her brain like an overexposed photograph. By the time her mare clip-clopped up the driveway, Abby felt physically and emotionally drained.

Daniel had heard the approach of her buggy and left milking his cows to come greet her. With one glance at her face, he grabbed the horse's bridle with a strong hand. "Whoa," he commanded. "What happened?"

She stepped down on wobbly legs and threw herself into his arms, forgetting about her bag of supplies and her clothes for the burn pile. "Oh, Daniel, I did everything I could. I did *more* than I should have, but we lost her...we lost the mother, Mrs. Fisher."

"And the baby? How's the child?"

"The baby is fine, but they waited too long to call an ambulance. I told Nathan Fisher to do so on the phone, but he refused. So I called 9-1-1, but because of the pileup on the interstate, they arrived too late to save her." Gulps and shallow breaths punctuated her words.

He pressed a finger to her lips to stem her rambling. "Easy now. Take a deep breath."

After she complied, gasping and hiccupping, he said, "You go take a hot shower and crawl into bed. You look faint from exhaustion. Anything more you want to tell me can wait until tomorrow...later on today, actually." The pink sun rising over the eastern fields heralded more good weather for Wayne County farmers. Without another word, she allowed herself to be led into the house.

Abby stood under the shower spray until the moist heat relieved her sore muscles and made her so drowsy she fell asleep with a bath towel still wrapped around her wet hair.

And, blessedly, she dreamed of nothing at all.

Two

One would think a person would be well rested after eleven hours of sleep, but Abby awoke tired in both body and spirit. Her back ached as she swung her feet out of the empty bed. Her legs felt heavy and stiff as she padded down the hall to the bathroom.

It wasn't until she was washed and dressed that she thought, *Where are my kinner?* A growing sense of alarm quickly replaced her grogginess. *Why didn't they wake me with their usual morning enthusiasm?* "Jake? Laura? Where are you?" She poured every ounce of her energy into her summons, but the sound merely echoed off the walls of the silent house.

"Daniel!" she called from the kitchen window. Her belly churned with unease. With great relief, she spotted her husband on the path from the livestock barn to the house.

"No need to holler yourself hoarse, *fraa*," he said while still twenty paces off. "All is well. I took them to the neighbor's house for the day so you could get some sleep. Telling those two to stay out of our room

would be like putting a stack of hamburgers on a doghouse and telling the dog 'no.'"

Abby grinned at the mental picture he described, feeling her heart
rate ratchet down to an acceptable level. "*Danki.* I suppose I needed
the rest, but I didn't mean to sleep so long. Have you had your lunch?
What about your breakfast? Surely you're not out there working on an
empty stomach."

Daniel followed her into the kitchen and lit the burner under the
coffeepot. "I know this will surprise you, Abigail, but I can fry up
bacon and eggs and make some ham-and-cheese sandwiches for my
lunch. I only allow you to fuss over me because I *like* it." He winked
at her mischievously. "Sit down. Let's have some coffee. You look like
you could use half the pot."

Abby set the pitcher of milk on the table along with two mugs. She
collected her thoughts while he filled their cups. Then, with as few details as necessary, she told Daniel about the events of the previous night.

He listened without interruption while sipping his coffee. "Do you
think the *boppli* will thrive?" he asked after she finished her tragic story.

"*Jah,* he was a sound baby boy. The paramedic said the baby was
healthy, but he still wanted to admit him at the hospital to make sure
he took to a bottle and formula. Mr. Fisher agreed and rode along in
the ambulance."

Daniel nodded with a sage pull on his beard. "Did the Fishers have
other little ones running around the house?"

"No, this would have been Ruth's first."

"How was the husband faring?"

"He was pretty shaken up. I don't think he understood her labor
was so far along and wasn't going well. He certainly didn't know his
wife was in any danger. At least, he sounded calm on the phone. During the time between talking to me and my arrival, he realized the situation had become dire."

"How did he get your phone number if you've never seen his wife
before?"

"From someone in his district." Abby took a gulp of coffee.

"How come they weren't under a doctor's care?"

She glanced up into his eyes. He was watching her curiously. "I have no idea about that, either."

"Who'll take care of that little one now? Didn't you say they had just moved here to find a place to farm?"

Abby held out her mug and he refilled it to the rim. "*Jah,* but he has an aunt living here in Shreve. So he does have someone to help. I stopped there on my way home to tell her what happened. She said she didn't know that Ruth Fisher was expecting, and she had never even met the woman in person."

Daniel grunted while studying the surface of his cup.

Abby sipped the coffee down so she could add milk and sugar. "I know Amish women never talk about their pregnancies, but I'm a midwife. Nobody wants to mention babies until they're burping on somebody's shoulder and then they can't stop talking about them. But that gal should have been talking to somebody."

"Hmm," he said.

She might be a midwife, but her *ehemann* didn't like discussing women's pregnancies, either.

"Iris Fisher seemed to think Ruth had been hiding from her, not wishing for them to meet face-to-face."

"Why would she hide from her husband's aunt?"

"I have no idea." She leaned back in her chair, feeling not much better even after two cups of coffee.

"Seems like there's more you *don't* know than do, so you probably shouldn't throw your suppositions into this pot of stew."

Abby's head snapped up. "I'm only talking to *you*, Daniel, in the privacy of my own kitchen. I know you'll never carry tales. It's not like I'm gossiping down at the fabric shop." She didn't try to hide her irritation.

"*Jah,* true enough, but this whole mess has me worried. Why didn't Doc Weller come to the farm?"

"He had responded to a hazardous situation in Ashland. They summoned all available medical personnel not on emergency call to treat possible toxic chemical exposure."

"He didn't show up later?"

"No, just the EMTs who transported Mrs. Fisher and the infant. Oh, and then someone from the sheriff's department and the coroner arrived."

"The sheriff's department?" he asked. His dark eyes flashed with apprehension.

"Of course they came. It's standard procedure when there's been a death from unknown causes. Women aren't supposed to die in childbirth." Abby closed her eyes for a moment silently wishing she could have stayed in bed all day with the covers pulled over her head.

"How come Nathan Fisher refused to call an ambulance?"

"He said his wife wouldn't let him. And I don't know why she wouldn't if that's your next question. Maybe she had a bad experience in a hospital at some point in time. Maybe she had an unreasonable fear of doctors. You told me not to muddy the waters with suppositions, yet you keep asking me questions I can't answer." She struggled to her feet to make something to eat. The bitter coffee was churning in her stomach. "All I know is that *I* called the ambulance when I got there, but I think her uterine wall tore during delivery before I arrived. I did everything I could to save her, Daniel."

He suddenly realized how his queries must have sounded. "*Mir leid, fraa,*" he apologized. "I know you did, but you delivering that baby by yourself doesn't bode well."

Abby sighed and bit back her retort. Arguing with Daniel would only make her feel worse. She tucked an apple into her apron pocket. "I'm walking to the neighbors to get Jake and Laura. They are probably wondering what's happened to their *mamm*. How does meatloaf and mashed potatoes sound for supper? I'll pick some fresh spinach with Laura when I get back. There should be enough ready for a salad."

"That sounds good. I need to finish cutting the hayfield before dinner." They walked outside together, and he pulled on heavy work boots while she laced up tennis shoes.

"I burned your clothes, Abby, so they would be done with. It must have been awful. I'm sorry you had to endure that. Maybe it's time for you to stop midwifing. Ohio doesn't seem to be ready to give you a proper license. Let the registered nurse-midwives do the delivering around here."

Abby stopped in midstride. "We've discussed this, Daniel. The nurse-midwives work at the birthing center where they make more money and have far more control over the situation. None of them want to follow Dr. Weller around on his rounds to homes and farms. Yet you know yourself many Amish women refuse to have babies anywhere but at home. At least our community is fortunate to have a physician still willing to make house calls."

"*Jah,* but for how much longer? Weller is getting up there in years."

"We must take life one day at a time. I've been praying for another licensed midwife to come to Shreve, one who is comfortable with Amish ways, and I've been praying some young doctor will find our part of the world simply irresistible and move here." Abby buzzed a kiss across his cheek and marched down the stairs. She was eager to stretch her rubbery legs and even more eager to rest the tired topic. Even though he was Amish, Daniel didn't understand. And surely no one outside their community understood why so many Plain women chose to give birth at home. Debate continued in the legislatures of Ohio and Pennsylvania to license trained midwives who weren't RNs, but resistance remained among other medical professionals. And yesterday's outcome would only increase the opposition. An Amish man or woman would conclude that the Lord chose to call Ruth Fisher home last night, but an *Englischer* might see her death as an avoidable and needless tragedy.

By the time she reached her neighbor's tidy yard, she forced thoughts of last night from her mind. Her children ran toward her from the garden with arms open wide. If she hadn't been ready for their embrace, they would have knocked her down.

"*Mamm,* come look in the barn!" cried Laura.

"New pups," added Jake as Abby lifted him off the ground and settled him against her hip.

"Let's hurry," said Laura, dragging her by the hand.

Her neighbor grinned and waved as she hung laundry on the line. Abby waved back and then followed her daughter into the dimly lit barn, smelling sweet from fresh-cut hay. The newborn spaniel pups tumbled and jostled as they vied for position to nurse from their mother. The cocker mom napped on a blanket-lined bed of straw in one corner of an empty stall. The pups, with eyes barely open, were heartbreakingly adorable.

"Miz Amy says we can look but not touch," whispered Laura. "We're not allowed to pick them up yet."

"That's right," agreed Abby, "they're still too little to be handled much." She knelt down in the stall for a closer look. The new mom seemed sound asleep until Jake bumped the stall wall. Then she eyed him suspiciously. Laura leaned close enough to be counted among the pups.

"Easy, Jake. Back up, Laura," cautioned Abby. "Let's not make the dog nervous by crowding too close." The children scooted back and crossed their legs Indian-style to watch the pups' antics with utter fascination.

"Could we ask Miz Amy if we can have one? They are so cute." Laura's face filled with joy.

"*Jah, mamm,* a pup! A pup!" Jake's enthusiasm managed to surpass his sister's.

"What about Boots? I thought you were fond of her."

"She always stays in the cabin in the woods, and it's been a very long time since old Betsy died," reasoned Laura. "We could use a new watchdog. I just know these will be good ones." Her grin made her dark eyes sparkle.

Abby chuckled at the idea of six months being a very long time in a child's perspective, and also about the idea of a floppy-eared spaniel being a watchdog. But the pups were quickly worming their way into her heart too. "We'll ask your *daed* during dinner, but don't badger him the moment he comes in from the fields. Let him wash up and eat his supper. Then he might be persuaded to take a cocker spaniel, even though he had his heart set on a springer."

"We'll just have to get two kinds of dogs," Laura said with the wisdom of a six-year-old. She gently scratched the dog behind the ears and was rewarded with a lick of her hand.

Abby loved watching the pups clamber over each other and could have stayed all afternoon, but her stomach growled loud enough to be heard. Standing, she brushed straw from her dress and pulled her children to their feet. "I know how you love sticking your fingers in your mouth, so let's wash your hands at the pump. And don't dawdle. We still need to pick spinach for supper."

For the remainder of the day—picking salad ingredients in the garden, fixing dinner, eating with her beloved family, and rocking on the porch swing while Daniel read Scripture aloud—Abby forced thoughts of Ruth Fisher from her mind. God would watch over Nathan and his new son. She let the last of her self-recriminations and doubts float up into the starry sky and again slept soundly.

Nathan had never been so happy to see anyone as he was his aunt when he returned from the hospital two days later. District members had come to the hospital to offer condolences and their help with chores at his farm. His cows had been milked, his chickens fed, and his horses cared for during his absence. Several nearby farmers had even cut his hay. The generosity of his new community touched his heart.

Especially because no one knew him very well.

This would have been a good place for his shy wife if she had lived. But God had other plans for Ruth, and Nathan had been left with a baby needing his *mamm,* not him. *What do I know about taking care of a boppli?* The pediatric nurses had spent several hours teaching him basic infant care and had sent him home with a question-and-answer booklet, but he still didn't feel comfortable holding the tiny child in his big, leathery hands. So when Iris Fisher walked onto his porch, drying her hands with a towel, Nathan breathed a sigh of relief and uttered a prayer of gratitude.

"Aunt Iris," he called, lifting the baby carrier from the hired van. "I'm very glad to see you." The bishop had thoughtfully arranged for a car and driver to bring them home from the hospital.

The middle-aged woman hurried down the steps to meet them. "*Guder nachmittag,* Nathan," she greeted as she peered into the carrier with one hand fisted at her throat. "Welcome home, little Abraham," she said as she peeled back the blue fleece blanket the hospital had provided.

"I have formula, bottles, and diapers, plus whatever else they packed up for me." Nathan looked into his aunt's face, hoping he didn't sound as desperate as he felt.

"With all the diapers and clothing your wife sewed and everything folks in the district dropped off, I would say your son will be set for some time to come. Why don't I take him inside and check his diaper while you carry in the remainder?" She barely waited for a nod of agreement before she took the baby carrier and marched toward the house. As Nathan watched her go, a tremendous wave of relief washed over him.

How would I have managed without her? It was hard enough to face each day without his Ruth, but an Amish man is sorely prepared to care for a *boppli.* "*Danki,* Lord God," he whispered, "*Danki.*" He unloaded the boxes and bags from the van and then reached for his wallet.

"Oh, no, Mr. Fisher. The fare has already been paid by your bishop, including my tip. I'll not take your money." The driver offered his hand, which Nathan shook heartily.

"Thank you for bringing me...us...home." Laden down with supplies, he walked toward the house as the driver hurried after him carrying the largest box of diapers ever made.

"I was mighty sorry to hear about your wife."

Nathan couldn't think of a suitable comment, so he kept walking with his eyes focused on what had been his home for the previous six months.

"Thanks again," he said at the back door. After setting his load down, he pulled the box of diapers from the driver's hands. Once the man had returned to his van and left, Nathan exhaled a sigh of relief and entered the back hall. His kitchen looked nothing like it had two nights ago. The floors, walls, and windows had been washed. Curtains he didn't recognize wafted gently in the warm breeze, while jars of fruit, vegetables, soup, and pickled meats lined the countertop. He supposed Iris had left them out for him to see before packing them away into the cupboards, pantry, and the cellar. The generosity of his neighbors appeared to have no limits. He contemplated looking for Iris and the baby, but an unbearable weariness came over him. He slumped into a chair in the pristine room without enough energy to lift a finger.

Ten minutes later his aunt bustled into the room. "*Ach,* nephew. You look as though you could use a cup of coffee. You probably didn't sleep a wink at the hospital." She lit the propane burner under the pot. "I know I'd like a cup too."

"*Danki* for coming, Aunt Iris. I am in your debt."

"Nonsense. I'm happy to make myself useful. Because my three daughters-in-law turned out to be industrious, I rattle around in the *dawdi haus* all day without enough to do." She winked one of her cornflower blue eyes. "Except when the garden produce comes in or on quilting days, there's not enough work for four women. One of my sons moved me into your guest room, so I will stay as long as you and little Abraham need me." She poured two mugs of coffee and carried them to the table.

"That could be a long while," he said softly, wrapping his fingers around a mug.

"Then so be it. I'll enjoy taking caring of your son, Nathan. My youngest *kinskinner* will start school in the fall, so the house will seem empty. Babies are such a blessing." She stirred two teaspoonfuls of sugar into her coffee.

He slanted her a wry glance, not feeling particularly blessed at the moment.

"They are, nephew. You're in mourning now; that is normal. But someday you'll see what a joy your son is. He's a living reminder of your wife, and she will go on through him."

He stared down at the oak tabletop and held his tongue, fearing he'd say something he'd later regret.

"This was the Lord's will." Her voice sounded soft and gentle.

"I know, and I accept the will of God." He tried to relax his fingers, which had curled into fists.

Iris waited to see if he would say more, but he remained quiet. "What's in your heart?" she asked. "Maybe talking to me would help."

"Yammering about stuff endlessly is the English way, not our way." He sipped his coffee, gripping the mug tight enough to crack porcelain.

"True enough, but holding in anger will eat a hole in an Amish stomach just as easily as an *Englischer*'s. Do you hold the midwife responsible? Is she the one you are mad at?" She studied him over the rim of her cup.

Her question caught him off guard. "Mrs. Graber? No, she's not to blame. She tried her best and did everything she could to save Ruth." Nathan focused on a freshly washed wall, noticing that the calendar displayed the wrong month. He waited, hoping his aunt would change the subject or offer another option besides the truth. But she sat patiently. After a few moments, he met her gaze. "I'm the one to blame. It's my fault Ruth is gone."

"Your fault? Oh, no, it couldn't possibly be—"

He held up a hand to stem her interruption. "Now that you asked, hear me out. Since the day Ruth and I married, I always said things like 'I can't wait until the *bopplin* start coming,' and 'I hope we end up with six girls for you and a half dozen boys for me.'" He grimaced remembering the joyous look on Ruth's face whenever they talked about a large family.

"That was just chatter, Nathan. All couples are filled with big plans and expectations."

"But she knew how much I wanted children, and…I pushed her to see a doctor when things didn't…happen for us right away."

Iris walked to the stove for the coffeepot, mitigating his discomfort from discussing a delicate topic.

"Ruth had found a lady doctor a couple towns away, so I drove her back and forth several times so she could run tests and whatnot. She even wanted to admit Ruth overnight once, but she refused. Ruth was afraid of hospitals. She didn't talk much about those appointments, but that was just her way—she didn't talk a whole lot about anything."

Iris nodded, her lips stretched to a thin line.

Nathan drew in a deep breath before continuing. "I thought the doctor would give her advice on how to…hurry things along." His breath caught, but he fought down the lump that had risen in his throat. "But that doctor told her she shouldn't *ever* get pregnant. That having a baby could jeopardize her life and probably cost the *boppli*'s life as well." His voice broke as emotion welled up against his resolve. "That's what the doctors had told her, but she didn't tell me any of this until afterward."

He lurched to his feet and stumbled to the sink. With the memory of that conversation, his feelings of helplessness and regret flooded back. He stared out the window at fields turning the color of lavender as the sun dropped below the western hills.

"When did your wife finally tell you?"

"After she was already carrying our child." He gripped the edge of the counter so hard his fingers began to cramp. "I would have said forget about *boppli* or we can adopt a child from somewhere. I never would have wanted her to take a chance with her life."

Silently, Iris crept up behind him and patted his back as though he were a child with a broken toy. "Of course you wouldn't have. And that's all the more reason why you can't hold yourself responsible any more than Abby Graber. You didn't know what the doctor had told her until she was already in a family way."

Nathan stared out the window as the evening star rose low in the sky. "She did this for me, Aunt. She sacrificed herself to make me happy."

"She did this because she wanted to have a child. She was willing to take a chance. After all, doctors don't know everything. Only God ultimately decides our fate. We all live and die by His hand."

"I know that, but I just wished she had asked my opinion about the risk. I would have told her that *she* was enough for me. Even without *kinner* we could have had a good life together. I loved her. I loved her so much."

Iris patted his back once more but said nothing. What more was there to say? They could discuss the matter like *Englischers* until the rooster crowed tomorrow, but it wouldn't change a thing.

"Come to your bedroom and see your son. He fell asleep almost the moment I laid him down in the cradle. It was as though he knew that cradle had been carved by his *daed* and the tiny quilt sewed by his *mamm*."

Nathan felt his back turn rigid under the palm of Iris' hand. "*My* bedroom? Why is his bed still in my bedroom? I don't want to sound ungrateful, but you'll be the one feeding and changing him and such. Don't you think the cradle should be next to your bed instead of mine?"

Iris walked around the table to set her mug in the sink. "That's where I found the cradle, so that's where I put him to sleep." Her voice was little more than a whisper.

"When he wakes up, I'll move his bed into your room." Nathan straightened his back and unclenched his hands, willing himself to relax.

"Why don't we go in there now? You could see him and we can move the bed together. I doubt that he'll awaken, but if he does it's almost time for his next feeding."

"No," said Nathan without hesitation. "I saw what he looked like at the hospital. He hasn't changed in the last six hours. I have animals to tend to in the barn. I can't expect my friends and neighbors to do my chores forever. They have enough work of their own." He strode to the door, and then he glanced over his shoulder at his tiny, gray-haired aunt, who couldn't weigh more than a hundred pounds. "*Danki* for the coffee. And I'm obliged to you for also cleaning this place up. I know we left the house in a terrible state that night, and I apologize for that."

Her face seemed to melt, and he thought she might cry. Nathan fled outside as though the house were on fire. He couldn't bear her look of pity and didn't want to be cajoled into standing around a cradle making cooing and clucking noises. Those were things that women did. Right now he wasn't cut out to be somebody's *daed*. How could he look into the sweet face of his son and not see his beloved Ruth staring back?

Tonight he would thank God for his aunt, who had been willing to leave her own family and move in with them. Having raised six children of her own, Iris Fisher knew all there was to know about *kinner*. Abraham would receive the tender loving care he deserved while Nathan could get back to work. If he was going to turn this place into a profitable farm again, it would take all of his energy and attention. A child was something he had desperately wanted with his wife, but now that Ruth was gone an infant became a confusing puzzle—like the first time he tried to use a cell phone. And he was sure he would never be able to look at that baby and not remember what she had given up for his sake.

Nathan hurried to the barn for evening chores. He cleaned stalls, spread fresh straw for bedding, scrubbed out water troughs and feed buckets, and groomed horses until it grew so dark he couldn't see two feet in front of his face. He worked until his back muscles ached and his stomach growled from hunger. But at least when he returned to the house to wash off the dirt and sweat of hard labor the kitchen was empty. A low-burning kerosene lamp cast dancing shadows across the walls. His plate of dinner had been left on the table—four pieces of cold and dried out chicken, fried potatoes in a similar state, and a large serving of pickled beets. Iris had thoughtfully spooned the beets into a separate bowl so the juice didn't stain the rest of his meal. But he could have easily overlooked red-tinted chicken as long as he didn't have to talk to his aunt or anybody else about recent events.

Or about what he planned to do with the rest of his life.

Three

Nathan heard a baby cry in his sleep. The sound had interrupted a pleasant dream in which he had been fishing in a rowboat on their farm pond back in Indiana. He had pulled several bigmouth bass from the water, one after another, while his father leaned back in the stern, watching him in amazement. "Haven't you any bait on your hook?" Nathan had asked his father in the dream.

"*Jah,* I have plenty of worms left," his father had said. "But the fish seem to like your line better today."

The sun had felt hot on his back and shoulders while a cool breeze across the water had kept them comfortable. He couldn't have imagined a more perfect summer day. Nathan remained in bed after realizing he'd been dreaming, burrowing deeper under the covers.

But the crying was real, the sound emanating from the next room. This was the third time the baby had awoken him during the night. Glancing at his windup clock, he punched his pillow and then swung his legs out of bed. He had only fifteen more minutes until his four thirty milking and figured he might as well get up.

As he passed the guest room—now the bedroom of his aunt—he heard soft cooing in an attempt to lull the child back to sleep. A twinge of guilt gripped his heart. *How much sleep will Aunt Iris receive if the* boppli *remains fussy night after night?* But Nathan had few options, considering he had signed a one-year lease on the farm. Because an Amish man kept up his end of a contract, it would be at least eight months before he could move back to Indiana where his *mamm* and sisters lived. They might be able to help with his son, but they couldn't solve the problem of few farms in the area available for lease.

A man needed to work to live. So he and his squalling child would have to stick things out here for the foreseeable future, as long as Iris didn't return to her decidedly quieter home with her own sons.

Nathan dressed and headed to the barn to immerse himself in the numbing oblivion of mindless chores. While he milked or watered or fed or cleaned, he concentrated on the task at hand and didn't allow his mind to wander. Today at noon his dear wife would be laid to rest in the small local cemetery. After the funeral, Iris' sons would host the mourners for the afternoon meal at their home. Because he and Ruth weren't well known, he expected only a dozen or so families at most to attend the graveside service.

He had refused to have the customary showing in his front parlor. He didn't want folks stomping in and out of his rented house all day. He'd never been an outgoing man, and his Ruth had been painfully shy, almost frightened of people. The sooner he put the final stage of this horrible ordeal behind him the better. Nothing would bring his sweet wife back—not prayers from the bishop or words of sympathy from the district members or a thousand tears shed over the next hundred lonely nights of his life. Only hard work and the grace of God would eventually take the pain and sorrow from his heart.

"Nathan? Nathan!"

He finally heard his name being called while moving hay bales down from the barn loft. "I'm on my way," he hollered from the loft window. On his way to the house he spotted Aunt Iris on the back porch. She was about to clang the rusty old farm bell when she spotted him on the path. She waved and then disappeared into the house.

Slipping off his muddy boots in the back hall, he padded into a kitchen smelling faintly of chicken soup.

"Good," she said. "I'm glad you heard me. You'd better eat some lunch and then take your shower. With the deacons and bishop meeting us at the cemetery, we shouldn't be late."

Nathan washed his hands before slumping into a chair. Iris set a plate of two sandwiches, sweet pickles, and a sliced apple before him. "I thought I smelled chicken soup," he said taking a bite of the sandwich. A simmering pot of beef, chicken, or twelve-bean soup had been Ruth's standard fare on Saturdays. Then they could reheat the leftovers on the Sabbath without much fuss.

"*Ach,* you're smelling chicken and dumplings. I put them in the big roaster to take with us to eat later at my son's house." She seemed to be avoiding eye contact and any direct reference that it would be a funeral they were attending today. "Would you prefer to eat a bowl of that now instead of sandwiches?" she asked while filling baby bottles at the stove.

"No, *danki.* These are fine—more than enough. I just wondered about the smell." He took a hearty bite. With all Iris had to do, he didn't want to appear finicky. "Aren't you eating? Would you like this other sandwich?"

"I've already eaten. I'll be right back," she said as she disappeared down the hallway.

Nathan sat eating in a house that no longer felt like his home, as though he were the guest and not Iris.

"Here we are," she said cheerily a few minutes later. "Little Abraham is ready for his lunch too." She set the baby carrier on the kitchen table next to his plate.

Nathan glanced into the folds of blue quilt and saw only a pink forehead and button nose. He continued eating bologna and cheese with no particular urge to get a better look.

"Go ahead," she said. "Say *guder nachmittag* to your son."

He locked gazes with her across the room. "He doesn't talk, Aunt, neither English nor *Deutsch,* and I don't see the point of babbling to infants."

"Well, just take a better look then. He's not going to bite you." Surprisingly, she walked over and poked Nathan in the shoulder.

He tamped down his rising irritation. Didn't he have to finish lunch and shower for the funeral? Hadn't she made a point that they shouldn't be late? He set the remainder of the sandwich back on the plate and put the plate in the sink. "I have to get ready to bury my wife. *Danki* for the meal." He walked into the bathroom without another glance at the baby carrier. At least the youngster wasn't kicking up his usual fuss.

Thirty minutes later he found his aunt still in the kitchen, packing baby bottles into a tote bag. A second cloth bag stated the obvious in large red letters: Diaper Bag. Iris was dressed from head to toe in mourning clothes, from her heavy black bonnet down to her black, lace-up shoes. Her dress reached her ankles, and a black shawl hung over the crook of her arm.

"It hasn't been cool at night for weeks," he said. "You probably won't need your wrap."

Her face looked pale and wan as she glanced up. "You never know, and this way I'll have it with me. Would you come back inside to carry Abraham after you get the buggy hitched?" She set the roaster of chicken and dumplings into Nathan's largest hamper.

"Of course," he murmured, tugging his black wide-brimmed hat down over his ears. Yet he couldn't help thinking that if he carried the heavy hamper and bags, she could manage a seven-pound tyke in a plastic carrier. He found himself tense with irritation while he hitched up the gelding. If he'd gotten to know some of his English neighbors, maybe one would have been willing to babysit and he wouldn't have to take Abraham to such a solemn occasion. How respectful would it be to Ruth's memory if sounds of wailing drowned out the bishop's Scripture readings?

Nathan turned his face skyward as he emerged from the barn driving the buggy. The intense color of the crystalline blue almost hurt his eyes. Not a cloud marred the perfection of the June day. Ruth had loved hanging laundry on sunny, breezy days, claiming that clothes dried in half the time without the humidity. But considering what lay ahead, it could have rained without cessation as far as he was concerned.

When he pulled open the back door, Iris pressed the handle of the baby carrier into his hand. "Let's be off then." She slung a tote bag over each shoulder and then lifted the hamper of food.

"Aunt Iris, let me carry that," he said. "It looks too heavy—"

"No." Her curt reply cut short any argument. "You haven't checked on your son since he came home from the hospital." She carried her burdens very gingerly down the steps while he closed the door behind them.

"The cradle is in the guest room. I don't want to invade your privacy by walking into your room."

"Nothing keeps you from going in while I'm fixing dinner at the stove." She glared at him over her shoulder.

"I suppose not, but I've been busy since we came home. Animals don't feed themselves. And my neighbors may have cut the hay, but it still needed to be raked. Now I must bale and get it stored in the barn before the next rain."

They reached the gate where the horse and buggy had been tied to the post. Nathan placed the baby carrier on the seat and then offered Iris a hand to step up.

She set the hamper and bags down in the driveway and crossed her arms. Her feet looked to be so well planted, Nathan was sure she wouldn't have blown away in gale force winds. "Hold on a minute, nephew. I want you to pull back that blanket and take a good look at your son."

Nathan crossed his arms too. "I've seen him, Aunt Iris. I sat with him on the ride to the hospital and held his carrier on the way back. You're being plum silly when we need to get to the cemetery."

"Then I suggest you stop wasting time and do as I ask, because we're not leaving until you do." When she lifted her chin, he noticed a dimple he'd never spotted before.

Nathan rolled his eyes. He knew he had no choice but to do her bidding. He owed her respect above all else. Had it not been for her, he didn't know what he would have done. He leaned over the seat and drew back the blanket. A quizzical pair of dark eyes peered up at him from a round pink face. The splotches evident on the day he was born had faded. One little fist kept opening and closing as though exercising his tiny fingers. After a moment the baby yawned with great exaggeration as though his day had been particularly tiring thus far.

Nathan watched until his son shut his eyes and dozed off, the fist coming to rest on the blanket. Then he slowly straightened his spine, one vertebra at a time. "All right, I took a good long look. I must admit he's changed in the past few days. As *bopplin* go, he's a fine-looking little tyke. Are you satisfied?" He again offered his hand.

Iris didn't budge from her statuelike stance. "So far you've referred to him as a *boppli,* little tyke, and a youngin. I would like you to call him by his name—Abraham. After all, you picked it out, so you should use it occasionally."

"If you continue with this nonsense, we'll be last to arrive at the funeral."

"Then do as I ask." The tiny woman grew more resolute by the minute.

Nathan leaned over the carrier and cleared his throat. "Hullo, Abraham. I am your *daed.* I trust you are comfortable in that contraption. Be sure to let us know by crying if you get hungry or need anything else along the way." Then he tucked the blanket snuggly under the baby's chin. "How was that?" he asked Iris with a smile.

"Harrumph," she huffed. "I guess it's not bad for a start." She accepted his hand and climbed into the buggy.

With his aunt finally seated, Nathan loaded the bags and hamper, climbed onto his seat, and clucked to the horse to get moving before she thought of something else to delay them. But with Abraham wedged between them, she seemed content to watch the passing scenery, and he had time to ponder the oddities of women.

They talked little on the drive other than to make cursory comments about the weather. But during the last half mile, Iris turned toward him on the seat. "Why didn't your wife ever want to meet me or come to my house?"

He gritted his teeth. *Can't she just let Ruth rest in peace? Why do folks have to figure out every what-for and why-not?*

He took a deep breath before he spoke. "She was very shy and nervous around people who weren't blood kin."

Iris furrowed her forehead as though deep in thought. "Then I'm surprised she wanted to move here."

"She didn't wish to move. I did. And since her place was with me, she agreed."

"Her family would have insisted she go to a hospital if they had been here."

He lifted a brow. "*If* she would have told them the truth about her condition, but that's all water under the bridge now." He pulled on the reins to slow the horse as they turned into the rutted cemetery road.

Several buggies of early arrivals were already parked near the entrance. Nathan pulled in line beside them. As the three of them stepped down into the bright sunshine, he spotted the hearse from the funeral parlor driving up the narrow lane. The bishop and deacon stood waiting under the sycamore tree with prayer books in hand. Over his shoulder Nathan saw several buggies approaching from the other direction. He glanced down at his sleeping son, bundled in blue fleece despite the warmth of the day, and then at his aunt. "Abraham hasn't peeped during the entire trip. Let's get this service over with before he wakes up. We need to put this sorrowful day behind us."

Abby had debated long into the night about attending Ruth Fisher's funeral. *Will people hold this young mother's passing against me? Will Nathan Fisher?* Though she knew in her heart she had done everything she could, most Amish men and some women didn't understand the risks of home births. Although thousands of babies had been born in

Amish bedrooms for hundreds of years, that didn't negate the risk a woman took not being close to modern medical equipment. In the end, Abby decided she needed to go for her own sense of closure.

After parking at the end of a long row, Daniel helped her down from the buggy. Far more district members had turned out than she'd expected. Because Amish funerals didn't last very long, no one had unhitched their horses. Abby appreciated the fact that Daniel had made sure their buggy was pointing toward the road should they need to make a hasty exit.

As Abby and Daniel approached the gravesite, six men lifted a plain pine box from the back of the hearse and carried it between the rows of uniform headstones. No flowers marked the graves, nor would any adorn Ruth's in the future. No wooden crosses, candles, potted plants, or stuffed bears had been left by grieving family members. When the Grabers joined the ring of mourners, the bishop, deacon, and most others nodded in their direction. Some reached over to shake Daniel's hand and then hers, whispering words of condolence despite the fact she'd never met Ruth before that awful night.

Abby felt a lump rise up her throat when she spotted Nathan Fisher. He stood at the head of the newly dug grave, staring down at the damp, rich loam of freshly turned earth. He held his hat between his large hands, while his bird-sized aunt waited by his side. She was holding a baby, swaddled in a handmade patchwork quilt.

Little Abraham Fisher.

How Abby longed to see his sweet face to be certain he was thriving. She wanted to count his fingers and toes, listen to his tiny heart, and watch life-giving air come and go from his healthy lungs. But she wouldn't intrude in their private time of sorrow.

Soon the bishop cleared his throat and began reading from the Scriptures. The entire funeral service took less than thirty minutes, including silent prayers for the repose of Ruth's Christian soul. Songbirds offered unbearably cheerful melodies high in the treetops, while the heavy scent of late rhododendrons and azaleas filled the air. Weather this agreeable didn't seem fitting for so a somber occasion. Of course, death was simply part of life—no less significant in God's design than birth. Abby glanced at the elderly English undertaker, looking dignified in his austere black suit. His occupation was the exact omega to her alpha vocation. *Does he enjoy his work as much as I used to?*

Daniel took hold of her arm, signaling it was time for them to depart. She uttered one final prayer, and then they started toward the row of buggies.

"Mrs. Graber," called a voice over her shoulder.

She knew who had hailed before she turned around. Nathan Fisher was striding toward them. Deep lines creased his pale face around his mouth and across his forehead, while dark smudges beneath his eyes spoke volumes about recent sleeplessness.

He halted in front of them, nodding to each in succession. "*Danki* for coming."

"We are sorry for your loss, Mr. Fisher. This is my *ehemann,* Daniel." The two men shook hands, and then Nathan crossed his arms over his starched black coat. He shifted his weight from foot to foot and appeared to be choosing his words carefully. If Abby could have vanished and reappeared in almost any other place, she would have done so.

"It was God's will, but also Ruth's choice," he said after a moment. "I wanted you to know you weren't to blame. There wasn't anything you could have done even if you had arrived sooner."

"I know I tried my best," she whispered as sweat ran beneath her *kapp* and down her neck.

"You say that now because it's still fresh in your mind. But some night you might lie in bed wondering and second-guessing yourself, and I don't want that to happen. My Ruth was told by a doctor in Indiana not to bear *kinner* because doing so might kill her. She chose not to listen to her. She thought maybe the doc could be wrong, or maybe God would take pity on her." He gazed off to the left where the undertaker's van was pulling onto the paved road. The crunch of gravel sounded unnaturally loud in the silent grove of hawthorn bushes and sycamore trees. "She never told me any of this until she was five months along."

Abby knew that this pregnancy talk was hard for Nathan, but still he continued for her sake.

"She wanted this baby more than just about anything else…for me and for herself. And once you delivered our son, she was all right with dying. Birthing him was all that mattered to Ruth, and you saved our little Abraham."

Abby forced herself to swallow and fought back tears. Crying would only make things worse. Nathan's eyes were also glassy with moisture.

"Don't get me wrong. She would have loved to watch him grow up, but giving me a son was worth the risk to Ruth. So if anybody should be held responsible here, it's me." A muscle in his jaw twitched.

"No one's at fault, Mr. Fisher," she said. "We can't blame ourselves for God's will, nor should we try to second-guess His plan for us." Abby felt Daniel's palm pressing against her lower back. He didn't like it when she voiced sentiments that should come from the ministerial brethren. But she couldn't allow this man to suffer unnecessary guilt if she could help it. "She must have loved you very much. Keep that in mind when *you* can't sleep at night." Abby shifted her body away from Daniel's touch.

"I will, and *danki* for coming today—both of you." He gave his beard a pull, nodded to them, and turned to walk away. Then he stopped short. "Would you like to see him? Little Abraham? He looks fine when his face isn't scrunched up from a throwing a tantrum."

Abby laughed, feeling her tension drain away. "I would love to."

"As long as we keep his belly full, he stays in a fairly pleasant mood," Nathan added. The three laughed while they walked toward a knot of people talking under the shady trees. Abby recognized Iris Fisher in the center of the group, holding the infant.

Nathan introduced them to his neighbors, most of whom Abby and Daniel already knew from barn raisings and other work frolics. Daniel shook hands with the menfolk while Abby approached Nathan's aunt.

"*Guder nachmittag,*" Iris greeted. "I suppose you'd like to see the little one." She held out the bundle for inspection.

"Good afternoon to you. *Jah,* I would love to." Abby pulled back the edge of the quilt and peered into the dark eyes of Ruth's newborn son. He grinned at her as though in recognition, which Abby knew to be plain silly. She reached to touch his downy soft hair with near reverence. "Hello, dear boy. You are looking very handsome today." When emotion began to constrict her throat, Abby stepped back and focused on the buggies by the road. One or two families were loading up to leave, while several horses stamped their hooves with impatience.

"Rest easy, Abby," said Iris. "Little Abraham is doing fine, and I plan to take good care of him."

Abby smoothed her palms down her skirt. "I know you will. It was nice to see you again, although I wish it had been under pleasanter circumstances." She voiced a particularly English expression she'd picked up from Dr. Weller.

"That's all right. We can't control circumstances, but at least you were able to see he's doing well." She shifted the boy to her other arm. "Why don't you stop by my son's house for a bite to eat? He doesn't live far from here. We have plenty of food." Iris looked her in the eye and held her gaze. "Do you remember the way?"

Abby considered accepting the invitation. If they attended, she would have a chance to hold the child and be assured he was thriving. And she might find out more about Ruth Fisher, but Daniel squeezed her shoulder.

"*Danki*," he said, "but we need to get home. Our two *kinner* are at a neighbor's house and I'm behind on my chores. We are real sorry for your loss." He nodded at Iris, grasped Abby's hand, and led her away from the mourners as though she were a child.

She felt oddly annoyed and yet relieved at the same time as they walked back to their buggy without speaking. She didn't wait for his help to climb inside. With a cluck of his tongue to the horse, the buggy rolled down the dirt lane in between closely packed graves. Once they reached the county road, she said softly, "I don't see what harm it would have done to stop by the Fishers'."

"Not a matter of harm, *fraa*, but what good would it have served? You got to see the *boppli* to set your mind at ease, but stopping there would only have prolonged your misery. You need to put this delivery out of your mind and concentrate on the hundreds of successful ones. Folk die. It's part of life. We might not like it, but upsetting yourself isn't going to bring her back or change a thing." He clamped his jaw closed the way he always did when he wished a subject dropped.

Abby swallowed down her reply. Arguing with her husband wouldn't help matters, and he was probably right. It just didn't seem so at the moment. She nodded and Daniel slapped the reins against the horse's back to pick up the pace.

On the way home she concentrated on the green hayfields waiting to be cut and the knee-high stalks of corn standing in neat rows. Sunlight sparkled off the clear blue water of ponds, while hawks wheeled on wind currents overhead, watching for tasty prey to make their lunch. Daniel's idea about focusing on the hundreds of successful births made sense. She would remember Ruth in her prayers for many nights to come, but her death shouldn't cripple her ability to serve her community.

"Do we have any leftovers in the fridge?" Daniel's question broke the long silence. "All that talk about food made me hungry. I'd better eat something before heading to the fields." He glanced over at her and they both burst out laughing.

"You're the one who passed up a free meal, Mr. Graber. Now you're probably stuck with a bowl of soup or a ham sandwich." She tugged the sleeve of his coat.

"Serves me right for not listening to my smart *fraa*." He offered a wink as he shrugged out of his coat. With their farm in sight, he would forgo his proper appearance.

"Good gracious, what is going on?" Abby's attention had focused on a vehicle in their driveway. The sheriff's cruiser was parked near their barn; its red and blue lights still spinning as the car idled.

"Git up there, Sam!" Daniel slapped the reins once more. "What on earth could the sheriff want at our farm?"

An icy chill pooled in Abby's belly. "Oh my. I hope nothing's happened to the *kinner*." She jumped down before Daniel brought the buggy to a stop and ran toward the cruiser. She saw no one inside or near the vehicle. With her heart slamming against her ribcage, she ran to the barn door and nearly collided with the exiting sheriff and his deputy.

"Easy there, ma'am. No need to knock us down."

Abby stepped back with fear and confusion. "What's wrong? Has something happened to my children? They were supposed to be next door at my neighbor's." Her voice sounded strangled.

"Your children are fine as far as I know. They're not why we're here." The man swept off his wide-brimmed beige hat and focused on Daniel. He was hurrying toward them with the horse still harnessed to the buggy.

Abby wrung her hands, casting glances between her husband and the sheriff.

The large man, with his belly straining the buttons of his shirt and noonday stubble darkening his chin, cleared his throat. He looked about as comfortable as she felt.

"Ma'am, are you Mrs. Abigail Graber, the midwife of this here Amish community?" He'd assumed a formal tone of voice.

The bottom fell from her stomach, and she suddenly felt weak in the knees. "I am. I'm Abby Graber."

Daniel dropped the reins and walked to her side. His arm protectively encircled her shoulders. "What's this about, officer?"

"I'm afraid a warrant has been issued for your arrest, Mrs. Graber." The sheriff set his hat back on, while his deputy shuffled his boot heels in the dirt.

Abby gasped. She tried to speak, but words would not come.

"For what?" Daniel asked. "What are the charges, sir?"

The sheriff gazed at Daniel with more pity than anything else. "Your wife has been charged with practicing midwifery without a license, involuntary manslaughter, practicing medicine without a license, and possession and sale of a dangerous controlled substance. Those last two charges are felonies, Mr. Graber."

He seems more comfortable addressing Daniel than me, she thought.

"Manslaugher? Practicing medicine?" Daniel's voice rose in agitation. "That's absurd. She doesn't kill people or practice medicine. She delivers babies."

The officer turned back to Abby. "Did you make a statement to the attending paramedic that you injected Mrs. Fisher with the drug Pitocin?"

Abby felt the blood drain from her head. "Yes. I wanted them to know so there would be no possible drug interaction with anything else or potential overdose. I did it in an attempt to save her." Her final admission was barely audible.

Daniel turned on the gravel and stared at her, his face a mask of confusion.

Excuses, explanations, pleas for understanding all swam through her brain, yet Abby couldn't think of anything to say to mitigate the wrong she had done.

"Then I'm afraid I must take you into custody, Mrs. Graber," the sheriff said.

His deputy brought forth handcuffs from his chest pocket, but the sheriff shook his head. "Bob, I think we can trust one skinny Amish lady to behave herself on the way to county booking."

With one last glance at Daniel, he turned back at her. "Ma'am, if you would be so kind?" He pointed toward the squad car.

Abby started to walk on legs threatening to collapse beneath her toward the police car on the second most terrifying day of her life.

Four

Abby bolted upright with a start following a particularly stressful dream. She had been running away from an unknown adversary. Each place she had chosen to hide from her pursuer turned into another trap of danger—gaping holes in the floor, stairs climbing into the clouds without end, and dangerously canted hallways in buildings that shook with earthquake intensity. Each time she felt that her nemesis had either lost her trail or lost interest in her, the faceless stalker would show up to send her fleeing to another condemned building or shifting sandbar.

When she awoke her heart was racing, her breath came in jagged, shallow gasps, and sweat was soaking through her nightgown. After perusing her surroundings, Abby realized the danger was real, not imagined. Even though no slippery slopes into dark abysses threatened her path, a cell offered an equal amount of anxiety to her jangled nerves.

She was in jail.

Abigail Graber, God-fearing woman and respected member of the

Amish community, had been locked up like a common criminal. She contemplated that fact as she knelt beside her uncomfortable bunk for morning prayers. At least she was alone in the sparsely furnished cell and the matron had allowed her to keep her well-worn Bible. Opening it to the book of Deuteronomy, she read a few paragraphs of Old Testament tribulations and changed her mind about the chapter selection. Perhaps Psalms or Ephesians could lift her spirits from self-pity and remorse—remorse for the effect her arrest would have on Daniel and her two *kinner.*

Would her husband hang his head in shame, keeping to their farm for fear of district censure for her actions? Crawling beneath a rock had never been his habit in the past. Would her children suffer embarrassment because of her arrest? At least school was recessed for the summer, but would other children point fingers or ask questions that would frighten Laura and Jake? The Amish were raised to not sit in judgment of others but to follow their *Ordnung.* How she longed to know how her *daed,* her district's bishop, would react to his daughter going to jail. Because it happened only last night, she doubted he'd even heard the news yet.

After her devotions, Abby dressed and was just lacing her shoes when suddenly the door swung open and a middle-aged woman entered carrying a tray. "Breakfast is served," she announced. "Nothing gourmet, but the eggs are real and the coffee is hot." She offered a pleasant smile along with the food. "From now on, you'll take meals in the common room with the other women, but you have a hearing in half an hour, so eat fast."

"*Dank*—thank you," Abby said, remembering to use only English. She looked over the tray—coffee with powdered creamer, scrambled eggs, two slices of white toast, margarine spread, and a plastic dish of fruit cocktail.

"I'll go get your own clothes," the woman said. "I suppose you'll be glad to get out of our duds for a while. Camouflage green isn't exactly an Amish color."

Abby's face flushed with shame. The matron probably meant no offense with her comment, but drawing attention to her mannish, ghastly outfit only made Abby feel worse. She took a bite of toast and looked up. "Will I be allowed to wear my own clothes from now on?"

"No, only during your appearance in court today. The judge will read the charges against you and set the amount of your bail."

Abby swallowed the dry bread and asked, "Then I can go home?" She reached for the coffee and drank half the cup, forgoing her usual cream and two sugars.

"No, then he'll ask if you have counsel to represent you. You know… a lawyer," she added upon Abby's bewildered expression.

She rubbed her forehead. "Amish folks don't usually hire lawyers. I wouldn't know who to call." *Because Amish folks don't usually get themselves thrown in jail.* "We try to settle our differences among ourselves and go to the ministerial brethren only if we can't come to agreement."

The matron looked sad and somewhat uncomfortable. "Yes, but this is Wooster, so I'm afraid if you don't have an attorney, the court will appoint one for you. That's what the judge will tell you today. I don't recommend you trying to represent yourself in court."

Abby nodded. "After I am assigned a court-appointed lawyer, then will I be allowed to go home?" She ate some of the bland, undercooked scrambled eggs, trying not to reveal her distaste.

"Mrs.—" The matron glanced down at her clipboard. "—Graber. Do you realize that you have been charged with a felony?"

"I understand the law says practicing midwifery in Ohio without the proper license is a crime, but Amish midwives have been delivering babies in our community since we settled here a hundred years ago."

"That may be, but it's still considered a crime. Usually you would have been charged with a misdemeanor. If that were the case, they would release you after your hearing and expect you to come back for your trial date. That is, if you didn't cop a plea. But it looks like you'll be charged with a felony, and that's much more serious. They must have something else on you other than just delivering a baby."

Abby swallowed as much of the eggs as she could stomach and washed them down with the rest of her coffee. She couldn't ask the woman about everything she didn't understand or the other inmates might not get their breakfast trays until lunchtime.

"So the judge will read the charges against you, assign a lawyer, and then set the amount of your bail."

"The bail is money I must pay to get out?"

"Yes, but you'll get the money back if you show up for trial."

"Why wouldn't I show up?"

The woman laughed softly. "Good question. I know *you* will, but some people hightail it and run. That makes them look guilty, and it also makes things go a lot worse when they're finally caught and dragged before the judge."

Abby nodded as she ate her fruit cocktail. Each fruit in the syrup tasted exactly the same. "I hope my husband remembers to bring whatever cash we have on hand if he comes to the courthouse today." She spoke more to herself than to her jailer.

The woman laughed again. "It'll take more than the proceeds from selling eggs and garden produce from your farm stand. Bail for felonies can run into a couple hundred thousand dollars."

Abby set the fruit cup back on the tray and stared in disbelief. Her appetite vanished while the food in her stomach started to curdle. "Then I guess I'll be staying here until the trial. We don't have that kind of money." Her calm tone of voice belied her inner turmoil.

"Nobody has that kind of money. That's what bail bondmen are for." She glanced at her watch and then over her shoulder. "Look, I can't spend any more time jawboning with you. I need to supervise the breakfast room so no food trays *accidentally* hit the walls. Your lawyer will explain about bonding and bail money." She walked out carrying Abby's tray but reentered within a couple minutes. "Here are your regular clothes," she said, handing Abby a plastic sack. "They want you to appear in court looking normal. You can wash up at the sink and change outfits. There's no time for a shower. If I finish up early, I'll stop back to explain more of the goings-on so you won't be afraid."

Abby glanced up to meet the jailer's gaze. "Thank you for breakfast, and for your kindness in speaking to me today." She didn't mention that knowing what would happen did nothing to alleviate her fear.

"Sure thing. For what it's worth, I'm on your side. There are too many laws telling us what to do in this country. They take away every personal freedom we once had in an effort to protect us from ourselves. Doesn't make sense to me." She marched out the door, shaking her head. At least no bolt clicked behind her as it had last night. Abby hated the thought of being locked inside a room. What if there was a fire?

She washed, changed clothes, and then tried her best to pin up her hair without benefit of a hairbrush. The guard's words swam through her mind like bees around a hive, making her more agitated by the minute.

Be still and know that I am God.

One of her favorite Scriptures helped to calm her nerves. As she contemplated the events at the Fisher farm, preparing to explain her actions to the judge, there wasn't a thing she would have done differently. If she was a woman faith, she needed to show some now as she waited for the hearing. Opening her Bible, she turned to the book of Genesis. "Might as well start at the beginning," she whispered and began to read.

By the time the deputy arrived to take her to court, God had created heaven and earth in six days and rested on the seventh; Adam and Eve had eaten the forbidden fruit and lost paradise; Cain had slain his brother Abel; a great flood had covered the earth; the Babylonians had erected the tower of Babel, separating people forever by language barriers; God had destroyed the cities of Sodom and Gomorrah; and the faith of the great prophet Abraham had been tested by the Lord. While walking the corridors of the Justice Center, Abby's problems seemed minor by comparison.

She walked into a courtroom filled with people, while many more stood along the back wall. She spotted Daniel and Dr. Weller but recognized no one else. "Who are all these people?" she asked the guard. "Have all of them come to hear my case?"

The question seemed to take the man by surprise. "No, ma'am.

The judge will preside over many cases this morning—some to set bail, some to request continuances, while others informed their lawyers they wish to enter or change a plea. But this sure isn't your lucky day. Judge O'Neil is sitting on the bench. He can be a tough one. Sit there, ma'am. You're next on the docket."

Abby did as instructed, wondering about this Judge O'Neil, who looked no different than most English folk to her. She stole a glance over her shoulder at Daniel. Dark circles beneath his eyes made him look as though he hadn't slept in days. He clutched his hat between his large hands, while his hair still showed the impression left by his hatband. He seemed as comfortable as a hen in a fox lair. She hoped she could go home with him after she explained to the judge that she'd tried everything within her power to save Mrs. Fisher. Did Jake and Laura wonder what had happened? Her little girl had trouble sleeping whenever her *mamm* was out on a call.

"Case number 9645287, the State of Ohio versus Abigail Graber."

Abby's head snapped up at the mention of her name. She felt a hand on her shoulder and heard a voice near her ear. "Stand up, Mrs. Graber." Her legs felt as though she'd run up a mountain and back as she rose to her feet.

The judge, a portly man with florid cheeks, studied her over his half-moon glasses. Most of his head was completely bald, yet his hair remained thick beneath ear level.

"Are you Abigail Graber of Shreve, Ohio?"

"Yes," she answered. Her words sounded more like the squeak of a rusty door hinge.

"Yes, Your Honor," he corrected, continuing to study her.

"Yes, Your Honor, sir."

"You are here today to enter a plea on the charges against you." He glanced down at his papers. "Abigail Graber, you have been charged with practicing midwifery without a license, involuntary manslaughter, practicing medicine without a license, and possession and sale of a dangerous controlled substance—the last two charges being felonies. How do you plead, Mrs. Graber?"

"I'm not sure how to plead, Your Honor."

While the judge rubbed the bridge of his nose with two fingers, his forehead furrowed into deep creases. "Do you have legal counsel? That is, do you have the means to hire a lawyer?"

"I don't know. I don't think I do." She desperately wanted to look back at her *ehemann,* but she didn't dare. The judge might interpret turning around as disrespect.

"In that case, this court will appoint legal counsel for you. Your pretrial hearing will be one month from now, and your bond is set at five hundred thousand dollars—cash or bond." He thumped his gavel halfheartedly. "Next case, Bailiff." He opened another folder from the stack in front of him.

Abby gasped. *Half a million dollars?* Their house, land, livestock, savings account, and everything added up wouldn't come close to being worth that much. And she would never allow Daniel to sell their farm to raise money. Where would her family live? What would he do for a living? Their farm was his livelihood as well as their home.

She felt a gentle tug on her upper arm. The deputy had returned to her side to lead her away from the raised platform. Her time before the heartless Judge O'Neil was apparently over, and she hadn't been allowed to explain anything.

"You will return to your cell now, but your lawyer will probably visit this afternoon," the deputy said. "He or she will tell you how your family can raise your bail through a bondman and all that. He might even file a motion to have your bail reduced, seeing that you're Amish."

They had exited the courtroom through a side door and stood in the chilly outer hallway. She slanted him a wary glance. "What does my being Amish have to do with the amount of my bail?"

"I don't think anybody could call you a flight risk. It's hard to make a fast getaway in a horse and buggy." His grin looked genuine.

"If you ever saw a standardbred horse get stung by a bee, you just might change your opinion," she said with a wry smile.

The deputy's hearty laughter echoed off the high ceilings.

Laughing felt odd to her, considering the stew of emotions

churning in her belly. There wasn't anything funny about the serious charges against her. Her hope that the nightmare would end once she explained what had happened faded the moment she looked into the judge's bland face.

She was just another criminal to him.

He thought she had killed Mrs. Fisher. Wasn't that what "manslaughter" meant?

He thought she had "practiced medicine" on a dying woman. But in a way she had, in an attempt to save her life.

And she certainly had been practicing midwifery without a license for several years. *Guilty as charged.*

Once she was back in her cell, Abby knelt in prayer to ask for relief from her stupidity, forgiveness for her sins, and clear direction as to what she should do next. Because never before in her life had she felt so confused.

Twenty minutes later she rose from her knees, took a pen and some paper she'd found in the common room, and began a letter to her sister. Catherine loved children and had worked as a nanny to an English family since leaving school almost nine years ago. Daniel would need help tending the children and keeping up with household chores. No better choice came to Abby's mind other than her *schwester.* He might not relish someone else in his house, but with bail set at half a million dollars, who knew how long Abby would be here?

■

Catherine spent the two-hour drive to her sister's home trying to concentrate on the countryside instead of her sad thoughts. At least her brother James had volunteered to drive her to Daniel and Abby's farm instead of her *daed.* Her father would have spent the time cautioning her on what constituted proper behavior in her brother-in-law's home.

Don't chatter at meals.

Keep busy with household tasks. Don't be idle.

Don't change your schwester*'s rules with her* kinner.

Keep your opinions to yourself about Abigail's troubles.

Instead, her brother talked about the ongoing dry spell and his hope for a downpour once his hay had been cut and stored. Afterward, he remained quiet for the rest of the drive.

Considering Catherine's frame of mind, his silence proved to be a blessing. After receiving Abby's letter, she had jumped at the chance for a change of scenery. A week or two with her niece and nephew would get her mind off a person better off forgotten. At twenty-three, she had some experience with courting. But after mustering the courage to ask a certain young man for a ride home from a singing, the result had been disastrous. The man of her dreams had agreed to give her a lift home—in the backseat. Another gal had apparently captured his heart and therefore the front seat at his side. Along the way home, he couldn't have hung onto Rachel Hawk's words more than if they'd been made of glue.

Life wasn't fair.

Rachel had her pick of beaus. Why did she have to pick the plum Catherine had been eyeing? Rachel was also younger, while prime marriageable age was about to pass Catherine by.

"I said, how long do you think you'll be staying at Abby's?" Her *bruder*'s question finally roused her from her mental replay of Sunday's heartbreak.

"*Mir leid,*" she apologized. "I was daydreaming."

"*Jah,* you've been doing that a lot lately." His dark hair, in need of a trimming, hung in his eyes.

She chose to ignore his comment. "I don't know how long Abby will be…gone. Maybe just a few days. But don't worry, James. I'm sure Daniel will drive me home once she's back." She couldn't bring herself to think about Abby being in a jail, let alone speak the words aloud. She had never known a person who'd been arrested. Her sister must be mortified with shame.

"That's *gut.* I need to rake, bale, and store the hay in the barn while the dry weather holds. But if you want me to come get you, call the Wainwrights on Abby's cell phone. They'll know how to get word to me."

"*Danki*," she murmured. As they rounded a bend, the Graber farm came into view. Catherine loved the three-story white frame house. With porches on all four sides and plenty of windows, there was always somewhere to sit and catch a cool breeze. It was one of the few Amish homes in their district that had never had a *dawdi haus* added during previous generations of residents.

As the buggy rolled to a stop, no friendly Graber faces came bounding out to greet them.

"Are you sure Daniel is home?" James asked, lifting her suitcase from behind the seat and setting it on the ground.

"Of course he is. He knew I would come as soon as I received my sister's letter. Don't worry. I see Laura peeking from behind the kitchen curtain."

"I'll look for Daniel in the barn. I'm not leaving here until I know there hasn't been some kind of mix-up."

"*Danki*, but I will be fine." She picked up her suitcase and some desserts her *mamm* had baked, and then she headed toward the house. The curtain had fallen back in place. Catherine pushed open the Graber back door and walked into an empty kitchen. "Laura?" she called. "It's your Aunt Catherine. Where are you?" She heard only the sounds of squirrels raiding the bird feeder for sunflower seeds. "Jake?" She waited a few moments and then went in search of her niece and nephew.

Their behavior struck her as odd. It wasn't as though she were a stranger. Abby once mentioned her daughter was very shy, but she felt assured that would change once Laura started school in the fall.

Catherine searched the front room, dining room, bathrooms, and the side and back screened porches before climbing the steps to the second floor. One of the bedroom doors had been closed, making that room the likely hiding place. "Hello, Laura? Jake?" She pushed open the door. "It's Aunt Catherine. Are you playing a game of hide-and-seek with me?"

Laura and Jake Graber sat on the floor near the window overlooking the backyard. Jake was playing with a barnyard building set while Laura rocked a faceless doll nestled between both arms. Both *kinner* looked scared and upset. "What's wrong, dear ones? Don't you remember me?" Catherine approached them slowly.

Laura shook her head affirmatively. "*Jah,* I remember you. You're *mamm*'s little *schwester.*" When the child turned up her face, her eyes were moist and round.

"That's right. I saw you on a preaching Sunday last month. You were eating peanut butter cookies after lunch. Your *daed* said, 'Save some of those for other folks.'"

Laura's lower lip quivered while a large tear rolled down her pale cheek. The girl's white *kapp* was wrinkled and in need of laundering. Her brother's shirt and trousers were equally unkempt. "*Jah,* I ate six cookies. You brought chocolate brownies with fat walnuts sitting on top." Despite the discussion centering on sweet treats, a second tear slid down the child's streaky face.

Their sadness broke Catherine's heart. She knelt down beside them on the braided rag rug. Looming over them like a giant wouldn't calm their fears. "Did you try one of my walnut brownies?"

After the child lifted one index finger, Catherine plodded on. "How did you like my baking?"

The girl shook her head furiously. "I only like my *mamm*'s cookies!" With that, her face crumpled with abject misery. Jake stopped snapping in logs to create the barn's second floor and stared at his sister. Seeing her tears, he decided to cry too.

Catherine felt somehow guilty for their unhappiness. "What's wrong, Laura. Tell me why you're crying and maybe I can help."

"I want my *mamm,*" she managed to say in between sobs. "*Daed* says she can't come home because we don't have enough money." Sobs nearly strangled her speech.

Didn't have enough money? What on earth? Catherine patted the child's knee gently. "What else did your *daed* say?"

"He said he didn't know when *mamm* could come back, but that you would live here and take care of us."

Jake soon tired of crying without knowing the reason and returned to snapping plastic logs together to create the barn loft.

"Because you came here to live, does that mean *mamm* isn't ever coming home?" Hiccups joined her sobs to create additional problems for Laura. "I want my *mamm*!"

Catherine wrapped an arm around her shoulders. "Of course you do. And she will be home as soon as she can. My being here won't prevent her from returning. She wrote me a letter and asked me to stay here while she's gone." She withdrew the folded sheet from her apron pocket, grateful for the intuition to bring it along. Opening the letter, she held it out for Laura's examination.

Although the girl couldn't read either *Deutsch* or English yet, Laura studied the paper with interest. Perhaps she recognized Abby's handwriting, but more likely she yearned for any reason to believe things weren't as grim as they seemed. "She will come home to us?" Laura sniffed as her nose began to run.

Catherine pulled out the clean handkerchief she kept up her sleeve and handed it to the child. "Dry your eyes and blow your nose. Everything will be all right. Your *mamm* will be home soon. In the meantime, you and I need to rustle up dinner in the kitchen. What would my sister say if we allowed the menfolk to go hungry?"

"She would get mad. My *daed* likes his supper on time. He says he gets hungry trying to keep crows from eating the corn all day."

Catherine laughed, rose to her feet, and stretched out a hand to her niece. "Then we'd better go downstairs and get something started. Do we need Jake's help or should he stay up here?"

Laura pursed her lips while considering the question. "He's not much help in the kitchen." To Jake she said, "You stay up here and work on the barn. Those *cuhs* need a roof over their heads before the next rain." She pointed at the plastic cows. "We'll call you when it's time to eat." Then she shyly accepted her aunt's hand.

Catherine marveled at the way the six-year-old readily assumed a near-parental role over her four-year-old sibling. Abigail's absence would affect these two, but she silently vowed not to let those changes affect them adversely.

When they reached the kitchen, they saw James sitting at the table drinking a Coke. "I found Daniel in the barn sharpening his cutting blades," he said. "I see you found the missing *kinner.*" He offered his niece an exaggerated wink and wiggled his dark eyebrows.

"Go wash your hands and face, Laura, before we start cooking." Catherine waited until the girl scampered off before addressing her brother. "They were afraid that if I stayed here, their *mamm* would never come home," she whispered.

James shook his head. "You have to wonder where youngins get their ideas." He took a long drink.

"What did Daniel say? Is he on his way up to the house?"

He met her gaze over the rim of the can. "*Jah,* I talked to him. He said he has two chickens plucked, cut up, and ready to fry for supper. They are in the fridge."

She waited but he relayed nothing else. "That's all you two talked about—a pair of plucked hens? What is the news about our sister?" She glanced at the closed bathroom door. "Should I walk to the barn to speak to him?"

James shook his head while slowly rising to his full height. "No, I think you should stay in here and fry up those chickens. Try to keep a low profile, if that's possible, Cat." He crushed the soda can with one powerful fist and tossed it in the blue recycle bin. "Our brother-in-law has never been a man of long speeches, but today he was downright uncommunicative. This whole mess with Abigail riled him up. He'll talk to you when he's ready. I wouldn't press him." James locked gazes with her for a long moment. "Tend to Abby's *kinner* and cut Daniel a wide swath. He wants his wife at home, not sitting in some jail cell. Until that happens, he probably won't be in the best of moods." He set his straw hat on the back of his head. "Now, I'd better head for home. Take care of yourself, sister. And send word or leave a message on the neighbor's answering machine if you need me." With a toss of his head, he motioned toward the barn.

The meaning of his cryptic gesture was lost on Catherine. "I will stay until Abby is back to care for her family herself." She followed James onto the porch. "Wait. There's one more thing. Laura mentioned that

Abby must stay in jail because they didn't have enough money. What could that mean?"

He glanced toward the driveway where his horse scratched impatiently in the dirt. "The court must have set her bail too high for Daniel to pay."

"Aren't there people to help with that sort of thing? I saw an ad in an English newspaper about loans against farm equity."

"That's Daniel and Abby's business, little sister. Don't go sticking your nose where it doesn't belong—it might get bit off." He started down the steps with Catherine on his heels.

"She's my *schwester* and I'd bet she's suffering in that cell. I'd say that makes it my business."

James stopped short. He turned around so fast she bumped into him. His facial expression needed no words of explanation.

"At least it's *somewhat* my business." She backed up two paces.

"Remember that I warned you, Catherine. But you'll probably listen the same way you heeded my warnings about the honeybee hive and the pond's thin ice. Just keep our neighbor's phone number handy, and I'll come get you—missing a nose and all." He strode toward his buggy with a broad grin.

She cupped her hands around her mouth. "Both of those incidents were more than ten years ago," she called.

"Tigers and willful sisters seldom change their stripes." With a wave of his hand, James left for home, leaving Catherine in the dusty driveway. She glanced toward the barn—still no sign of her brother-in-law—and then she looked at the house. Her niece was peeking from behind the kitchen curtain again. Catherine walked back to the house to chickens that needed frying and a niece and nephew who required reassurance. But a tiny seed of unease took root in her heart and began to grow.

Five

Daniel Graber had always been content with his life. The Lord had blessed him with a good wife, healthy children, and acres of productive land to farm. He grew most of the food they ate, raised dairy and beef cattle, and owned good-laying hens. For water he had a deep well, a spring-fed pond stocked with trout, and access to a fast-flowing river for summertime dips. He loved his wife. She had never given him one sleepless night in ten years of marriage. Now, through a misjudgment on her part, a misstep that broke an English law, she was locked in a jail cell instead of being home where she belonged.

Why would an English judge require half a million dollars to make certain Abigail would appear in his courtroom? If he asked her to come back another day to state what happened at the Fisher farm, she would show up—not that she hadn't already explained the events several times to the EMTs, the sheriff, the coroner, Dr. Weller, and to her court-appointed attorney. Did *Englischers* who ran afoul of the law pay such sums to the court? He couldn't fathom it. Abby's fancy-dressed lawyer had stopped over to explain the bondman's business, and it smacked of money-changing in the temple in Daniel's estimation. Plain folk didn't put up titles to their farms to strangers in exchange for a guarantee that a man would appear in court, except that this person was a woman—and his wife, no less.

In all his life, Daniel could count on one hand the number of Amish folk who had ever been arrested. And the crimes committed had usually been for *rumschpringe* pranks of mischief.

Never a woman and certainly not the daughter of a bishop.

Each time he thought about the situation, he was filled with shame and anger. If that newcomer Nathan Fisher had called for an ambulance the way he should have, Abby wouldn't be sitting in jail for doing nothing other than delivering a baby. Tomorrow, the bishop would visit with the other ministerial brethren to discuss what should be done. They would know how to get Abby back home where she belonged.

With tired muscles and a weary spirit, Daniel finished feeding the livestock and washed up in the former pump house. The old copper bathtub still leaned against the wall—a nostalgic reminder of Saturday night baths before the days of indoor plumbing and propane hot water tanks. His *grossmammi* used to heat kettles of water on the wood-fired stove and then scent the steaming tub with bayberries and cloves. Now they showered with soap-on-a-rope, and their Plain lifestyles had grown easier but not simpler.

When Daniel entered the house, he found Laura and Jake already seated at the table. His sister-in-law was pulling a fry pan from the oven with giant mitts. "*Gut nacht,* Catherine," he mumbled, hanging his hat on a peg. He ruffled the downy blond hair of his son and pulled one of his daughter's *kapp* strings.

"Good evening to you, Daniel. I was about ready to look for you. Laura said you liked to eat earlier than this, and everything has been finished for an hour."

"I must finish chores before settling down to a meal." He cast her an appraising glance. Was she scolding him on her first day in his home? Catherine was younger, smaller, and more opinionated than Abigail. It didn't surprise him that no man was seriously courting her. Besides an ornery temperament, her dark hair was drab, whereas Abby's auburn mane was as fiery as an autumn sunset. And Catherine's eyes were a watery shade of blue instead of the rich sapphire of his wife's.

"I said shall I scoop some noodles for you?" She hovered next to his chair with Abby's favorite ceramic bowl in hand.

"*Jah,* give me a spoonful." He speared two pieces of chicken from the platter and then placed a drumstick on each of the *kinner's* plates. "Abby doesn't use that bowl for everyday. She saves it for good."

Catherine served noodles to his children and then sat down in his wife's chair. "Why not? Using a bowl won't wear it out like table linens or bed sheets." She looked genuinely perplexed.

"I don't know. You'll have to ask your sister that question." He bit into a chicken breast. The breading was greasy yet the meat tasted dry. "Is there nothing to drink with this meal? Some cold milk or iced tea?"

"Sure, I'll get the milk, but I didn't make any tea. No one told me you favored it over milk or water."

"I don't particularly favor one over the other. Abigail sets both on the table and lets me decide."

"I'll keep that in mind." Catherine took four glasses from the cupboard and the pitcher of milk from the refrigerator.

"The young ones use plastic cups, not glass." Daniel watched her while trying to swallow the dry meat.

Her shoulders stiffened as she filled two glasses with milk and returned to the cupboard for another selection. "Will these red, white, and blue ones suffice or are there *particular* plastic cups I should learn about?"

Daniel glanced up to see if she was teasing him. She appeared earnest while waiting for his reply. "The stars-and-stripes will do fine."

She poured the milk and then sat down to her own dinner. She'd taken small helpings compared to Abby's.

"What did you put in this salad?" he asked.

A smile bloomed across Catherine's face. "I found some cooked bacon strips in the fridge. So I crumbled them up and tossed it in with the spinach. That's how they fix spinach salad in fancy restaurants. The only difference is that I didn't see any mushrooms, but I did mix up a fresh garlic-and-buttermilk dressing."

"We seldom have mushrooms on hand because we don't have a cave on the farm." After a moment, a thought occurred to him. "Is this the bacon from the green Tupperware container? I was saving that for bacon, lettuce, and tomato sandwiches for tomorrow's lunch."

"Oh, my. I'm sorry, Daniel. I'll fry some extra bacon tomorrow at breakfast. And pick another tomato if any more are ripe." Her focus fell on the chopped tomato ringing the edge of the salad bowl.

"All the rest are still green," Daniel whined. He wasn't sure why he was making a big deal out of a vegetable, but he didn't like the way Abby's sister had just taken over his kitchen.

Catherine set down her fork and dabbed her mouth with a napkin. "You don't have a problem with Abby inviting me to stay here, do you?"

"No. I'm grateful you are here. Jake and Laura need someone to look after them while I work the fields. And I don't have time to wash clothes and cook meals along with the farm chores, even if I knew how." He glanced at his daughter. Laura was listening to their conversation with great interest. "I didn't mean to sound like you're not welcome, Catherine, because you are."

"*Danki* for that. I'm happy to help out until Abby returns." She looked directly at Laura. "But I must admit, I'm rather poor at reading folks' minds. So if you will leave notes on what you don't want touched, I'd be much obliged." She smiled, displaying a mouthful of gloriously white teeth.

Daniel decided to let the matter drop. It was only day one with their houseguest. As he had no idea how long this arrangement would last, it would be better to not get off on the wrong foot over bacon strips and ripe tomatoes. He ate everything on his plate, including a second helping of buttered noodles so there would be no hard feelings. Women loved to see clean plates.

While Catherine scraped dishes into the slop bucket, Daniel fixed another plate from the leftovers and poured milk into a travel mug.

She eyed him nervously. "You're eating more, brother? I wouldn't have started clearing the table if you weren't finished."

"No, I'm done. I'm fixing this plate for my cousin." He dumped the rest of the noodles onto the plate and poured her spinach concoction into a small bowl.

"Your cousin? Is he here?" She drew back the curtain and peered out the window toward the driveway.

"He lives out back in a cabin by the river. You can't see his place from the house. The barn, orchard, and woods block the view."

Catherine approached, wiping her hands on her apron. "Why didn't he come up for supper? I would have set another plate."

Daniel gritted his teeth. *Hopefully, every Graber family custom won't be brought up for discussion and review.* "He likes keeping to himself. He usually takes his meals on the back porch, but if he spotted you in the yard earlier today, he'll stay away until full dark."

Following her perplexed expression, he added, "He's shy, that's all. He doesn't like strangers." Daniel tucked silverware and a napkin into his back pocket. "It's nothing for you to be concerned about. Besides, this is the time Abby gets the *kinner* into the bathtub."

He forced a pleasant smile, snapped a lid on the travel mug, and headed outside before the next round of questions. He knew that telling Catherine to pay something no mind was like telling a thirsty man to ignore an oasis, but because she was Abby's sister and was doing them a favor, he would try to overlook her constant questions. Daniel had grown accustomed to his wife's quieter nature, which didn't have the need to rehash everything to death.

As he walked the well-worn path around the barn and through the orchard toward the river, he knew much of his dissatisfaction was with himself. The look on Abby's face when they had led her from the courtroom had nearly broken his heart. He didn't understand what she had done to be charged with a felony. The authorities generally ignored midwifery that was confined to the Amish community. How could they charge her with practicing *medicine* without a license? That was absurd. Did the fact that Mrs. Fisher had died change the situation?

Surely they wouldn't keep Abby locked up until the trial…that could be months from now. His tenderhearted wife wouldn't last among worldly, hardened criminals. If he had to mortgage his farm to bring her home, then so be it. But her *daed,* their bishop, would have an opinion in the matter.

The slanted rays of the setting sun reflected off Isaiah's cabin as Daniel rounded the last bend in the path. Early settlers in Wayne County had cleared this patch of land on the bank of the Tuscarawas River and constructed a crude cabin. After his cousin had come to live with them and discovered the ramshackle shack, he had seen possibilities among the cobwebs and entwining grapevines. Isaiah had laid hardwood planking over the original dirt floor and installed double-paned windows purchased from a resale shop. He'd added a wood-burning stove bought at auction for cooking and winter warmth. Cool breezes through the pinewoods stretching high into the hills kept even the hottest July days bearable. His reclusive cousin had dug his own well, built a flagstone fireplace into one wall, and replaced the rotted roof with steel sheeting from the salvage yard. Then he'd crawled onto the roof and painted the metal dark green to blend in with the forest. The bishop probably wouldn't approve of so fancy a roof, but Isaiah loved the fact that it would last forever.

Daniel knew his practical cousin wasn't half as simpleminded as folks thought him to be.

"Isaiah?" he called at the clearing, but he heard only the faint rush of the river and birds high overhead. Then Daniel saw his cousin round the back corner of his cabin carrying an armful of firewood. His constant companion, a large yellow dog, loped by his side. Isaiah's thick, straight hair was combed back from his tanned face and, as usual, his hat was nowhere in sight. With bare feet and his shirtsleeves rolled up to his elbows, he looked more like a Native American from schoolhouse storybooks than an Amish fellow. But he didn't need to conform exactly to the Plain style of dress because weeks would pass without his seeing anybody other than family members.

He added his load to the neat stack near the front door for his old-fashioned stove. He had no use for the propane Daniel and Abby used at the main house. "Hullo," Isaiah called with a grin. Daniel was one of the few people the younger man ever tried to communicate with.

"You didn't come up to the porch for supper," said Daniel, "so I brought it to you." He held up the food containers and travel mug.

Isaiah sprinted to the pump to wash while Daniel set out his meal in the outdoor dining room—a rough-hewn picnic table and two hand-made benches under the slanted porch roof. Isaiah dried his hands on a gingham towel that hung from a tree branch and slipped onto a bench, graceful as a cat. He could sneak up on a deer and pull her white tail, he moved so silently.

While he bowed his head, Daniel pulled the plastic wrap from the plate. "Sorry about the dried out meal," he said. "Abby isn't home. Her younger sister cooked this, but the buttered noodles aren't too bad."

Isaiah glanced up quizzically while biting into a piece of chicken.

For some reason, Daniel prattled on whenever he was in his cousin's company, knowing full well the man couldn't hear and didn't understand a word he said. Yet he seemed happier when folks spoke to him—grinning and nodding his head—so Daniel talked whenever they were alone. Isaiah grunted a sound that meant pleasure, so apparently Catherine's cooking didn't fall short of the mark for him.

Daniel patted Isaiah's strong shoulder with affection. "No need to hurry." He made a slow, undulating motion with his hand. "Bring the dishes up to the house tomorrow." He touched the plate, bowl, and cup, pointed in the direction of his house, and then toward the sky and made a forward rolling motion that both men took to mean "to-morrow." They had devised a similar backward movement to indicate "yesterday." Over the years Daniel and Isaiah had developed their own simple form of communication.

When Isaiah nodded in understanding, Daniel slapped his shoulder once more and started for home. As darkness fell around him, he paused a moment to pray for guidance. With Abby gone, he felt like a boat adrift without anchor or paddle. Now more than ever, he needed to stay strong for the people living here who depended on him.

Catherine watched from the kitchen window as Daniel sauntered off, carrying supper to his mysterious cousin. Shy Amish people might not talk much at meals, but she'd never known any to hide from folks, especially not from their own family. While she washed dishes, wiped down countertops, and swept the floor, her mind invented half a dozen reasons for someone turning into a hermit.

Had he broken the *Ordnung* so grievously that the district had cast him out? District members could not take meals, conduct business, or socialize with those who had been shunned, but they could provide food, shelter, and basic necessities. *Is that what Daniel is doing—providing subsistence to someone who has been shunned?* By the time she had finished cleaning the kitchen, no other explanation seemed logical.

"Laura, Jake, come take a bath," she called from the doorway to the front room. "Your *daed* said it's time. Laura, you put the toys away in the box while your *bruder* bathes first."

Jake scampered to his feet, carrying a yellow rubber toy.

"*Mamm* lets him bring Ducky in the tub," said Laura, looking pensive.

"Then Ducky can come for a scrubbing too." Catherine took the boy's hand, feeling a measure of relief as Laura began tidying the room without a word of argument. Maybe the *kinner* would adjust to her presence quicker than their father.

After Jake was bathed, dressed in his sleep shirt, and headed up the steps with an equally clean duck, Catherine called Laura for her turn in the bathtub. Daniel hadn't returned from his delivery yet. While the girl splashed around in the bubbles for a few minutes, Catherine started the kettle for tea, watching the back door for his arrival. Fifteen minutes later, her niece padded out in a fresh nightgown and sopping wet hair. Catherine left her window-side vigil to towel dry Laura's waist length tresses and brush out the tangles.

"Tell me, niece, how old is your cousin who lives out behind the barn?"

The child shrugged her shoulders. "I don't know."

"Is he young like you, old like me, or somewhere in between?"

Laura looked up at her and considered. "He's old like you, but not old like *daed*."

"Hmm, that's interesting. Do you know his name?" She glanced into the back hallway.

Laura giggled. "Of course I know his name. It's Isaiah."

"I don't think I've ever met him," Catherine said softly, working her fingers patiently through a nasty snarl.

The girl lifted and then dropped her shoulders.

"I wonder why he doesn't come to preaching services or why I've never met him at any social occasion. I don't think my sister has ever spoken about a cousin living at her farm." With care, she plied the brush through another tangle, not wishing to cause pain on her first day.

"Abby doesn't talk about him because there's not much to say… unless a person is interested in gossip." Daniel leaned on the door-frame of the back hallway. His arms were crossed over his chest, and he wasn't smiling.

"Daniel! You startled me. I had been wondering when you would get back." Catherine finished brushing the child's long hair and then braided it into a loose plait.

"Put that wet towel in the hamper and go upstairs, daughter. It's thirty minutes past your bedtime. I'll be up to say *gut nacht* in a few minutes." After Laura did as instructed, he turned his hard-edged dark eyes on Catherine. "If you have any questions, ask them of me instead of a six-year-old."

She stood and walked to the stove while her back arched like a cat. "I was curious as to why you have kept your cousin hidden away in a cabin instead of letting him mingle with other people. Would you like a cup of tea, Daniel? The water's hot."

"*Jah*, tea, *danki*." Daniel walked across the kitchen and settled his tall frame against the counter. "Isaiah isn't hidden away. He chooses to live by himself down by the river. He's happy keeping his own counsel without folks asking nosy questions or giving him advice he doesn't need."

"Honey or sugar?" she asked, dunking tea bags into both cups.

"Honey, two teaspoons." His pique changed to an expression of bafflement.

"My, you like things sweet," she murmured, while measuring the precise amount of honey into his cup. "I asked because I'm filling in for Abby for a while, and I would like to know the number of mouths to feed. And if the arrangement is to set a plate of whatever we're having on the porch picnic table, or send a hamper of sandwiches tied to a pack mule down the back path, please just let me know." She handed one cup to him, keeping her gaze locked with his.

Daniel was struggling not to smile as he accepted the cup. "We don't own a pack mule, Catherine, only Percherons, standardbreds, and one Shetland pony." He singed his lips when he sipped his tea.

"No mule? All right then, that question has been settled. You should let that tea cool a tad."

"If you put a plate of food on the porch after breakfast and dinner, that would be fine. Cover it with plastic wrap. It doesn't bother him if the food gets cold. Fill a travel mug with coffee in the morning and milk in the evening and snap the lid on tight."

"What about lunch?" She blew across the surface of her cup.

"Two sandwiches, any kind. Mustard, no mayonnaise. Sliced tomatoes if we have them, and any variety of fruit. And if you've baked cookies, he'll take as many as you can spare. Just put his lunch in one of those cooler bags with a can of cola and leave it on the table. He'll come for it by-and-by. Sometimes he gets busy cutting deadwood in the hills or working the back fields, but he always comes eventually."

Catherine sipped her tea. "Good to know. That's useful information and not idle gossip."

Daniel nodded. "Abby bakes him banana nut bread whenever the IGA puts bananas on the reduced rack. She buys all they have and freezes the extra loaves." He took a gulp of tea. "Don't be surprised if he avoids crossing your path, Catherine. He's simpleminded and keeps to himself." He tapped his temple with an index finger. "He's not all there, but he's a fine man and takes good care of himself in his cabin. You don't have to worry about him except for setting out his meals. *Danki* for the drink. I'm going to read in my room for a while. *Gut nacht.*" He left the kitchen before she could ask any more questions.

While finishing her tea, she pondered the cousin who had grown only more mysterious with Daniel's explanation. If the Graber family was concerned about gossip, the young man must have been shunned for some past transgression. She wandered onto the porch. With Daniel and the children already upstairs, she knew she should also retire to her bedroom, but she wasn't sleepy and felt too addled to read. Setting the empty cup on the rail, she grabbed the flashlight from the steps and started walking from the house at a brisk pace. Walking always brought peace whenever her siblings were annoying or *daed*'s rules thwarted her plans. If she hiked for a while, sleep would come more easily to a weary body. She headed around the barn and down the path toward the river for some much-needed exercise.

She wasn't spying on Daniel's cousin.

She hadn't planned to pick her way through the increasing gloom in the orchard, fending off low-hanging branches with an upraised arm. Mosquitoes feasting on her face and hands were no reason to turn back. After all, the moon rising low on the horizon would soon flood the fields with light to illuminate her way home. The evening breeze carried the sweet fragrance of honeysuckle and jasmine, while whippoorwills and owls joined the serenade of tree frogs and cicadas.

Catherine paused on the narrow path to catch her breath. With the orchard behind her, she spotted a line of swamp willows a quarter mile ahead. Those trees loved moist rocky soil. In between, briars and spiny shrubs encroached on the path on both sides. Who knew what critters lurked in the brush? She considered turning back, contemplating what her brother-in-law would say if he spotted her flashlight beam from his bedroom window. But Catherine Yost had always been a curious child. As a grown woman, that particular characteristic hadn't diminished. With a final glance over her shoulder, she inhaled a deep breath and forged ahead, concentrating on where she walked as sharp black-berry thorns threatened both eyes and clothes.

As the path entered the woods and shadows soon enveloped her, Catherine stood still for several moments. The flashlight became more hindrance than help because it revealed too small an area to gain her bearings. Switching off the narrow beam, she waited patiently for her eyes to adjust to the darkness. Soon the well-trodden path dimly reappeared between the trees.

What am I doing here? Why am I spying on someone who wishes to be left alone? Haven't I annoyed Daniel enough my first day in his house? But Catherine inched forward until scrub forest gave way to the tall syc-amores and willows that grew near water. She paused and listened to the faint but distinctive sound of a rushing river, trying to ignore the chilling cries of a coyote up in the hills. Beyond the line of trees she spotted a black void, warning of the steep drop-off of a riverbed. She gingerly picked her way along the path, illuminated only by the light of a full moon overhead.

As she pushed aside some low tree boughs, she gasped. Yellow light from a kerosene lamp flickered through the wavy glass of a window. She had found the cabin—the residence of Daniel's reclusive cousin, Isaiah. Though she yearned to peek inside his home, to discover the tastes of a man who lived by his own design, she didn't dare. She'd already wandered from her sister's home and had been gone too long. Feeling a shiver of excitement snake up her spine, Catherine watched spellbound for another minute. Then she turned and began the pains-taking journey back to her new home.

Creeping along the path, darker now than on her way in, tiny hairs on the back of neck suddenly stood on end. She peered off to her left into the brush, maybe ten or twelve feet. Sitting motionless in the thicket with ears at full alert sat a very large yellow animal. His eyes reflected the moonlight with an evil, netherworld glint. The beast neither barked, nor howled, nor made any menacing approach, yet Catherine's heart stopped beating within her chest for several seconds.

Was it a fox? Or a coyote? Perhaps a lone wolf that had wandered down from Canada across a frozen lake?

She didn't stick around to ask questions or gather additional canine details. She picked up her skirt and ran pell-mell for the house. She didn't stop until the porch loomed before her eyes, and then she doubled over, panting like the species she had encountered.

Despite her best effort, Catherine hadn't been remotely unobtrusive. Alive to the nuances of the night, Isaiah Graber had sensed her approach from the moment a blackberry briar had first caught the sleeve of her dress and she'd muttered in dismay. Overcome with his own curiosity, he'd circled around in a wide arc to watch the stranger approach his cabin.

He knew she was afraid—he'd caught the scent of fear—but on she'd crept.

He could tell she had little experience in the great outdoors, yet she hadn't turned back when the path left the sparse orchard and entered the dense, dark woods. Little illumination reached the forest floor until a person reached the clearing for his cabin, but the woman had waited for her eyes to adjust to the darkness and then kept going. *Will she boldly let herself in and sit down on my sofa? Maybe fry up a few eggs for a late night snack?* At the spruce tree she had paused and approached no farther. She stood staring at his cabin, watching what he couldn't fathom. Then she'd tripped over the same rocks and been scratched by the same briars all the way back. Utterly perplexed, Isaiah followed her until she reached the orchard without breaking her neck.

This was the same woman who had arrived this afternoon with a bulging a suitcase. He'd seen a buggy pull up to the house while he'd been repairing fences in the high pasture. Little happened on his cousin's farm that escaped his notice, unless he was off hunting in the autumn or buried under a blanket of snow during winter. Was she the one who had cooked the delicious fried chicken, buttered noodles, and spinach salad with pieces of bacon? He'd watched Abigail climb into a car with flashing red and blue lights and not come back. Isaiah couldn't imagine what Daniel would do without his wife. And he'd been rather curious about the woman ever since her arrival. But now that she had bravely ventured down the path, all the way to his cabin, he was down-right mystified.

Six

Nathan Fisher paid no attention when the late model sedan drove up his driveway. English folks often pulled into the yard to ask directions or to see if they were selling eggs, cheese, or garden produce. Once an elderly *Englischer* asked if he had any cuckoo clocks for sale. When he had been dumbfounded by the question, the woman explained that because the Amish originally came from Switzerland, she thought he might have maintained an old-country trade.

Cuckoo clocks. Just when you think you have heard it all.

Whoever this person was, most likely he or she would soon leave when no one came out with things for sale. He had chores to do. His recently baled hay needed to be stacked in the barn loft out of the weather. Cows needed milking and garden vegetables were ready to be picked. Although Ruth had managed their garden on her own, he couldn't expect his aunt to keep house, cook meals, care for his son, and do outdoor chores too. He needed to do more than his share because she owed him no lifetime commitment. Besides, he couldn't drop what he was doing in his present condition. He was dirty from head to toe and probably smelled worse than their sow after a roll in fresh mud.

Pulling on the rope with all his strength, Nathan raised another pile of bales up to the loft. Two more loads and his latest cutting of hay should be finished. He would cover the remaining bales with plastic and leave them outdoors to supplement pasture grass for the next few weeks.

"Hello? Mr. Fisher?" A female voice called from the barn doorway.

Nathan clenched down on his back teeth. "*Jah,* I'm Nathan Fisher, but I'm busy right now. We have no eggs for sale if that's why you're here. And if you're collecting donations, my aunt's up at the house. Tell her there's some money in the canister by the door."

The woman chuckled, stepping inside rather than going on her way. "I'll remember that come time for the March of Dimes drive, but today I'm not soliciting money. I'm here to talk to you."

He glanced over his shoulder at her from the ladder. The woman was as skinny as a fence pole, with curly yellow hair standing out from her head like a lion's mane. But her manner of dress was all business—gray suit, white blouse, and high-heeled shoes. As Nathan stared, she ventured deeper into the barn. "Careful there, ma'am, in those fancy shoes. There are things in here you do not want to step in."

She instantly stood still. "Right, then. I'll wait for you outside in the shade." She pivoted and headed to the pasture fence, where low dogwood trees offered cool relief.

Because she did not appear to be leaving, Nathan had little choice but to tie off the pulley rope, wipe his dirty hands on a rag, and walk out into the oppressively hot sunshine. He shielded his eyes from the glare. "What can I do for you, Miss…"

"Mrs. Patricia Daly," she said, digging in her purse. "I'm a social worker with Children's Services. I'm here to make a home inspection regarding the care of an infant, Abraham Fisher." She smiled pleasantly and held out her identification card from a brown wallet.

He blinked once or twice like an owl. "What kind of inspection?"

She slipped the wallet back into her shoulder bag. "Just routine.

Nothing to worry about. Your son was admitted to the hospital for observation following your wife's passing. In these situations, the case is
assigned to Children's Services. A follow-up visit is scheduled to make
sure the baby is receiving proper care and nutrition. And please accept
my deepest sympathy for your loss."

What she just said took a moment to sink in, but when it did
Nathan felt his back go rigid. "You've come to check if I'm feeding my
boy?"

"Put in those terms my job sounds awful, doesn't it? And I am sure
you're taking fine care of your son, Mr. Fisher, but not everyone, especially not every widower, faced with so enormous an undertaking rises
to the occasion."

Nathan shifted his weight and tucked his hands under his suspenders. "You would be better off speaking plain English, ma'am, so I don't
misunderstand your meaning."

She nodded after a moment's thought. "Some fathers looking after
a baby alone for the first time don't care for them properly. They don't
change diapers often enough or maybe they can't handle a fussy eater.
My job, my responsibility, is to the children of this county—Amish or
English. I've been sent to observe Abraham and fill out a report." She
pulled out a pad on a clipboard from her leather bag and stared at him
with more determination than he'd ever seen in a woman.

He looked away to gaze at the sow slumbering in her pen as her tiny
piglets nursed in a neat row. "All right, then. Had I known you were
coming, I would have made myself more presentable. I wouldn't walk
downwind of me on the way to the house, if you take my meaning."

She laughed much too loudly. "I do, but don't worry, Mr. Fisher.
I'm not here to describe you in my report, only your son. And we're required to make our assessment visits unannounced."

"So nobody puts on a dog and pony show just for your benefit?" He
sounded caustic and hadn't meant to. This *Englischer* was just doing her
job and he had no cause to be surly. He'd heard that some folks didn't
take good care of their *kinner,* but thought none of them were Amish.

Mrs. Daly didn't seem to mind. "That's right. Some people clean up their act when somebody's watching but go right back to their neglectful ways once my tires hit the pavement."

As they walked toward the house, the social worker gave him a wide berth, and then she paused at the porch steps.

"Go in," he said. "The door's open."

She went up the steps, pushed open the screen door, and entered his kitchen. Iris had opened every window and door in the house, and a battery fan rotated on the countertop. The room smelled of ripe peaches and brown sugar.

"Hello. Come on in," said Iris, glancing up with flour dusting her cheeks and nose. "I'm baking peach pies before my fruit turns mushy. You're right on time. The first batch is ready to come from the oven."

Mrs. Daly took in the entire kitchen with a quick, perusing glance. "I don't want to interrupt what you're doing, and you might not want to offer pie when you know why I'm here." She introduced herself and then repeated everything she'd explained to Nathan by the barn, omitting the reference to a dog and pony show.

Iris listened wide eyed and bewildered. "Do you think we would let a *man* fend for a baby by himself?" Her tone betrayed how ridiculous she found the idea. "Amish men don't know much about infants, and they don't have time to sit around reading books sent home by the hospital." She talked over her shoulder while washing her hands. "That's what his family and the community is for. And if he didn't have me, some other woman in the district would have stepped in to help." She dried her hands and then offered one to shake. "I'm his aunt, Iris Fisher."

"I'm pleased to meet you."

"Likewise, I'm sure. Why don't you have a seat?" Iris pointed toward the end of the table not covered with baking supplies. "And that's I-R-I-S for your report." She nodded at Mrs. Daly's clipboard.

Patricia grinned and lowered herself into a chair. "Let me write that down right now. And if you don't mind, I'd like to ask you some questions."

Iris supplied Patricia with her permanent address, an emergency contact phone number, and the expressed assurance that she would remain in Nathan's home for as long as she was needed. Mrs. Daly wrote fast and asked few questions because Iris volunteered plenty of information.

Nathan stood in the doorway watching the interview like a reluctant bystander. Fancy-dressed *Englischers* made him nervous. The only *Englischers* he could relax around wore bib overalls, Carhartt jackets, and ball caps advertising a particular brand of tractors.

After a short while, Mrs. Daly glanced up at him. "If I can see little Abraham, I won't take up too much more of your valuable time."

"Sure thing," crowed Iris. "Just follow me. He's asleep in the front room because the kitchen gets stuffy on baking days."

Nathan watched the social worker trail after his aunt, subtly peering left and right to see if any wild beasts lurked in dark corners or if other hidden dangers waited to befall an innocent baby. He followed after them, too nervous to return to his chores. What would happen if this overdressed inspector saw something she didn't like? Would she snatch up Abraham and run out the door to her car, maybe sticking a receipt in his mailbox like an English dry cleaners? He wouldn't take his eyes off her until she left his property.

"There he is." Iris pointed toward the bay window. "Inspect all you want."

Mrs. Daly peeked into a portable crib where the baby slept in blissful repose. The bed had a wind-up mechanism that would rock back and forth, usually long enough to put the tyke to sleep. "Oh, my," she whispered. "He is a handsome boy."

"Of course, he is. He's a Fisher, ain't he?" Iris grinned at Nathan over Mrs. Daly's head.

"I'm very sorry, little Abe, but I must lift you out of there." She reached beneath the lightweight blanket.

"You're going to wake him?" Iris didn't sound pleased.

"Have to, I'm afraid. I must estimate his length and weight to make sure he's gaining weight as he should be. Also, I need to check him for diaper rash."

"*Diaper rash?*" Iris' pique rang out loud and clear. "He doesn't have diaper rash!"

When Mrs. Daly lifted the baby free of the swinging contraption and pulled off his covering, Abraham began to wail with indignation.

"Now you've done it," said Iris. "I'll fetch a fresh diaper so you can make yourself useful while inspecting his bottom." Off she hurried, leaving the social worker cooing and jiggling the *boppli* like a proud grandparent.

"I'll be on the porch if you have more questions for me." Nathan marched off without waiting for her response. This was a woman's affair, if it was anybody's business at all. He couldn't believe his tax dollars paid a person's salary to check baby bottoms for a living.

Pouring a cup of coffee, he drank it cold on the porch glider. The longer he rocked, the more irritated he became. What right did the government have sticking their noses in how Amish families raised their *kinner*? Didn't he already have enough folks looking over his shoulder, making sure he didn't paint his barn too bright a color or attach too flashy a battery light to his buggy? He also had the rules of the *Ordnung* and his Bible—the Word of God had never led him astray before. Why did a fancy-dressed woman in high heels have to come snooping around his barn, his home, and his son? Nathan exhaled through his nostrils like an angry bull denied access to a spring pasture. And he hadn't cooled off much by the time the nosy woman bustled back to the porch alone. His aunt must have returned to her chores.

Mrs. Daly beamed at him as though they were long-lost friends. "There you are, Mr. Fisher. Your Aunt Iris is a delightful woman. I sampled her pie and thought it could win blue ribbons. You and Abraham are fortunate to have her."

He rose to his feet, never comfortable sitting if a woman stood before him. "*Jah,* that we are." He pulled his beard slowly and waited.

"Your son looks perfectly healthy. I left the card of a local pediatrician on the table. He'll need a medical checkup down the road. Shall we say at six months, if not sooner?"

"Okay, we'll take care of it." He clasped his hands together behind his back for something to do with them. After an uncomfortable pause, he asked, "Was there something else you needed to know about Abraham? What arrangements we've made for his schooling?"

She looked anxious. "No, not about the baby. I was just wondering how *you* were doing." She met his gaze and held it.

"Me? I'm eating fine. Iris is a good cook, if you're worried about my size and weight." He almost added something about his lack of diaper rash but caught himself in time. That would have been inappropriate.

Mrs. Daly hefted the strap of her bag higher up on her shoulder with a smile. "I'm not inquiring about your physical state, Mr. Fisher. I'm concerned about your mental outlook since your wife's unexpected passing."

He narrowed his gaze. "Wayne County wants to know about my mental state?"

"No, no," she said, shaking her head. "I'm not approaching this correctly." She pulled a business card from her jacket pocket and held it out to him. "In my spare time I'm a lay minister for my Christian church in Wooster, and I'm a trained counselor. I conduct grief therapy sessions in my home for those like you who have lost spouses. I'd like to invite you—"

He interrupted her. "I'm a farmer and Amish, in case you haven't noticed. I don't have time to sit around somebody's living room sipping tea and telling folks how much I miss my wife. Plain folks don't question the will of God. We go about our business and mourn our loved ones in private. You *Englischers* love to chaw everything to death. And you probably don't feel much better once you're done pouring your guts out to each other."

If she had been shocked by his outburst, she hid it well. "Coffee," she said.

He glanced back at her. "I beg your pardon?"

"We usually drink coffee sitting around my living room, not tea. And you're right—sometimes we don't feel any better after sharing our grief." She waited until he met her gaze. "But every now and then we do." She put the card on the plastic table. "Tuck this into a kitchen drawer for now, just in case you change your mind." She started down the steps toward the driveway. "Oh, I almost forgot. Abraham looks healthy and robust, and the home you and your aunt have provided is more than adequate. That's what I intend to say in my report. I commend your care and diligence." She nodded, strode to her car, and drove away with barely a stirring of driveway dust.

Nathan sat on the porch glider and began to rock. He stared down at floorboards in dire need of paint, not feeling the least bit caring or diligent.

Daniel Graber spent the night in his buggy, parked behind the Wayne County jail. He didn't want to miss visiting hours for those awaiting trial. With Catherine home watching the *kinner* and Isaiah to tend to his chores, he was able to see Abigail. Never had he missed his wife as much as during the previous week. He didn't think it possible to miss a person so much. He'd come to Wooster yesterday, tied up in the back parking lot, fed his horse hay and a bucket of oats he'd brought from home, and filled another bucket with water from plastic jugs. Arrangements for him weren't quite so luxurious. He ate his meal cold from a small cooler and slept curled up under a blanket behind the seat. Today his back rebelled with painful spasms from his cramped sleeping position.

Daniel washed his hands and face in the public washroom and then found a vending machine to buy coffee. After inserting a dollar, he pushed the button and waited. When the cup fell crookedly, the stream of hot liquid missed by a quarter inch. He tried again with a second bill and burned his fingers correcting the cup's position.

The morning was not off to an auspicious start. For the first time in longer than he could remember, he hadn't begun with prayers of thanksgiving or pleas for guidance. With hat in hand, Daniel waited in line for the appointed hour. When the door opened at the appointed time, a guard with a clipboard asked his name and then pointed across the room. Midway down a table sat Abby, so still that pigeons might have mistaken her for a statue if this had been a park.

Daniel saw something that turned his blood cold—they hadn't allowed his wife to keep her traditional Amish outfit of a navy blue dress with white apron and *kapp*. To be seen in public in the atrocious green, mannish clothes must cause her unbearable discomfort and shame. As he approached, she glanced up with an expression of both joy and sorrow. Dark hollows lay beneath her eyes, and she appeared at least five pounds thinner.

"*Guder mariye, ehemann.* You look like you slept in your clothes." The corner of her mouth turned up in a familiar and heartening smile.

"Good morning to you, *fraa.* That's because I did. I drove here yesterday so I wouldn't miss visiting hours."

"You came by horse and buggy?" She lifted an eyebrow. "You should have called the hired van. There's extra money in the coffee can in the cupboard for occasions like this."

For occasions like this? "I doubt you had planned to use your egg money for visiting day at the county jail." He glanced nervously around the room at the odd assortment of humanity.

"No one plans for emergencies, no matter what their nature."

"True enough, but let's not quibble about nonsense on our first meeting." He reached for her hand. "How are you faring, Abby? Are they treating you well?"

She allowed her hand to be enfolded with little response. "*Jah,* I'm fine. The lady guard is nice to me. She explains how things are done here so I won't be unduly shocked." She inhaled and exhaled with practiced control.

"Anything else?" he asked, desperate to understand what had transpired since her arrest.

Her face turned pale. "They took my photo, Daniel. I ask them not to, but they said it was mandatory. Then they fingerprinted me and took away my clothes and worldly possessions, including my *kapp.*" Her fingers reached up to her uncovered head.

She shook her head, as though dislodging an unpleasant thought. "At least they let me keep my Bible, so I started reading the Old Testament. Did you know that the first chapter of Exodus talks about midwives? Pharaoh, king of Egypt, had enslaved the Hebrews. When he grew concerned about their increasing numbers, he ordered the midwives to kill the male children. Because the midwives feared God more than Pharaoh, they refused and were rewarded for their faith. Later, when the Hebrews continued to multiply, Pharaoh ordered every boy to be thrown into the Nile. Baby Moses was placed in a basket and sent downriver and saved by Pharaoh's daughter. She adopted him as her own son. Much later, he led his people out of bondage into the promised land."

Daniel blinked several times. "You've been locked away from your family for days and you wish to tell me *Bible stories*?"

Abby's eyes filled with tears. "If I start asking about Laura and Jake, if I hear they have missed me and suffer because of my absence, then I'll go mad. I must stay strong by distracting myself from the circumstances and using my time wisely." She swiped at her face with her sleeve. "Tell me that my sister has arrived and cares for my family."

"*Jah*, Catherine has come to look after our young ones, but she's not…you."

"No, I suppose not. Each woman has her own way of cooking, baking, and ironing clothes. But I hope you're not being too particular, Daniel Graber. If she stomps home, back to her own life, you'll be stuck with cooking scrambled eggs three times a day."

Daniel fought back bitter tears from his selfishness. Abby was worried about him instead of herself. "If I chase her off with my peculiar demands, it'll serve me right. When does your lawyer think you can come home?" His voice crackled with emotion.

"When you pay the court half a million dollars." She lifted her chin. "Because I don't pose a flight risk, the attorney requested another hearing to reduce my bail, but we can't be certain it will be granted. Hopefully, I won't draw sour-faced Judge O'Neil next time."

Don't pose a flight risk…draw a sour-faced judge? His sweet wife sounded like a city *Englischer*. Even her *Deutsch* accent had diminished. "Your *daed* and the ministerial brethren visited me the day before yesterday," said Daniel. "They are undecided on the idea of using a bail bondman. They must hold a congregational meeting after the next preaching service. Your father fears the district will be divided on the matter. There's never been anything like this before to set a precedent."

Abby nodded, withdrawing her hands and folding them in front of her. "That is true, Daniel, but tell me about my father. How is he handling the shame of a daughter in jail? He's not a young man anymore." As visitors at the other tables stirred up a commotion, her words became barely audible.

Daniel considered how much to tell her. He couldn't lie, but should she hear that her *daed* looked ten years older than the last time Daniel had seen him? "Don't worry so much about others. Your father is a strong man whose faith will carry him through this ordeal. He is of the opinion that we should put the farm up as collateral. He's even willing to offer his own home as collateral so that you could be free until the trial. It's the ministers and the deacon who are undecided. And a bishop cannot behave in a certain fashion just because the member in question is his daughter."

She sighed, her mouth turning down at the corners. "*Jah,* I suppose not, but I'm glad he hasn't disowned me."

"He loves you, Abby, but he must follow the *Ordnung*." Daniel glanced up at the large clock hanging on the wall. He couldn't remember how much time he would have with his wife. He sighed and inhaled deeply. "There is talk among the people. Word got around about the charges against you. No one understands how you could be charged with 'practicing medicine without a license' *and* 'practicing midwifery without a license.'" He gazed at a multitattooed woman consoling an equally tattooed family member at the next table, wishing he didn't have to broach this subject. When he turned back, Abby sat waiting, pale and deflated. "Is there more to what happened at the Fisher farm that night?"

She nodded with downcast eyes. "I knew if I couldn't stop Mrs. Fisher's hemorrhaging, she would die. So I gave her a shot to stop the bleeding. But the drug didn't work, or it simply came too late. Ruth's blood pressure fell so fast that her heart stopped."

Daniel leaned across the table and gritted out his words between clenched teeth. "You have no idea that's what happened. You couldn't see inside that woman's body." He tried unsuccessfully to keep his voice down.

She shrugged. "That's what the books say happens when a person bleeds to death, so I'm assuming that's what took place with Mrs. Fisher. But it doesn't matter now. She's gone and nothing will bring her back."

"It matters for you, Abigail, and for our family. I take it you weren't supposed to have that drug in your possession," he said. All this medical talk felt as alien to him as discussing the migratory patterns of wildlife on the African plains.

"No, but I told the paramedics. They had to know the dosage I gave so they could treat accordingly. I didn't know what amount would be too much, or if the drug reacted badly with other medications."

"Of course you wouldn't know. You're not a doctor."

"I never said I was." She jutted out her chin.

Her defensiveness began to irritate him. "Who else did you tell?"

"I told Dr. Weller when he called me the next day." She began wringing her hands as though lathering them with soap.

"Didn't you tell the sheriff when he arrived at the Fishers?"

"No, but not on purpose. Mr. Fisher was very upset—one minute sobbing incoherently and the next minute talking baby names as though nothing bad had happened. When the sheriff began writing up his report, I answered his questions but forgot to mention the shot of Pitocin."

"Oh, Abigail, that's what these charges are about. You had no business injecting a drug into a woman you didn't even know and who wasn't even a patient of Doc Weller. You shouldn't have done that." He felt foolish restating the obvious. "When did you tell the sheriff what you had done?"

"When he arrested me. You were standing right there."

Daniel slapped a palm down on the table.

She glanced up with confusion. "I had to tell him what I'd done.

I wasn't about to lie. Is that what you would have me do—bear false witness?"

"No, of course not, but you shouldn't have given that woman a shot in the first place. Administering medications to folks is business for English doctors, not Amish midwives. Your *daed* will not like hearing this."

Her expression of confusion changed to alarm. "You plan to tell my father?"

"I don't have a choice. He asked me to speak to you. How can he and the other brethren make a decision without knowing everything? Nobody understood why the charges against you were so serious."

She sighed. "Tell whomever you wish." She glanced around the room as though the discussion failed to hold her interest.

Daniel couldn't fathom how a gentle soul, separated from her family, could remain so lackadaisical. "Abby, if you're convicted of a felony, you could be sent to prison for many years. Do you fully understand the situation?"

"I think so. I might be convicted of dispensing medicine, of which I am guilty. But if I had to do it over, I don't think I would have done anything differently."

Daniel grabbed her hand. "You can't be serious! If the judge hears you're not sorry, that you don't regret your lapse of judgment, he may…" Daniel tried to remember the English expression, "…throw the book at you."

She stared at him blankly. "The apostle Paul wrote several books of the Bible while locked away in a Roman jail, including the book of Philippians. In that book he outlined the steps to obtain true joy in life."

It was Daniel's turn to stare. *Has a week in jail been long enough to change Abigail into a stranger?* "Do you fashion yourself to be an apostle? Do you see some connection between Paul's persecution as a Christian and your present circumstances?"

Her pale complexion flushed to an unnaturally deep hue. "Oh, no. I didn't mean it like that. I only meant that if God wants me locked up for attempting to save Ruth Fisher's life, then I intend to use my time wisely. I've begun studying the Bible from the beginning. I wish to know more about the Hebrew prophets and the events before the Savior's birth that determined His life on earth."

Daniel noticed the other visitors hugging and rising to leave. He knew his time with his wife was almost over. "At least listen to your lawyer, Abby. I don't want you to lie or withhold information, but please accept his counsel." Daniel never thought he would be saying words like that. "If not for your sake, then for the sake of Laura and Jake."

With the mention of her *kinner*, Abby's face clouded with pain. "How are they? Do they miss me?"

"They are well, but of course they miss you. It takes great effort and many bedtime stories for Laura to fall asleep. Your *schwester* tries her best, but she is not you. Not with the children and certainly not in the kitchen."

A ghost of a smile flitted across her face. "I hope God will forgive my vanity, but it does a wife's heart good to hear she's not easily replaced."

"And I hope I'll be forgiven for capturing my *kinner*'s image with a camera." He drew out an old-fashioned Polaroid snapshot and passed it to her, blushing a bright hue. "I asked a tourist looking to buy eggs if she would take their picture and she did. I wanted you to have something to look at, to keep your spirits up while you're in here."

Abby looked shocked at first, but she smiled when she gazed on Laura and Jake playing on the swings. "*Danki*, but you shouldn't have done this." She tucked the photo into her pocket.

"It's time. Let's go, folks." A harsh voice made the announcement over the loud speaker.

Daniel's heart dropped into his stomach. There was so much he'd wanted to say, but he had used the time to prod, complain, and deliver advice. "We all miss you, *fraa*—me most of all, and not just your cooking. Please don't be stubborn or willful. Come back to your family."

"It's not my choice that I remain here, Daniel. There is the small matter of half a million dollars."

He struggled to his feet, while she rose with the smooth grace of a swan. "I'll do what I can," he said. "You have my word."

"Tell Catherine I am in her debt. And be patient with her, *ehemann.* She has a gentle spirit and is easily hurt by strong words." Abby offered a smile and walked toward the metal door across the room, calm and composed.

What goes on in this loathsome place that has so affected my wife?

Seven

Catherine had mulled over the recluse last night while waiting for sleep to come, as she had each evening since seeing his tidy cabin in the woods. During the last couple of days she had set out his meals as she'd been instructed. Yet, despite her attempts to get a look at him, the man evaded observance. She had been in the cellar washing clothes, breaking up a dispute between siblings, or cleaning up after dinner when he claimed his meal. Now, as the sun rose over dew-kissed fields and purple-hued hills, Isaiah Graber again occupied her thoughts. She washed and dressed quickly because Daniel liked his breakfast early, and then she checked on Laura and Jake in each of their small bedrooms. Laura's faceless doll had fallen to the floor and the sheet had tangled around her legs. Jake's nightshirt was sodden with perspiration because she'd forgotten to open the window in his room. Yet both slept the deep slumber of those who knew no worries in life.

She pulled Jake's thumb from his mouth and pushed damp hair back from his brow. He barely stirred in his dreams. She paused to utter a silent prayer to be shown the correct course in her sister's home, a way to serve without her own will getting in the way. Once the matter of her adjustment was turned over to God, she headed downstairs with a lighter heart.

In the kitchen she found that Daniel had already started coffee. Another note—the fourth since her arrival—waited for her on the table:

> *Gone out to milk cows. Be back around six thirty for breakfast. Get kinner up around that time. Don't let them sleep in so late.*

Catherine poured a cup of coffee and then began frying a pound of bacon and chopping peppers, onions, and tomatoes for the eggs. She mixed orange juice; peeled, diced, and boiled potatoes for hash browns; and toasted half a loaf of the whole wheat bread she'd baked yesterday. By the time she heard the screen door slam, signaling Daniel's arrival, cheese was melting over the omelet while crisp bacon drained on paper towels. Catherine dumped the seasoned potatoes into a sizzling skillet.

Daniel shrugged out of his chore coat and toed off his boots in the back hall. "Something smells good," he said, entering the kitchen.

She buttered another slice of toast, adding it the stack already on the table. "Laura, please get your *bruder* from the front room. It's time to eat." She turned to Daniel. "I got them up twenty minutes ago."

Daniel poured himself coffee and topped off her mug. "Those two would sleep till noon if you'd let them," he said. His eyes widened as she set the platter of bacon and bowl of eggs on the table and nearly bugged from his head when she carried over the hash browns. "Good grief, Catherine. This is a lot of food for an ordinary Wednesday," he said. "Bacon and eggs *or* toast and oatmeal will suffice in the future."

"Good to know," she murmured as they bowed their heads in prayer.

Once the Graber family began eating, Catherine surreptitiously glanced out the window to the back porch. "It looks like rain. Do you think we should invite Isaiah inside for breakfast? We don't want him or his food getting wet." She concentrated on pouring milk for the youngsters.

"Nice of you to worry, but that porch has a roof. His food will stay perfectly dry until he comes up to eat." He scooped a hearty portion of fried potatoes. "I don't think Abigail has ever made spuds like these. They're very good," he said after sampling a forkful. He preferred his eggs without all the peppers, onions, and who-knew-what-else, but he remembered Abby's request for patience and kindness toward her sister. He took five strips of bacon, just to be polite.

"*Danki.* A little bacon grease adds plenty of flavor." She ate almost twice her usual amount just to keep herself from asking questions about Daniel's shy cousin. Laura ate some eggs but spent most of her time pushing onion and peppers to the side of her plate. Jake played with his bacon strips, trying to stand them on end.

"Jake usually eats corn flakes, Aunt Catherine," said Laura. "Is it all right if I pour him a bowl?" She looked from one adult to the other. Catherine also glanced at Daniel, uncertain of the correct reply.

"*Jah,* go ahead," Daniel said to his daughter. Then to his son he said, "Stop playing and eat your bacon, Jake. You always eat *mamm*'s. And drink your milk and juice." He returned to his own breakfast as though competing in a race. "If you should need me today, I'll be out in the east fields spreading manure."

She knew what manure-spreading days smelled like, so barring an emergency she planned to stay indoors with the east-facing windows closed. "I'll catch up on laundry in the morning and save ironing for the afternoon. By three o'clock a breeze usually picks up from the south, cooling off the front room. Let me fill your thermos with coffee." She rose from the table as he walked into the hallway.

"Put a couple extra sandwiches in Isaiah's cooler for my lunch too. That'll save me from coming to the house and interrupting my work."

Catherine followed him to the door, carrying the thermos. "I'll put plenty in the cooler bag." She watched him pull on boots and grab his hat.

"Before I forget, your sister sends her regards and thanks you for filling in for her. She will write another letter soon."

Her chest tightened around her heart until it became painful to breathe. "Does she look well?"

"Like I told you last night, she looks as well as can be expected." He opened the door and peered up. "There's barely a cloud in the sky. I think you're mistaken about your forecast of rain." He reached for his thermos and hurried down the steps.

Actually, he'd told her little since his return from visiting Abby in Wooster. He'd rambled on about the charges being more serious than they had thought, and that he needed to talk to her father after Sunday's preaching service—updates about the unfortunate circumstances, but not much about her beloved sister. Yet Catherine knew Daniel missed his wife terribly. Several times his eyes had filled with tears while relaying the details of his trip.

Catherine loaded a plate with eggs, potatoes, and several pieces of bacon, and then she topped the mound with four slices of buttered toast. She balanced the breakfast on her forearm so she could carry mugs of coffee and juice to the porch too. But her mind was on Abby. How she must suffer away from her family, surrounded by dangerous *Englischers*. As Catherine pushed open the screen door with her backside, she hadn't expected to find Isaiah at the table, waiting with a fork in one hand and a knife in the other. She nearly dropped his plate of food.

For several moments they merely stared at each other. Time suspended as she took in his unusual appearance—long, straight hair combed back from his face without the customary bangs, a tanned complexion with nearly black eyes, and large muscular arms and hands. Because Amish men wear wide-brimmed hat and long sleeves, they seldom became tanned. However, both of Isaiah's shirtsleeves had been torn off above the elbow. She gasped, even though she had seen men's arms before.

He gasped too, several times. Then she realized he wasn't gasping but speaking to her. "*Guder mariye*," she greeted.

He voiced a similar pattern of sounds.

She repeated again the *Deutsch* words for "good morning."

He grinned and issued the same strange, guttural sounds.

Catherine realized he was trying to mimic her words. She set his breakfast on the table and pulled off the plastic wrap. "Eggs," she said, indicating the appropriate food on the plate. She chose the easier-to-say English word and exaggerated its pronunciation with lips and facial contortion.

"Agggs," he repeated and speared a forkful to eat.

She nodded, smiling enthusiastically. "Bay-conn." She pointed to the food and repeated the English word several times.

Isaiah tried to emulate her pronunciation with little success. It seemed as though his lips couldn't form the correct position. She tried just the first syllable, shaping and then relaxing her mouth. Each time she would point at her lips while saying the syllable. She felt like a fish in an aquarium trying to gulp a large amount of algae.

He watched her curiously. Then he picked up a slice of bacon and shoved it into his mouth. Catherine slipped onto the other bench and allowed him to eat while the food remained warm. As he forked up some hashed browns, she said "poe-tay-toes" with slow, deliberate enunciation.

He swallowed his food, drank some coffee, and dabbed at his mouth with a napkin. "Pah-tah-tohs," he parroted. This time when he repeated her word, the approximation was very close to the correct sounds.

Catherine pointed at the other items on the table—knife, fork, plate, mug, and lantern. But Isaiah had tired of her game and ate his breakfast without watching her distorted expressions. From time to time he looked up and smacked his lips and rubbed his belly.

She accepted the gestures as high compliment. "*Gut?*" she asked.

"*Gut,*" he agreed.

When he smiled, thin lines webbed his eyes, probably from not wearing his hat in the hot sun. She judged his age to be between twenty and twenty-five years old. Catherine pointed to the center of his chest. "Eye-zay-ahh," she enunciated.

"Eyes-zah," he repeated.

She attempted to stretch his name into three syllables without success. He grew restless and hooked a thumb to his chest. "Eyes-zah," he said firmly, leaving no room for discussion.

She changed the conversation to her own name. "Cath-ther-inn," she said, pointing at herself. She repeated the name three times. He studied her and then shrugged his shoulders. "Cat," he said, as though anything longer wasn't worth the effort. He finished the mug of juice in two long swallows.

She threw her head back and laughed. "Close enough. That's what my brothers call me anyway."

While Isaiah ate, a crow in the apple tree by the steps cawed loud enough for Catherine to jump. But Isaiah didn't move a muscle with the unexpected noise.

Because he didn't hear a thing, she thought. If her intuition was correct, Daniel's cousin was stone deaf. To test her theory, she blocked her mouth with her hands and began reciting the breakfast foods on the top of her lungs. The young man didn't glance up from his meal. However, her bizarre behavior did not go unnoticed.

"What are you doing out here?" Daniel asked. He walked onto the porch, letting the screen door slam behind him.

"I thought you went to the barn," she said without thinking.

"I came looking for Isaiah. I need his help."

Isaiah sipped his coffee, looking from one to the other with mild interest.

"Oh, Daniel. I've discovered he's deaf." Catherine turned her face to whisper, not wishing to be rude to the young man.

Daniel crossed his arms over a soiled jacket. "That's not much of a discovery. His *mamm* figured that out years ago."

"But don't you see? I can teach him. With my past experience as a nanny, I can help him." Excitement swelled inside her as possibilities flooded her mind.

"Help him do what, Catherine? He will till between the soybean rows today, and later he'll help me plant a late crop of corn. He doesn't need help with his chores. He already knows what to do. But if he decides to become a bank teller in Wooster, I'll let you know."

Catherine chewed on her lip to keep from responding to Daniel's sarcasm.

"Isaiah." Daniel touched his shoulder because a squirrel in the bird feeder had diverted his attention. "Hurry up and finish eating." Daniel made a chopping motion with one hand against his forearm.

"That is *not* 'hurry up' in sign language," Catherine said quietly.

Daniel looked surprised before his expression faded. "Maybe not, but he and I understand each other and that's what matters." He pointed at his cousin and then the barn, and made another chopping motion.

Isaiah nodded with comprehension, scraping the rest of his eggs onto toast to eat like a sandwich. He rose from the picnic table with the grace of a mountain lion.

"I could teach him to communicate," she insisted as her stubborn streak made an appearance.

"We'll discuss this another time, Catherine. Right now I have work to do." Daniel strode from the porch without another word.

She stared at his retreating back and started counting to ten. Before she got very far, Isaiah reached out to tug one of her ribbons. He yanked so hard he pulled her *kapp* askew. After uttering a grunt, he picked up the egg sandwich and loped off the porch. He might have been saying *danki* or perhaps the grunt had been only indigestion.

Catherine straightened her *kapp* and hollered, "You're welcome" in both English and *Deutsch*. She watched him follow Daniel toward the barn like a dog that had been chastised for chasing a rabbit. Halfway down the path, he turned and waved at her. She waved back like a tourist from a bus window, and then she hurried into the kitchen to start her morning chores.

As she washed dishes, swept floors, and put loads of laundry through the propane washer, ideas swam through her mind. Her years as a nanny for an English family would come in handy. Both of the youngsters, a set of twins, had been born deaf. Catherine had learned sign language to communicate with them. Once the twins learned to read lips, she had to remember to face them squarely while speaking. Although she never became as proficient as their mother, Catherine usually understood their speech patterns. Many words were difficult to master if a person had never heard the correct pronunciation. When the children turned eight, the family moved to Cleveland so that the twins could receive a better education than what their rural district offered.

Catherine still had the booklet she'd used to learn sign language. If she wrote to her younger sister, Meghan would send it to her. What if Isaiah wasn't simpleminded? What if his brain operated perfectly well, but he hadn't learned to communicate with his fellow man? Plain schools adequately prepared students to farm, keep house, and work in shops, factories, or construction trades. Apprenticeships taught skills such as woodworking, weaving, roofing, carpentry, and plumbing to young people. But for those with handicaps, Amish schools were woefully inadequate.

In the early afternoon Catherine put Jake down for a nap under a shady tree and gave Laura green beans to snap on the porch. She needed to hang the last load of wet laundry. The Graber yard sloped away from the house, and someone had installed a clever system of lines and pulleys between the house and the eave of the barn. From the side porch, a person could pin clothes on the line and send them out to flap in the breeze up high and away from the people below. It was an ingenious set-up—unless a kink in the rope jammed the pulley—as was the case now. She could neither haul back the dry clothes to fold, nor hang the last load of wet garments. After several attempts to unjam the pulley, Catherine marched to the cobwebby cellar to hunt for a stepladder. She dared not interrupt Daniel with his chores.

When she returned fifteen minutes later without finding a ladder, the pulley was operating smoothly. The load of towels and blankets on the line had been taken down, folded, and set in the basket. Someone had also left a nosegay of daisies on the porch steps.

Simpleminded, my foot, she thought. Holding the wildflowers to her nose, she arched up on tiptoes to scan the pasture, the vegetable garden, and the cornfield for her elusive admirer. She saw no one.

Catherine felt a stirring in her heart—a heart long thought shriveled and dormant from disuse. But she knew better than to fan the small flame of hope. Daniel Graber would never allow a friendship to grow between her and his protected cousin.

Each day Abby awoke to a different world than the one she'd known on her farm. Her jail cell was really a sparse room with two bunk beds, a toilet, and a small sink. She could take a shower down the hall, but no bathtub had been provided for muscle-soothing soaks. Between ten p.m. and six a.m., she and her roommate were locked inside, but their door remained open throughout the day. During the first hour of the morning, they cleaned their cell, which was then submitted to an inspection at seven fifteen. Each prisoner wore the same dull green jumpsuit emblazoned with "Wayne County Jail" in case she forgot where she was. Her roommate referred to their accommodations as Hotel Wooster. Inmates who earned the deputies' trust washed everyone's clothes in the laundry room down the hall. Women who possessed culinary talents prepared their meals. Other trustworthy inmates washed the dishes. Abigail wasn't awarded any chore to relieve her boredom.

After breakfast, while the other women watched TV in the common room or exercised, Abby closed her door and read her Bible. After Daniel's last visit, she continued to study the Old Testament. In the book of Leviticus, God called Moses from the tabernacle and gave him detailed instructions regarding how the Israelites were to live. There were complex procedures for burnt offerings, grain offerings, and peace, sin, and guilt offerings; complex rules about unclean animals, people, and houses; specific ways to celebrate holidays and festivals; and what constituted disobedience. The punishment usually was death. By comparison, the Amish *Ordnung* no longer seemed difficult to follow.

Abby didn't like the book of Numbers very much. It detailed the organization of the twelve tribes into armies while they lived in the Sinai Desert after fleeing from Egypt. But she loved the book of

Deuteronomy, which told the story of the Jews traveling through the wilderness, and about Moses receiving the Ten Commandments etched on stone tablets. God had provided for their every need, and yet they had showed no faith and continued to sin. The Israelites' lack of faith so angered God that, with the exception of just two people, Joshua and Caleb, no one old enough to fight in battle when they left Egypt crossed the Jordan River into the Promised Land, not even Moses.

This morning Abby picked up where she'd left off, taking courage from Scripture. Compared to the Israelites, her woes seemed small. *How a person takes comfort for granted, not appreciating God's gracious gifts of tranquility and peace of mind.*

Suddenly the door opened and the woman guard stuck in her head. "Visiting day," she announced.

"Thank you, but I won't have anyone today." Abby knew Daniel wouldn't have made the trip again so soon, not in the high season for farm chores.

"Oh, but that's where you're wrong." The deputy winked one green eye. "Someone has signed in."

"Who's come to see me?" Abby asked with growing anticipation.

Deputy Todd glanced at her clipboard. "Dr. Gerald Weller. He's on your list of potential visitors."

"Dr. Weller is here? I used to work with him..." Abby's explanation hung in the air because the deputy had already left.

She thought of several questions on her way to the visitation room: *Will Dr. Weller be angry with me? Did he land in trouble because of my behavior? Will he pity me and feel sorry for my circumstances? Or will he feel I deserve everything I got and much more for overstepping my bounds?*

When she arrived, the small, distinguished doctor was already sitting at the table. His gray hair was windblown from the parking lot, his sport coat looked too warm for the July heat and humidity, and his folded hands were age-spotted and paper-skinned. But his cool blue eye met hers without a shred of animosity.

"Abigail," he murmured as he rose clumsily to his feet.

"Dr. Weller. It's good to see you, but you shouldn't have come. You probably left an office full of patients, many who need you more than me."

"I rescheduled them. I'm sorry I haven't been here sooner."

"Thank you for coming to court for my bail hearing. I saw you in the…audience." Abby didn't know correct courtroom terminology.

"I wanted to make a statement on your behalf, but I was told I had to wait until the pretrial hearing."

"You wished to speak for me?" she asked, as hope stirred deep in her chest.

"Of course I do. Mrs. Fisher wasn't my patient and therefore she was not *your* patient. From what I could find out, she wasn't under a doctor's care, so she had no business calling you instead of an ambulance."

"I told her husband to call the EMTs, but he refused."

Dr. Weller held up his hand. "I know. I spoke with him at the hospital the next day. He stayed overnight in the waiting room so they could keep an eye on the baby. He doesn't like courthouses any better than his wife liked hospitals, but I believe he will testify on your behalf. How far along was Mrs. Fisher when you arrived at their farm?"

"She had dilated nine centimeters and was in tremendous pain. Her contractions were worse than any I've ever witnessed."

"And you called the ambulance before setting foot in Mrs. Fisher's bedroom?"

"*Jah,* as soon as I reached their house."

"Then, in my opinion as a physician, you were acting not as a midwife but in a Good Samaritan capacity."

Abby's forehead furrowed with confusion. "But I am a midwife. That's why Nathan Fisher called me. His wife got my number from someone in their district."

"You were also trying to save the life of the child. If you had stood by and waited for medical personnel to arrive, most likely the baby would have also died. And nothing you could have done would have saved Mrs. Fisher. She shouldn't have chosen home delivery with her medical condition. In fact, she'd been advised back in Indiana not to get pregnant in the first place."

Abby glanced left and right to make sure no one was listening. She'd discussed birthing matters with Dr. Weller often enough to not be embarrassed, but she wouldn't like anyone overhearing them. "That's what Nathan told me at the funeral."

"In my professional opinion, you saved the life of Abraham Fisher. The county prosecutor might not agree. He might call expert witness to the contrary, but I don't think he will. A healthy, thriving child delivered from a dying woman is strong evidence." Dr. Weller smiled for the first time since arriving. "Now tell me again what you did for the baby."

Abby's head began to throb as she remembered Ruth's cries, the oppressively hot bedroom, and the overwhelming smell of blood. "A few moments after I examined Ruth she was fully dilated, so on one of her contractions I was able to pull the baby free. But her contractions grew weaker as she lost more blood. After I cleaned mucus from the baby's nose and mouth, he started breathing and crying. I wrapped him in a blanket and handed him to Mr. Fisher. I told him to keep the child warm while I tried to help his wife." Tears were streaming down her face. "But I couldn't save her," she croaked. "There was too much blood."

Dr. Weller covered her hands with his. "No, you couldn't save her. It's doubtful that I could have either without proper medical equipment, IVs, and an accomplished surgeon. You shouldn't blame yourself for that woman's death."

Abby removed one of her hands from his to wipe her face with her handkerchief. "I don't, not really. God called her home. That's what I believe happened."

Weller nodded in agreement. "Your attorney should have no trouble with the charges of 'practicing midwifery without a license' in this emergency situation, and he certainly should be able to get 'manslaughter' dropped at the pretrial hearing. That one is ridiculous anyway." He glanced across the room and sighed. "But the 'practicing medicine without a license' and 'possession and sale of a dangerous controlled substances' charges are a different story. Did you really give Ruth Fisher an injection of Pitocin?"

Abby met his gaze without hesitation. "*Jah,* I did, but I didn't sell any drugs."

"Ah, Abigail. If you'd planned to accept payment for your services, it's the same thing. Mrs. Fisher's uterine wall had torn during delivery. She needed emergency surgery to save her life. That drug will usually slow or stop bleeding with minor tears, but not like what Ruth Fisher had."

Abby's back ached from sitting so stiffly, but she said nothing.

"You had no way of knowing that. In desperation you tried something you had heard about. But this is very serious. I suppose I already know who supplied you with the syringe and medication."

She lifted her chin and ground her back teeth, willing herself not to cry. She refused to drag another person into the mess she had created.

"Well, it really doesn't matter now. The drug didn't save the woman, but by giving her that injection, you have landed into a heap of trouble. I will do what I can, Abigail. I know your heart; you meant no harm. And nothing you did harmed that woman. God's will had been set into motion before your buggy turned up the Fisher driveway. Let's hope a judge with compassion in his heart can see beyond the letter of the law." He tightened his grip before releasing her hand. "Stay strong, stay well, and as my grandmother used to say, 'This too shall pass.'" He rose wearily to his feet.

He is an old man. When did he become so stiff and aged?

"Thank you for coming, Dr. Weller, and thank you for your words of support." She forced a smile for her friend and mentor, feeling pangs of guilt and sorrow as he shuffled away from the table. She was causing grief and heartache for everyone close to her, but she didn't know how to stop. *What could I have done differently?*

Later that night, staring at the ceiling when sleep wouldn't come, she prayed for those around her who suffered because of her actions. And she prayed to be shown the correct path out from this thorny maze.

Eight

Sweat ran beneath Nathan's hat, pooled at the base of his neck, and soaked into his shirt collar. Wiping his brow, he watched two turkey vultures floating effortlessly on wind currents, with only an occasional flap of their wings.

Oh, to have been born a bird instead of a farmer. But he probably would have been born a hummingbird instead of a vulture, eagle, or hawk. Then he would have to beat his wings all day long, continually searching for food to maintain strength. And if that weren't bad enough, he would have to fly south every year down to Mexico with only a two-inch wingspan.

Most of the time Nathan Fisher loved farming, but today was not one of those days. After he'd managed to mire the plow into mud near the riverbank, he broke two harnesses trying to pull his equipment free. In so doing, he ended up in foul-smelling muck up to his hips. He thought he might have to hitch another team of draft horses to pull himself out. Then his driving horse threw a shoe and he had to call a farrier to stop at the farm, costing him money he didn't have. Paying for Ruth's funeral expenses and the hospital bills for Abraham had left him without enough to pay this month's rent. So when a wasp stung his neck on the way to the house, he wasn't surprised. Nathan opened the screen door at lunchtime not in the best of moods.

"What happened to you?" asked Iris.

"I got stung by a wasp," he answered, heading toward the bathroom. He felt a painful lump swell beneath his fingers as he dabbed on antiseptic.

She followed him to the bathroom doorway. "Did you get out the stinger?" She arched up on tiptoes for a better look.

"A wasp, Aunt, not a bee. No stinger." He pressed a cold washrag to the lump and searched for some anti-itch medicine Ruth had bought. When he found the bottle, he sprayed liberally, bringing a searing pain to the tender area. "This hurts like the devil, worse than any bee sting."

Iris paled, glancing around the room. "Do not invoke the evil one's name. You may just compound your troubles."

"Hard to imagine this day getting much worse," he groused. "I mired the plow in mud, got myself stuck, and broke two harnesses. And my standardbred threw a shoe." He sprayed his neck a second time as the area began to grow numb.

"Is that why your clothes are soaking wet?"

"I had to wash the mud off in the pond."

"And that's when the wasp decided to frost the cake." Her eyes twinkled with suppressed mirth.

"Are you laughing at my misfortune, Aunt Iris?"

"*Jah,* I suppose I am. *Mir leid.*"

"Don't be sorry. I'll laugh at myself too once this pain goes away."

She clucked her tongue. "I'll get you some dry clothes. There's a folded pile on the steps, waiting to be taken upstairs."

By the time she returned, the throbbing in his neck had begun to subside. "*Danki,*" he said, sitting down at the table.

"You're welcome." Iris ladled beef soup into two bowls. The broth smelled deliciously of onions and celery, but he spotted little meat among the carrots and potatoes.

"Is there no beef left in the freezer?" he asked, feeling guilty. It was one thing to ask her to cook meals and quite another to ask her to spin gold out of straw.

"Not too much, so I'm trying to stretch it until you're ready to take a cow to the meat processor. I know you need all your milking heifers."

"I'll bring you a chicken for supper." He ladled up vegetables and broth.

She leveled her gaze over the kerosene lamp. "Don't you need your laying hens for eggs? I can sell extra eggs to your English neighbors to bring in a little money."

Shame rose up this throat like acid indigestion. "We need to eat, Aunt Iris. Man…and woman…cannot live by potatoes and carrots alone." He took a long drink of water. *At least spring water is still free.*

"I'll send a note to my son to bring over a beef quarter. He took one of his steers to the packinghouse last month, besides the male spring calves. The freezer in his cellar is full."

Nathan sopped up broth with half a slice of bread. "All right, but I'll reimburse my cousin for the meat. I'm not taking handouts. Folks in the district have already done enough by taking care of a large chunk of the hospital bill. I intend to pay my own way in this world."

Iris buttered a piece of bread. "In that case, you can go to town and buy more baby formula. I need both the powdered kind and the pre-mixed to take along when we leave for the day."

"More formula already? We just bought fifty dollars' worth." Nathan didn't begrudge food for his son, but the cost of English baby products was ridiculous.

"That boy has a healthy appetite. I can't very well feed him chicken and dumplings yet."

With the mention of solid food, Abraham started crying in the other room. Before Nathan had a chance to enjoy his bowl of canned peaches, Iris retrieved the noisy child and foisted him into his father's arms.

"I'm still eating, Aunt Iris," Nathan complained, positioning the child into the crook of his elbow. But Abraham didn't stop crying.

"So am I," she said. "Try your best while I finish, and then I'll feed him his lunch." She smiled sweetly and returned to her soup.

"He doesn't like being held by his *daed.*" Nathan set down his spoon and began bouncing the child on his knee.

"Only because he's not used to you." She spooned up one piece of carrot. At this pace, she wouldn't finish lunch until Christmas. "The more time you hold him, Nathan, the more he'll grow accustomed to you. Then he won't cry so much."

"I can't very well strap a *boppli* onto my back like a papoose while I work the fields. *Bopplin* are a woman's business, not a man's."

"All my sons take pride in their *kinner.* All have spent time walking the floor with colicky babies and when teething makes for plenty of sleepless nights. The Lord provides *two* parents for a reason."

"Your sons never had to bury a wife. They don't know what that's like, and God willing, they'll never have to find out."

Just then, Abraham stopped fussing for a short while and gazed at his father. But Nathan didn't notice his son. He met the gaze of his aunt instead.

Iris picked up her bowl and drank the broth. Then she speared the remaining carrots with her fork. "True enough, but your son needs a father, not just his old *gefunden.*"

The sound of crunching gravel beyond the kitchen window broke the stalemate between the two. "A car has pulled up to the house. I'd better go see who it is. Maybe that English social worker has come back to check for diaper rash again." He passed the baby to Iris. Upon the exchange, the boy began to wail as though he'd been pinched.

Actually, Nathan secretly hoped it was Patricia Daly. He regretted how he had treated her when she had only been doing her job. Her compliment about his care and diligence had been unjustified. *What do I have to do with my son's health and well-being?* He'd told Iris about the social worker's comment, and she had had little reaction.

And why did I bite Mrs. Daly's head off for suggesting grief therapy sessions? Couldn't I have just said, "No, that's not for me"? Maybe he did need his head examined after all. He'd considered writing a letter of apology, but his penmanship and knowledge of English grammar left much to be desired.

Halfway down the walkway, he knew his apology to Mrs. Daly would have to wait for another day. A thin young man stretched his tall frame from the driver's side.

"Mr. Fisher?" he asked. "Nathan Fisher?" The man approached the porch, glancing down at the gravel path with each step, as though un-accustomed to anything except concrete.

"I'm Nathan Fisher. What can I do for you?"

"I believe I can do something for you, sir." He pulled a business card from his billfold and held it out. "My name is Jack Boudreau. I work for a law firm in Canton."

Nathan glanced down at the card he'd accepted. It revealed nothing beyond what the man had already said.

"First of all, let me say our firm would like to express our deep-est condolences. We understand you lost your wife in childbirth." He paused a moment before continuing. "She was a very young woman, wasn't she?"

"*Jah,* she was twenty-three." Nathan shifted his hat back on his head and tucked his hands beneath his suspenders.

"Oh my. That is too young to die. We are so sorry for your loss." He pulled on his necktie to loosen the knot.

Nathan wondered why the man talked in plural while he stood alone in the driveway. "*Danki.* God decides who to call home. He doesn't ask anybody's opinion beforehand."

"That is what I was taught too. My mother is a Sunday school teacher and my wife helps out at VBS."

Nathan arched an eyebrow.

"Vacation Bible School," explained Mr. Boudreau. "So they would readily agree with you. But for myself, I think there are times when people should be held accountable for their actions. And this is a per-fect example of one of those times." He turned his focus skyward.

"Would you mind if we talked in the shade or maybe inside the house? This sun is a scorcher today."

"Sure, come up to the porch." Nathan led the way, wondering why *Englischers* insisted on beating around the bush. They tried to use the maximum number of words to express whatever was on their chest. He waited while the lawyer sat down, pulled off his tie, and unbuttoned his top shirt button.

"That's better," said Mr. Boudreau with a grin.

"Suppose you tell me who this perfectly accountable person is." Nathan lifted a boot heel to the bottom step.

"Mrs. Abigail Graber, of course. That woman doesn't possess a license to midwife in the state of Ohio. She's had only hands-on training and maybe a few classes beyond her eighth-grade education. She had no business coming into your home and attempting to medically administer to your wife."

"I called and asked her to come." Nathan stared in the man's watery blue eyes.

"Notwithstanding, your request doesn't mitigate her actions. She's culpable, Mr. Fisher, and liable in this situation. She broke the law." Boudreau imbued his final four words with special emphasis.

"What would you have me do?"

"My law firm and I feel you are entitled to damages from Mrs. Graber to compensate you and your son for the loss of companionship of a wife and mother. This sum of money can be used to pay funeral expenses, medical bills for the baby, and future long-term childcare. That little boy no longer has a mother, and that's just not right." Boudreau's voice lifted with indignation.

Nathan pulled on his beard. "So you wish to sue…am I following you right?"

"That is correct, sir. That Graber woman doesn't have liability insurance like she should have had—we've already checked. But she and her husband do own a two-hundred-fifty acre farm that's worth quite a bit of money in this market."

Nathan held up a calloused palm to stem the tide of words he'd rather not hear. "And this 'we' you keep talking about—this office full of other lawyers—what would they get out of this?"

"Our standard legal contingency fee is one-third of monies received. Which means if we don't get you anything, you don't owe us a dime."

His smile rubbed Nathan the wrong way. "And this money you think you can squeeze out of the Graber family—it'll bring my wife back?" He leaned close enough to smell the man's spicy aftershave.

"No, nothing will do that. But like I said, your son will have expensive needs now that he has no mother. You're entitled to funds for your hardship too, the same as your boy." He lowered his tone so it was soft and melodic.

Nathan stared a moment at an ant carrying a kernel of corn across the flower bed. Then he said, "I don't want to take up any more of your time, so I'll speak plainly. I don't want the Graber farm. Amish folk don't go around suing people, for one thing. And for another, Mrs. Graber tried her best with my wife—license or no. It's not my place, or yours, to question the will of God."

"Did you know Mrs. Garber injected your wife with medication? A drug that was illegal for her to possess?"

Nathan squinted from the sun's glare, slanting over the roof. "If that's true, that's a matter for the law. That's probably why she's still in jail. But that's not my concern. Now, I ask you to be on your way. I have chores to do."

Mr. Boudreau tried to argue, to offer additional reasons, but Nathan lowered his head and stared at his dusty boots. After a moment, the lawyer strutted back to his car and left in a cloud of dust.

Attorneys and sums of money, illegal drugs and contingency fees... Nathan wished it would all just go away. If only he could close his eyes and when he awoke, his sweet Ruth would be there with a tray of corn bread fresh from the oven.

But she wasn't coming back.

And nothing seemed to be able to pull him from the nightmare world that he was living in.

"Not like that, Jake!" Laura's shrill voice rang out across the garden. "Aim the hose higher or you'll knock the new cabbage plants from their holes."

Catherine looked up from kneading bread dough and smiled. How Laura loved to mother-hen over her younger *bruder*. Just the way Abigail did over herself and Meghan. Once, when the three sisters had been peeling apples to run through the cider press, Catherine had up-ended the bowl of peels over Abby's head in sheer frustration.

Those peels are too thick. Those peels are too thin.

Abby's admonishments rang in Catherine's ears. *Mamm* had sent her to bed right after supper, but at the time it had been well worth it.

"The spray is still too strong, Jake. Aim the hose so the water falls down like rain, not like a blast from a fireman's hose."

Laura remembered the spring event last April when area volunteer fire departments staged a controlled burn on an abandoned house. Amish and English folk came from all over the county to witness the training session. Children and adults watched awestruck at how quickly a building burned to the ground.

"Now you're wetting the side of the house," she screeched. "Give me the hose. Let me show you how—"

Laura screamed and then started to wail as Jake turned the hose on her instead of the garden. Apparently the Graber siblings matched the Yost *schwestern* in temperament.

Catherine covered the dough ball with a damp towel so it would rise and walked outdoors. By the time she reached the *kinner,* they were rolling around in the wet grass while the hose writhed between them like an angry snake. "Laura! Jake! Stop that right now." She hauled them up by their arms. They were drenched from head to toe. Laura's *kapp* had fallen into a mud puddle. "Look at you two," she scolded. "What's this about?"

"I was only trying to teach him, Aunt Catherine, and he refuses to do it right."

"She's always bossin' me!" Jake's red face scowled with frustration. "She acts like she's *mamm,* but she's not."

"What on earth?" Daniel's voice thundered over Catherine's shoulder. She flinched while the combatants shrank beneath her grip. "You two should be ashamed. If you don't stop your squabbling, I'll spank both of your backsides. Is that what you want?"

Catherine thought not, judging by the way they paled to the color of skim milk.

"Get in the house and put on dry clothes. And don't give your Aunt Catherine any more trouble."

The two ran for the house while she followed behind at a slower pace. She could have handled the crisis without Daniel's intervention, but she held her tongue. After all, he was their father.

"I'll get washed up for lunch, Catherine," he called, heading to the pump house. Using the hand pump and old washtub kept much dirt out of the house. "After I eat, I'm driving to the grain elevator. I need more seed corn because some of mine has turned moldy. Give me a list if you want anything."

She nodded in agreement and then went inside to fix lunch. After setting out a plate of sandwiches along with jars of pickled beets and chow-chow, she checked on the *kinner* before Daniel returned. They were in the bathroom. Jake sat on the closed commode, streaky faced but wearing clean clothes. Laura sat on the edge of the bathtub in a fresh dress with her head buried in her hands. She sobbed as though her young heart would break. Catherine perched beside her on the tub, snaking an arm around her shoulders. "There, there. It's all over now. No one gets through childhood without an occasional scolding from their *daed.*"

Laura glanced up, her face awash in misery, and laid her head against Catherine's side. "I wish *mamm* would come home. I miss her so much." Her tears resumed with full force while Jake began to sniffle.

"Of course you do, and she misses you. I'll check to see if you could visit her some time. Would you like that?"

Laura's head snapped up. "*Jah,* I would so much! When can we visit her?" She dragged Jake into their embrace as though he were a rag doll. The boy climbed into Catherine's lap.

"I will ask your father, but not right now. Let's wait until he simmers down a tad."

Laura thought for a moment, and then joy bloomed across her face. "After supper, while he eats pie with ice cream," she said. "Ice cream always puts him in a good mood."

"That's an excellent idea, but now it's time to eat, so dry your eyes." Catherine stood, lifting the boy up to her hip. After wiping her face on a towel, Laura grasped Catherine's hand and the three walked from the room with renewed composure.

Daniel sat distributing sandwiches between the lunch plates. "I wondered where you had gone." He glanced from one to the other. "Everyone in clean clothes?"

Three heads nodded while Catherine settled Jake on his chair. Laura sat and bowed her *kapp*less head. After prayers they ate turkey-and-tomato sandwiches, but no one faster than Daniel.

"Is your list ready?" he asked, taking another spoonful of beets.

"*Jah,* it's by the door." She hoped he wouldn't mind buying her favorite strawberry shampoo. The Graber house brand left her hair a mass of tangles.

Daniel wrapped his second sandwich in plastic for the drive. "I'd better take off if I want to get home by supper. Feed them at six if I'm not back yet." He picked up her list on his way out.

For some reason, Catherine breathed easier once her brother-in-law left for his errands. Though his tirade hadn't been directed at her, she'd been as nervous at the table as Laura.

When his buggy pulled onto the roadway, she turned to her niece. "What do you say we deliver lunch to your cousin instead of letting it sit on the back porch? We could see how he's spending this fine summer day."

Laura clapped her hands. "Can we go to his cabin? We haven't been there since last fall." She jumped up and down for the second time within an hour.

"I don't see why not. But remember, he might not be there. Maybe your father gave him work to do while he went to town." Catherine fixed Isaiah's sandwiches and packed the small cooler with soda, fruit, and oatmeal cookies.

"No, *daed* doesn't like Isaiah to work with equipment alone. He might get hurt."

"He could be up in the hills cutting firewood."

Laura smirked at her aunt. "Not in the middle of summer. That's autumn work."

"In that case, let's be off." As Catherine put extra water in the cooler, anticipation began to build in her veins. "I wonder which one of you can reach the back path first," she said, closing the door behind her.

She hurried to keep up as the siblings bolted through the grass like jackrabbits. They barely slowed their pace as the trail wound through the apple orchard. "Hold up there. Let's rest a minute." Catherine leaned against a tree trunk to catch her breath.

Laura pulled down a low branch to sniff the dead blossoms. "Don't expect Isaiah to talk much, Aunt Catherine, because he doesn't."

"All right. What else can you tell me?" Her heart pounded more than exertion warranted.

Laura released the tree branch and pulled buttercups up by the roots. "When he does try to talk, he sounds real funny, so don't be surprised."

Catherine knew as much, yet she yearned to hear anything the child had to say. "Why do you suppose that is?"

Laura chewed on a weed for insight. "*Daed* said he never heard how words should sound, so he can't say the ones he knows, and he doesn't know many because he didn't go to school much."

"Because the teacher didn't know how to help him?" Catherine started walking along the path.

That explanation did not make sense to a six-year-old. "No. A couple of boys laughed at him, so he stopped going. Isaiah doesn't like people laughing at him." Jake tripped but Laura pulled him upright before Catherine could intervene. "Even if something looks funny, like Jake or a squirrel in the yard, remember not to laugh, okay?"

Catherine smiled down on a child who possessed the sage wisdom of an elder. "I promise to keep that in mind." As the trail entered the briar thicket, bees and insects buzzed around their heads. Catherine picked up Jake so he wouldn't get scratched or stung.

Laura also stayed close, grasping a tight fistful of Catherine's skirt. "*Daed* says that Isaiah talks to those who cannot talk back," she whispered as the path turned to follow the river.

Catherine stopped in midstride. "What do you think he meant by that?"

The child gazed up. "I dunno, but I hope we find out today." Her grin expanded to fill her face.

The aunt and niece didn't have long to wait for their answer.

The deeper they ventured into the forest, the quieter they became. Soon they were creeping like mice past a sleeping cat. Even Jake watched with owl-round eyes as he clung to Catherine's neck.

In a sun-dappled clearing with pine needles for carpet and blue sky peeking between the treetops, Isaiah Graber stood motionless with his hand outstretched. A single black crow perched on his shoulder, cocking his head from left to right. A large doe with huge eyes and twitching tail nibbled dried corn kernels from Isaiah's palm. Two speckled tan-and-white fawns stood on spindly legs beneath their mother's belly. The braver of the fawns timidly approached some fallen corn, even though he was too young to have been weaned.

The attention span of a four-year-old only lasted so long. "Hi, Is-sah," called Jake. He squirmed to be set down. The deer family ran off into the woods while the bird flew to an overhead branch with an annoyed *caw*.

"Hullo," said Isaiah, not appearing surprised to see them.

When Laura and Jake ran to him, he stooped to give each a loose embrace. Laura tugged on his sleeve. "Can we go to the swing?" She made a half circle pendulum motion with her hand through the air.

"*Jah, jah.*"

"Can we go, Aunt Catherine?" Laura asked as an afterthought.

"Well, I don't know." Suddenly, the hot sun was making her sweat despite a breeze through the trees. "Is the swing safe?"

The girl looked baffled. "I guess. It's not high off the ground."

"All right, then." Catherine thought to add, "Stay where I can see you" too late. They had already run off. She walked to where the doe had stood, feeling Isaiah's gaze on her. Finally, she looked up and drew in a sharp breath. He was chuckling at her—not smiling or smirking—but laughing, at what she didn't know.

With a sweep of his hand he indicated the direction the *kinner* had gone. Catherine marched down the path as though on a mission… right to the log cabin with the green metal roof and comfortable wide porch.

Isaiah easily kept pace by her side. While she breathed heavily and perspired, he remained cool and unaffected by the heat or humidity. At the steps he went around her to open the front door, and then he motioned for her to enter.

Her heart rose up her throat as she looked into the unknown interior. She knew she shouldn't go in. She had no business here. Daniel had gone to town, and no one knew her whereabouts. She was supposed to be the responsible person in the group. Yet maybe Jake and Laura were already inside. Inhaling deeply, Catherine walked past him into the dim, cool, sweet-smelling cabin. She waited for her eyes to adjust, and then she perused the room with fascination. Her eyes landed on a small wooden platform under the window. Twin aluminum bowls sat side-by-side, nestled in the recessed openings of the stand. The first bowl contained water, while kibble filled the second to the rim. Someone had burned the word "Boots" into the face of the wood, as though with the tip of a hot poker. Catherine stared as the memory of the phantom yellow dog provided explanation for the handmade apparatus. *A feeding station so the dog wouldn't have to bend down.* Duly impressed, she scanned the rest of the room.

Isaiah owned no curtains, upholstered sofa, or comfortable recliner to read by the fire. *Because nobody lives close enough to peek in windows and Isaiah can't read anyway,* she thought. But the furnishings he owned were tidy, functional, and possessing their own charm and beauty: an oak table and two chairs with slat backs and woven rush seats, two bentwood rockers that must have taken someone months to make; and a rough-sawn bedstead with four high posts and an intricately carved headboard. Catherine crept deeper into the room to examine the woodcarving on the headboard. It was of a deer family like the one they had seen in the forest clearing. A backdrop of tall pines and knee-high wildflowers indicated Isaiah hadn't journeyed far for his inspiration. A thick multicolored quilt, probably sewn by her sister Abigail, covered the rustic bed, while a plump pillow leaned against one bedpost. A braided rug in soft, muted colors lay beneath her feet. The sparse room looked inviting in its simplicity.

She suddenly felt shy and embarrassed by her intrusion. Wheeling around, her gaze locked with Isaiah's. He stood in the open doorway, silhouetted by the light, with his arms crossed over his dark shirt. The no-longer-mysterious golden Labrador lay at his feet.

He tucked a lock of shoulder-length hair behind one ear. "*Gut?*" he asked.

"What?" she croaked, transfixed by his black eyes.

"*Gut?*" He gestured with his head toward the corners of the large cabin.

"*Jah, gut,* very nice. I must be going now." Catherine set his lunch bag on the table, and strode past him out the door, practically jumping over the dog. She ran around the cabin on the narrow band of yard next to the river, where she found the *kinner.* Jake sat in a tree swing while Laura pushed him from behind.

"There you are!" She swept the boy up in her arms, grabbed Laura's hand, and didn't stop running until she almost reached the apple orchard. She ignored their questions as to what was wrong and why were they hurrying so fast.

Because Catherine Yost didn't have a clue.

Nine

Abby had curled up on her bed after lunch with her Bible. Today she was reading out of the book of Joshua. After Moses died, the Lord told Moses' servant Joshua that he should lead the Israelites across the Jordan River into the Promised Land. Great battles were fought and the conquered territories divided up between the twelve tribes. God told Joshua's army to march around the fortified town of Jericho for six days. On the seventh day, they marched around the walled city seven times, and then the priest blew a loud horn and the people began to shout. Suddenly, the walls of Jericho fell to the ground and Joshua's army stormed in and destroyed the city. No one was spared except a prostitute who had helped Joshua's spies.

Frankly, Abby didn't enjoy reading about wars and bloody battles, but the amazing power of the Lord revitalized her spirits. She loved learning about the ancient cities of refuge, created for those who had killed someone unintentionally. The accused person would be protected from those out for revenge until their trial. *How much simpler life was when God spoke to His people directly,* she thought.

"Abby," a voice called. "Your attorney is here to see you."

She glanced up to see Deputy Todd standing in her doorway. She'd been so engrossed in reading that she hadn't heard the cell door open.

"Thank you, Deputy." Setting down her Bible, she hurried into the common area, where most of the women spent their days. Her lawyer, a young man with blond hair and pale skin, stood as she approached the table.

"Hello, Mrs. Graber. How are you doing?"

Abby bit back her initial retort. "Very well, thank you, Mr. Blake. How's the weather? Humid today?"

"Yes. That rain last night didn't cool things off one bit."

It rained last night? Has the dry spell finally broken or will Daniel's corn shrivel on the stalks, stunted from lack of water? She shook off thoughts of home and focused on the man with a folder of papers before him.

Mr. Blake cleared his throat. "The grand jury met yesterday and indicted you for practicing medicine without a license—a fifth-degree felony. That charge we were expecting." He peered at her through thick-lensed glasses. "They also charged you with possession of a dangerous drug. That one I was hoping to avoid."

"Dangerous drug? Pitocin isn't a dangerous drug. It slows down bleeding until the woman can get to a hospital."

"Yes, I agree, but the grand jury doesn't because Pitocin requires a doctor's prescription to obtain and a medical license to administer."

Abby stared at her hands. "I know I shouldn't have had it."

"Regarding the other two charges, 'practicing midwifery,' is a misdemeanor and shouldn't give us much trouble. And after reviewing statements from the EMTs and the medical examiner's report, the county prosecutor decided to drop the charge of involuntary manslaughter." He grinned with pleasure. "That is *very* good news. Apparently, nothing in the evidence indicated you were responsible for the woman's death."

"Mrs. Ruth Fisher," said Abby.

"I beg your pardon?" he asked while shuffling through his papers.

"Her name was Ruth Fisher."

He glanced up. "Yes, ma'am. Mrs. Ruth Fisher. I didn't mean to sound callous." He extracted the sheet he'd been searching for. "Now, for the bad news. The two felonies carry minimum sentences of one year on the first charge and eighteen months on the second. If you are convicted—and, based on your signed statements made in the sheriff's office, that's highly likely—you could face two and a half years in prison if they run consecutively." He tugged on the cuffs of his shirt-sleeves beneath his coat.

Two and a half years away from my family? Away from the little ones whose lives change in countless ways every day? And apart from Daniel, who I have pledged to love, honor, and obey? How can he manage that long without his wife?

She shook off the idea like a chill from an open window. "Two and a half years, Mr. Blake? I can't be gone from my family that long." Her voice was barely a whisper over the nearby television set.

"I understand. And your sentence wouldn't be served here in Wooster. You would be sent to a women's correctional facility in the western part of the state. Too far to go by horse and buggy," he added unnecessarily.

Abby felt sick to her stomach. She gripped the table for support as the whole room swam before her eyes for several seconds.

"Are you all right, Mrs. Graber? Can I get you a glass of water or something?"

"No, thank you. I'm fine," she lied. She wasn't fine. She'd never felt so afraid in all her life. Laura would be almost nine and Jake nearly seven by the time she got out of jail. A common criminal—that's all she was. She would be treated like an outcast if not outright shunned by her district. Tears filled her eyes but she forced them back. *Inmates in the Wooster jail do not sit around crying.*

"That's the worst-case scenario—the one we're trying to avoid. I don't wish to scare you, Mrs. Graber, but you must understand what we're up against."

She blinked several times. "I won't stand up in court and lie, Mr.

Blake, if that's what you mean. I won't say I didn't give that shot when I did."

"No, no, I understand that. But the jury will be curious as to where an Amish lady without a car or easy access to a pharmacy came by a syringe of Pitocin. I'm advising you to cooperate with the judge and the prosecutor in this case. And I don't always tell my clients that," he said rather smugly. "But you should do exactly that. Tell the truth when the judge starts asking you questions at your pretrial hearing." He tucked the papers back into her file folder. "Just answer his questions and things will go much better for you."

He glanced around at the other inmates. "How are you doing in here? Are any of the ladies giving you trouble?" He focused on one particular woman who looked to be in a permanent bad mood.

"No, everybody's been nice enough. Some ask rather nosy questions, but most *Englischers* are like that." Abby realized the rudeness of her words the moment they left her mouth. "Excuse me, Mr. Blake. That was an awful thing to say. Here I am complaining about rude behavior by others, and I say something like that."

"Not to worry. We are a nosy bunch. Just ask movie or television stars."

Abby waited, unsure how to respond.

"What's going on with your bail?" he asked, closing her folder. "I thought your husband would have arranged bail once the judge granted my motion reducing the amount to one hundred thousand. Any bondman would loan him that against your farm."

Abby's lightheadedness increased twofold.

"My bail has been reduced?" she asked.

"Yes, ma'am. I left a message for you. And I called your husband to let him know."

"My house has no phone." She supported her head with her fingertips.

"I called your cell phone and he picked up. I talked to him personally about the reduction of your bail amount."

She shook her head with growing comprehension. "The elders must have decided not to allow Daniel to post bail. Borrowing money for such purposes is not done in our community."

Blake met her gaze and held it. "All right. Would you like me to see if any women's groups might want to raise the money on your behalf? Maybe a midwife's society, if there is such a thing?"

Abby struggled to her feet. "No, please don't do anything like that. I appreciate the thought, but if the leaders of my district want me to remain behind bars, then here I will stay. Now, I must return to my cell. I don't feel well." She braced her palms on the table for balance.

"Sure, but don't worry, Mrs. Graber. I won't do anything you don't want me to. I will request a speedy trial as it looks as though you'll be stuck here until then. I'll do what I can to hurry things along."

"Thank you, Mr. Blake." Abby shook his hand and walked back to her cell on legs that could barely support her weight. Other inmates said hello or asked questions, but she couldn't pause to chat. She needed to get back to her bunk to lie down.

Two and a half years in a woman's prison on the other side of the state? How would her family manage? Certainly Catherine couldn't stay that long to raise her children. Wasn't she entitled to a life of her own? She would never find a suitable husband shut away on the Graber farm without her circle of friends nearby.

Worries circled around her head like birds of prey over carrion. Finally she dozed off, and when she awoke she went to the desk in the common room where paper and pens were kept to begin a long overdue letter.

Dear Catherine,

It is my fondest hope that you are well and enjoying your stay with Daniel, Laura, and Jake. Words cannot express my gratitude for your sacrifice. A woman your age wants to think about social events and courting, not keeping house for her big *sister. I will be in your debt until I draw my dying breath.*

My lawyer has requested a speedy trial. Please pray that the trial comes soon, and that the judge will have a merciful heart.

Do not work too hard. A house is just a house. Providing meals and comforting my family are more than enough. And please pray that my faith sustains me in the difficult decision I must make.

Your loving schwester,
Abigail

With the letter addressed, sealed, and stamped, her headache faded. She managed to eat some odd-tasting beef chili and drank two glasses of iced tea. Back in her cell, away from the other prisoners who talked, watched TV, and read magazines, Abby found a sense of peace. As she lay in bed, her choice became easy.

Living with the repercussions of that choice was what would prove difficult in the dark days ahead.

Catherine could not have felt sillier about her behavior toward Isaiah if she tried. She was the one who had been curious about the inside of his cabin. Yet, given the chance to satisfy her curiosity, she had acted like a foolish little girl. Her niece wasn't afraid of Isaiah, and neither was her nephew. But inside in his austere cabin, with his dark eyes boring holes through her back, she had panicked. She had planned to apologize, but she saw neither hide nor hair of the elusive man for several days. Twice he'd failed to come for his lunch bag, and she'd fed his sandwiches to the hog. And twice he'd come for his dinner plate after dark, when she'd been busy bathing the children and putting them to bed. She might have feared her behavior had offended him, but remembering his laughter and warm, tender eyes in the cabin doorway told her otherwise.

So on this hot July day, with her housework and garden chores finished, she planned a summer outing. And Catherine aimed to include Isaiah in the fun.

"*Guder nachmittag,*" she said when Daniel came to the kitchen for lunch.

"Good afternoon, sister." He hung his straw hat on a peg and wiped his brow. "It is really a hot one. You could fry an egg on the concrete patio. I'm not working those horses anymore today." He poured two tall glasses of iced tea.

"Indeed, that's what I wanted to talk to you about." Catherine spread tuna fish salad on slices of white bread.

"Do you think talking about the weather will cool things down a bit?"

It took her a moment, but she laughed at his rare attempt at a joke. "No, but I know what will. Mrs. Corey has invited me several times to bring the *kinner* to her pond for a swim. She said it has a sandy shallow end and no algae. I think today would be perfect to accept the invitation. My chores are caught up, the garden is temporarily weed free, and the youngsters could use a treat. They have been good for days on end." She set the sandwiches and jars of pickled vegetables on the table. "I thought I would pack lunch into a hamper along with cold drinks and take the path through the pasture." She waited for him to squash her plans.

Daniel bit into his sandwich and popped a small gherkin in his mouth. "Sounds like a good idea. You have been working hard too, and I've been meager with the appreciation. An afternoon off will do you good. Although, if those two young ones squabble, it won't be much of a vacation day." He grinned over his glass of tea.

"I'm prepared for any and all eventualities. I baked a pan of banana bread. Those who misbehave will get none." She waited until he started his second sandwich to continue. "Tell me, Daniel. How did Isaiah end up living here with you and Abby? I've been curious."

He pondered while he chewed and then frowned as though remembering something unpleasant. "My aunt was the only one who could handle Isaiah when he was little. And she was the only one who didn't think him slow-witted. My uncle had no patience. His other two sons were much older and weren't deaf. Isaiah was a late-in-life baby." Daniel's frown deepened into a scowl. "When my aunt died of pneumonia one winter, my uncle was left with Isaiah to raise alone. Things for him became much worse. Once, when we were visiting my uncle's farm, I saw him take a stick to Isaiah because he didn't do what he'd been told. He didn't understand." He looked up at Catherine before glancing away. "I told Abby what I saw and she agreed with me. We brought him home to live with us that day." He rose from the table abruptly. "Curiosity satisfied?" he asked.

"Somewhat. I would like to leave him a note in his lunch bag to join us at the pond. I'm sure he could use a reprieve from the heat." She held her breath.

Daniel narrowed his gaze. "He can't read, Catherine. Writing him a note would be pointless."

"But I thought you said he went to school for a few years."

"He did, but he never learned to read. The teacher didn't know how to teach him. He was…special." Daniel filled a bottle with the remaining tea. "Anyway, Isaiah is a farmer, same as me. We have work to do. Soaking up the sunshine and sticking your feet in ponds on a summer day are for women and children." He headed for the back door with Catherine practically on his heels.

"But you had planned to rest the horses this afternoon because it was extra hot."

"There are other chores in the barn to occupy our time." His hand was already on the doorknob.

She tugged lightly on his sleeve. "Now, Daniel, I know you're fond of your cousin or you wouldn't have intervened with your uncle. Barn chores will still be there this evening after the hottest time of day has passed. That boy could use a swim and so could you. Why don't you both come and cool off? It will make you a happier man."

He turned to face her as his lower jaw dropped open. "Have you always been like this, Catherine? When you were a child growing up and as an adult with your friends?" A small smile twitched the corners of his mouth.

"*Jah,* pretty much. Isn't it a blessing you married the more agreeable of the Yost sisters?"

"I'll count that particular blessing twice tonight." They both laughed as he pulled open the door. "I'll send Isaiah over to the pond as soon as I no longer need him. He can eat his lunch with his cousins. I, myself, prefer a nap in the shade in the hammock when chores are done. But be mindful—the pond has hungry fish that love to nibble toes." Daniel strode off without a backward glance, but somehow she knew he was smiling.

Laura and Jake needed no convincing about a dip in cool water. They changed into swimming attire and appeared at the door with towels, inflatable water wings, and Jake's yellow rubber duck. Catherine set Isaiah's cooler on the porch, hoping Daniel would keep his word. But after she and the *kinner* had been wading along the pebbly shore for forty minutes, she began to have doubts.

"Can't we eat yet, Aunt Catherine?" asked Laura. "I'm starving." She rubbed her tummy for emphasis.

"I am too. Let's get started. I was waiting for cousin Isaiah, but he must have too many chores."

The two children followed her from the water like ducklings after their mother. Catherine spread an old patchwork quilt on a grassy slope and opened the hamper. Laura and Jake sat cross-legged with their towels across their laps.

"Tuna salad sandwiches, pickles, chips, grapes, and cold Cokes," she announced. "How does that sound?"

They offered an enthusiastic round of applause. Laura grabbed a sandwich and started eating quickly. "Yummy!" she declared.

If it had been just butter on day-old bread, Catherine doubted the girl would have complained. "Everything tastes better when you're hungry," she said with a smile. Just as she unwrapped her own sandwich, a horse thundered over the hill separating the Graber farm from the neighbor's. Isaiah galloped up to the picnic spot and reined his horse to a stop a few yards from the quilt. He rode bareback and barefoot and was wearing an old pair of trousers, suspenders, and the white shirt with its sleeves torn off at the elbows. But at least he'd remembered his hat. The large yellow dog trotted alongside the horse.

Not a fox or coyote or lone wolf that had crossed Lake Erie over the frozen ice, but a Labrador retriever. Catherine smiled, remembering her foolish fears along a dark path in the night.

He slid smoothly from the mare to the ground and tied the reins to a mountain laurel bush. "Hullo," he said, sauntering up to the group.

"Hi, Isaiah. Hi, Boots," called Laura.

"Is-sah," added Jake around a mouthful of sandwich.

Isaiah pulled a sandwich and a small bag of chips from his pocket. After settling on the quilt, his focus didn't leave Catherine for a moment.

"Good afternoon," she said in English, mouthing the words with exaggeration.

He repeated the greeting with some semblance of accuracy, waved to his cousins sitting two feet away, and began eating his flattened sandwich. He poured the smashed potato chips directly from bag to mouth. The dog settled next to her master. After a moment, Isaiah stopped eating. "Boots," he said, tapping the fingertips of his hands and then pointing at the dog's paws.

Catherine nodded with comprehension. "Boots," she said. "Her name is Boots."

The Lab trotted over, sat down on her haunches, and lifted a dainty white paw.

"She wants you to shake, Aunt Catherine," explained Laura. Catherine hesitated, not wishing to touch the dog's fur before eating her meal.

"Boots won't leave until you shake hands. She'll just sit there forever, holding her paw in the air." Laura looked up with childlike expectation.

Seeing no way out, Catherine complied and shook the paw. "How do you do, Boots?"

Her duty complete, the dog wagged her bushy tail and trotted off to investigate scents in the tall grass.

Catherine took a bite of her tuna sandwich but soon set it down on the wax paper. It stuck in her throat despite having used a liberal amount of mayonnaise. It wasn't fear of dog fur that made her nervous, but the close proximity of Daniel's cousin. She nibbled a few grapes instead, uncertain how to behave. *Should I make small talk with the* kinner *or would Isaiah deem this rude because he can't understand the conversation?*

She need not have worried.

As soon as Isaiah finished eating, he tossed his trash into the hamper, his hat on the grass, and sprinted toward the pond. He circled past the sandy shallow area and headed straight for the fishing dock. When he reached the end of the twenty-foot wooden platform, he dove smoothly into the blue water. Sea lions she'd seen at the Cleveland Zoo couldn't have acted more at home. He dove deep, swimming underwater for long periods, and then he resurfaced to shake hair and water from his face. Other times he crisscrossed the pond with uniform strokes of his powerful arms. When he would reach one end, he flipped upside down and started back underwater.

Catherine couldn't take her eyes off him. Even Jake and Laura watched while they ate, mesmerized by the show. "I wish I could swim like that," said Laura. "I can't swim well at all."

"Maybe when you're finished, Isaiah could teach you."

"Let's go ask him!" Laura stuffed her remaining fruit into the hamper and finished her drink with one long gulp.

"Only in the shallow water," Catherine ordered. "And only with your water wings on." She picked up one set of wings and began to inflate them with air.

Laura grabbed her *bruder*'s pair and applied her lung power to the valve. While the females inflated the wings, Isaiah swam back and forth across the pond with abandon—sometimes a lazy butterfly stroke, other times flat on his back with the barest attempt at propulsion. He seemed to be making up for lost time or missed opportunities in his zeal.

By the time Catherine slipped a life ring around Jake's waist and attached water wings to both children, Isaiah was heading toward them with his black hair slicked back. His smile couldn't have been grander.

"*Wadder gut,*" he pronounced.

It took her a moment, but she realized he had spoken English. How confusing it must have been to watch his family mouthing *Deutsch* words, while his schoolteacher used only English in the classroom. No wonder he'd never learned to communicate well. "*Jah,* water good," she agreed. Then she pointed at her niece, shrugged her shoulders with exaggeration, and mimicked a person swimming. She repeated the gestures, but this time she pointed at Isaiah and mimed him swimming gracefully. Then she stood back, hoping for the best.

He thought for a moment to find meaning in the antics. Then he nodded, took Laura's hand, and walked her into the pond. Catherine picked up Jake and followed after, fearing he would take Laura into water too deep. But when the water rose to the child's waist, he stopped and knelt down on the hard-packed bottom. He began a patient learn-to-swim program that should be in textbooks. First, Isaiah drew a deep breath and ducked his face into the water. He demonstrated this twice and then allowed Laura to duplicate the action. Each time he would hold his breath a few seconds longer. When it was her turn, he held firmly onto Laura's arm so she remained stable and confident. Laura and Isaiah were soon holding their breath for a full minute, while Catherine watched near the shore as her nephew splashed around.

Next Isaiah gestured for Laura to join Catherine close to the shore, while he demonstrated treading water in slightly deeper water. When he returned for the child, he allowed her to practice the activity in water up to her shoulders. Laura was a quick study, and no fear of water slowed her progress. And Isaiah turned out to be a natural born teacher—patient, repetitive with movements, and offering security to ease his pupil's anxiety.

Too bad no one offered any of that to him, Catherine thought. Without warning, something bit her big toe and she howled like a dog.

Isaiah couldn't hear. Jake was splashing up a storm, while Laura was enjoying the lesson too much to pay attention. But the person standing on the hill heard the yelp, loud and clear.

"I warned you about the biting fish, Catherine," called Daniel. "They mistake toes for bait." He turned his focus back to the swimming lesson.

She carried Jake back to the quilt, wrapped him snuggly in a towel, and then inspected—and counted—her toes. "At least they didn't break the skin," she said when Daniel joined her at the quilt.

"They wouldn't eat much if they had." Daniel grinned with his second joke of the day. "With two ponds so close to the house, I'm glad Laura is learning to swim. And nobody could teach her better than Isaiah." Daniel's facial features and tone of voice softened, perhaps by a distant memory. Then he picked up his son and settled him on his shoulder. "But that's enough for today," he said. "Time to get them home and start dinner." Daniel headed in the direction of his house.

Catherine hadn't noticed how low the sun had fallen in the western sky. "Laura, come out of the water. We must go." Once the girl acknowledged with a wave, Catherine bent to repack the hamper and fold up the quilt. When she stood up, Isaiah, dripping wet, was standing behind her. He was close enough for her to see reflected sunlight dancing in his eyes.

"*Danki,*" he said, one word of *Deutsch* he knew well. "*Danki,*" he repeated. Then he strode to his horse, who had been munching on tall weeds, shimmied onto her back, and rode off in the direction Daniel had gone.

Catherine and Laura stood staring for several seconds after he disappeared over the hill. "Is he good at everything he does, except talking?" asked Laura.

"Apparently so, dear girl." And it took great effort for Catherine not to grin all the way home.

Ten

Abby tossed and turned that night, as she had every night since her attorney's visit. She knew what he'd meant by "make sure you tell the whole truth when you're asked a question in court." Mr. Blake wanted her to reveal where she had obtained the anti-hemorrhage drug she gave Mrs. Fisher. But how could she possibly do that? The licensed midwife who had entrusted her with the syringe made it clear she was breaking every rule in doing so. She had emphasized that the injection was to be used only in an emergency—a case of life or death. That night, Mrs. Fisher's situation had certainly qualified.

The retiring midwife had been awarded the distinction of Midwife of the Year many times. She'd enjoyed a long, successful career, bringing thousands of babies into the world. What was the point in ruining the woman's reputation, stripping her of her nurse's license, and maybe landing her in jail too? Nothing would bring back Ruth Fisher. One life destroyed should be enough. *Two and a half years in jail.* How could she withstand separation from her family that long? Yet she remembered her last conversation with the retiring nurse as though it had been yesterday:

Please, Margaret. Let me keep a syringe or two of Pitocin. Nothing works as well when a woman is bleeding too much. It can buy enough time to get the patient to the hospital.

Margaret had frowned, her lips pursing with unease. *You know I can't do that, Abby. It isn't an over-the-counter drug. I have to account for the doses in my possession. Anyway, you'll always be assisting Dr. Weller or another registered nurse, so you won't need your own supply.*

Doctors usually arrive well after us and might come too late. And which nurse are you talking about? The job opening for your replacement has been posted for months and still no takers. No one is eager to live in a rural community, apart from the conveniences Englischers *hold dear, not to mention miles from the nearest large hospital.*

Margaret had closed her eyes and rubbed her temples with the beginnings of one of her commonplace headaches, while Abby held her breath.

Please, I'm pleading with you. Having that drug could save someone's life.

Margaret had remained silent for what seemed like a long time. When she finally spoke, the toll of working long hours along with the chronic pain of arthritis were evident in her face. *All right, one dose of Pitocin—to be used only in an emergency, and only if you're certain medical personnel can't arrive in time.* She had wrapped the single syringe in sterile gauze, placed it in a bag and handed it to Abby with near reverence. That had been almost three years ago. Margaret hadn't requested protection from possible repercussions. She hadn't demanded Abby's future silence. But the look in her eyes had said it all: She hadn't wanted to share the medication.

Now, as Abby lay awake, listening to the resonant snores of her roommate ring in her ears, she knew she couldn't divulge the truth. She would pay the price for this and other mistakes she made in life, but extending the misery to an unwilling participant wouldn't solve anything. Unable to sleep, she prayed for guidance, turned on the small light above her head, and opened her Bible.

Lately, she'd been reading the book of Judges. Although she enjoyed the story of Samson and Delilah, she couldn't understand why the Israelites continued to sin and disobey God despite all He had done for them. They worshipped the pagan idols of the people they had been sent to conquer. In the book of Samuel, she read the story of a poor shepherd boy, David, who slew a giant Philistine warrior named Goliath. Without sword or shield, David had brought down his foe with a rock and sling, and then he had cut off Goliath's head with his own sword. As David's reward, the king gave him one of his daughters in marriage.

So much bloodshed in the Old Testament, she thought and turned to the New Testament to read about how a large crowd had heard of Jesus' miracles and had followed Him to where He was in a remote area. That evening Jesus told His disciples to feed the hungry people, but they could only find two fish and five loaves of bread. After Jesus blessed the food, the disciples distributed it among more than five thousand people. After everyone had eaten their fill, twelve baskets of scraps were left over. The disciples had been skeptical, even though they had witnessed great miracles firsthand.

I need to turn this problem over to God. If I have faith and trust the One who fed thousands from so little, surely He can solve the problems of one insignificant Amish woman sitting in a Wayne County jail. With that thought, she closed the Good Book and slept the deep, blissful sleep of a baby.

"*Daed,* I want to learn to ride a horse. Is that okay?" asked Laura at the supper table.

If her niece's question took Catherine by surprise, it downright flabbergasted Daniel. "*What?*" He dropped his spoon into his soup bowl. They had all been enjoying a pleasant supper of chicken noodle soup with corn bread and deviled eggs. Conversation had centered on the weather, the outlook for the corn crop, and how poorly the newest Cleveland Indian pitcher had been doing since midseason. Occasionally, Daniel listened to a ball game on his transistor radio while driving his team of draft horses through the fields. His father-in-law wouldn't approve if he knew, but other than his fondness for baseball, Daniel was a pious and humble man.

Instead of eating, the *kinner* were sulking and picking at their food. Daniel had still not inquired about a visit to their *mamm* in Wooster. Laura seemed intent on drowning a carrot by pinning it to the bottom of her bowl. "I want to learn to ride a horse like Isaiah," she repeated.

"You are only six years old," Daniel pointed out.

"How old do you have to be? How old was Isaiah when he first rode a horse?" The girl finally ate the submerged carrot.

Daniel thought a moment and frowned. Apparently, the answer didn't suit his argument.

"Probably about that age, but let's not forget that Isaiah is a boy, not a girl."

This comment drew a stare from Catherine, but she chewed on the inside of her mouth to avoid trouble.

"Do you mean girls don't ride horses?" Laura's forehead furrowed with wrinkles. "I thought that Aunt Meghan rode around barrels in races with other girls." She drew a figure-eight pattern on the table's oil-cloth cover with her finger and peered up at her other aunt.

"That's true," said Catherine. "She did. I believe she even won a race one summer." She smiled at her niece. "But she used a saddle with bit, bridle, and stirrups, which is not the way Isaiah rides. It's much harder to stay on the horse when riding bareback, not to mention getting on and off the beast. He probably used a saddle when he first learned."

This gave the girl something to ponder. In the silence that followed, Daniel cleared his throat. "May I have another ladleful of soup, Catherine? I like how you added lima beans to the other vegetables. And it might be time to slice that apple pie I've had my eye on in the windowsill."

She rose to her feet to get his soup, but Laura wasn't so easily distracted. "*Daed*, you have a small saddle in the barn. I saw it hanging on the wall. Can I use it to learn to ride?"

He released an exasperated sigh. "I'm sure your Aunt Meghan wasn't six when she started. You're too little, Laura. Your legs won't reach the stirrups even if we shorten them to the highest notch. Maybe in a few years. Why don't you ask Aunt Catherine to teach you to embroider? That's a good female pastime." He began eating his second helping with gusto.

Laura's lower lip protruded and then began to tremble. Large tears pooled and then poured from her brown eyes like a faucet. "You say no to everything! I couldn't stay overnight at my friend's house, then you wouldn't let me go see *mamm,* and now I can't even ride a horse around my own *backyard*!" She emphasized the last word to make sure he understood she wasn't asking to ride to Wooster. Then she laid her face down on the table and sobbed, her tears quickly forming a puddle.

Catherine clenched her teeth to keep from intervening between a father and child. She took a knife to the pie, hacking it into six mismatched pieces.

Daniel rolled his eyes and clucked his tongue. "Okay, Laura, stop bawling. I'll ask Isaiah to saddle up his mare. She's the smallest horse on the farm." He pushed away his empty bowl.

"You will?" she asked, lifting her head.

"You will?" Catherine's tone expressed an equal amount of disbelief. She set the largest slice of pie in front of him.

"*Jah,* I will if he's still in the barn cleaning water troughs."

"I can learn to ride tonight?" Laura stared at him.

"*If* Isaiah hasn't gone back to his cabin, and *if* he feels like teaching you. But only inside the paddock, with Aunt Catherine leading the horse by the reins and Isaiah keeping you in the saddle. I won't have you falling off and breaking an arm. How would I explain that to your *mamm* when she comes home?"

Laura flew from her chair and into her father's lap. With her arms around his neck and her face buried in his shirt, she spoke in a muffled voice. "*Danki, daed. Danki* so much." From her gratitude an outsider arriving at the door would think she had been awarded a treasure chest of toys.

Daniel patted her back. "You're welcome. Now finish your soup and corn bread. I'm sure Aunt Meghan never rode a horse on an empty belly."

He turned to his son, who'd been listening with interest. "Jake, you can ride the porch swing with me after supper. How does that sound?"

The boy nodded his head vigorously.

While Laura devoured her meal, Catherine found her own stomach fluttering with anticipation. *I will see Isaiah again.* That same visitor might assume Catherine was the one getting to climb into the saddle, because she was as excited as her niece.

With supper dishes done and Laura pacing the porch, Catherine resorted to counting cows in the distance to settle her nerves. They didn't have to wait long, however. Within the hour Isaiah appeared coming from the barn, leading his mare outfitted with a saddle.

"Hullo, Laura. Hullo, Cat."

He wore clean dark pants, a navy shirt, and black suspenders, and he had replaced his everyday straw hat with his black felt. Catherine knew he hadn't just finished barn chores, and considering the pink flush to his cheeks, he'd probably showered with the barn's cold water.

"Hi, Isaiah," both females chimed as they ran to join him in the paddock.

"Cor-rah," he said, patting the mare's neck. He made a calm, still-water motion with his hand.

"Cora is a gentle horse," interpreted Catherine.

"Hi, Cora." Laura greeted the mare while lightly patting her neck. "Pick me up, Aunt. I want to see her face better."

When Catherine lifted the child higher, Laura leaned so close that beast and child were eye to eye. She kissed the mare above the nose. The girl possessed no more fear of horses than swimming in a pond filled with feet-nibbling fish.

Isaiah laughed at the affectionate gesture as he pulled Laura from Catherine's arms. He effortlessly swung her into the saddle, and then he also planted a kiss on Cora's nose. Laura found this worthy of applause. Isaiah held up one stirrup. "*Fut,*" he said, and Laura slid her boot into place.

Catherine noticed that a recent hole had been bored through the leather, higher and not in line with the others.

"*Fut*," he repeated on the other side. Then he handed Laura a short set of reins, and to Catherine he gave the longer lead rope. "*Tie-ette*," he enunciated, tapping the child's leg.

"You want me to hold tight with my legs?" asked Laura, squeezing rather ineffectively in her long dress.

He nodded and tapped her leg again, harder. Laura practiced gripping with her legs while Isaiah steadied her in the saddle.

Suddenly, Laura shrieked. Isaiah might not have known if the animal hadn't sidestepped. "Spider!" the child cried, pointing to a harmless daddy longlegs sitting on Cora's mane.

Isaiah leaned in to inspect, and then he gently nudged the bug onto the back of his hand. Without releasing his hold on the saddle, he transferred the spider to an overhead tree branch.

Catherine watched, enchanted by his kindness toward God's lowest of creatures, and also by the patient instruction of someone who had spent little time in school. Once he was satisfied that Laura understood what to do, he made a small clicking sound with his tongue—a sound so soft Catherine could have missed it. But the brown Morgan heard, shook her magnificent black mane, and began to walk. Catherine hurried a little to get out in front of her with the lead rope. Around the fenced paddock they went—man, woman, child, and horse. And all seemed to be enjoying themselves.

Catherine caught Isaiah staring at her more than once when she glanced over her shoulder. When their gazes met, he blushed and focused on the child, adjusting Laura's position on the saddle or correcting her posture. But Catherine could sense his attention even with her back turned, and she walked taller and smiled more than usual. *Hopefully, I won't break into a song of joy,* she thought, tamping down her emotions.

"Let's go faster, Isaiah," demanded Laura. But because he didn't hear the child, he kept plodding along at a snail's pace. Laura gave Cora a small kick with her heels, causing the horse to lurch forward.

Isaiah pulled the short reins with a quick "whoa." Laura reached over to tap his shoulder and almost fell off the horse. He pushed her back in the saddle with a frown.

"Faster," she begged and made a quick, staccato movement with her hand.

He shook his finger at her and said, "*Fass-nuff.*"

No problem with his communication today, thought Catherine.

After twenty minutes of going in circles in the paddock, Isaiah took the lead rope from Catherine and led the mare to the back steps. After wrapping the rope around the rail, he lifted Laura off the horse and set her on the porch.

"*Danki,* Isaiah." The child offered a quick hug and ran to the door, calling "*Gut nacht*" as the screen door slammed behind her.

"*Danki,* Isaiah. Nice of you," said Catherine, beaming and pointing at his chest. "Good night." She started up the steps, but he grabbed her elbow before she got too far.

"No." He gestured for her to follow as he led the horse toward the barn.

Catherine stood stymied on the bottom step, wondering what he needed her help with at this hour.

"Come," he demanded, halfway down the path.

What could she do but obey his command? After a hesitant glance over her shoulder, she picked up her skirt and hurried after him, hoping Daniel wasn't watching from the window.

With his long strides and no child on Cora's back, Isaiah disappeared behind the barn before Catherine could catch up. She slowed her pace to avoid panting like a dog. By the time she rejoined them, Isaiah was adjusting the length of the saddle's stirrups. He perused her from head to toe, set the buckle into a notch, and then readjusted the other side. Catherine watched, mesmerized, as Cora stood stock-still without being tied during the saddle adjustment.

"*Dun,*" he said and motioned for her to come closer.

"Me?" she asked, even though no one else was there.

"*Jah,* you, Cat." He winked when he spoke her name. Patting the saddle with one hand, he offered his other hand to her.

Comprehension of what he wanted finally registered. "Oh, no," she said, shaking her head vigorously. But she couldn't stop grinning.

"*Jah,* Cat." He grabbed her hand and dragged her to Cora's side.

She didn't know what to do, having never ridden a horse before. Her sister Meghan might own a small trophy to prove her expertise, but Catherine had always been afraid of large beasts with flies buzzing around their heads.

But no flies buzzed around Cora when she focused one gentle brown eye on Catherine as though to say: *What's taking you so long? Get on already.*

She couldn't possibly climb onto the horse—she was wearing a dress! And what if she fell off? How would she explain a broken arm to Abby, not to mention Daniel? But how could she not comply and still preserve a friendship with the man she wished to help? Without another thought, Catherine lifted her skirt, put her shoe into the stirrup, and accepted Isaiah's hand. From the other side of Cora, he pulled hard while she transferred her weight from the ground into the saddle.

It was not a pretty sight if anyone had been watching. And once seated, no matter how she tugged and pulled at her long dress, quite a bit of her black stockings showed on both legs.

What would daed *think of me now?*

"*Fut.*" Isaiah held the other stirrup in a position she could reach. Once she complied, he ordered, "Legs *tie-ette,*" and slapped her exposed black stocking.

Catherine blushed to the roots of her hair, thinking she might die of embarrassment from the touch of his fingers. She forced thoughts of her father from her mind before she fell off Cora into a disgraced heap.

However, Isaiah didn't seem to find anything embarrassing as he led the horse down the path toward the orchard. He maintained the same slow pace he'd used with Laura inside the ring. Catherine concentrated on holding the reins and the saddle horn, and gripping with her thighs as well as a person could in a dress.

After a few minutes of perfect behavior by Cora, Catherine glanced up toward the sky. Stars twinkled overhead in the purple-black sea as the breeze carried the sweet scent of honeysuckle and jasmine. Venus was low on the horizon, while a crescent moon hung lopsided like a forgotten English Christmas ornament. As they walked, melodic crickets, tree frogs, and hoot owls began their nightly chorus, sounding much louder in the pasture than from the open window of her bedroom. Ahead, Catherine saw the orchard, and to her shock, spotted the outline of a second horse.

Isaiah planned this little escapade, confident I would comply, she thought, giddy with excitement. *There's nothing simpleminded about him at all!*

When they reached the tree where the horse had been tied, he tugged the reins from the low branch and mounted effortlessly, never releasing his hold on Cora's lead rope. Once he was settled in his saddle, Isaiah leaned over to Catherine, who was clinging to her saddle horn with both hands. "*Gut?*" he asked, meeting her gaze.

She briefly considered the possibility of broken bones, Daniel's aghast reaction should he find out, and her personal shame if she fell into a mud puddle. After a moment, she drew a breath and nodded affirmatively. "*Gut,*" she said in a voice crackling with animation.

And *gut* didn't come close to describing the nighttime ride through apple orchard, open pasture, and scrub woods of mountain laurel and hemlock. Although Isaiah avoided the dark paths of the deep forest, he took her on an adventure through a world of unknown sights, sounds, and smells. Neither spoke. No one had to. The night was alive with hoots, cackles, croaks, howls, and whispers. Isaiah was at home in the shadowy darkness, with only the moon and stars to point the way. So Catherine relaxed in the saddle and gave herself up to the unexpected.

At no point was she ever afraid.

And if she lived to be one hundred and ten, she doubted she would ever again enjoy herself so much.

Nathan awoke from fitful sleeping to the sound of a coyote howling up in the hills. He bolted upright in bed and scrubbed his face with his palms; then he realized it was no coyote. His son was kicking up a fuss in the next bedroom. He settled back on damp warm sheets in a hot, airless room and heard his windup clock tick…tick…tick. No breeze stirred the curtains as he listened, overtired from long hours in the relentless sun and strung out from worry. How would he pay off all the money he owed? Amish folks weren't supposed to be in debt, yet Nathan Fisher owed money to just about everyone. The district members didn't wish to be repaid for their contribution toward the baby's medical bills or Ruth's funeral. Instead, he would be expected to chip in for future expenses, such as barn raisings or unexpected surgeries. But Nathan couldn't imagine himself staying in this district once his one-year lease was up.

Not without Ruth. The memory of that horrible night trailed him around the house like a malevolent shadow. He would never stop hearing her cries of anguish as long as he lived here. So he planned to pay the district and that hospital every dollar he owed and then he would leave this land of painful broken dreams.

In the meantime, how could a man sleep with this racket? He needed to rise at four o'clock for milking and then cleaning stalls while the horseflies were still asleep. Plus, he would have a full day if he wanted to finish cutting hay. After another minute of listening to Abraham wail, Nathan swung his legs out of bed and shrugged into his robe. "What's wrong with him?" he asked in his aunt's open doorway.

Iris paced the length of the room with the red-faced infant on her hip. "I'm not sure. He has some heat rash on his back and legs, so that's probably why he's fussy." The boy appeared oblivious to her attempts to soothe or comfort. "I'll pick up ointment tomorrow when I'm in town."

"Is there nothing you can do tonight? A man needs to get his rest."

She knit her brows and glared at him. "So does a woman, I assure you."

Nathan blew out his breath with a whistle. "True enough, I suppose." Although he didn't sound wholly convinced.

"Here, nephew. Hold him while I use the bathroom." Before he could object, Iris foisted the crying child into his arms and marched from the room.

He peered into his son's pinched, beet-colored face, uncertain what to do. He tried rocking him in his arms to no avail. He lifted him up and down while making the silly noises he'd heard women do at social events. But Abraham Fisher was having none of it.

As unknowledgeable as Nathan was, he knew the heat wasn't helping the situation. He carried the child down the hall and out the front door, despite it being the middle of the night. By the time Iris found them, the boy had settled down as Nathan rocked in the porch swing.

"Looks like you're managing," she said, slumping into a plastic chair.

"*Jah*, as long as I keep rocking him out here where it's cooler. What do you suppose will happen if I lay him down in his cradle?"

"I imagine he'll start crying again." She answered without a moment's hesitation. "That's part of being a parent."

"I am not cut out for this, Iris. I need to milk cows in the morning." He continued rocking, afraid to stop.

"Then you'd better get *cut out for it*, Nathan Fisher. You worry more about those Holsteins than your own flesh and blood." Her tone revealed more than simple discomfort from a hot, humid night.

"That's because I know how to deal with cows. This baby was Ruth's idea. She wanted a *boppli* to fuss over like the other women. With her gone I can't step into her shoes."

"Shame on you! Your wife died giving you a fine son, and yet you fret and moan and feel sorry for yourself."

Anger spiked through his blood, but when he opened his mouth to deny her allegations, to lash out against her unfair judgment, no words came to mind. Instead, his eyes filled with moisture, and despite every attempt to control his emotions, two tears ran down his face.

"I know you're hurting, Nathan. I know you miss your wife," she murmured. "But your son knows nothing about that. He needs his *daed*. He needs you."

It was a good thing she couldn't see his face, because Nathan sat with tears falling freely. Soon his whole body was racked with sobs. Iris lifted the *boppli* from his arms and then sat back in her chair. The child, blessedly, drifted off to sleep in the crook of her arm. "How long are you going to carry around this anger toward Abraham?"

Hearing her speak his name filled Nathan with shame. After a little while he spoke with a mouth gone dry. "I don't want to blame him, to be mad as though this were his fault, but I don't know how to stop." He buried his face in his hands and cried.

"I don't know how to help you, but that lady social worker does. Maybe you should give her a call. The business card she left behind is in the drawer with the pot holders."

He glanced up. All the fight had gone out of him. He couldn't argue because every word his aunt spoke was true. "I'll walk to the neighbors' tomorrow and call her."

"No, you'll be watching your son tomorrow. My daughter-in-law is picking me up in a hired van to take me to the doctor's office. After that, I'm buying her lunch at the buffet restaurant and then we'll do a little shopping."

He stared at her through the near darkness, but her expression didn't waver. "I know this will be a trial by fire for you, nephew, but that's your own fault. You should have been learning about diaper changing and whatnot along the way. I'll leave his bottles ready in the fridge with instructions on how to warm them." She paused to take in a breath. "I won't leave until after your cows are milked. I do understand the importance of *that* chore." She offered a wry smile.

"*Danki,* Aunt. And don't worry. I will do whatever needs to be done."

She rose to her feet with the sleeping child. "To save you some time, I'll call the social worker while I'm in Wooster. I'll ask her to stop out when she can. You have to start somewhere."

Nathan watched her carry Abraham inside. He hoped the boy would sleep until morning so Iris could get some rest. He, however, would sleep no more that night. He had to figure out how to be a *daed* by tomorrow.

Eleven

July

Abby awoke with a start. The nightmares that had plagued her since her incarceration had grown more unsettling. Images of sick children, husbands reaching the end of their patience, and stern fathers shaking their fists conspired to provide another restless night. Kneeling beside her bed, she prayed for strength. Later today she would appear again in court. Her lawyer indicated there was a chance she could be released on her own recognizance.

Home. Reunited with Daniel and Laura and Jake. Thinking of loved ones filled her with a tangible ache that neither food nor water could satisfy. Yet, as the specters of her nightmares retreated to the shadows, Abby doubted the judge would be merciful. Her fellow inmates often spoke of his harsh sentences and brusque treatment. Why would her case be any different?

Opening her Bible to the book of Daniel, she read the story of someone far braver than she. Daniel had lived in Jerusalem. After the Babylonians captured the city, he was taken back to Babylon, where he would spend the next sixty years of his life. During this time of great warring tribes, the Persians marched on Babylon and captured the city. Although Daniel was forced to work for the conquering king of Persia as an adviser, he continued to serve God faithfully. Jealous associates plotted to have him thrown into a lions' den, but God protected faithful Daniel from the hungry beasts. The following morning he walked unscathed from the den.

Abby tried to remember Daniel's devotion when the deputy arrived at the door carrying her Amish clothes. Today they hung from a hanger instead of being rolled up in a plastic sack.

"Did you launder my dress, Deputy Todd?" Abby asked, surprised.

The woman blushed, her cheeks turning bright pink. "Yes. They wouldn't have fared well in the jail laundry because the fabric isn't permanent press. We can't have you looking a mess when you stand before the judge." She laid the outfit across the bed.

"Thank you," Abby said. "I am in your debt."

After showering and pinning her hair beneath her *kapp,* she left the cell common area flanked by two deputies. They didn't handcuff or bind her wrists, yet nevertheless she felt oddly constrained. Even her steps mimicked someone whose ankles had been shackled. At least the court appearance didn't require a long, jarring car ride. The Wayne County Justice Center housed both jail cells and courtrooms. On the night of her arrest, she'd become nauseated in the backseat of the sheriff's cruiser.

Mr. Blake, a fresh-faced, shiny penny of a man on this hot July day, sat with her in the hallway. He repeated his warnings of potential consequences if she didn't comply with the judge's requests. However, as they waited Abby's mind drifted back to summer afternoons picking raspberries with Laura and then making gooey cobblers and pies. She remembered other warm days when she would take them swimming in the creek. Once Jake had caught a crayfish and kept it all summer as a pet. Laura helped him to collect dead flies trapped behind the barn windows to feed the critter.

"They have called us, Mrs. Graber. Are you ready?" Mr. Blake broke her reminiscence with a tight grip on her elbow.

She shivered, either from the air-conditioning or from apprehension of what was to come. "As ready as I ever will be," she said, staggering to her feet. They entered the courtroom and headed toward the polished wooden tables and the railing that separated those whose lives hung in the balance from those who had come to watch. She spotted the woman who typed into a machine and the same gray-haired judge, whose mood hadn't improved since her previous visit, if his scowl was any indication.

After being seated, Abby scanned the crowd in the packed court-room. A knot of pain tightened in her chest when she found Daniel, her beloved *ehemann*. She yearned to reassure him that God would make this and all things right again in His own perfect timetable, but how could she? How could she tell him she wasn't afraid, knowing what she must do? Forcing a smile, she lifted her hand in a wave. Daniel waved back, looking haggard. Then Judge William O'Neil spoke and Abby's legs turned weak and rubbery.

"Please stand, Mrs. Graber."

Abby complied with Mr. Blake at her side. Hearing murmurs behind her, she focused her attention on the man who held her earthly fate in his hands. The judge flipped through and scanned the papers before him while she waited for what seemed like an eternity.

"These are very serious charges against you. Has your attorney explained them adequately so that you understand these proceedings?" he asked.

She nodded. Her tongue felt as though it was glued to the roof of her mouth.

"You must speak in my courtroom, Mrs. Graber. A nod of the head will not suffice for my court reporter."

She swallowed hard. "Yes, Your Honor."

"I see you have been a guest of the county for a couple of weeks now, despite your attorney successfully petitioning the court for a reduction in your bail to a fraction of the original amount." He peered at her over the glasses resting on his nose.

"Yes. Thank you," she answered, uncertain of the correct response.

"What I'm curious about is *why* you're still here." He leafed through the folder again and sighed. "Does it run contrary to Amish laws or customs to raise money against the equity in one's property?"

Abby looked into the man's eyes while her hands turned clammy. He studied her like a bug under a magnifying glass. "Yes, sir. I believe it does. It's left up to the district leaders because…this seldom happens to people in my community."

"I'm sure it doesn't. But the reality of the matter is that although the Amish live by their own rules, you're still in the state of Ohio and subject to our laws also. I'm well aware that local midwives have operated outside the legal system for years—flying beneath the radar—primarily because the Amish don't carry health insurance. I might be an advocate for freedom of choice, but certain lines cannot and will not be crossed. Dispensing medications is one of those lines. You cannot interpret the law to fit your particular situation."

"Your Honor, Mrs. Fisher wasn't my client's patient. Mrs. Graber was functioning in a humanitarian…"

"Save it for the trial, Mr. Blake," the judge interrupted. "Today I'm not interested in what extenuating circumstances prompted your client's actions." He glared at Abby, not the lawyer. "But I'll tell you what I am interested in. The grand jury would like to know where you obtained that syringe of…Pitocin." His gaze drifted to the paper in his hand. "It's not as though you can drive your buggy to the local drug store and pick some up. It's a controlled substance available only by prescription."

Abby felt the weakness in her legs spread throughout her body. She feared she might crumple into a ball if she didn't do something. Clearing her throat, she spoke in a calm voice. "No, Your Honor, I did not purchase the medicine. It was a gift." She focused on the American flag instead of his stern face.

"A *gift*?" He frowned at her word choice, and then he shook his head. "Because I do not consider you a flight risk, and because you are a mother of two young children with strong ties to your community, I may be inclined to release you on your own recognizance until the trial date on one condition." He set the paper back on the pile. "I want the name of the individual who gave you that drug. I won't have medical personnel in this county breaking the law besides the ethical standards of their profession." He waited a few moments and then added, "You could go home to await your trial."

He uttered the words she had longed to hear since her arrest. *I could go home today with Daniel, to my* kinner *and my house, back to my world.* She could sleep in her own bed, wash with soap that smelled of fruit instead of disinfectant, and wake up in the fresh country air of her farm. Tears rushed to her eyes while Judge O'Neil tapped the papers into a stack and returned them to the folder.

Abby hung her head, staring at the floor. "I cannot say, Your Honor."

"*What?* Speak up, Mrs. Graber."

Despite her tears, she lifted her head and met the gaze on the learned man of the law. "I cannot tell you who supplied the medicine."

A voice from somewhere behind her spoke a single plaintive word: "No!"

Abby knew exactly whom that voice belonged to.

"You cannot or you will not?" The judge's voice rose with indignation.

"I will not. My life has been ruined by my misjudgment. I won't ruin another life too." Without a handkerchief, she wiped her eyes with her sleeve.

"This court hereby orders you to release that name. Do not compound your problems by sheltering another criminal. Whoever supplied the drug was well aware that they were breaking the law."

"She did so on good faith, despite her personal reservations."

"*She* showed good faith? I don't think so, not if she ever witnessed what improperly administered pharmaceuticals can do in inexperienced hands. The wrong dosage of a lifesaving drug can kill a person. And a medical professional would know that."

Abby bit the inside of her jaw, mortified that she had revealed the nurse-midwife's gender. *I'm not good at answering questions without time to consider or pray on the matter.*

"Mrs. Graber, I could hold you in contempt of court and throw you in jail for thirty days. But as you're already incarcerated, I don't see what good that would do." He shook his head with resignation.

The courtroom crowd had grown restless; their chatter had steadily increased. "Order in the court!" He banged his gavel. Abby flinched from the sharp noise.

"Should you change your mind about testifying before the grand jury, contact your attorney. I shall set your trial for the earliest available date on the docket. We might as well get this over with, no?"

She nodded despite his request for audible replies and watched her chance to be restored to her family slip away, feeling powerless to do anything about it. Another rap of his gavel—this one a half-hearted tap—set off the start of a headache. The deputy clutched her upper arm, indicating it was time to go. Her day in court was over. Now other criminals would take their turns before Judge O'Neil's bench. Oddly, she felt no animosity for the man. He had a difficult job to do. Upholding English law couldn't be easy.

Turning, Abby caught sight of Daniel's face as she left the courtroom. And the sight would stay with her for weeks, if not for the rest of her life. His eyes looked moist and sorrowful, but his lips had thinned to a hard line. He was angry, hurt, and confused.

How could I disobey a direct order from the English judge? Haven't I been taught to obey the laws of the land?

How could I place an English nurse-midwife before my ehemann *and* kinner*? Haven't I taken an oath to obey my husband and believe that he, not I, is the head of the family?*

She would write to him when she returned to her cell to ask for forgiveness and understanding. She loved Daniel with every fiber of her being. He deserved a wife worthy of his tender devotion, not a willful sinner who acted impetuously without consideration of the consequences.

On the long walk back to her cell, through drafty corridors, elevators, and many locked doors, she considered the person who hadn't been in the courtroom today—her *daed*. He could have appeared in support as either her father or her bishop, yet his absence spoke volumes to the once-favored daughter—the practical, dutiful, solemn Abigail Yost. Now Abigail Graber had become a pariah, an embarrassment to the man who had taught her to fly a kite and catch tadpoles in a jar. Maybe her district would choose to shun her, making her an outcast even after her years in jail were finished. Maybe even Daniel would turn cold to her. Although the Amish didn't divorce, a shunned wife would receive only the barest necessities from a spouse. Could she live without his love?

As Abby reentered her cell, words from Scripture came to mind: *I will never leave you, nor will I forsake you. We will be together until the end of time.* If a woman has God the Father and His Son, Jesus, what else could she possibly need?

Nathan drummed his fingertips on the table, waiting like a condemned man for the executioner. His aunt had wasted no time in calling the social worker. She must have made the call as soon as she arrived in town and had reached the woman immediately. No answering machines or messages left with family members that could easily go astray had stood between Iris and the grief therapy counselor. Mrs. Daly had been delighted to hear from the Fishers, according to Aunt Iris. And she'd promptly volunteered to pick him up for the next session, which just happened to be today. *Why couldn't the meeting be the following week or sometime next month? Am I ready to spill my guts in front of strangers?*

Nathan didn't think so.

It wasn't as though he doubted the usefulness of such sessions…for *Englischers.* Most of them and some Amish women liked to talk. They could blab about any subject all day long until the air in their lungs ran out. But he and Ruth had always been folks of few words. He remembered when they had been courting. He had driven her home after a singing for the fourth time that summer. He'd pulled down a farm lane off the county road so they could marvel at a night sky filled with stars.

The moon shone so bright it nearly hurt their eyes. A breeze from the west carried a chill, heralding autumn.

Ruth had scooted closer on the bench for warmth, and he'd draped his *mamm*'s old quilt across her knees. She nodded but had kept her gaze on that moon. Beneath the patchwork he found her fingers, and with a thrill, he wrapped his hand around hers. She neither pulled her hand back nor admonished him for his boldness. When her tiny smile grew into a full-fledged grin, he *knew*. She was the one for him, and he for her.

Bravely, he turned to her and asked, "Well, then. What say you about a wintertime wedding?" While waiting for her answer, his heart had thudded against his ribcage loud enough to be heard.

She cocked her head to ponder the notion before replying. "I reckon I would like to marry you this winter, Nathan Fisher." Then she had refocused on the moon until it scuttled behind a cloud. A little while later, they had headed for home.

Ruth and Nathan Fisher had been people of few words. That night might have been years ago, but he hadn't changed in that regard. Yet he couldn't disappoint his aunt, who so wanted him to heal. As a widow herself, surely she understood that losing a spouse was different from breaking your arm or cracking your skull. Some wounds festered for a lifetime.

"Slice of pie while you wait?" asked Iris, bustling back into the kitchen. "You didn't eat that much of your supper."

"No, *danki*. My appetite isn't up to par today." He slouched lower in the chair.

She filled the sink with soapy water to tackle the dishes. His son was nowhere in sight.

"And Abraham?" he asked. "Where is he?"

"Sleeping. I fed him his bottle a tad early so you wouldn't be held up for your meeting." She parted the curtains to peer down the driveway. "You did fine yesterday while I was in town. You put the diaper on the correct end, and fed him the proper number of bottles. The boy seems no worse for the wear." She winked at him over her shoulder.

"I only had to refer to that hospital booklet five or six times. Not too bad, if I say so myself." He returned the wink. "How is his heat rash since you bought that tube of ointment?"

"The skin is still red and blotchy, but his discomfort seems to have gone away. He's not crying nearly as much today."

Nathan realized he would prefer an evening filled with his son's squalling to what Patricia Daly had in mind. "That's *gut* to hear," he said. After a moment, he asked, "Do I look acceptable?" He had donned his Sunday best, down to his lace-up shoes and black felt hat. Because he owned no in-between clothes, his only choices were this outfit or his tattered work clothes.

She glanced back at him. "You look fine. Stop fretting."

He overheard a chuckle once she turned back to the dishes. "I'm not sure how fancy folks can sit around and yak the night away," he said.

"Amish folk spend every Sunday afternoon talking up a storm. Just pretend you're standing around somebody's barn after a preaching service."

He was about to debate the issue when he heard a car pull up the driveway. "Whew. Time to go. Don't wait up, Aunt Iris. No telling how long these things last." He tugged his hat down over his ears and marched outside to meet his fate.

Patricia jumped out of the car and waved her hand. "Good evening, Mr. Fisher. My, you look very nice. I have my personal car tonight instead of the county's sedan. I hope you don't think it's too small."

"Please call me Nathan, and no, your car is just fine." He ducked his head and folded himself into the two-seater sports car. It felt as though he was sitting mere inches above the ground while his knees pressed hard against the dashboard.

"You can slide that seat back some. There's a gizmo on the side. And please buckle your seat belt."

Nathan didn't like the seat belt. It made him feel trapped inside the tin can. However, once he was situated, he forced a pleasant expression. "Is it a long drive to your place?"

"We're not going to my house, although that's where we usually hold these meetings. Once I told a few members you were coming, another woman who doesn't live far from you volunteered her home. Plus, she had a blackberry cheesecake recipe she wanted to try out."

Little hairs rose on the back of his neck. "This is a *social* gathering—a coffee klatch of women getting together?" he asked. It wasn't too late to ask her to turn the car around and take him home.

"No, no, it's a therapeutic session, I assure you. Other men will be there. But we *Englischers* tend to include some kind of dessert or refreshment when we gather, no matter what the occasion." She glanced at him.

Begrudgingly, he nodded. "I suppose the Amish are the same. We have almost as much food after a funeral as a wedding." He tried not to think about the sliced ham, fried chicken, barbequed beef, cold salads, and hot vegetables served by his cousins after Ruth's funeral. He tried but did not succeed.

"I want you to relax tonight, Nathan." Patricia seemed to sense his unease. "These are all fine Christian people who, like yourself, have recently lost a loved one. Although you may not have met them before, you can be certain you'll be among friends." She kept her focus on the highway. Cars and trucks zoomed past the tiny car at incredible speeds. "And one of the requirements to join the group is complete discretion. Nothing you share with us will ever be repeated to other people, and the same will be expected from you." She met his gaze briefly.

He pulled on his beard, trying to shift to a more comfortable position. "I don't know if I'll say anything a'tal. I thought I'd just listen to what other folks have to say."

"That's perfectly fine. You're under no obligation to talk tonight or ever. But you might be surprised. There's something about people sharing their burdens that may make you choose to unload a few of your own."

He grunted and clenched his teeth. *Missing my wife is no burden.* "You say these folks are Christians? Do they all go to your church?"

"They are all Christians, but they go to a variety of churches—Baptist, Methodist, Lutheran, Catholic, and non-denominational, like mine."

"Am I your only Amish?"

"You will be our first, but I hope not our last."

Nathan stared out the window without comment. As usual, he didn't know what to say or think about any of this. But his time for contemplation ended as her little red car pulled up the long drive of a beige ranch house with green shutters. A ceramic deer with glass eyes watched their approach from the flower bed, while a metal sunflower spun wildly in the breeze.

"This is the home of Carol Baker," announced Patricia.

"Mrs. Baker sure loves red geraniums and purple pansies," he said, unfolding himself from the car. Dozens of each plant bordered the concrete walkway leading to the front door. Nathan walked behind Mrs. Daly on legs stiffened from the soup-can car and from fear of the unknown.

A middle-aged woman in bright purple greeted them at the door. "Hello, Patricia. And you must be Mr. Fisher. Welcome," she said. "Everyone else is already in the living room. Shall we join them?"

Nathan nodded, following the ladies into the front room, where four women and two men waited. Some were sitting on the couch or in upholstered chairs, but metal chairs had also been set up. All eyes fastened on him and their chatter ceased when they entered.

"Everyone, this is Nathan Fisher," said Patricia. "I'll let people introduce themselves, and talk a little about the loved one they have lost. I'll go first and then you can be last, Nathan."

After he sat down in the chair closest to the door, the social worker cleared her throat. "My name is Patricia, and I've been widowed for two years. I met my husband in high school and we dated throughout college, marrying after graduation. We were blessed with two daughters. One is at college in Toledo and the other is married and living in New York. My Jim worked hard as a plumbing contractor to provide for his family. And he never wanted to go to sleep without patching up a disagreement. Because he passed over in his sleep, I was very grateful for his little rule." Patricia smiled directly at Nathan. "That gets easier and easier the more times I repeat it."

Nathan tried to exhale the breath he'd been holding. *This will not be easy.*

A young woman spoke next about a baby who had died. The infant had been born prematurely, with lungs that hadn't had a chance to fully develop. When tears filled the woman's eyes during the telling, Nathan's heart swelled with pity. It had been nearly three years, yet the woman still suffered. He wondered if she had other *kinner* but didn't dare ask.

Just when he thought the woman had finished her story, she blurted out, "My husband says I've been neglecting my two little girls and not paying them the attention they deserve. I don't mean to, but I can't stop thinking about the son I've lost."

Nathan's mouth dropped open. *She is neglecting two other children because of her memories?*

The next speaker was an older woman who had lost her sister. She spoke at length about how this sister used to torment her while young—blame mischief on her, flirt with her boyfriends, and even steal her possessions. As adults, the women still hadn't gotten along. The deceased sister had often criticized the woman's housekeeping and cooking skills and constantly mocked her for her weight problem. Although she had tried to think of the positive aspects of their relationship, she couldn't forget that her initial reaction to her sister's death had been relief. Nathan squinted his eyes, thinking that all this family history should have been buried with the dead.

The younger of the two men had lost his brother in a car accident last year. The brother had been drinking late at a bar and had tried to outrun the police. They would have undoubtedly arrested him for his third DUI. Instead of avoiding arrest, his brother failed to negotiate a curve and had died on impact with a tree. Nathan said a silent prayer for the man's soul, and then he put him out of mind because any further thoughts about him would be unkind and judgmental. *Wasn't his behavior an abomination before the Lord?*

The other man—elderly, white haired, and stoop shouldered—spoke lovingly of his wife of forty-nine years. They had had children, grandchildren, and even great-grandchildren together. He sounded angry because plans had been underway for a huge, catered reception to celebrate their golden wedding anniversary. He spoke of their travels to Europe, Africa, and more cruises through the Caribbean than he could count. "But why, oh why couldn't she have lived long enough for the tour of China in the spring? Maddy had always wanted to see the Great Wall. We had already paid our deposit, and although the money was refunded, I still wish God had given us more time together. There were still so many more things Maddy and I had wanted to see and do."

Indeed. Nathan clenched his jaw and squirmed in his chair. He had no business here with these *Englischers.* He had nothing in common with them.

"Nathan?"

His head snapped up. Patricia and the others were staring at him.

"I asked if you would like to comment on Bob's story. Something he said seems to have touched a chord. Or maybe this would be a good time for you to share your story."

Nathan breathed through his nostrils like a bull and considered running for the back door. But the fact that his horse and buggy weren't parked outside kept him in his seat. "My wife, Ruth, died in childbirth a few weeks ago. Our first baby. My son is fine. His name is Abraham." He spoke in quick, short sentences. When it felt as though he hadn't spoken for his allotted time he added, "We met at a church social. That's it. End of story."

Eight pairs of eyes watched him, expecting more details. After an uncomfortable silence, Patricia asked, "Is there something you wanted to say about Bob's sharing?"

He closed his eyes, feeling irritation gather deep within his gut. "It seems to me that if the good Lord gave you and your wife forty-nine happy years together, that should be enough. What's so important about seeing some fancy wall in China or spending a lot of money on some golden party to impress your friends? You should be grateful for what you had. Period."

Bob cleared his throat. "I know that's how I *should* feel, but some days I just can't. I miss her so much. I always thought I would go first. I don't know how to live without my Maddy."

"You get up and go about your day. You do your work and fall into bed at night too tired to think about things." The words bubbled forth of their own accord. He felt color rise in his face like turning up a kerosene wick.

"Nathan, take a deep breath and try to relax." Patricia Daly spoke in a soothing tone usually used to quiet rambunctious children. "You're getting yourself worked up, and we're all friends here."

He shook his head. "You are all friends here. And that's fine. This sort of thing probably works for *Englischers,* but it seems to me that you're telling family secrets that you shouldn't and you're spending far too much time dwelling on the past." He struggled to his feet. "What's done is done. Nothing is going to change the past or bring back the people who died. I don't care if you talk from now until the sun comes up tomorrow." He set the hat he'd been fiddling with back on his head. "I'm going to walk home, Mrs. Daly. Please stay with the group. I appreciate what you're trying to do here, but frankly, the exercise will do me far more good than sitting here chawing all night."

He practically ran for the door. Whatever new recipe Mrs. Baker had for cheesecake would remain a mystery to him. He strode down the pebble driveway, past the red geraniums and purple pansies, past the silly ceramic deer smiling from the garden, and past the spinning sunflower. The cool night air felt wonderful on his overheated skin. A full moon rising above the horizon would light his path home. But the first of many prayers he uttered on that long walk was one of gratitude that the meeting had been moved from its usual location in downtown Wooster to a home closer to his own.

Twelve

Abby waited at her usual table in the visitation room. Her thirty-minute visit would begin as soon as her guest walked through the doorway. But no matter how she stared at the metal door, no loved one for her appeared. Her new cellmate, Rachelle, a young woman with blond hair and crooked teeth, was seated nearby, chatting away with her boyfriend. She had been arrested for shoplifting for the second time and would spend sixty days here before being allowed to go home. The girl explained that if her ex-husband would pay the back child support he owed, she wouldn't be forced to steal the new clothes and video games her kids needed. Abby chose not to mention that video games weren't necessities of life, and neither was new clothing. Even though shoplifting broke the Eighth Commandment, perhaps Rachelle wouldn't appreciate advice from a person charged with two felonies, including drug possession.

Each time the door swung open Abby's heart skipped a beat. How she longed to see her *ehemann*. She had begged for understanding in her last letter but received no reply in return. *Does he still love me?* Because she had refused the judge's offer of awaiting the trial at home, she wondered if Daniel's heart had hardened during the past week.

With the sound of a scraping door, Abby glanced up to find her wait for answers would soon be over. Daniel Graber entered the common room and strode toward her table. Then, with a breath-stealing rush, she saw he held the hands of her two *kinner*. Laura and Jake let go of his hands and ran toward her wearing bright smiles and their Sunday best.

"*Mamm!*" they chimed in unison and flew into her arms.

She hadn't expected this. She wasn't prepared to feel their arms around her neck or smell their sweet baby-fine hair. And she certainly wasn't ready to answer their questions.

"They can only stay a few minutes," said Daniel, his expression somber. "Then they will sit with Catherine in the hallway while you and I talk."

While her face lay buried against Laura's neck, Abby asked, "My sister is here? Let her come in too. There are more chairs, and I have so much to thank her for." She hugged Jake until he squirmed in protest.

"She can't, Abby. There are limitations. This isn't a quilting bee, where it's the more, the merrier."

He didn't raise his voice, yet she heard the bitterness in his soft words. "Yes, of course," she said, keeping her focus on the children. *Has Jake grown taller during the past weeks? Is Laura thinner? Hasn't she been eating properly?* For five minutes, however, she asked no questions. Instead she listened to jumbled tales of spilled ice cream, swimming lessons in the neighbor's pond, loose teeth, and burnt cupcakes. Abby tried to divide her attention equally as both clamored to fill in the details of their lives…lives she was missing.

All too soon their visit was over. "All right, that's enough. Laura, take your *bruder*'s hand and go back out to your aunt."

Abby clung tightly to her children until Daniel pulled them from her grasp. Slumping into her chair, she forced air into her lungs with deep, hard breaths to regain control. They waved their little hands until

Daniel nudged them through the doorway. "*Danki* for bringing them to see me," she said once he sat down opposite her.

"I thought seeing your *kinner* might do you some good—and maybe bring you to your senses."

She closed her eyes for a moment. "I'm not sure if it helps me forebear or makes things worse." She felt her throat turn dry and raw. "It's good to see you, Daniel. I know it's a long drive on busy roads to come here." She reached for his hand. It felt limp against her palm, but at least he didn't pull back from her.

"It's not that far. I left early this morning. Good thing your lawyer called me on your cell phone or I wouldn't have known what to bring." He clucked his tongue. "I had to find the *kinner*'s birth certificates or they wouldn't have been allowed to see you. I had to *prove* they were my children. What did they think? That I would pick up just anybody's kids along the route to bring for a jail visit?" His expression reflected utter confusion.

Abby understood his frustration. So many of the English ways were confusing, but dwelling on them wouldn't help. "Guess who came to visit me?" she asked, changing the subject.

"I would expect your attorney."

"Besides him." When Daniel offered no second guess, she continued. "Dr. Weller. I had added him to my initial list on a lark, never thinking he would really come."

Daniel shrugged. "If he would have shown up that night, then you wouldn't be sitting here right now."

Abby gripped her trousers beneath the table. "It wasn't his fault. He had an emergency to attend to that night."

"Why did he come see you?"

"To tell me that nothing could have saved Mrs. Fisher, and that I did nothing to harm her. He came to set my mind at ease."

Daniel rubbed the bridge of his nose. "And did he succeed? Is your mind at ease, Abigail? Do you feel better knowing that you're likely going to prison for helping a woman who would have died anyway?"

"I'm glad I didn't make matters worse." Her shirt began to stick to her back. "What would you have had me do? Sit there and do nothing while she bled to death?"

"I think you should have called an ambulance before you left our house, despite what Nathan Fisher said. Then this mess would have fallen to the paramedics instead of you."

She had often wished the very same thing. "What I chose to do is in the past, and God's will prevailed with Ruth Fisher."

He leaned across the scarred tabletop. "You're right. Nothing can be solved by rehashing the past, but you need to start thinking about the present." He pulled his hand from hers and grasped her sleeve. "Your children need you. Your sister works hard, but she's not you. They need their *mamm*." Silence spun out between them while the other groups talked quietly. "I need you, Abby. Come home to us. Let's put this behind us, at least until your trial. You don't belong here with these other people."

She scanned the group of inmates and visitors. Some were laughing, some teary eyed, while others appeared as relaxed as though chitchatting over pie in their kitchens. Were these women any different from her? As time wore on, she didn't think so.

"Apparently, I do belong here. The judge will only release me if I ruin another's reputation. She will lose her license, Daniel, and may face jail herself. That's not fair."

"Not fair? That nurse had no business giving that syringe to you. She *should* lose her license. You weren't trained to give injections."

"I watched her do it so many times." She rubbed the back of her knuckles.

"I watched the vet deliver a foal by cesarean section a couple times, but that doesn't mean I'm ready to try that myself."

"Giving up her name won't affect the outcome of my case. My trial will be set within a couple months. My lawyer won't try to delay it for any reason."

His complexion darkened. "Your loyalty rests with an English woman you used to work with? A nurse who has already retired? What does she care about her license anyway?"

"She had planned to fill in at the birthing center when they are short on staff. Besides, the court will go harder on her than me because she's a registered nurse."

Daniel's head reared back. "Have you given no thought to *your* reputation in the community? And what position this has placed your *daed* in? What if the district decides to shun you? What will that do to your children? Doesn't my opinion as your *ehemann* count for anything?"

Abby didn't meet his gaze. She couldn't look him in the eye without breaking down. Truth was, she hadn't allowed herself to think about the Amish community or her father. She had blocked them out to stay strong, but her avoidance wasn't fair to Daniel. "I shall deal with the elders in due time. My *daed* has not visited me, nor has any Amish person other than you."

He slicked a leathery hand through his hair, which had become more peppered with gray. "Do you not love me anymore, *fraa*? Do you no longer respect me or my opinions? Are you not willing to honor the vows you took before God?" His voice grew harsher with each subsequent question.

Abby couldn't hold back her tears. They ran down her cheeks and dropped onto her drab green shirt. "I still love you, Daniel, with my whole heart. I'm the one who's no longer worthy of respect. Forgive my weakness and indecision. I long to be restored to my family...to come home."

"Your thirty minutes are up, Mr. Graber," a guard called from the doorway.

Abby flinched, first from the interruption and then from Daniel's expression. "Titus chapter three instructs believers to submit to the government and its officers. If you want to come home so badly, then do the right thing." He glanced at the guard. "I need to be on my way, but I'll return as soon as possible."

For one brief moment, their gazes locked and she saw the heart of the man who had picked her wildflowers in spring meadows, thrown pebbles at her bedroom window when she was sick with the flu, and cried at the births of their children. Then he put on his hat and strode from the room with a stiff-legged gait. He didn't look back.

Abby shuffled to the other door across the room. After a short tap, she was taken back to her cell. Her stomach churned with hollow emptiness while her eyes couldn't seem to focus. She stretched out on her bunk and closed her eyes. The solitude didn't last for long. Her young cellmate flounced into the tiny room within ten minutes.

"Hi, Abby. Got a headache?" asked Rachelle.

"*Jah,* I guess I should have eaten some lunch."

Rachelle emitted a snort. "Yeah, right. My old man gives me a headache too, as well as in another part of the body." She stepped onto the bed frame and swung up to the top bunk. "I saw your old man giving you grief during visitation."

"That wasn't my father," Abby corrected. "Daniel is my husband."

"Both breeds of men have been known to wreak havoc wherever they go. You need to stand up for yourself. He doesn't understand what it's like in here. This ain't exactly a day spa."

Abby rubbed her eyelids with her fingertips, wishing the woman had chosen TV over female bonding. She had only a vague idea what a day spa was, but she didn't want an explanation. "Daniel only wants me to put the needs of my family first." She struggled to a sitting position. "To mind him the way I promised I would."

"*Mind* him?" Rachelle squawked like a crow. "Or what, you'll get a spanking?" She shifted onto her belly so she could hang over the edge and peer at Abby.

"It's part of the marital vows."

"Not in most weddings anymore," said Rachelle, shaking her head. "I realize you drive a horse and buggy and wear old-fashioned clothes, and that's all well and good. I respect that, but obeying somebody for no reason other than because they are male has got to go. You must stand on your own two feet, even if they are wearing high-top shoes." She grinned before pulling back to a prone position, restoring Abby's semblance of privacy.

And it was a good thing, because her tears returned with a vengeance.

Abby pressed her fist to her mouth to keep from screaming. Her cell-mate was yet another person telling her how to think or feel or act.

This *Englischer,* as well-meaning as she might be, couldn't imagine what her world was like. And though she'd been gone barely a month, Abby was having difficulty remembering the familiar details that had sustained her for years.

Catherine Yost had known better moods than the one she was in. Yesterday she had traveled over bumpy roads to downtown Wooster and never saw her sister. She would have appreciated five minutes even if Daniel had wanted the lion's share of the time. Seeing that Abby was thriving would have eased her mind. While they were young, her sister never ate properly if she was upset. Hopefully, Abby hadn't wasted down to skin and bones with her current circumstances.

During the drive home, Daniel had answered her questions with grunts, sighs, and one-word responses. He had said only that Abby looked well but wasn't listening to reason. "You would do well not to become as stubborn and willful as your *schwester,*" had been his final words on the subject. Jake and Laura, buoyed by their brief visit, received no more information about their *mamm* than she did.

Daniel Graber set his jaw so tight, a nervous tick in his cheek appeared. And he had clenched the reins as though expecting wild mustangs to suddenly bolt for freedom. The children soon grew tired and dozed off in the backseat, so Catherine stared at the passing scenery with no desire to irritate a crabby man. She'd slept fitfully last night, dreaming of building snowmen with Abby on crisp winter days and then drinking cups of cocoa by the woodstove while their socks and gloves dried.

This morning at breakfast, her brother-in-law's mood hadn't improved. He remained cordial but silent as he wolfed down oatmeal and toast like a starving stray dog. She might not have minded a few complaints about burnt bread or too much maple syrup in the oats, but Daniel was a troubled man with no relief for his woes in sight.

Her disposition was in for a treat, however. After she fed the children and fixed a plate for Isaiah, she found him already on the porch. Two shirt buttons were open, his sleeves had been rolled to the elbow, and his damp hair again sported no hat. But the quiet man was wearing a smile as he waited at the table, fork and knife in hand.

She regretted not spraying on a little body mist, a birthday gift from Abigail. "Good morning, Isaiah," she mouthed, setting down his food.

"*Gut* morn!" He nodded and pulled the plate and bowl closer.

Catherine perched on the edge of the bench. For some reason, watching him eat fascinated her, despite the fact that he did so same as everyone else. Midway through his meal he gestured with his fork toward the porch steps. Four pails had been lined up by size—two large and two small.

"Buckets," she said, stating the obvious. She walked over to look into the first. A thin layer of blackberries, plump and juicy, lined the bottom. "Yummy," she declared before the first ripe berry passed her lips. She didn't speak again until she had consumed half the contents. "I love blackberries," she mouthed, returning to the table. "They're my favorite fruit." He might not have been able to read lips well, but her licking each fingertip managed to convey the message.

When Isaiah finished breakfast, he gazed at her with a crooked grin. "Pick today," he stated. Twin dimples gave away his enthusiasm.

Catherine glanced into the empty pail and back at the other three. "You want to pick berries today with Laura and Jake and me?" She had difficulty reducing verbiage, even when she understood his ideas.

Isaiah downed his coffee in two swallows and wiped his mouth with a napkin. "*Jah*. You, Cat, Lorr, and Jake pick." He peered from under his dark lashes. His eyes could have drilled holes through her if she hadn't broken the connection.

The way he looked at her…*it is the look that passes between lovers, between those who are courting and will someday marry.* Catherine shivered, even though no breeze stirred the wind chimes overhead. She held up an index finger, made a swishing motion over his empty plate and bowl, and then fled inside with cheeks ablaze. What was happening here?

Wasn't she supposed to be improving his communication skills? Bringing the man out of his reclusion to enjoy the camaraderie of family and friends? Daniel had long since left for his chores, yet nevertheless she kept glancing over her shoulder while she washed the breakfast dishes. She knew for certain *he* wouldn't like the way Isaiah looked at her.

Drying her hands, Catherine dismissed the notion. No doubt she was imagining things. How many times had she misinterpreted a simple act of kindness or a sidelong glance during a preaching service that had been intended for another?

At twenty-three I might be older but no wiser, she thought. "Laura, Jake, where are you? Let's go berry picking."

The children bounded into the kitchen at speeds that belied their short legs. "Blackberries? Is it that time?" Laura jumped up and down. "*Mamm* always takes us to the back pasture fence. Then we make blackberry pie and blackberry pancakes. And she stirs some into our milk too."

Catherine didn't think she would appreciate anything floating in her milk, but Laura's excitement knew no bounds. It only increased when she spotted Isaiah on the porch through the screen.

"Isaiah," Laura shrieked and ran out the door, followed by her shadow, Jake. She threw her arms around his waist.

Catherine tucked stray hairs beneath her *kapp* and sprayed insect repellant on her neck instead of body mist. She slipped it into her apron pocket to use on the *kinner.*

"Hullo, Lorr," said Isaiah, returning her hug shyly. He handed her a bucket.

"Ready, Cat?" he asked, meeting her eye. His words were low and guttural, yet recognizable. Considering he had never heard two barn cats howling at each other, she didn't mind the nickname.

"Ready," she said, picking up a pail. Catherine thought the walk to the berry patch would be a perfect opportunity to gauge Isaiah's lip-reading abilities. She would ask short, direct questions without a companion action to see which words he recognized. Perhaps by day's end she would have determined which vowel sounds were harder for him to discern.

Too bad Isaiah couldn't read her mind. With his long strides and the *kinner* running beside him, she was soon left in the dust on the pasture lane. As Laura chattered away, oblivious to the fact no one was listening, Isaiah loped along, taking in the sights and smells of a summer day. He sniffed low-hanging dogwood branches and plucked buttercups growing along the fence line.

Catherine, however, marched as fast as she could without running. She had no wish to sweat heavily during the outing. When the threesome disappeared around a bend in the path, she grew annoyed. *Am I not the nanny? Aren't these children my responsibility to keep safe? Hadn't Isaiah extended the invitation to include me?*

She fumed until she rounded the bend and discovered her companions waiting in the shade. Each held a different colored nosegay of weeds—Jake's were purple ajuga, Laura white yarrow, while Isaiah presented yellow buttercups he'd pulled up by the roots. With a blush, she accepted the gifts.

"Hurry, Aunt Catherine," demanded Laura, "before the birds eat all the berries."

Catherine held her skirt up with one hand to keep pace with the group. "Looks like we won't have to worry about sharing," she answered as they reached the pasture fence. Stretching for fifty yards, briar bushes hung over the split rails. "Oh, my," she gushed. She'd never seen such a rich harvest. Honeybees buzzed in and out among the late flowers while the fruit glistened with the last of the morning dew. And not a single blue jay in sight!

Isaiah hooted as he handed Jake his pail. The four spread out and began picking. For the first twenty minutes, they ate as many as they gathered. When they had eaten their fill, they concentrated on filling the buckets with berries to take home. Abby kept an eye on the youngsters to make sure they didn't entangle themselves in the thicket, but both knew how to pluck the low berries without encountering too many thorns.

"Enough?" asked Isaiah, over Catherine's shoulder.

She started, not realizing he'd come up behind her. "*Jah,* more than enough. I had no idea the Grabers owned this goldmine."

He plucked one firm berry and inspected it carefully before pressing it to her lips. Without thinking, she chomped down like a fish taking a baited hook. "*Danki,*" she murmured, hoping Laura wasn't watching. But the child worked diligently as Isaiah fed Catherine berry after berry as though she were incapable of eating on her own. She felt a rush of exhilaration as she plucked a ripe fruit for him. She should discourage his boldness, yet she couldn't seem to muster the energy. When she fed him a second berry, he bit lightly down on her fingertip. He laughed while she flushed with embarrassment.

"Stop that," she hissed under her breath. "Load your bucket, and then we'd better head back." *Before Daniel notices we're gone.* They picked for another ten minutes, swatting at mosquitoes and wiping the back of their necks. Then Isaiah took Laura's hand. "Come," he instructed and lifted both children over the fence. He climbed over effortlessly and made a motion for Catherine to follow.

"Come where?" she asked, her brows knitting together above her nose.

Isaiah strode toward the scrub pines, holding his bucket and Jake's hand. Laura ran ahead, spilling berries as she swung her pail like a pendulum.

"Where are you all going?" She hollered to no avail. "There are still plenty more here to pick." But because Isaiah couldn't hear her and the *kinner* didn't appear to want to, she had no choice but to climb over the fence too. It was neither a graceful nor ladylike maneuver. By the time she caught up with them, she was perspiring and had a horde of gnats swarming around her head.

"Where are you going?" she asked, catching Isaiah's sleeve.

He stopped abruptly to face her, holding up his index finger as she had done this morning to signal patience. Then he flicked the tip of her nose and resumed hiking.

After a quick glance over her shoulder, Catherine grabbed Laura's hand and followed. Curiosity had gotten the better of her. They walked not in the direction of Isaiah's cabin but toward the neighboring property. A fast-moving stream separated the two farms, more or less creating the property line. Tall sycamores and cottonwoods lined the riverbank, while the namesake white fluff floated on the breeze as they drew close. On the western side, catching plenty of sun while being sheltered from the strong burning rays, stood another stand of briars. Although smaller than the first patch, its location along the river provided optimum conditions. The berries were the largest she'd ever seen.

Catherine began picking as though part of some race or competition. Soon they had all filled their buckets to overflowing. When she glanced over at Isaiah, he was watching her. He pressed his finger to his lips and said, "*Ssshhhh.*"

She didn't have to ask him what he meant. This patch of blackberry bushes would be their secret. He wouldn't bring anyone else here and neither should she. She nodded eagerly, loving that she shared a secret with him. She'd become his trusted confidante. And judging by the way he walked at her side on the way home, she'd also become his friend. Although he attempted no conversation, his sparkling eyes told plenty.

Back in the Graber yard, Catherine took everyone's berries to the porch to be washed and sorted later. The ripest would be eaten tonight with sugar and cream, and then the remaining would be baked into pies or canned. When she came back to find Laura and Jake, they were taking turns on the swing. Isaiah pushed one, then the other on the oak slat hanging from the tree. Patient and careful were his efforts so that Jake didn't fall off or Laura swing too high.

Catherine watched them from the shade, wishing she didn't have to start cooking or get the two children washed up for supper. Truthfully, she wished this idyllic summer day would never end. But before she could curtail their playtime, Isaiah sent them inside the house in his special nonverbal manner. Neither child argued but headed toward the porch hand in hand.

She scrambled to her feet, planning to thank him for the afternoon.

"Cat," he voiced and pointed at the swing.

"Oh, no. I'd better go inside and start—"

"Cat," he insisted. He pointed again at the swing.

After three seconds of consideration, she plopped down on the wooden slat and gripped the chains. *After all, what difference will five minutes make?*

Isaiah clamped his fingers over her hands and began to push. His touch sent her heart soaring into the clouds. For a short while she lost herself with childlike abandon. He pushed while she swung higher and higher. The breeze lifted the strings of her *kapp* and loosened a few tendrils of hair. Closing her eyes, she savored the exquisite sense of flying...of freedom.

Then without warning, Isaiah slowed the swing with a firm grip on both chains. When she turned her face to thank him for the enjoyable afternoon, he leaned in and kissed her. Not a brush of his lips against her cheek as *Englischers* loved to do or a buzz across the top of her *kapp*. It was a smack right on her mouth.

And there was nothing childlike about it.

Catherine jumped off the swing and ran toward the house, hearing his laughter ring in her ears until she closed the kitchen door behind her.

Thirteen

Are you up there, nephew?"

Iris' shrill voice could be heard clearly from the bottom of the narrow staircase. Nathan punched his pillow before burying his head beneath it to block out any sound. He contemplated ignoring his aunt's question and hiding from her like a child. Perhaps she would assume he'd gone to the fields or to one of the barns and he would be able to catch another hour of vital sleep. The walk from Mrs. Baker's house had nearly killed him. Because he'd worn his ill-fitting dress shoes, the short distance by car had turned into a nightmare on foot. He had blisters on top of blisters by the time he reached his driveway. But Nathan was an adult, not a boy playing hooky from school. He sat upright and swung his sore legs out of bed.

"I'm up here, Aunt," he called, scrubbing his face with his hands. "I'll be right down."

After slipping on clean work clothes, he staggered down the steps like a ninety-year-old man. His legs burned from the excursion, while his knees and ankles felt swollen to twice their usual size. The sweet smell of sizzling bacon reminded him of how long it had been since last night's supper. His stomach grumbled with hunger. Iris took one look at him and dropped her wooden spoon. Apparently, he looked as bad as he felt.

"What happened to you? Why were you still upstairs? Were you *sleeping*?" Her inflection on the final word revealed how unbelievable she found the idea.

Nathan poured coffee and drank half a cup before attempting to answer. "I went back to bed after milking the cows and filling feed and water troughs. I needed a little more shut-eye today than usual." Right now, he needed more coffee, probably more than what remained in the pot. He quickly downed his first cup and refilled it to the brim.

"You went back to bed?" She pulled the pan of eggs off the burner.

"That's what I said. *Danki* for frying bacon this morning. I'm hungry enough to eat a whole pound myself." He lowered himself to a chair and grabbed two slices of toast.

"Did you stay at your meeting very late? Folks wanted to keep talking until the wee hours, eh? It probably did you some good, hearing you're not the only one with sorrows. A person can always sleep—"

"Aunt Iris!" he interrupted. "Hold up there. You're running away like a stampeding herd. That's not what happened." He ate the toast almost without chewing.

She set the scrambled eggs, plate of bacon, and coffeepot on the table. "All right, then, why don't you tell me what took place. I prayed for you all evening that the meeting would go well."

"God chose not to answer that particular prayer, Aunt. It didn't go well at all." He scraped a hearty portion of scrambled eggs onto this plate and began eating.

She sipped coffee, studying him over the cup's rim. "What happened? Talk to me, Nathan."

He set down his fork and dabbed his mouth with his napkin. "Those *Englischers* are rather odd. They dwell on the past, rehashing events to keep them alive in their memories. They won't let themselves move on." He reached for another slice of toast.

"Are you saying you would prefer to forget Ruth?"

"No," he said, raising his voice. "But these people neglect living children to focus on one who died." Remembering that young mother's story still tightened his belly into knots. "One man still mourns a brother who drove home drunk from a bar and smashed into a tree. He died from his own irresponsibility and bad decisions. Luckily, he took no innocent people along with him."

She narrowed her gaze. "His brother still has a right to grieve for him, and maybe he mourns the fact the man was an alcoholic. It was a tragedy. I've never heard you so critical, Nathan. Judgment is best left up to the Lord."

He devoured his plate of food, organizing his thoughts to make a clearer case for the therapy fiasco. "One other man sounded mad at God for calling his wife home after forty-nine years of marriage. He had that much time with her and still it wasn't enough. He wanted to throw some fancy party and go touring walls in China!"

"You're saying that because he had forty-nine years, he wasn't entitled to grieve for his wife? He had that much more time to grow attached. He's probably lost without her companionship." Iris nibbled a cold slice of toast.

"Grieved, yes, but mad because they didn't have even more years together is pure greediness."

"You're angry because you had so *little* time."

"True, but that's not why I can't abide with the therapy sessions. Those *Englischers*...they bare their souls about things meant to remain private. Family business, things shared between two parents...they tell anybody who'll listen their deepest, darkest secrets." Nathan closed his eyes trying to blot out the woman who initially rejoiced upon news of her sister's death. Or the young mother who admittedly neglected her daughters because she so favored her lost son.

"Wasn't that the point of the meeting?" Iris asked. "They weren't telling their secrets to just anybody. They were sharing with like-minded folks who understood."

Nathan stared at her. She was taking the side of the self-centered

Englischers? Why had he thought she would understand *him*? "All well and good for them, but their meeting didn't help me one bit." He shoved two slices of bacon into his mouth at once.

While he chewed, she studied him. "If the therapy went poorly, then why were you so late coming home? You must have slept little last night to return to bed this morning after chores."

"When my turn to speak came, I told my story and then I left."

"Left? How could you leave? You rode with Mrs. Daly." Her brow furrowed with confusion.

"I didn't want folks asking me questions. I didn't want to wait around while they ate their dessert. And I didn't want that social worker to leave her group. So I walked home."

"You walked home?" Her cup clattered onto its saucer.

"Aunt Iris, must you repeat everything I say? Can't you just believe me the first time around?"

She wrinkled her nose. "Well, that explains why you can barely walk this morning."

"I wore my dress shoes. If I'd worn my boots, it wouldn't have been so bad."

"You walked all the way from Wooster?"

He rolled his eyes. "No, not that far. Some lady invited the group to her home so she could try out a new recipe."

After a moment's contemplation, she said, "I guess I'm having a hard time understanding why anyone would walk home instead of waiting for his ride."

Nathan's voice rose with irritation. "Because I lost my temper. Those people got under my skin, so I stormed out of the session. I didn't want to listen to that pushy social worker on the way home. She would have handed me a pile of reasons and excuses, sort of what you're doing now."

"What do you know about losing one's temper?"

He thought for a moment. "Something about it being a sign of our pride and arrogance. I admit I didn't handle the situation very well, but I shouldn't have gone in the first place." He sighed with resignation.

Iris pushed away her plate of eggs, barely touched. "So why did you? Why did you agree to go if you had no desire to give therapy a chance?"

Nathan swallowed hard, washing down the bacon with more coffee. The caffeine was making him agitated but not energized. "I went because you asked me to go."

"You did it for my sake and not for your own?"

"*Jah.* I knew it was important to you." He dumped the remaining eggs onto his plate and ate, still hungry after his first helping.

She waited until he had finished and said, "Then the plan was doomed from the start. You can't do this for someone else, Nathan. You must be the one who wants to heal."

"I'm not sick, Iris. There's nothing wrong with me. I'm going about my life and tending my farm. You're starting to sound like one of *them.*"

She slapped a flat palm down on the table. "There's plenty wrong with you. Your idea of checking on your son is peeking at him from the doorway. You handle him as seldom as possible and hold him as though he might break. You might be tending your farm, but when did you last talk to a neighbor? Or maybe checked to see if someone needed *your* help for a change? When was the last time you went to a preaching service or read your Bible? God might lead you to helpful Scriptures if you opened the Good Book once in a while. I see you bow your head, but do you pray? Or are you merely passing time, thinking about your list of chores?"

His head reared back while his mouth dropped open. "You speak too sharply, Aunt. This is still my home, and I won't be dressed down like a schoolboy."

She clucked her tongue. "We all need to be set back on the straight and narrow once in a while."

He drummed his fingers on the table. "I'll ask around at the grain elevator if any work bees have been scheduled, or if somebody can use my help getting their hay cut and stored. Folks helped out around the time of Ruth's funeral and brought all that food here and to your son's home."

She refilled both cups. "That's good for a start. When we're suffering, we sometimes can't see beyond our own noses. And I'm speaking from personal experience. What about church services?"

"I can't go back to preaching. We hadn't had a chance to know folks much before Ruth died, so this district is a pack of strangers."

"And they will stay that way until you do something about it." She cocked her head. "Should I ask the bishop to schedule a service here? Then you wouldn't have to walk far for worship or to be sociable, for that matter." Her sly smile gave her away.

"Absolutely not. Don't even joke about that. I won't have people here without my Ruth." Then he added softly, hesitantly, "I can't face them if gossip has spread from that midwife…if everyone knows."

"Knows what?" Her face pinched into a frown.

"That Ruth had been advised never to have *kinner*—that any pregnancies would endanger her life." He stared at the ceiling, unable to meet her eye. *Patricia Daly is wrong. Voicing the words doesn't get any easier.* "Ruth did it to make me happy, to give me a son."

"You can't blame Abraham for his *mamm*'s death. He's an innocent baby!"

"I know that. I don't hold anything against him." Fog lifted from part of his brain. "Is that why you have been so pushy about my son? You thought I was still taking this out on him?" He shook his head back and forth like a stubborn nag. "I don't pick him up much because my hands are too rough and clumsy. I'm afraid I might hug him too tightly or lose my grip and drop the little fella. I stand in the doorway of his room so I can listen while he sleeps. I hear his sighs and tiny snores and know he's all right. I'm not good with *boppli,* Aunt Iris." He pushed away his plate. "Remember the other day when you made me feed him? I ended up with more formula down the back of my shirt than in his belly. But I promise you—when he's older and I don't feel like such a goat in a gift shop, I will be the best *daed* around. I'll make you proud."

Iris folded her hands, softness returning to her gentle brown eyes. "I know you will, but you shouldn't blame yourself either about Ruth. She wanted *kinner* as much as you did. Amish women are raised to assume that someday they will marry and have a houseful of little ones. When God has other plans, the news is hard for a woman to accept."

"She might have accepted it easier if I hadn't been hounding her. I took her to see an herbalist who made her drink four cups of bad-smelling tea per day. Next I took her to a chiropractor to straighten her spine, hoping that would help. Then I made her ask advice from a woman in our district who had borne fifteen children. *Fifteen.* I just couldn't let the matter drop. Finally, we drove to the city for a full examination and series of tests. Ruth never told me the final results, but when she said she was in a family way, I assumed they had fixed whatever had been wrong."

They sat listening to the hum of the propane refrigerator for a minute or two.

"I know you feel guilty, but you need to overcome these feelings. If she were here, she would say she forgives you. Maybe returning to church or talking to the bishop will help you—"

Couldn't she give it a rest? His aunt was like a bulldog with a firm grip on one end of a stick. "No church, no talking to the elders, no rehashing this sad tale anymore. I'm tired of repeating the details. It doesn't do a bit of good. Leave me be on this matter. In time I'll heal on my own, if that's what you insist on calling it."

"No."

It was just a one-word answer, delivered without exclamation or frenetic gesture, but the arrow hit its target. Nathan stared at her, fear creeping up his back. "What do you mean, no?"

"I'll not *leave you be* on this matter. If you don't want to go to preaching or talk to one of the brethren that's your choice, but I won't make it easy for you to wallow in your grief and self-pity. If you don't do something to pull yourself together, then I'm leaving. I'm going home to my own family, who appreciate my counsel. I'll take Abraham if you'll permit me, but either way, I'm putting you on notice, Nathan Fisher."

One small, gray-haired grandmother brought goose bumps to his forearms. He inhaled a strangled breath. "Okay, I'll start praying... praying for real. And I'll open my Bible tonight."

She studied him for any hint of insincerity, and then she shrugged her shoulders. "All right. I'm going to feed Abraham and get him up for the day."

Nathan marched from the house to his fields, feeling mule-kicked. *What an insistent, pushy woman! She's not my* mamm *and has no right issuing ultimatums. If she decides to return home, Abraham and I will get by. Or I'll pack up and return to Indiana. Breaking a lease isn't against the law. I'll find some way to pay the landlord.*

For the rest of the morning and into the afternoon, he fumed and pouted. But when his pique waned, he turned his eyes toward the heavens. A flock of geese had drawn his attention. Or the heavy clouds had suddenly given way to sunshine. For whatever reason, Nathan Fisher began to pray. He was rusty at first, but after a while his heart began to swell with emotion and then anticipation. Tonight, after supper and chores, away from interruptions, he would open his Bible and see what would happen.

Catherine's emotions ran the gamut for the next several days. She vacillated between sheer joy that someone *finally* was in love with her to fear that Daniel would put a stop to the fledgling relationship, and then to shame that this would somehow lead to disappointment and further alienation for Isaiah.

But wasn't he a grown man, not a child, and as such capable of giving and receiving affection? Yet each night as she tossed and turned, unable to sleep, anxiety sat heavily on her heart. Was she breaching Daniel's trust by sneaking around behind his back? The fact was that she knew little about his cousin other than the man couldn't hear. Was there another reason for his avoidance of people? Along with the first rays of dawn came the realization that she needed advice before this romance proceeded any further. Second-guessing only went so far. At times like these a woman needed her big sister. Jail or no jail, Catherine had to talk to Abby.

Of course, Daniel saw no reason for an in-person visit. "A letter would work just as well," he said. "I haven't got time to take you. I should cut hay while the good weather holds. Maybe in a few weeks, once all the hay is stored away." He finished his bowl of berries and ice cream, licking the spoon for the final drop.

Catherine couldn't afford to wait even a few weeks, so she considered her reply carefully. "I'm in need of her advice about…womanly matters. There's no need to interrupt your work. I'm capable of driving a buggy by myself. With a county road map I can leave at first light and be in Wooster by the start of visiting hours." She lifted her chin higher. "I'll park behind the courthouse in the back parking lot, where you tied up."

She might have asked to travel alone to Missouri, judging by his reaction. Daniel listed no less than ten things that could go wrong on her trip, but Catherine countered each with a logical solution. All except, "You might suffer from heat stroke and faint behind the reins. Then the horse might take you far in the wrong direction."

That one had left her speechless, as she'd never known heat stroke in her life. In the end, he agreed to her solo visit as long as she traveled by hired van at his expense. Avoiding a long ride on dusty roads in heavy traffic was fine with her.

On Sunday the van picked her up at eleven thirty and dropped her in front of the Justice Center by twelve fifteen. The driver promised to return at two after finishing some errands in Wooster. She sat on a hard bench for forty-five minutes, contemplating how to broach the topic of Isaiah with Abby. *Englischers*—some well dressed, some not— passed by without paying her any attention. By one o'clock, the start of visitation hours, a crowd had gathered in the hallway. When a guard opened the heavy metal door, people formed a line before him. Catherine joined the queue, not knowing what to expect. One by one, the officer checked the ID of visitors against the list provided by each inmate.

"Catherine Yost," she stated when her turn came. "I'd like to see Abigail Graber." The balding man flipped through his binder of papers, and for a moment she feared Abby hadn't added her name to the list.

Then with a nod he said, "Thirty minutes, Miss Yost. You'll find your sister seated far to the right." After thanking the guard, Catherine entered the overly air-conditioned room filled with inmates and their family members. She located her sister easily, but she wasn't prepared for what she saw. Abby wore a drab olive green shirt with matching trousers, both several sizes too large. Although her hair had been bound in a traditional bun, she wore no *kapp* for modesty. And she had on the same battered tennis shoes she usually wore in the garden.

But her appearance was far more unsettling than her English clothes. Abby must have lost fifteen pounds since her arrest. And she hadn't needed to lose an ounce. Gaunt and hollow cheeked, her chin jutted at a harsh angle. Her peaches-and-cream complexion had washed out to the color of unbleached sheets. Dark circles and deep lines ringed her still striking blue eyes.

Catherine's shock must have been apparent. "Don't look so worried," said Abby. "I am fine, truly. It might not be the same as *mamm*'s home cooking, but the food is good here." Abby gestured toward the empty chair across from her.

"Then why aren't you eating any of it?" asked Catherine, once she was seated.

Abby giggled. "My appetite has abandoned me. I start eating but fill up quickly." When she smiled, Abby looked more like her old self. "It's good to see you, Cat. Is Daniel here, waiting out in the hallway?"

Catherine reached out to grasp her hand. "It's good to see you too. I have missed you, as have your children. But no, Daniel had to cut hay today. It's ready, and by midweek we're supposed to get heavy rains. I came by hired van."

If Abby's heart was breaking, she hid it well. "That's good. We'll have the entire half hour to ourselves."

Catherine stole a glance around the room. Faded torn jeans, bright tattoos, work boots, motorcycle ad T-shirts, flannel shirts in the height of summer heat—the attire of *Englischers* resembled what she saw at Saturday afternoon flea markets. She turned back to her sister with a shudder.

"It's not that bad. Everyone has been very nice to me. Sometimes the women ask some nosy questions…" The corners of Abby's mouth turned up. "But they don't mean any harm. They're curious, that's all. Everybody wants to know what an Amish woman did to land in here."

Abby sounded matter-of-fact, almost casual about the matter. Catherine stared at her. "When are you coming home? Your *kinner* miss you so much. Not that they're not well. I don't want you to worry, but they miss their *mamm.* If you can come home, at least until your trial, they'll be overjoyed. After that, this whole business will be settled. Mr. Fisher knows you did nothing wrong and holds nothing against you."

Abby's smile faded. "I see Daniel has been explaining things his way. God's will shall be done at my trial. That's all we can hope for." Abby gazed around the room as though they were discussing someone else.

"I will pray for you every night," Catherine said, with growing uneasiness.

"*Danki,* but I don't want to harp about my troubles. I wrote you a full update and mailed the letter yesterday. Let's not waste our precious time by chewing our food twice."

"You don't wish to talk about your situation?"

"No, I don't. Tell me about my children. What have they been up to? I hope they have been minding their aunt." A ghost of a smile appeared, revealing a bit of her former self. "And then tell me about yourself. How are you faring in my home? Is Daniel critical or too demanding? I'm afraid I have spoiled him over the years."

"Oh, no. He's been quite agreeable once we got past the first couple days, even when I overcook his eggs or burn the biscuits. And your children—they make me long to marry and have some of my own."

Abby's smile stretched from ear to ear. "Is Laura helping you in the garden? I hope you're not letting Jake stay up too late. He loves to creep out of bed and play with his building blocks with a flashlight."

Catherine arched an eyebrow. "I'll be sure to double check he's still in bed before I go to my room. I thought he'd fallen asleep quickly, like a little angel. *Danki* for the warning." She relaxed against the chair. "You would have been so proud of Laura. When we went to the pond next door, she asked Isaiah to teach her to swim. Because she had no fear of the water, she caught on quickly. Soon she was floating on her back without anyone holding her up. Jake and I played in the shallow water, and he built a sand castle of sorts. He turned brown as an eggshell by day's end. And because Isaiah had ridden his mare to the pond that afternoon, Laura became intrigued with horseback riding, especially bareback. At first Daniel said she was too young to learn, but after some convincing he changed his mind. That very evening Isaiah let her ride in the ring on his gentle horse. She clung to the saddle horn and reins while I led the horse around with a rope. Isaiah held her in the saddle because her legs couldn't quite grip the mare's flanks." Catherine drew in a deep breath before continuing her update. "Then, after we sent them inside to get ready for bed, Isaiah took me on a short ride down the pasture trace. I must say I liked it much more than I did when we were young."

"You got on a horse?" Abby's forehead creased with wrinkles. "On the same horse as Isaiah?"

"No, he had brought along another horse. I rode his mare." Catherine felt her cheeks grow warm.

"Funny how I can remember you calling horses fly magnets."

"True, but his mare is really sweet, and there are almost no flies out after dark."

"You went off riding in the dark?" Abby straightened up in her chair.

"It was just getting dark, and anyway we were only around the pasture. We didn't go to his cabin."

Catherine realized her mistake the moment the words were out. "Anyway, I'm getting off track. Let me continue my story. A few days ago, we picked blackberries along the pasture fence to serve over shortcake with ice cream. The next day Laura and I baked four pies, and I canned the rest for you to use this winter." Catherine didn't mention the secret patch down by the river.

"You picked enough to can with just you and the *kinner*?" Abby cocked her head.

"Well, no. Isaiah helped us. And he's quite good at picking."

"I didn't know Isaiah knew where the patch was, but then again, I didn't know *you* knew Isaiah." Mischief twinkled in Abby's eye. She'd always been good sniffing out mysteries.

"Of course I met him, as I'm the one setting out his meals." Catherine decided to change the subject. "I packed up one pie to bring here, but Daniel said gifts are forbidden. No food or personal items, and not even paper or pens to write letters."

"Don't worry. Daniel deposited money in my commissary account to buy whatever I require. And I find that other than my Bible, my needs in here are few." A wistful expression flitted across her face. "I am in your debt for taking such good care of my family. But tell me…are you lonely living at our farm? Do you miss your friends back home? If you were courting a special man, he might not be able to drive so far out. Tell me what's new with *you*, Cat."

Catherine stared into her sister's eyes and sighed. *Where to begin? Surely I can't blurt out I'm in love with Daniel's cousin, especially as I'm not sure if I am.* "I'm not missing home very much. I see *daed, mamm,* and our *bruders* at preaching. But I don't stay long after lunch. I want to come home to fix something for Daniel to eat."

Abby's expression turned intense. "Do you mean you're taking Laura and Jake to church while Daniel stays home?"

Catherine wished she had chosen her words more carefully instead of riling things up between a husband and wife while separated. "Sometimes, if a service is far away, he will drive us. He…has plenty to do around the farm this time of year."

"Not on the Lord's Day, he doesn't. Daniel has never worked on the Sabbath before, other than tending to the basic needs of the livestock." She scrutinized her sister as though gleaning clues in a mystery. "Tell me what's going on with my *ehemann.* Please, Catherine."

"Don't worry yourself. He just needs some privacy from folks pestering him with questions he can't answer. You know how he hates being in the center of controversy. And I think he might not want to face our *daed* every other week."

Abby pursed her lips and nodded in agreement. "*Jah,* I suppose that's true, but he should think about you too. If you're driving the horse and buggy, then there's no chance of some young man bringing you home at night."

"Don't worry about me, either. Truthfully, I needed a little break from singings and socials. Turns out the person I had my eye on back home had set his cap for another. It's a good thing I left before I made a complete fool of myself." She felt the sting of regret and shame in the back of her throat. "I'm in no hurry to jump back into the frying pan."

Abby laughed, tightening her grip on Catherine's hand. "I've never heard anyone describe courting quite like that, but trust me, no one grows up without suffering some kind of embarrassment. Otherwise we might become prideful and vain."

"Then I don't have to worry about those two sins." The sisters laughed, and for a moment it felt like old times. "I do want to know something, Abby." Catherine inhaled deeply. "Tell me about Isaiah. I know he's deaf, but I might be able to help him if I knew how far he went in school and how much training he received for the hearing impaired. Why does Daniel keep him locked away in the woods?"

Abby looked aghast. "Daniel doesn't keep him locked away. Isaiah chooses to live on his own. His life with his father was very difficult. The man had no patience, and he thought Isaiah wasn't trying to learn to talk. He couldn't accept his deafness. Isaiah didn't do very well in school and never learned to read. The teacher tried her best, but she was ill equipped to handle special needs along with students in eight different grade levels. She taught him to speak some, but only English words. He doesn't recognize much *Deutsch.*"

"So Isaiah fell by the wayside, discarded and thought to be simpleminded."

Abby nodded. "Unfortunately, that's pretty much what happened until Daniel became aware of the boy's neglect while we were visiting for a wedding. He invited him to live with us, and his uncle quickly agreed. Isaiah was an embarrassment to him." She frowned at the memory. "Living with us, the boy learned farming from Daniel. He caught on quickly once things were demonstrated. By the time he was fifteen, he had cleared the brush around that old log cabin in woods. That shack had been falling down, but Isaiah rebuilt it with timber he cut himself and then aged the lumber. Daniel only needed to help with the beams and roofing. When he finished the cabin, Isaiah moved in. He loves being alone, surrounded by God and nature."

"Does he know God?" Catherine asked.

Abby blinked several times. "What do you mean? God watches over and protects Isaiah the same as everyone else."

"Of course, but you said he never learned to read. So he can't read the Bible and can't hear the sermons in church or Scripture read aloud in the evening."

"When he shares a meal at our table, he bows his head in silent prayer along with everyone else."

"He's mimicking your behavior. He's never *heard* a prayer, Abby. And maybe his *mamm* never taught him about God because she didn't know how."

"Now I'm the one embarrassed. I never thought much about it after he found his…safe place in the world."

Silence prevailed while each woman collected her thoughts. "Isaiah is a good man. I'm sure God won't hold it against him on Judgment Day because he hadn't followed a Christian path. After all, He gave Isaiah the disability in the first place." Abby shrugged her shoulders and glanced at the clock, satisfied with her conclusion.

Catherine pressed on. "It's not too late. He could learn to read at that school our English neighbor enrolled her twins in."

Abby's chin lifted while she wrung her hands. "Oh, I don't know about that. Daniel's very protective of his cousin. I don't think he would permit Isaiah to be sent away to strangers, considering his past experiences in school."

Catherine opened her mouth to argue, but the guard looming behind Abby's chair interrupted. "Time's up, Miss Yost. You can come back next week." He crossed his arms over his starched uniform.

Catherine thought better of pleading for more time. "I'll be back as soon as I can," she said, rising to her feet. "Please don't worry about your family or me or Daniel's cousin."

Abby grinned. "I'll try my best about the first two, but you have been thinking about Isaiah's best interests plenty lately. I won't worry about him." Her grin turned sly. "It sounds to me like you know him better than just 'Daniel's cousin from the back cabin.' You must have mentioned his name at least a dozen times since you arrived."

With her cheeks burning with embarrassment, Catherine leaned over to kiss Abby's cheek. "Forget I said anything. You know how I love to run on about the most inconsequential topics." She strode toward the door before she melted into a puddle in the middle of the visitation room floor.

Fourteen

When Abby returned to her cell, Rachelle hadn't come back yet. Blessedly, this gave her some time alone to mull over her sister's visit. As happy as she was that her *kinner* were thriving, her heart ached. She was missing so much of their precious young lives. Learning to swim, riding a horse for the first time, picking berries on warm summer afternoons—these were memories every mother cherished. How many milestone events would she miss while locked up in here? The sour taste of bile filled her mouth as she realized she might spend *years* separated from them. *How they will suffer due to the sins of their mother.*

And was something happening between Catherine and Isaiah? Or were boredom and her weariness making her see things not really there? And what about Isaiah? Catherine's questions convicted her of neglecting the young man over the years. When they had moved him to their farm, they had certainly seen to his physical needs. She made sure he ate three balanced meals a day and even baked his favorite banana nut bread on occasion. She had sewn his clothing and provided him with warm winter gloves, boots, and the head coverings he needed—even though he refused to wear hats even on the coldest January days. Daniel had taught him farming—to milk cows, train horses to pull equipment, and how to bring in the harvest. He'd taught him to hunt, fish, and use building tools. Daniel had taken the boy ice skating on frozen winter ponds, swam for hours during the summer, and helped him build a home that would shelter Isaiah all his life.

Abby had felt satisfied, almost smug, that they had provided him with a loving, supportive family when his own family couldn't be bothered. But what had she done for his spiritual health? It had not even occurred to her that Isaiah didn't know God.

What good is it if a man gains great riches if he loses his very soul? Isaiah might not find the salvation promised to believers upon their deaths. And in the meantime, he didn't know the one true Helper, our Guide and Teacher, the One who promised to remain at our side all our lives. Shame rose up her throat, adding to the already bad taste in her mouth.

Catherine had been right. Isaiah went through the motions but didn't know how to pray. He had never read nor heard Scripture—the only solace for a troubled heart. People in their district assumed Isaiah had been born too slow-witted for religious instruction, but Abby had known the truth and done nothing about it. Sitting in jail, she could no more help Isaiah than she could the rest of her family.

She picked up her Bible, but for several minutes she just clutched it to her chest. Tears streamed down her face, unstoppable, relentless. They soaked her shirt and closed off her throat. Her head pounded, her stomach churned, and her lungs burned from staccato breathing. Her hysterical crying might have soaked through the mattress if her cellmate hadn't returned and intervened.

"Abby, what is it? What has happened?"

Abby tried to speak but her vocal cords refused to cooperate. She gasped and coughed with a ragged wheezing sound.

"Oh my." Rachelle pulled hard on her forearm. "Sit up. You can't lie there like that. You might choke to death." When Abby didn't budge,

Rachelle pried the Bible from her fingers, set it on the window ledge, and dragged Abby into a sitting position.

Abby bumped her head on the upper bunk, adding to her woes. "Thanks, I'm okay now." She couldn't look at her friend.

"Tell me what's wrong. What are you crying about?" Rachelle handed her a Kleenex and sat down beside her.

Abby dabbed her eyes and blew her nose, feeling a modicum better. "I was thinking about everything I'm missing in my children's lives. What if they keep me locked up for years? Laura and Jake will forget about me by the time I get out." She held the balled tissue under her nose to stem the tide.

"Don't be ridiculous. Kids never forget their mothers." Rachelle handed Abby a box of Kleenex and then moved the wastebasket next to her legs.

"But they change so much within a few months. What will they be like in several years? The best times of their childhood will pass by while I'm locked up." Abby pulled out several more tissues.

Rachelle pondered this and frowned. "That really does stink, so you can't think about the future. Stay focused on the moment. Isn't that what Dr. Phil always says?"

Abby didn't know a Dr. Phil. She sighed and glanced around the tiny room. "Stay focused on *this* moment?"

Rachelle's gaze traveled the same path. "I meant you should concentrate on remembering the details from their last visit. And wasn't that your sister today? Think about the stories she told you about home. Picture it all in your mind. Don't let yourself think too far ahead." She gave Abby's shoulders a shake and smiled. "Okay?"

Abby nodded. "Good advice. Thanks."

"You're welcome. Now, I believe you were going to read until dinner." Rachelle retrieved Abby's Bible from the ledge. "I'll watch TV in the common room to give you peace and quiet until it's time to eat." She flashed a toothy smile and sauntered out, closing the door behind her.

Abby watched the doorway long after she'd gone, composing herself.

Then she wiped her face and opened the Good Book. The photo of Laura and Jake fluttered out. She stared at their faces until love replaced her sorrow and then tucked the picture away. *No Old Testament wars or tribulations today.* She needed some of the advice Jesus gave His apostles and they, in turn, imparted to the early Christians. She turned to the book of Ephesians and started to read. Before long, her eyes fell on chapter 5:22-23: "Wives, this means submit to your husbands as to the Lord. For a husband is the head of his wife as Christ is the head of the church..."

She stopped reading. There it was—specific instructions that she should listen to Daniel and take his advice. Yet she had refused to do so. Her reasons were valid. Her motivations to protect another person seemed sound, but maybe every sinner trotted out excuses for his or her behavior. Daniel had the responsibility to follow Scripture and their *Ordnung.* She only had the responsibility to follow him. But could it be that simple? In this day and age, could a wife, even an Amish wife, blindly do whatever her spouse instructed? Rachelle would laugh at such an old-fashioned notion, but would her *mamm*? Abby thought about how her *mamm* enjoyed far more serenity compared to her own turbulent life. Her *mamm* trusted her *daed,* and trusted that God wouldn't allow a Christian husband to stray too far from the path.

Once again Abby stretched out on her bunk and clutched her Bible to her chest. But instead of weeping uncontrollably, racked with physical pain besides emotional turmoil, she closed her eyes and stilled her brain, forcing thoughts of any kind away. Quiet suffused her soul.

All Scripture is inspired by God, she remembered. *Make it your goal to live a quiet life.*

Bits and pieces of Bible verses she'd learned over the years flitted into her mind and out again as she silently prayed for direction. She asked for God's grace to fill her heart.

Her headache diminished and then vanished altogether. Moments later, she drifted into blissful, dreamless sleep.

"Abby, wake up." Someone's voice pierced the calm place where Abby dwelled. She clamped her eyes tightly shut to block out the intrusion.

"Please get up. You have to see this!" The insistent voice grew louder while somebody worked her arm like a hand pump.

She opened one eye to peer up at Rachelle. "What is it that can't wait until morning?" she asked softly.

"Morning is a long way off. I let you sleep through dinner and brought you back a sandwich. I know you are exhausted, but I can't let you miss this." She pulled again on Abby's hand. "Come take a look."

Abby swung her legs off the bunk, licking her lips and swallowing to try to moisten her parched throat. She rose to her feet to follow her roommate. Rachelle was already at the window, looking down on the street below. Abby heard the faint sound of hymns before she reached the tinted glass.

Lining the sidewalk, two and three people deep, Amish men and women stood shoulder to shoulder, their voices raised in song. Each person held a candle, and the flickering light along with the yellow streetlight cast shadows across their faces. Yet, even poorly illuminated, the crowd seemed to be focused on *their* window. Abby stared, unable to make sense of what she saw. Her chest lifted and fell with each breath as she mutely watched.

"Don't you get it?" asked Rachelle. "Those people have come to Wooster to support you." Her grin filled her face. "It's a candlelight vigil in your honor." She hooked her arm around Abby's waist.

Abby leaned closer, her nose nearly pressing against the window-pane. "Can they see me?"

"I don't think so. This tinted glass makes it tough to see in even though we can see out."

"Then how do they know I'm in here?" The idea that these people had come to town on her account was baffling.

"Some guard probably told them your cell number. Then it's not hard to count the windows. This isn't exactly the state pen." Rachelle leaned on the glass and appeared to be counting. "Forty-five, forty-six, forty-seven…looks like almost fifty people are down there." Her voice dropped to a whisper as the throng began another hymn, this one louder and more upbeat.

Abby recognized "Just a Closer Walk with Thee" and felt a surge of joy. It was one of her favorites. "But *why* have they come? I'm nothing more than a common criminal. I did exactly what the judge accused me of."

"You had your reasons and they must know that. I heard that you Amish stick together—helping out and supporting each other. So that's what they're doing. You seem surprised."

Abby met her roommate's gaze. "I am surprised. I've received no Amish visitors other than my husband and sister. My father is our district's bishop, but he hasn't come to see me. I took that to mean the members of my district had turned their backs on me."

Rachelle rubbed her sleeve against the glass, clearing away some condensation. "Looks like you figured it wrong. The crowd is growing. A bunch of English women have joined them now."

"My *daed*," whispered Abby, thinking aloud. "I wonder if my *daed* is down there?" With only candles and the thin streetlight, it was hard to recognize anyone. Abby stared, holding her breath. She focused on several taller figures in the back row who were drifting in and out of the light. Then suddenly she spotted the long, snowy beard of her father and the distinctive broad shoulders and long neck of her *ehemann*. His floppy hat brim gave him away. "It's them—Daniel and my father. They have come to the vigil." A lump the size of a boulder formed in her throat.

"See, it's always darkest before the dawn…or something like that." Rachelle pulled something from her pocket. "You need to eat while you watch to keep your strength up. You must be hungry."

"Thank you, Rachelle. You've been a good friend. I'm in your debt." Abby unwrapped the ham-and-cheese sandwich.

"It's not much, but when this is all over with, maybe you can teach me how to knit someday. I always wanted to learn that."

"It would be my pleasure." Abby took a bite and then ate ravenously, her appetite returning.

The two women kept their own vigil by the window for almost an hour. Abby's spirits soared hearing the voices lifted in song and prayer.

When the assembly finally blew out the candles and began to disperse, she waved her hand frantically, despite Rachelle's comment that no one could see inside.

Folks came from Shreve to Wooster...for me.

She felt unworthy of their support and yet so grateful. The tall man with floppy hat brim had been in the last group to leave. He didn't extinguish his candle while on the sidewalk, but had walked away with it still burning. Abby stared at the small yellow glow until it disappeared around the corner.

That night after lights-out, she lay in bed with a sense of peace and sent prayers of thanks to the Great Physician, who knows our needs even before we do. She had a lot to be grateful for and much to contemplate. Before she drifted back to sleep, her path at last became clear.

Of all the days for Daniel to finish work in the fields early, this had to be the worst. Catherine couldn't believe it when she spotted him walking toward the porch from the pump house. He had rolled up his sleeves, and his arms, face, and hair were dripping wet. That could only mean he'd finished for the day. She was elbow-deep in cornmeal, battering chicken to fry. The green beans still needed to be cleaned and potatoes boiled for potato salad. At least she'd washed fresh greens and chopped garden vegetables for a tossed salad. She sighed while moving the coffeepot onto the burner to reheat.

"*Guder nachmittag,*" he said upon entering the kitchen. Daniel grabbed the towel to dry his face and hands.

"Good afternoon to you. I saw you in Abby's flower garden earlier. What were you doing out there? I thought you once said that flowers were women's business." She glanced up while pouring oil into her skillet.

"I wanted to cut back her rhododendrons and azaleas. It needed to be done before they set buds for next year. My *fraa* sets great store by those flowers." He tossed the towel down on the counter.

"If there's still more work in the garden, we have plenty of time before dinner. It won't be ready for another hour."

"No, I'm done for the day. I'll just relax for a while, maybe read to my *kinner* in the front room." He offered her a pleasant smile.

She pondered the best way to approach a delicate subject. "Were you still moving hay bales today?"

"*Jah.* Isaiah and I stored what we could fit in the barn loft. The rest we lined up close to the pasture gate and covered with plastic."

Catherine arranged breaded chicken pieces in the frying pan and then turned up the burner. "Isaiah works hard for you? He has no problems understanding the chores?"

Daniel poured coffee into a mug. "He does just fine. You only have to show him a task once and he remembers. People don't give that boy enough credit." He added a splash of milk and sipped with appreciation.

"He's not really a boy anymore, is he?"

"I s'pose not. He must be twenty-four or thereabouts." Daniel pulled sagely on his beard. Plenty of gray peppered his shade of dark brown.

"But I'm sure there are some chores you don't dare allow him to do alone, like feeding cornstalks into the grinder for silage, for instance. That could be dangerous. A person could lose a hand if they didn't understand the machinery." She continued coating pieces of chicken without meeting his gaze.

"Isaiah comprehends as well as anybody else. Accidents can happen to anybody, but there's nothing slow-witted about that man's mind. Offhand, I can't think of any job I wouldn't trust him with. Some just require two people."

She looked him in the eye. "So Isaiah has learned everything he needs to about farming?"

"He knows enough to get by."

"And he obviously understands construction."

"His cabin isn't exactly a five-bedroom house with attached *dawdi haus,* but *jah,* he knows how to put…and fix…the roof over his head."

Daniel rubbed his chin. "What's on your mind, Catherine? If you have something to say, I wish you would spit it out."

"Well, because, other than his deafness, Isaiah is just as bright as any average person. I don't see why he should be ostracized from his kin." She deftly flipped the browned chicken in the skillet.

"He's not being ostracized." Daniel's face scrunched into a frown. "Nobody keeps him apart from his kin."

"That's good to hear, because I invited him to share supper with us in the kitchen." She pointed at the oak table so there would be no confusion.

Daniel walked back to the stove for a refill. "He won't come, sister. You can leave his plate on the picnic table, same as usual. Isaiah *prefers* solitude at day's end, surrounded by only trees and hoot owls. I'll take my second cup into the living room."

"He's already agreed to join us. In fact, he looked quite pleased about the invitation."

Daniel halted in the doorway. "How in the world did you get that ridiculous notion?" he asked over his shoulder.

"I spoke to him at breakfast this morning. I watched for him to come for his plate. We have a way of communicating with hand gestures and pantomimes. Plus he somewhat reads lips of the words he knows."

He stared at her in disbelief. "You and Isaiah have found a way to talk?"

"In a manner of speaking." She grinned at her word choice. "It is all right then that he comes inside for supper?"

"*Jah,* Catherine. I wouldn't dream of telling you no." He walked out, leaving her an hour to cook a delicious meal that would make Isaiah disavow cold leftovers forever. She began to consider how best to deal with Daniel and Isaiah in the same room.

Will my feelings be written across my forehead like an old-fashioned barn advertisement? Will Isaiah's? How will Daniel react to a real friendship between us?

Catherine peeled, cooked, and diced potatoes and eggs faster than ever before and then chopped celery and onion. With the salad chilling in the refrigerator, she snapped and steamed the beans. She glanced at the two loaves of banana nut bread she'd baked that morning. They were Isaiah's favorite—one for dessert tonight and one for him to take home. She lifted the last batch of fried chicken from the grease with tongs. With enough food to feed a small village, Isaiah could eat the leftovers tomorrow for lunch.

Stop it, before you sew up a last-minute shirt and make a complete fool of yourself.

But Catherine couldn't help herself. After setting the table, she hurried into the bathroom for a sponge bath and then she changed into a fresh dress. *Let Daniel think whatever he pleases.* She emerged half an hour later, smelling faintly of lavender and vanilla. Daniel sat nibbling pickles and olives from the relish tray. "Are we ready to eat yet? We're mighty hungry."

Jake and Laura nodded their heads in agreement. They too were waiting at the table with fists full of carrot sticks.

"Of course. I'll get the chicken from the oven." She placed the brimming roaster pan on the table.

"Good grief. We'll be eating chicken all week. I thought you said you invited Isaiah, not Paul Bunyan and Babe the Blue Ox."

The *kinner* laughed, even though she felt certain they didn't know who Paul Bunyan was. "Hardworking men need to eat." Catherine divided the salad into five bowls and placed the potato salad on the table. She dawdled while pouring glasses of milk because she didn't want the meal to begin yet.

"Sit down for prayers, Catherine," ordered Daniel. "Looks like Isaiah didn't quite catch your drift. You can leave his food on the table as usual."

She tugged her apron over her head, tossing it onto the counter. "I don't know why we can't be patient for—"

At that moment, Isaiah opened the screen door and strode into the kitchen. He grinned as he hooked his straw hat on a peg. He'd worn a hat to dinner. Catherine and Daniel stared, wide eyed.

"Hello, Isaiah," she mouthed, pointing to the empty chair. "We're ready to eat."

Isaiah pulled Laura's *kapp* ribbon, chucked Jake under the chin, and nodded to his cousin. Daniel reached across his son to shake Isaiah's hand. "Long time no see," he said, amused.

Isaiah reached for a chicken leg while the other four bowed their head in silent prayer. "No, Isaiah," said Laura, gently patting his arm. "First we must pray."

He glanced up at Catherine instead of at the youngster.

She smiled and then bowed her chin to her chest and folded her hands. For a few moments the ticking of the battery clock was the only sound heard. Catherine whispered her words of gratitude for the food, and then she discretely opened one eye to see what Isaiah was doing. At first, she thought he was praying, same as everyone else. Upon further perusal, she noticed his eyelashes flutter as his head turned left and right, almost imperceptivity. When Daniel murmured a quiet "amen" and lifted his head, Isaiah did the same, although his sounded more like a grunt.

She had been right! He was only mimicking behavior he'd witnessed. He didn't know to pray. As she passed the bowls and platters around the table, Catherine silently pledged to teach him. *But in order to pray, a person first needs to know God.*

"Please pass the salad dressings," said Daniel, studying her.

"Sorry. I was daydreaming." She handed him three bottles of store-bought dressing, regretting not making her own from buttermilk, herbs, and minced vegetables.

Isaiah watched Daniel add ranch dressing to his and Nate's salads, while Laura added French and Catherine topped hers with Italian. When the bottles reached Isaiah, he poured a drop of each onto his finger to taste, and then he selected the Italian. Isaiah winked at Catherine as he poured on a liberal amount.

His gesture didn't go unnoticed. Daniel cleared his throat and speared a cherry tomato with sufficient force to spatter his shirt with seeds and juice. Isaiah and the *kinner* laughed. Catherine merely smiled, but Daniel aimed his peevish glower in her direction just the same. "Eat your dinner, Laura," he then said to his daughter. "Let's not dawdle tonight." The child complied, but she continued to giggle each time she looked at the array of seeds on her *daed*'s shirt.

Catherine rapped on the tabletop. The vibration attracted the attention of the guest of honor. Isaiah glanced up from his enjoyment of the chicken breast.

"More green beans?" She mouthed the words with exaggeration, while the verbal sounds were only whispers for the hearing folk at the table.

"*Jah,* thanks," he replied with an ear-to-ear grin. He accepted the bowl and scraped the remaining beans onto his plate. The size of the heap warmed a gardener's heart.

Laura knocked on the table next, offering the potato salad in the manner she'd observed. Isaiah pulled her other *kapp* string and took a large spoonful of spuds.

Daniel squinted his eyes. "Enough of that, or the boy will eat until he explodes just to be polite." He bit into a chicken leg with a frown.

"Perhaps he simply *loves* my cooking," Catherine said, not hiding her wry tone.

"Your cooking might be better than average, but I would bet he simply loves all the newfound attention." He met her gaze and held it, broadcasting his meaning without words or table raps.

"He's been eating alone for years. Everyone deserves some attention and to feel consideration and compassion from their family members." Catherine sliced her tomato, popping half into her mouth without breaking eye contact. The two in-laws circled around each other like wary dogs.

Isaiah, oblivious to the contention he was causing, enjoyed his supper with finger-licking appreciation.

"All well and good, but no one should be led down a dead-end road." Daniel dropped his chicken bone on the plate with a thud.

"I don't see how this road could be considered a dead end. Isaiah enjoys eating with the family and he's done just fine. He doesn't have poor table manners despite his years of seclusion." She regretted her words as soon as she said them. *Wait…this is Daniel's house, not mine. He sets the rules in his home.* And even worse, she'd spoken about a person sitting at the table. Although he may not have heard their exchange, somehow he'd sensed the discomfort of the situation at last. He looked between Daniel and her with a bewildered expression.

Catherine blushed to her hairline. "Who's ready for banana nut bread?" she asked.

"I am," chimed Laura and Jake in unison.

"None for me. I'll eat my dessert later." Daniel concentrated on his remaining dinner.

Catherine sliced one large and three small pieces of banana nut bread. When she delivered Isaiah's to the table, his nervousness had vanished. He looked joyous as he broke off a corner and popped it in his mouth.

Daniel mumbled something about water troughs and left the kitchen while the others enjoyed dessert. She exhaled slowly and leaned against the back of her chair when he was gone, overall happy with how the meal had turned out. When Isaiah finished his dessert, he nodded to her, mouthed his thanks, and walked to the wall peg for his hat. Before the screen door slammed behind him, their eyes met and held for a long moment. The look that passed between them made her stomach turn cartwheels.

But Catherine's joy lasted only midway through washing the dishes and kitchen cleanup. It faded as she mulled over something Daniel had said. *No one should be led down a dead-end road.* With a shiver, she realized he hadn't been referring to tonight's dinner or any meal at all. But it didn't matter. Catherine's road was to help Isaiah find God. And to do that, she needed to keep communicating with him. He needed to learn to talk and to read lips a whole lot better before anyone could teach him to read.

Fifteen

At breakfast, Abigail noticed on the bulletin board that a Bible study for female inmates was scheduled for that evening. The idea of sitting around a table and studying the Bible with *Englischers* had never appealed to her before. Scripture reading, silent prayer, and meditation were usually private matters for the Amish or within your family, sitting around the woodstove or fireplace—not among strangers with varying levels of Christian commitment.

But by dinnertime, after reading and contemplating to the point of exhaustion, she felt ready to try something new. Abby decided to attend the session and invite her roommate.

Rachelle had asked a few shy questions about Abby's faith since moving into the top bunk. The woman had been raised in a home without much religion whatsoever. Her grandmother had occasionally taken her to church whenever Rachelle's mother left her overnight. And she remembered attending Vacation Bible School for a full week during one summer. Her grandmother had registered her, picked her

up, and then driven her back home afterward. Rachelle's mother hadn't
been keen on the notion, but she had finally agreed. "Just a pack of do-
gooders telling you stories about burning bushes, sending babies down
the river in baskets, and nasty Roman kings. None of it will do you
a-hill-of-beans worth of good in the real world," had been her mother's assessment. But Rachelle had loved the week, including the camaraderie with the other kids. Looking back, she was still curious about
what she'd learned.

*There is a powerful God who knows us and what we've done, but still
loves us anyway?*

*He sent His only Son as a sacrifice for our sins, and if we believe in Him
we'll be allowed into heaven?*

Rachelle couldn't grasp where heaven was or what it would be like,
but she understood it was far superior to the alternative. She also didn't
know if there was a tally system for sin.

Is stealing a car worse than cheating on your income taxes?

*Is premeditated murder the most evil thing a person can do, or is there
a sin even worse than that?*

Abigail had no clue about the hierarchy of sin either, but she showed
Rachelle the Ten Commandments in the Bible. "This is a good place
to start," she said. "These are the most important things to concentrate
on. Oh, and the Golden Rule."

Rachelle held up her hand. "Whoa, slow down. You mean there's
this list of commandments plus a whole other bunch of rules?" She
crinkled her forehead with dismay.

"No, only one rule, but it's important. Basically, it's do to others as
you would have them do to you."

Rachelle exhaled with relief. "Okay, I've heard that one." Relief
washed over her face. "I'm going to copy down these ten before we go
to the Bible meeting. I'm not walking in there empty handed." She
perched on Abby's bunk to copy the list onto a sheet of ruled paper.

Abby glanced at the clock in the hallway, waiting patiently. They
would be late, but she didn't want to hurry the girl. When Rachelle
stood at last with list in hand and handed Abby her Bible, they walked

to the small chapel off the common room. Abby felt nervous anticipation begin to build.

"Come in, ladies. Have a seat," said a woman at the table. "I'm Mrs. Jarvis, and we have just begun." She had a gentle face, warm smile, and blue eyes the shade of a robin's egg.

Abby and Rachelle sat, stealing surreptitious glances around the table. All of the faces were familiar, yet a few were a surprise in their current setting.

"Today we are studying First Corinthians, chapter thirteen, for some ways to improve your personal relationships while you are in here and to prepare you to rejoin your lives down the road. This chapter is commonly referred to as the 'love chapter' and is often read during weddings. But Paul's instructions to the people of Corinth are helpful to improve *all* our relationships, including those with our mothers, sisters, neighbors, bosses, and even nasty coworkers who try to stab us in the back." A few women giggled and nodded while Mrs. Jarvis's gaze spanned the small room.

"Who was this Paul guy?" asked Rachelle, shifting in her chair.

Two women laughed aloud, while Abby felt mortified. But Mrs. Jarvis' smile didn't falter. "He was a man who once persecuted the followers of Jesus after His crucifixion. But God appeared to him while Paul was on a journey, and He talked to him. Paul spent the rest of his life converting people to Christianity like the other apostles. But we'll learn more about Paul another day. Let me read what he had to say about Jesus' message about love:

"'If I could speak all languages of earth and of angels, but didn't love others, I would only be a noisy gong or a clanging cymbal. If I had the gift of prophecy, and if I understood all of God's secret plans and possessed all knowledge, and if I had such faith that I could move mountains, but didn't love others, I would be nothing.'" Mrs. Jarvis paused for a moment before continuing on to the end of the chapter.

Abby listened, absorbing the words like a dry sponge.

"'If I had such faith that I could move mountains, but didn't love others, I would be nothing…Love is patient and kind. Love is not jealous or boastful or proud or rude. It does not demand its own way. It is not irritable, and it keeps no record of being wronged. It does not rejoice about injustice but rejoices whenever the truth wins out…When I was a child, I spoke and thought and reasoned as a child. But when I grew up, I put away childish things.'"

Abby found comfort and simplicity in Paul's teachings. And the other inmates seemed to like them too because everyone had an interpretation. Some seemed off track, but Mrs. Jarvis encouraged the conversation and didn't correct anyone's application.

"You shouldn't be jealous if you're really in love," said one woman.

"Being smart and a good talker aren't going to get you places forever. If you forget to love anybody along the way, you have just wasted your whole life," offered a multitattooed lady.

"You always need to be patient with your kids if you love them as much as you say you do." This was spoken by a girl who looked not much older than a child herself.

Abby heard the practical applications only vaguely. Her head was spinning with new thoughts. She knew she could keep Margaret's name out of her case. It wasn't right to get the licensed midwife in trouble for a choice she had made, but what about the truth? *Love rejoices whenever the truth wins out…Three things will last forever—faith, hope, and love—and the greatest of these is love.*

She loved Daniel and her children. She also loved her parents and respected their guidance over the years. She loved her Amish community, including the few women who tended to gossip more than sew at quilting bees. Hadn't members of her district come to town for the candlelight vigil in her support?

Abby sighed. There was only one response to all that she had heard this morning. Although she loved her friend and mentor too, she had to tell the truth and pray that the English system of laws would be merciful with Margaret.

After discussing the women's applications, the session was over. Abby wished it had lasted longer.

"Who would ever think we'd talk about loving people during our first Bible study?" asked Rachelle on their way back to their cell. "I figured we would learn more about Moses parting that ocean and all those chariots racing across the dry bottom. Then *whoosh*…this huge wave comes to swallow up the chariots after Moses gets his people on the other side. I saw it on TV." She gestured wildly with her hands. "I always felt sorry for the horses. What did they do to deserve a watery grave?"

Abby shrugged, not wishing to picture drowning horses at the moment. "I liked the love chapter. It gave me something to think about while trying to fall asleep tonight."

"That's for sure. I'll be planning my exit strategy with ol' Al once I get out of here. That man is not capable of love. He's always been about me-me-me. I need to live with only my kids for a while to get my head on straight. Then maybe I'll think about falling in love with a *nice* guy for a change. Maybe he won't turn out as boring as they all look." Rachelle laughed so, Abby did too, but she wasn't sure what boring men looked like. They had reached the door of their cell, but it wasn't lockdown time yet.

"What are you going to do?" asked Abby. "I'm just going to read."

"Oh, no, you don't. This is our night to stick together. First, Bible study—I'm going again next week—how about you?" Without waiting for an answer, Rachelle continued, "Now we'll both watch TV in the common room. Don't worry. It's a Hallmark Channel movie. Some guy gets this letter from his long-dead father and it changes everything in his life." She hooked her arm through Abby's elbow. "Sounds pretty good, no? It'll be good to relax for a night."

We haven't done much other than relax in here, Abby thought, but she smiled at Rachelle. "That does sound interesting. Okay, I'll come with you. And I'm coming to Bible study next week too." She patted her hand as they headed toward the sound of laughter and a loud television set. Abby ended up enjoying the movie and appreciated the company of her English roommate and friend. After lights out, she fell asleep with Paul's words running through her brain like a skipping record.

The greatest of these is love.

Try as she might, Catherine thought of no easy way to teach Isaiah about God. Hand gestures, pantomimes, and artistic sketches were woefully inadequate to impart so powerful a truth. The man needed to learn to read. There was no way around it. But first he needed a better grasp of common English words and phrases. His lip-reading seemed to improve each time they were together, but they weren't together enough as far as she was concerned. *That is about to change,* she thought. Because she and Isaiah were adults, Daniel had no right to keep them apart.

Catherine marched toward the barn in search of her brother-in-law as soon as her laundry was hanging on the line. Her niece and nephew trailed behind her, trying to catch butterflies with little success.

The barn yielded nothing more than an amazing number of flies. Every cow and horse, and even the sow with her piglets, had opted for the outdoor pens on such a breezy day. "Stay close," she instructed the children, "and mind where you step. We're going in search of your *daed*." The two siblings grasped hands and skipped along as though on a grand adventure.

Catherine spotted Daniel repairing the fence that separated a field of soybeans from the cow pasture. She waved and cupped her hands around her mouth. "May I have a word with you, brother?" Her heartbeat quickened upon noticing Isaiah a hundred yards farther down the fence line.

Daniel wiped his neck with a handkerchief as he walked toward them. "Is something wrong, Catherine?" His gaze flickered over the *kinner* with concern.

"No, nothing's wrong, but we have run out of coffee, sugar, and mayonnaise. And we're almost out of yeast, baking powder, and laundry detergent. Plus I need some personal items. I can't postpone a trip to the grocery store another day."

He swept off his hat to dab his brow. "I wish you would have told me sooner. I could have stopped on my way home from the bank yesterday." His eyes focused skyward at a vulture soaring on wind currents. The sun had reached its zenith.

"*Danki,* but I prefer to do my own shopping. Besides, I need a change of scenery today," she said. "And so does Isaiah. He needs a break away from farm chores. He kept working yesterday in the fields while you went to town on errands." She tried to keep accusation from her tone.

Daniel cocked his head and narrowed his gaze. "I asked him if he wanted to ride with me and he shook his head no."

"It's not good for him to work without any leisure."

"Leisure? We're farmers, Catherine. We'll have plenty of time for leisure in January when the fields are buried beneath a foot of snow." He squinted at her even though the sun's glare was at his back.

"Even so, I'd like to ask him if he would drive me to town. I'd prefer not to go alone because I'm unfamiliar with your horses."

Daniel set his hat back on, nodding. "True enough. You can ask him, but I'll take you if he doesn't want to go."

Somehow Catherine knew he would and so did Daniel. She marched to where Isaiah was pulling out rotted rails and stacking them in the wagon. She worked hard to pantomime the actions of driving the buggy and grocery shopping, and he readily agreed once her meaning became clear. They walked back to where Daniel was planing the end of a fence rail to fit snugly into the post, the children standing quietly by as they watched him work.

"He said he would take me," she said, unable to hide her enthusiasm. Perhaps the fact Isaiah's smile was wide enough to reveal most of his pearly white teeth had something to do with her joy.

"All right," said Daniel, barely glancing up. "I'll see you all at suppertime then."

"You won't, but I fixed a plate of roast beef and potatoes to reheat in the oven whenever you get hungry."

His head snapped up with full attention. "Where will you be?"

"I'm dropping Jake and Laura off for the afternoon at the neighbor's house. Mrs. Miller has invited them several times this summer to play with her *kinner.* I'd like Laura to play with other girls for a change and

Jake with little boys. They spend too much time in only each other's company. We'll pick them up on our way home this evening."

"*This evening?* I thought you said you needed to grocery shop." His tone turned sharp.

"That's right, but I also want Isaiah to practice his lip-reading. That would be easier to accomplish without little ones interrupting our talk."

Daniel's focus landed on Isaiah, who waited patiently during a conversation he couldn't hear. "And how do you propose to teach him more English words?" He lifted one boot heel to the lowest fence rail.

"I intend to treat him to dinner in Shreve. Has he ever been in a restaurant? I'll shape my mouth to form the names of common foods and point out the item on the menu. It might be the start of word recognition."

Daniel grunted with disdain and picked up the next replacement rail. "You're trying to move mountains during one supper at a local diner." He shook his head like a mule. "I don't think this is such a good idea, Catherine."

"Are you saying we're not allowed to stop to eat when our errands are done?" She shifted her weight from one hip to the other and crossed her arms over her apron.

"Oh, no. Like I said before, I wouldn't dream of forbidding my wife's sister from any harebrained notion she might have." He started to plane the end of the next rail with renewed vigor.

"*Danki,* Daniel. I'm pleased to hear that." She grinned at Isaiah, pointed toward the barn where the open buggy had been parked, and picked up Jake's hand. "We'll be off then."

"At least give him one of my clean shirts to put on," Daniel hollered when they were almost to the pasture gate. "He shouldn't eat his first restaurant meal in a sweaty shirt."

Catherine waved to indicate she'd heard him and then changed direction for the house. While Isaiah changed clothes, she filled water bottles and packed ice into the cooler. At the neighbor's driveway, her niece and nephew jumped down from the buggy, overjoyed to play with other children. Mrs. Miller waved from the front porch.

"We'll pick them up before dark," Catherine called. After another wave from Mrs. Miller, Catherine and Isaiah were headed toward Shreve in an open buggy on a perfect summer day. They sat close together on the bench, and she caught him watching her several times from the corner of his eye. If his expressions were any indication, he was glad she'd invited him along.

She pointed out landmarks on the way, and he attempted to vocalize the words she formed. The approximations weren't bad for a start, but she wished she'd had more training. Isaiah didn't seem to mind repeating the words until either his enunciation improved or she gave up on the word. He was curious about many things they saw along the road. He pointed at a hawk soaring overhead, the lap robe they were using for a seat cushion, and a mosquito feasting on his arm, and then he waited for her to mouth each word. He found the game entertaining until they reached the grocery store. As she found each item on her shopping list, she would hold up the package and form the word.

Isaiah glanced around and then rolled his eyes. He motioned for her to hurry along as he pushed the cart up and down the aisles. Catherine assumed he was eager to get the chore over with. Few men enjoyed the usually female activity, so she filled the cart with staples and a few treats without slowing down for speech lessons.

After they loaded cold items into their ice chest and the rest into the back of the buggy, Isaiah offered his hand for her to step up.

She shook her head vigorously and pointed toward the restaurant across the street. His gaze followed to where her outstretched hand indicated. Bringing his attention back to herself, Catherine rubbed her belly and then mimed a person eating an ear of corn on the cob. He laughed and shrugged his shoulders. With relaxed familiarity, she gestured for them to cross the street.

After a moment's contemplation, Isaiah nodded, rubbed his belly, and offered his arm. She hooked a hand in the crook of his elbow, and they entered the diner like any other courting couple. She tried not to think of them as such. She was afraid she would lose her nerve otherwise. Once inside, they were met with delicious smells and convivial conversation. After finding seats at a booth toward the back, Catherine picked up the menu to study.

Isaiah seemed content to study *her*. He tried to take her hand, but she pulled it back quickly and picked up her glass of ice water. She was pleased to note that many of the items had photos beside them, and she turned her menu around so he could see. When she pointed to the picture of roast beef, she mouthed the word "moo" like a heifer. For the fried chicken, she flapped her arms as though they were wings, and she did a fairly good imitation of swimming fish for the fried perch dinner. Both spaghetti and meatballs and stuffed roast turkey left her stumped, but she said "baa" like a spring lamb while pointing to the daily special of lamb stew.

It was too bad she wasn't as good at reading people as she was at pantomiming food dishes.

Isaiah pulled the menu from her fingers, closed it, and laid it on the edge of the table. He was no longer smiling, and his cheeks had flushed to near purple. He glanced around the room and then met her eye with obvious discomfort. His own gestures indicated he wished his meal to be the same as hers...without further discussion on the subject. Then he crossed his muscular arms over Daniel's shirt and leaned back.

She had embarrassed him. Upon the realization, shame washed over her. When the waitress returned for their order, she ordered them each a burger with fries with a blush almost matching his. By the time their meals arrived, Isaiah seemed to have forgotten his anger. He dipped fries into catsup, added steak sauce to his burger, and devoured both with obvious lip-smacking pleasure. She had difficulty swallowing the dry bun and greasy potatoes, but waited until they had returned to the buggy, away from observers, to attempt to apologize.

Her expression managed to convey her contrition better than any gestures. After a moment, he pressed a finger to her lips to stop her apologies. His eyes softened when she held her fist to her remorseful heart. He tipped up her chin and said clearly, "Okay, Cat. It's okay." Then he kissed her.

His lips remained on hers longer than any acceptance of an apology warranted. When he finally pulled back, she was gasping for air. Calm, cool, and collected, Isaiah released the brake, shook the reins over the horse's neck, and started for home.

Catherine didn't attempt further conversation during that drive to the Graber farm. For a change she'd been rendered speechless.

Nathan Fisher sat on his porch swing, reading the newspaper, and rocking his son's cradle with his bare big toe. This was the most pleasant evening in a long while. A short afternoon thunderstorm had washed away the dust and oppressive humidity that had hung in the air for weeks. A cool breeze blew from the south, bringing the soft scent of pine, which was so much nicer than the scent from the sow pen he'd scrubbed out earlier today.

Iris had taken the pony cart down the road to sew with some of her lady friends. She'd left a large slice of cherry pie under plastic wrap on the kitchen table. He planned to enjoy his dessert with a cold glass of milk before bed. Birds were chattering in the nearby maple tree as they settled down for the evening with their customary fuss. The familiar sounds soothed him.

However, the sound of crunching gravel in the drive produced the opposite effect.

Nathan craned his neck around the porch post, frowning when he saw Patricia Daly exit her sedan. "Oh, mercy," he mumbled, but he managed to feign a smile. He rose to his feet and tipped his hat. "Good evening, Patricia. What brings you to our neck of the woods?"

"I'm here to see you, of course. And what a nice night for a drive." She climbed the steps to the porch. "Mind if I have a seat and chat for a while?"

"Sure." He noticed she'd brought along her Bible.

"I was wondering how your family has been getting on. I see little Abraham is putting on weight. He'll turn into a big bruiser at this rate." She peered into the cradle, clucking her tongue and making cooing noises, even though the boy was sound asleep. Straightening, she walked to a chair and dragged it closer to the swing. "You have been on my mind since the grief therapy session. I wished you would have let me drive you home."

He turned his gaze skyward for a moment. "I'm sorry I ran off like that. I had no call to lose my temper and behave like some hot-headed child."

After an uncomfortable pause, she asked, "Why did you?"

Nathan continued rocking the cradle while he thought. "Because I was uncomfortable. I realized I didn't belong with a group of *Englischers*. It's not the Amish way to spill our guts like that."

"The *Ordnung* says you are not to talk during group therapy?"

"No, not to my knowledge. We just don't do it."

"Amish people are supposed to wallow and suffer in their misery?"

He glanced up. "I'm not wallowing. Those other folks were wallowing by rehashing the past. I prefer to grieve for Ruth in my own way."

She nodded but her expression didn't change. "And you want to make sure you don't forget your wife."

"Of course I don't want to forget her. She's my son's *mamm*." He focused on the sleeping infant, who would never hear the sound of his mother's laughter or feel her soft lips against his cheek. "Why would I want to forget?"

"You shouldn't, but let's see what the Good Book says about sorrow…about grief. Get your Bible, Nathan. I'll wait for you here and sit with the baby."

He sat temporarily paralyzed. *Who is this bold woman to walk onto my porch and begin barking orders?* Nevertheless, he stood, strode inside the house, and retrieved his Bible from the mantel. If not for Iris' fastidious housekeeping, it would be dusty from neglect.

When he returned, Patricia had slipped off one sandal and was rocking the cradle with a barefoot big toe as he had done. "Turn to First Thessalonians and read chapter four, verses thirteen and fourteen. Tell me what it says in your own words."

Thinking of no polite alternative, Nathan opened the book and silently read the passage. "It says that God wants us to know what will happen to believers when they die. Because Jesus was raised to life after death, when He comes back he's bringing all the believers with Him."

Patricia nodded in agreement. "That's heartening to hear. So you will see Ruth and I'll see my husband again. Why does the apostle Paul remind us of this?" She spoke in little more than a whisper.

"So we will not grieve like those who have no hope. Grief is natural, but if we grieve too long or too hard, God may think we've lost our faith." He leaned back in the swing. "But it's hard to stop. You can't turn sorrow off like a faucet. Sometimes I get mad at God, even though I know that's not right." He thought she would rail against such blasphemy, but she actually smiled.

"I was mad for a while too. I guess that's normal, but our fellow Christians can help us overcome our anger if we let them. I understand that our English meetings weren't your cup of tea, but what about your Amish community? Can you talk to a deacon or to the bishop of your district?"

Nathan stared off at the crimson sun, dancing just above the treetops. Soon only the fiery glow would remain. "Like I told you before, we were new here. I'm a stranger to those men."

"So they'll turn a deaf ear since you haven't been a member long enough." She clucked her tongue with disapproval.

"I didn't say that. It's just not easy to show up at preaching after I haven't gone since the funeral."

She nodded at the closed book between his hands. "In that case, turn to Ephesians 4:11-14 and tell me what you think it means."

"You sure came here prepared, didn't you?" he muttered. Nathan found the Scriptures and read them over twice because he'd never heard them before. The sooner he met her demands the sooner she would go home. When he finished reading, he looked up to meet her gaze. "It says we're supposed to keep going to preaching and listen to what the teachers and pastors say to build up the church. We can't stop until we measure up to the full standard of Christ."

"Are you there yet, Nathan?"

He shut the book with a snap. "No, ma'am. I'm not there yet."

"Neither am I," she said, grinning. "I'm still a long way off, I suppose."

He couldn't help but smile too.

"You're on the right track though. At least you didn't run in the house and hide when you saw my car, pretending not to be home."

"Don't think that didn't cross my mind." He gave his beard a pull.

"Go back to church services, Nathan. Take your son and your aunt, and let your Amish community reach out to you in Christian love."

He ducked his head as shame filled his heart. *It took an English woman to set me back on the right track.* "I will, I promise. My aunt's been threatening to go home if I don't do something. Preaching is a good place to start. I don't know what I'd do without her."

Abraham stirred in his cradle, signaling the adult conversation might soon be interrupted.

"I'd better head back to Wooster. I don't like driving on twisty roads after dark, but later tonight after I leave, read the book of James, chapter two. James tells us that faith without good deeds is dead. We are to reach out to others and lend a helping hand as long as we live. You can't hole up alone and keep your faith. And when you involve yourself in good works, you'll lose the guilt that's keeping you miserable. You'll never forget Ruth, but punishing yourself won't bring her back. Let go of your misguided sense of responsibility. Everything in our lives happens according to God's plan, even the untimely deaths of loved ones." She placed a gentle hand on his shoulder, squeezed, and then walked down the steps to her car.

Nathan mumbled his thanks, but he couldn't lift his head. His face streamed with tears long held in check.

Sixteen

When Abby and Rachelle returned to their cell from morning church services and lunch, Rachelle was upbeat and talkative. She'd joined in the singing of "Rock of Ages" with passion. Her enthusiasm more than made up for the nasal, off-key tone of her voice. She said that hymn had been her grandmother's favorite. From her expression of pained nostalgia, Abby assumed her grandmother had passed on.

"Oh, no," Rachelle corrected. "She lives in Tennessee in a little town called Soddy Daisy. Aunt Wanda is always bugging Gram to move in with her since my grandpa died. Gram has a hard time keeping up with yard work. I've always wanted to see what a place called Soddy Daisy looked like. I picture tons of flowers blooming in people's yards besides lining every sidewalk and road median leading to town."

"Do you mean you've never visited her?" asked Abby. "You said you owned a car called an Escort."

"Yeah, I do, but I've never driven down since she moved there ten years ago. Big Al said he doesn't do old-lady houses filled with doilies, knickknacks, and cat hair. And he said I was too stupid to find my way by myself. I *do* get lost pretty easily."

Abby lifted a brow. "That's why they make maps. I can't fathom not seeing your grandmother for a decade."

"I know it's not right, but all that is about to change. No more Big Al telling me what I can and cannot do." Her green eyes sparkled. "Besides, one of my friends bought a Garmin and she said I could borrow it whenever I needed to. My kids and I are heading south."

Abby had no chance to inquire about a Garmin because she spotted Deputy Todd with her clipboard, talking to several inmates. "Excuse me a minute, Rachelle. I must speak to the deputy. Today's visiting day, and I'm hoping to see my attorney. I've made a decision and need to talk to him before I lose my courage."

Rachelle shrugged her shoulders. "Your lawyer doesn't have to wait till Sunday to see you. He can request a meeting anytime he wants. Did you call his office?"

"*Jah,* Friday morning right after breakfast, but he wasn't in. I left a message on his voice mail to come see me, but I haven't heard back."

"Yesterday was Saturday. He'll probably pay you a social call on Monday. Lawyers don't work on weekends, so I wouldn't get your hopes up about today."

"Okay, thanks." Abby hurried to catch the guard before she retreated from the common room.

"Deputy Todd?" she asked. "If that's the visitor roster, could you check if anyone has signed in to see me?"

The kind woman smiled as she flipped through the sheets. "Hmm… Here we are. A Mr. Daniel Graber has come to visit. I think that guy might have a crush on you," she teased. "He's come back so soon."

"Daniel?" Her husband was even better than her lawyer. She wanted so much to begin mending the fences between them before facing another sleepless night.

Abby couldn't sit still at the metal table. She cracked her knuckles, straightened her shirt three times, and squeaked the chair against the linoleum until she drew stares from the other women. Finally, her beloved *ehemann* walked through the doorway, his felt hat in hand. She smiled in warm welcome and received the same response in return.

"*Guder mariye, fraa,*" he said softly, slipping into the folding chair across from her. The web of lines around his eyes and mouth had etched deeper into his ruddy complexion. He reached for her hand, and she allowed it to be enveloped, savoring the human touch.

"It's so good to see you, Daniel. I didn't think you would come again so soon. This is such a busy time on the farm, and Jake isn't old enough to help."

"I have Isaiah. He works harder than two men. And I came because I have something to say, Abby. Something that won't wait."

She felt a twinge of anxiety that she refused to acknowledge. "I spotted you in the crowd the night of the candlelight vigil. It warmed my heart to see you and members of our district out there. I heard the hymns, Daniel, and they sounded so sweet. Rachelle and I stayed at our window until the last candle was gone."

"Your *daed* was out there too. When he heard the women were organizing this, he hired two vans to bring them to town, paying out of his own pocket. He wouldn't take any money toward the fare."

Abby exhaled with a *whoosh*. "That is a pleasant surprise. He can be hard-nosed at times."

Daniel nodded. "The women wished to voice their support. You delivered their babies, Abby. Every one of them was a grateful mother."

His tone conveyed the same pride surging through her blood. "Hearing that might make what I must do harder, but my mind's made up."

He lifted his leathery palm. "Hold on. I've come today with something to say and I want to be heard. Then I'll listen to you until the guard drags me out by my ear."

Abby's twinge of anxiety expanded as her skin grew clammy. The air-conditioning had turned the room into a cellar in January.

He blew out his breath through his nostrils. "I've been stubborn and hardheaded the whole time you've been in here. I took an oath to love and honor you. Then, when times get tough, I make things worse for you instead of better. That's about to change." He paused, meeting her gaze with eyes soft and moist. "You are my wife and I love you no matter what. Listen to your own heart about what to do about Margaret. I'll stand behind your decision. Folks are divided in our district. Most are with you, but a couple say you deserve whatever you get. If those few people make your life uncomfortable later on, we'll sell the farm and move to some place new. I heard that Minnesota has plenty of farmland a family can still buy for less than an arm and a leg." He squeezed her fingers.

She stared at the love of her life in disbelief.

"Stick to your convictions, Abby. You have always had a good head on your shoulders, and I trust your judgment in this situation. I'm sorry I've given you a hard time about this. I love you, plain and simple."

She shut her open mouth with a snap and shook her head. "Daniel Graber, just when I thought I had everything figured out, you throw in a monkey wrench." Her laughter drew smiles from those sitting at nearby tables. "I love you too." Then she lowered her voice. "And I love my *kinner* and parents and sisters and brothers. That's why I want to put this business behind me. I phoned my lawyer, asking him to stop by. There's no reason to drag this out with a jury trial. I'm ready to plead guilty and put myself in God's and Judge O'Neil's hands. The sooner this is resolved, the sooner I can serve my time and return home to my family."

"What did he say?"

"He hasn't come to talk with me yet, this being the weekend. But if the judge still demands to know who supplied the Pitocin, I'm ready to comply. I'll pray that Margaret will someday forgive me."

Daniel dropped his head, running both hands through his longish hair. "Let's hope it doesn't come to that." He sounded hoarse from worry and fatigue.

"Let's have faith that God will deliver the best solution for everyone involved. And before I forget, you need a haircut. Ask my *schwester* to give you a trim. You're starting to look like one of those teenaged *Englischers* who hang out at the auction barn."

"Is her haircutting skill similar to her cooking and baking?" His question teemed with impish irony.

"Pretty much, but I don't see you losing any weight."

"Maybe I'll stop on my way home and shell out ten bucks at the barber shop."

"Suit yourself. Now, how are the young ones and Catherine and Isaiah? Has she made any progress with him? She sounded bound and determined to teach him to talk."

While he rubbed his eyes with his fingertips, Daniel told her the family vignettes and travails of daily farm life. Abby could tell he chose his words carefully to describe her sister's insistence on taking Isaiah to a restaurant for dinner. Abby tamped down her growing excitement for Catherine's project, deciding to let this matter play out on its own accord. Daniel's opinion of the liaison was apparent, despite his diplomatic phrasing.

After he filled her in on the news, he did something quite out of character. Just as they spotted the guard heading in their direction, he leaned over and kissed her squarely on the mouth. Such bold public demonstrations of affection were rare in the Amish community.

Her *daed* would be speechless.

The other brethren would be aghast.

But Abigail Graber felt as joyous as a brand-new bride on her wedding day.

Catherine tried not to think the worst about people, but it sure seemed as though Daniel was trying to keep Isaiah and her apart. She never saw him at breakfast, yet she found his empty plate on the porch by the time she finished morning chores. His lunch sack never went unclaimed, but Daniel usually insisted on delivering his noon meal when he retrieved his own sandwiches and fresh thermos. And apparently Daniel found too much work for his cousin to do, preventing him from sharing dinner at the kitchen table again with the family. She certainly hoped this was Daniel's handiwork instead of Isaiah avoiding her. But by the fifth day, she had her doubts.

I embarrassed him in the restaurant. I drew attention to us and to what I was trying to accomplish. If I've learned anything about him, Isaiah shuns the limelight at all costs.

When she set his plate of meatloaf, lima beans, and carrots on the picnic table, she didn't bother scanning the yard for his tall, lithe form. He was avoiding her, like a cat to water. Grim thoughts filled her mind as she washed the dinner dishes that night. So total was her pitiful self-absorption that she almost didn't notice the soft tap on the kitchen window. Moving aside the curtains, she gazed on Isaiah, who was sitting with a napkin tucked into his shirt collar and eating his dinner with his usual hearty appetite. He grinned and motioned for her to join him on the porch. She held up a soapy plate and then her index finger and closed the curtain, but not before she offered a dazzling smile. Catherine yearned to leave the sink full of dishes for later that night, but that would only draw Daniel's suspicion.

After hanging up the dish towel to dry, she rinsed out her mouth with mouthwash, pulled off her soiled apron, and walked onto the porch with as much dignity as a breathless person could muster. "Good evening. Dinner good?" she asked, smoothing her *kapp*.

"*Jah, gut.*" He patted his flat stomach and sprang to his feet. With gestures they both understood, he conveyed his desire for her to walk toward the back pasture to see something. She controlled herself from jumping up and down and asked how long would they be gone.

Picking up the flashlight from the steps, he indicated a medium-length time period. Catherine stashed his dirty plate, glass, and silverware behind the potted fern and reached inside for her shawl. Goose bumps rose on her arms that had nothing to do with any cool breezes.

The *kinner* were spending the night at their friends' homes. Daniel had taken his hunting dog for a walk and would probably stop at the neighbors' for a late cup of coffee. He would be gone for more than an hour. She had time to herself…they had time to themselves. Anticipation rose inside her like a stack of presents on Christmas morning.

Once they were behind the barn, with little chance of being seen, Isaiah took her hand. It felt massive wrapped around hers; the calluses warm and oddly comforting, as though someone who worked so hard must be strong and protective. They swung hands like children as the path skirted the pasture and wound its way through the scrub brush. As daylight waned, the meadow came alive with sounds from indiscernible creatures that crawled, flew, or slithered. She stayed close to his side to avoid unexpected encounters with black snakes or skunks. Once she had crossed paths with a red fox and screamed as though her life hung in jeopardy. The unfortunate fox had bolted on sight, equally frightened by her.

Isaiah occasionally glanced over his shoulder as though he too preferred not to run into his cousin along the way. Catherine tugged on his suspender to get his attention. "Where are we going?" she asked.

He winked slyly and put his finger to his lips, as though keeping a secret.

Soon the trail left the scrub brush and entered the cool, dim woods. Darkness fell earlier in the forest because little light pierced the tall canopy even at the sun's zenith. Isaiah switched on the flashlight and tightened his grip on her hand. Although she couldn't see very well and heard strange noises around her, she didn't worry. Utterly safe—that's how she felt in his company.

He quickened their pace as they skirted around his home. The cabin looked little more than a dark shadow in the gloom. They hopped a row of flat rocks to cross the creek, and then the path turned steeply uphill beyond the riverbank. Catherine breathed deeply, trying not to sweat or pant like a dog, but she had to take two steps for each one of his long strides. Just when her lungs began to burn and she was about to demand a slower pace, Isaiah stopped short and pulled her to his side.

A clearing in the forest, formed by the death of several formidable trees, opened before them. The dead wood had been cut up and hauled away, leaving a mossy glen where wildflowers, mountain laurel, and wild dogwood grew. Though well past the blooming season, new growth had created a private grotto hidden to all but Isaiah…and now her. Light from the setting sun dappled the forest floor. Purple violets and white trilliums were bathed in gold, lending a mystical quality found usually only in storybooks.

"Oh, my goodness," she breathed, stepping into the glade. He followed close behind her, his hand resting on the small of her back. He flicked his flashlight beam across the clearing, illuminating a bench— a handmade wooden bench for two, sanded and stained for protection from the weather. She ran toward it as though it were a pot of gold beneath a rainbow. Plunking down on one end, she patted the spot beside her. Isaiah needed no invitation. He plunked down and draped an arm around her shoulders.

"Did you plant those?" she mouthed, pointing at the magnificent dogwood shrubbery, prized by gardeners everywhere.

After a moment's consideration, he indicated two of them.

"Did you make this?" she asked, patting the bench where they sat. She tapped one fist on top of the other to mean "build" or "work."

He nodded affirmatively, his pride obvious even in the thin light.

"*Wunderbaar!*" Her expression underscored the meaning of her word.

"*Danki,*" he said as two white rabbits crept into the glade to nibble on tender young shoots. For a few minutes the couple watched the diners until Isaiah turned to face her on the bench. His sudden movement sent the rabbits scurrying into the brush. Hooking a thumb toward his chest, he patted the location of his heart with a fist and pointed at her.

She *knew* what this meant. He liked her. Or he *loved* her. Either way, the sentiment filled her with joy as she repeated the gesture to him.

He shrugged his shoulders and nodded, as though he'd known that particular tidbit for quite some time. Stretching out his long legs, he seemed content to sit in the growing darkness as the bunnies ventured from hiding once more.

She smelled the scent of pine drifting on the breeze and the familiar fragrance of Ivory soap. He must have bathed in the river or showered in the barn just before showing up for supper. Whippoorwills called to one another from nearby trees while crickets and cicadas began their evening chorus. Catherine pulled up the shawl around her neck, not because of any chill but to keep mosquitoes from feasting on exposed skin. She was glad she'd forgotten to grab the can of bug repellant. Somehow its odor might have intruded on the idyllic serenity in Isaiah's secret garden.

Inhaling a deep breath for courage, she peered into his chiseled face—his high cheekbones and strong jaw, his clear olive skin and dark, shadowy eyes—and broached a subject she'd been mulling over for days. After several misunderstood pantomimes, she finally managed to ask, "Would you go with me to a party?"

It took her a while to convey that other people would be there, men and women around their ages.

He realized that there would be plenty of delicious things to eat and drink, besides a bonfire for roasting marshmallows.

At last, she expressed that the drive wouldn't be very far by horse and buggy. But she couldn't convey the concept of a volleyball game— the main purpose of the social event—no matter how hard she tried. He scratched his chin and shrugged his shoulders in confusion.

Catherine decided that a man with Isaiah's strength and agility would be able to catch onto any game easily, so she dropped her ineffective playacting. "Will you go with me or not?" she demanded.

He stared at her for a long moment, pondering a question he understood perfectly.

"Please?" she begged, with growing fear she had misinterpreted his affection.

"Okay, Cat," he said. "For you."

Light had faded in their hidden garden as the sun dropped below the horizon. Isaiah picked up her hand, switched on the flashlight, and led her down the path with the assurance of one who had spent ten years in the woods. Twice she stumbled on unseen rocks. More than once Catherine glimpsed the yellow eyes of critters that wondered who the intruders were in their domain. A flashlight beam illuminated a pitifully small area in absolute darkness. Yet Isaiah hiked back at nearly the same speed they had maintained on the way there.

She clung to his hand, following close on his heels, content that she had a date to a young people's event before she was no longer young. Without tumbling into the ravine, twisting their ankles, or suffering too many bug bites, they emerged from the forest. And all too soon they rounded the path behind the barn.

Isaiah hesitated, pointing toward light streaming from the barn windows, and motioned to stop.

"Ah, you left the battery light on." She nodded as he sauntered toward the open doors. Then on impulse, she followed him inside, despite the outbuildings being her least favorite spot. This main barn, with a loft bulging with stored hay bales, had an open ground floor so that buggies could be driven inside during foul weather. Catherine pivoted in the center of the room, scanning the walls and shelves in all directions. Farm tools, gardening implements, and children's toys hung in neat rows from pegs. After a moment, she spotted what she sought—a beach ball, muddy and forgotten, but serviceable.

"Isaiah!" she called as he was halfway to the shower light. She tossed the ball at him.

Of course, he couldn't hear her so the ball bounced off his head, knocking off his hat. He turned quickly, picked up the ball, and threw it back at her with an amused laugh.

She clamped her palms together, bent her knees, and returned the ball as though it had been a volleyball serve. Too bad she seldom demonstrated such athletic ability during actual games. The ball arched upward and then descended toward her target. He duplicated her movement without hesitation, sending the beach ball soaring toward the rafters. Catherine positioned herself underneath, and then she sent the ball back to him with open, flat palms. He lunged to copy this new hand position, returning the hit with a high, arching ball.

Doves and swifts roosting in the rafters didn't appreciate the nighttime commotion one bit. They cooed and ruffled their feathers in protest. But Isaiah enjoyed the game. They volleyed back and forth until Catherine's prowess finally gave out. Her missed shot flew into the sow's pen and disturbed the slumbering family of pigs. Isaiah leaned over the gate to retrieve the ball. When he straightened up, he met Catherine face-to-face.

"Voll-lee-ball," she pronounced slowly.

He repeated the word with some similarity, tossed the ball back to the corner it came from, and then switched off the lights. They walked from the barn hand in hand halfway to the house, where Isaiah nodded and headed toward his path.

But not before he placed the lightest and sweetest of good night kisses on Catherine's lips.

Sweat soaked through Daniel's shirt and ran down the back of his neck. His hat brim was sodden and would need replacing as soon as Abby returned home. But he wouldn't stop working until he plucked every Japanese beetle from her roses and every slug from the hostas. He'd already pruned back the lilacs and forsythia, pulled up the dried tulip and daffodil stems, and deadheaded the spent rose blooms. Abby set great store by her flower garden, and he wouldn't have it looking neglected no matter how his back ached.

Besides, the physical activity took his mind off his sister-in-law. He had seen Isaiah and Catherine walk from the darkened barn last night from his bedroom window. What had they been up to?

He truly liked his sister-in-law and was grateful for her help in his family's time of need, yet he didn't want her friendly desire to also help his cousin turn into something more serious for Isaiah. Daniel didn't want to see him hurt. It was time to pray about the situation.

He had just come to that conclusion when he saw that Catherine was headed his way with a glass of iced tea in hand. Maybe it was also time to say something directly to her.

"You look like you could use this," she said, handing him the cool drink.

"*Danki*." He drained the contents in four long gulps.

"I wanted to speak to you about Isaiah," she said, smoothing her palms down her skirt.

Daniel wiped his mouth. *Well. Perfect timing.* "That's probably a good idea."

"I'd like him to come with us to preaching on Sunday. It's time he gets to know the Lord."

He blinked as though he'd seen snowflakes falling on the cornfield. "What would the point in that be? He can't hear the sermons or hymns, the ministers don't know sign language, and Isaiah couldn't follow signing even if they did. It would be a waste of time." He handed back the empty glass and focused on pulling up weeds by the roots.

"Maybe he would enjoy being surrounded by people, for a change."

He didn't glance up. "I assure you he would *not* enjoy that. I took him to a livestock auction once, and he hightailed it out of there as soon as the room filled up with buyers. I found him waiting in the buggy, taking a nap."

"Well, I'm buying him his own Bible on my next trip to town, an English Bible because that was the language he'd started to learn in school." She crossed her arms, standing with that annoying hipshot posture she often took when arguing.

Daniel sighed. "Why waste your money, Catherine? Isaiah can't read. Why can't you get that through your head? He will *never* read, so I wish you would stop torturing him."

"I'm not torturing him. I'm apparently his only friend, and as such I invited him to the district volleyball party on Saturday. You don't need to hear or be able to read to join in the fun. I showed him how to play last night in the barn. He caught on quickly."

"Is that right? I was wondering what you two were doing out there."

Her rosy cheeks paled considerably. "I explained about the game, told him that folks will bring plenty of good eats, and about the bonfire when it gets dark. He seemed interested in all of it."

"Only because *you* were so interested. He would probably follow you onto thin pond ice in winter if you smiled at him." Daniel pulled up a clump of stinkweeds by the roots.

She huffed like an angry hen. "Why can't he just *try* a social event to see if he likes it? If he runs back to the buggy to take a nap, I'll never ask him again."

Daniel shook his head and straightened up. He saw no way out but to tell her the truth. He looked her in the eye. "Who will be hosting this social event?"

"The Joshua Miller family, two roads over." Her weight shifted over to the other hip.

"Joshua Miller was one of Isaiah's classmates a long time ago. If the party is at his house, you can be sure his cousin Sam Miller will be there too."

She waited for him to wipe his brow without interrupting. Sweat had run into his eyes, causing them to burn.

"Sam Miller might have turned out okay, but he went through a mean spell. He used to make fun of Isaiah, mocking him when he tried to repeat the teacher's words. At first Isaiah didn't know this was happening behind his back. But eventually he caught on that some kids were laughing every time he spoke—Sam Miller most of all."

Catherine's face grew even paler. "How did you find this out?"

"My aunt said he came home one day all upset. She could tell he'd been crying. The next day he refused to go to school. My aunt went to talk to the teacher, and she told her what happened. The teacher was young, inexperienced, and felt real bad about the situation, but the damage had been done. He wasn't ever going back to that school." Daniel picked up his bucket of soapy water, pruning shears, and long-handled digger. "What do you plan to do if Sam Miller is there on Saturday and he hasn't grown out of his mean-spirited nature? Are you prepared to subject Isaiah to that kind of torment again?"

He didn't wait for her answer but marched to the barn to put away his tools and take a long, cleansing shower. He wanted to rid himself of the odor of stinkweeds and bad memories. And, perhaps, wash away his bad intuition of what was to come.

Seventeen

Abby had thought she was ready for today. Her lawyer had finally returned her phone call a week ago. He had requested the next available court date on the docket and would meet with her beforehand to discuss the case. Now, as she waited for him in the small chamber dressed in her traditional Amish garb, her courage began to wane.

Please hurry, Mr. Blake, before fear creeps back into my heart.

Suddenly the door swept open. "Sorry, Mrs. Graber. I was stuck behind an Amish hay wagon and then two school buses. I didn't think I'd ever get here. Isn't it fitting? The hay wagon part, I mean." He pulled a manila folder from his satchel and sat across from her at the table.

"*Jah,* I suppose. Probably a third cutting going to market." Abby folded her hands primly.

"But don't you worry. We have plenty of time to prepare before your case is called." He tugged on his shirtsleeve cuffs beneath his coat.

She could hear car doors slamming beyond the window and then a horn blast followed by unintelligible shouting. A disagreement over a parking spot might have sparked tempers. "Like I told your answering machine, my husband and I have agreed on my course of action. I wish to plead guilty to all charges. There's no reason to drag this out with a jury trial, and no reason to implicate anybody else. I am the sole responsible party. The sooner I am sentenced, the sooner I can serve my time and put all this behind me." She stared at the table-top, which smelled faintly of lemon furniture polish. Smeary fingerprints had somewhat dulled the shiny finish. The rest of the room had a musty, air-conditioned odor.

"Abby." He tapped her forearm to get her attention. "I have better news than that." He was grinning like a contest winner. "I've heard from the prosecutor's office. Based on the evidence, Judge O'Neil might allow you to plead guilty to reduced charges—every one of them misdemeanors, no felonies. Do you know what that means?"

She looked into his clean-shaven young face and shook her head.

"The felony convictions could have gotten you nearly three years in Marysville. But with no felonies, you might be going home *today.*" He adjusted the knot of his already perfectly straight tie. "I say 'might.' Judge O'Neil's mood tends to change with the barometer. The hotter and stickier it is, the crankier he becomes, and then his sentences aren't as lenient as I would like. But the prosecutor's office agreed to reduced charges, and I haven't heard any further mention of the grand jury's request." His eyebrows lifted with anticipation.

"What's the weather like outside today?" she asked, her palms damp and itchy.

He smiled. "It's warm, but there's a light breeze. It should have been lovely when the judge drove to town this morning."

Abby felt some of her tension drain away. She slumped against the back of her chair. "Then I'm glad you didn't return my phone call right away."

He laughed. "Weather was pretty nasty last week, wasn't it? I can't say for sure, but I think that candlelight vigil a few weeks ago also had something to do with bringing this matter to a close. Both the county prosecutor and Judge O'Neil are up for reelection in November. That show of support outside the Justice Center made the Ohio newspapers. The AP also picked it up, and several TV stations ran the story on the nightly news. Nobody likes to see an Amish lady sitting in jail. Not under these circumstances."

Abby could barely focus on the remaining preparations and instructions. Her mind filled instead with images of her *kinner* and what she would do first when she got home: *Hug Jake and Laura until they squirm away in protest? Cook Daniel all his favorite foods for supper? Eat a piece of cheese that doesn't come in individually wrapped slices? Take a long soak in my own bathtub? Maybe get down on my knees and thank a merciful God?*

She entered the courtroom on wobbly legs when her case number was called. After she was seated at the defense table, she glanced briefly over the packed courtroom. But in that moment she saw the faces of the English midwives who had stood for hours on the sidewalk along with members of her district. She spotted several children she had delivered and then the weathered, lined face of her father. And she saw her beloved *ehemann* in the front row, looking weary but smiling.

Judge O'Neil cleared his throat, causing Abby to swifty focus on the stern-faced judge. "I have written affidavits that have been entered into evidence from just about everyone who knows you, Mrs. Graber. But it's the statements from Dr. Weller, the responding paramedics, and the Medical Examiner that are most convincing in your case. It's the sworn testimony of these gentlemen that your actions did not cause or in any way contribute to Mrs. Fisher's death. In light of this evidence, I'm willing to amend the charges against you to one count of attempted unauthorized practice of medicine and one count of possession of a dangerous drug. Do you require a postponement of these proceedings to confer with legal counsel?"

"No, Your Honor," said Abby, with her heart beating in her throat.

"Do you understand the new charges against you?"

"Yes, Your Honor. I do."

"Then do you wish to enter a plea to these charges?"

A hush fell over the room. "I do. I am guilty, Your Honor." Abigail spoke in a soft but clear voice.

Judge O'Neil dropped the statements back into the file. "Then I hereby sentence you to three hundred sixty-five days in jail, suspending all days but time already served in favor of three years probation. As a condition of your probation, you must prepare, have printed, and distribute a pamphlet outlining the risks of home births versus hospital deliveries to be used within the Amish community. Two different obstetrical medical personnel must approve this pamphlet for accuracy and a copy must be submitted to this court. In addition, you are hereby ordered to pay a five-thousand-dollar fine. In lieu of the cash amount, you may choose to assist a physician or licensed midwife during deliveries throughout the probationary period as community service. The key word being 'licensed' midwife or physician. You can accept no payment or gratuities during the entire three years."

The gallery of onlookers broke into a round of applause. A few Amish men waved their hats.

"Silence!" The judge underscored his order with a rap of his gavel. "This is not a television show. I demand order in my courtroom." After the crowd quieted, he refocused on Abby. "Do you understand the sentence I am about to impose, including the terms of your probation? Any noncompliance could result in the reinstatement of the full one-year jail sentence."

She tried to sort things out, but her brain refused to cooperate. "Do you mean I don't have to return to my cell?" She croaked like a frog.

"That is correct. Today's proceedings will be transcribed and you will receive a copy outlining the terms of your probation in the mail. On the paper you'll find the name and address of the Wayne County Probation Department. You must register by the date listed on the sheet to be assigned an officer to whom you'll report." He placed her file on the left-hand pile and was already reaching for another file on his right.

"Do you mean I can continue helping to deliver babies?"

The frosty expression he leveled over his wire-rimmed glasses did not coincide with the day's mild weather. "*Help* to deliver, Mrs. Graber. 'Help' being the important word in that sentence. Under no circumstances are you to deliver a baby on your own. You are to wait until medical personnel arrive before entering a patient's room. If no help is available, 9-1-1 is your sole option. And, of course, you are never to handle pharmaceuticals during any medical procedure again. Have I made myself perfectly clear about that?" He leaned forward in his chair, his eyes capable of boring holes through steel walls.

"Yes, Your Honor, I understand. I don't intend to ever break the law again." She had said that she understood, but when she turned around and gazed over the sea of friendly faces, she wasn't so sure. *Will I be allowed to walk out of the courtroom with Daniel? Do I have to wait until the court session concludes and everyone's case is heard? Should I return to my cell to clean out my meager possessions and say goodbye to Rachelle?*

Like a child afraid of the dark, Abby took a few steps as though walking in her sleep. Then her eyes met and held her *ehemann*'s. He was grinning so broadly, his face would probably be sore tomorrow.

"Come, Abby." His beckoning wave broke her paralysis.

"You can join him, Mrs. Graber," Mr. Blake said, prodding her with his shoulder. "A deputy will speak to you in the hallway about receiving your personal property."

His nudge galvanized her to action. She crossed the short distance to Daniel's waiting arms. He enveloped her and drew her tightly against his chest as though someone might try to pry her loose. Hands reached out to slap her back or squeeze her arm. One well-wisher patted her head as though she were a young child. Cradled against Daniel's crisply pressed shirt, she heard welcoming greetings in both English and *Deutsch*.

"All right, folks, take your celebration out to the hallway. We have other cases still to hear. Bailiff, clear those people out of my courtroom." Yet the judge's voice had softened considerably when he delivered his final pronouncement in the case of Abigail Graber versus the State of Ohio.

The Grabers, their district members, and their English friends couldn't comply fast enough. Abby was caught up in the tide that moved through the doorway, down the steps, and then spilled onto the street. All around her she heard words of encouragement and support.

The Amish spoke in *Deutsch* so reporters couldn't write down what they said. Daniel did his best to shelter her from some rather zealous newspaper people.

"What do you think about Judge O'Neil's ruling?" one man asked.

"Are you ready to reveal who supplied the anti-hemorrhage drug, Abby?" A young woman in a short suit pushed a microphone toward her face.

"Are you anxious to get home, Mrs. Graber? What do you think you will do first?" This particular question from a petite redhead she chose to answer. She'd thought about nothing else since the meeting with her lawyer. "I believe I'll close my eyes and thank God for His grace, and then I'll rock in the porch swing with my children."

Daniel hustled them through the crowd to a van idling across the street. When he rolled back the door, Abby saw her father and mother already inside. She climbed in, followed by her husband and several other neighbors. The van's driver swung the door closed, blocking out more inane questions from the media. As he tried to shoo them away, Abby peered into her *daed*'s face. The ordeal seemed to have aged him a decade. "Welcome back to us, daughter. Your *mamm* and I have been worried about you." He lifted his arms, garbed in his black Sunday coat, and she leaned gratefully into his embrace.

It was difficult to accept the hug within the vehicle without sitting on her father's lap. But as clumsy as she looked, she felt utterly relieved. Her mother whispered endearments in her ear, commenting on her weight loss and what she planned to do about it. Daniel took the seat next to the driver as she settled into the space between her parents. Other folk wedged into the third row as the van crept carefully into Wooster traffic.

"Jake, Laura?" she asked, trying to hold back tears.

"Waiting at home with your *schwester*. No sense bringing them into the fuss," said her *mamm*, still assessing her skinny frame. Abigail nodded in complete agreement.

The van soon turned onto the expressway, leaving the tall Victorian buildings of Wooster behind. However, before her mother had a chance to fill her in with the latest district news, the van exited the freeway onto a local township road. She leaned around her father for a better look. Parked close to the road on the side of someone's driveway was a horse and buggy, oddly familiar.

"Is that *our* buggy?" she asked, staring out the window.

Daniel glanced over the seat as the van turned into the driveway. "It is, *fraa*. You and I will travel the rest of the way like a normal Amish couple. Once we get home, the *kinner* and Catherine will surround you for days, demanding your undivided attention. You and I have been separated for months. This is my chance to spend some time with my wife, alone."

The van stopped and Daniel jumped out. When the driver opened the back door, she climbed over her mother into the late summer sunshine. Daniel picked her up like an English newlywed and carried her to their buggy. Then he went back for the animal's feedbag and water bucket.

"There's nothing wrong with Abigail's legs!" The bishop hollered out the window, but his light blue eyes were twinkling.

Daniel waved as they drove off toward Shreve. All the way home they talked and laughed and whispered the endearments special to every couple in love. He even kissed her once or twice in his shy fashion. By the time the gelding trotted up their driveway, Abby thought she was ready to face the rest of her family.

But she'd been wrong. When Laura and Jake ran pell-mell from the house, with arms flailing and legs pumping, Abby felt the depth of her love rise up her throat and nearly cut off her air. She dropped to her knees to accept their embrace.

I'm home. At long last, I'm truly home.

"What do you see up there?" Nathan asked, stretching out on the quilt, flat on his back next to his son. He received only arm waving and leg kicking in response, but he didn't mind. This was a good day to savor a lovely summer afternoon, fleeting as they soon would be. He stared skyward, seeing hawks soaring on wind currents known only to them. Down below, the still air hung heavy with humidity and the promise of rain. It was too hot to weed the garden or pick ripened vegetables for supper. Because the livestock all had plenty of food and water, he would wait until evening to clean out barn stalls.

Just above the two Fishers, a butterfly fluttered her colorfully patterned wings. Abraham laughed with glee. His tiny fist opened and closed as though trying to capture his first jar pet. Dressed in something Iris called the "onesie"—a combination garment of shirt and pants—he worked his arms and legs energetically. He would soon grow into the tiny trousers and plain muslin shirts his great-*gefunden* had been busy sewing.

Nathan rose up on one elbow, supporting his head with a palm. He watched the *boppli* with fascination, pride, and sheer joy. *He will look like me some day. Maybe he'll have my chin or jawline and, of course, my eyes.* But he hoped the boy retained some of his *mamm*'s features so that Ruth would live on through him. Nathan brushed away a fly that dared to land on his son's pudgy leg and offered one calloused finger for the child to grasp.

"What a grip!" he exclaimed. "I can't wait to put a baseball bat between those strong fingers."

"What makes you think he'll take a shine to that silly game?" Iris stood with one hand on her hip, while the other clutched a basket of folded laundry to her side.

Nathan glanced up. His aunt's face was filled with "smile wrinkles" as she called them. "Because he is his father's son. A Fisher male grows up to love apple pie, pickled eggs, fire roasted corn, and baseball."

Iris approached until she loomed above the quilt. "Nice to see that you finally ran out of chores to do, nephew." She transferred the basket to her other hip.

"Didn't run out. That'll never happen around here. But with this heat, my helper and I decided to take a short break."

"What, may I ask, has he been helping with?"

"Fly chasing. They don't dare light when Abraham waves those arms around."

"Well, if you two are hungry, come up to the house. I'll fix you a sandwich and feed him his bottle. It's about that time."

"We'll be up in a minute, *danki.*" After Iris headed for the house, Nathan paused to study his son a little while longer. All too soon he would be crawling and pulling himself up on the curtains. Then he'd be toddling after Iris, following her from room to room like a dog. Before too long he would venture into the barns and silos, discovering countless places to play or hide. A close eye would need to be kept on him then. Nathan dreaded Abraham's first day of school without siblings to offer advice on what was to come. But he also yearned for the spring he could work with him in the fields, sticking young plants into each freshly dug hole. The years would pass quickly. And throughout each passing season, God would watch over little Abraham Fisher until he was little no longer. He would be there to guide and sustain him throughout his life until he drew his dying breath. Perhaps Ruth would watch over him too, proud of the son she'd given her life for. But for now, Nathan savored these perfect summer moments with the tiny helpless baby. His heart filled with so much love it might burst.

"*Waaah!*" Abraham's empty belly signaled the end of father-son introspection. Nathan swept him into his arms, grabbed the quilt, and hurried toward the house. Inside the kitchen, Iris pulled the highchair to the table and placed jars of peas and creamed beef on the tray.

"I'll feed him those," he said, settling the boy in the chair.

Iris handed him a bib with a parade of dancing Holsteins. "Start with the peas first. Otherwise he'll fill up on beef and potatoes and refuse the vegetables. He loves the stuff."

Nathan opened the jar of peas, took a whiff, and made a face. "A brave man, my son. After his nap, I'll take him to the barn in his stroller. He can shoo away flies while I milk the cows."

Iris clucked her tongue. "He'll have the tougher job of the two this time of year. I'll be in the garden if he gets cranky. I need to pick the last tomatoes before they rot on the vine. Tomorrow it should be cooler, so I'll have two days to finish canning before the Sabbath." She set out their sandwiches, pickles, and iced tea.

"Speaking of which, we're going to preaching service this Sunday... all three of us." He took a long swallow of tea.

She cocked her head to one side. "That Mrs. Daly finally set you straight?"

So like her not to let a matter slide without comment. "*Jah,* I couldn't argue when she resorted to Scripture to make her point." He took a bite of turkey and then resumed spoon-feeding green mush into Abraham.

"I think you underestimated that *Englischer,* nephew, right from the start."

He didn't look up but had to smile. "Yep, I surely agree with you there."

Catherine must have changed her mind a dozen times during the past few days. After her conversation with Daniel, she'd decided not to subject Isaiah to Sam Miller. Isaiah's painful memories of his final school days probably had faded little over the years. Seeing a former nemesis could tear open old wounds.

However, she then considered that Mr. Miller was now an adult... no longer a taunting, troublemaking child. He might regret his hurtful behavior and would welcome a chance to make amends. Because Isaiah lived like a hermit, Sam's opportunities to apologize had been few and far between. The seeking and acceptance of forgiveness would benefit both men's characters.

But how can I be certain that's how this day will play out? Sometimes cruel children simply grew into mean-spirited adults. Not everyone learned the lessons of love, kindness, and mercy. Would this jeopardize the progress Isaiah had already made in socializing with his family? *How much do my own selfish desires to spend an evening away from the farm like any normal courting couple influence my decision to take him to this party?*

And so she vacillated…back and forth until she practically drove herself crazy. By Saturday morning, Catherine realized she had no choice but to follow through as planned. Isaiah had come to the porch for his lunch bag bouncing the beach ball up and down with short precise taps with his wrist. He waved at her through the window and then practiced ball control all the way back to the cornfield. If she were to cancel the date now, *she* would be the one to hurt his feelings. And that she couldn't bring herself to do.

After baking a double batch of peanut butter walnut bars and a batch of banana nut bread, Catherine dressed for the occasion with care. Her dress was a flattering shade of cornflower blue, and she donned a freshly starched *kapp.* Packing the desserts into a hamper, she grabbed her shawl and headed toward the barn before the Grabers returned from the pond. Daniel and Abby had taken their *kinner* swimming after lunch. Cold-plate suppers waited in the fridge for whenever they became hungry.

Ten paces from the porch, she realized there would be no chickening out. Isaiah waited next to the open carriage with a clean blue shirt, straw hat, and a toothy grin. He'd put on sneakers as she had and had placed a quilt in the buggy for cool evening breezes. He clutched a bouquet of daisies, larkspur, and gladioli in one massive hand. Boots sat at his feet, patiently waiting to see if she would attend the party too. She wagged her tail and then lifted her paw when Catherine drew near.

"Evenin', Cat," said Isaiah, tipping his hat. He held out the massive bouquet.

"Evening. *Danki* for the flowers," she said with a shy smile. She set the flowers on the seat and bent to shake Boots' paw. Isaiah had tucked one daisy into her collar.

"Home," he ordered when Catherine straightened up. Boots looked from one to the other, and then she trotted toward the path through the forest, wagging her tail.

Too bad we can't follow the dog back to the cabin. We could eat the desserts sitting on the bank of the river, with only annoying mosquitoes to contend with, she thought climbing into the buggy. By the time Boots reached the cabin, they would be halfway to the Millers. Along the way, Isaiah whistled without an ounce of anxiety as Catherine worried, fidgeted, and perspired.

"Lord, give me strength," she whispered when the buggy turned up their hosts' driveway. They parked at the end of a long row of buggies and approached a party already in full swing. Catherine placed her desserts on the snack table under a canopy while Isaiah studied the action from the sidelines. Two volleyball matches were underway, with at least a dozen people per side. After rejoining him, she watched too, waving at a few acquaintances that called out her name. Finally, she touched his sleeve to get his attention. "Play?" she asked, secretly hoping he would decline the idea. Then they could head straight for the bonfire, roast a few marshmallows, and go home.

"*Jah*," he said, angling his head toward the right-hand game.

Catherine assessed their play, noticing the sides were mismatched, with one team holding an unfair advantage.

Isaiah rolled up his sleeves as they approached the players. With far less enthusiasm, she called out, "Hello, everyone. I'm Catherine and this is Isaiah. Just so that everybody knows, he's deaf and doesn't talk much, but he plays volleyball pretty well."

"Catherine, Isaiah, come join our side!" Several members of the weaker team called out a warm welcome.

They took places in the back row and the game resumed. Catherine's description of "pretty well" turned out to be woefully inadequate. Isaiah played the game as though he'd practiced every day for years. Catherine? Not so well. He served and returned, volleyed and spiked, bumped and saved, and more than once rescued her feeble hits by diving for the ball and sending it soaring over the net. He sacrificed the knees of his trousers to keep the ball in play. Their team not only caught up, but surged ahead and won by five points.

Isaiah mastered game strategy the way only the athletically gifted are able to do. He and the man on his right developed and perfected the two-man spike setup that led to their team's victory. By the end of the third game Catherine and most of the other women were breathless.

"Let's take a snack break," shouted one girl, while the others followed her away from the net.

As the crowd wandered toward the tables under the tent or in the shade, Isaiah's impromptu partner lingered behind. "Hi, I'm Sam Miller," he said to Catherine, while mouthing his name wordlessly to Isaiah.

She blinked several times. *This is Sam Miller? The tyrant who had caused hurt feelings and a curtailed school career?*

Sam stepped forward, tipped his hat to her, and then shook Isaiah's hand.

If Isaiah remembered Sam, he hid it well. He pumped the man's hand heartily and slapped him on the back, mimicking one of their game-winning setups.

"Hopefully we'll play again before dark," said Sam. "Let's get something to eat. I'll introduce you two to my fiancée, Becka." He pointed at the tent, rubbed his stomach, and grinned.

Catherine hooked her arm through Isaiah's elbow. "We'll join you in a minute, Sam. I look forward to meeting Becka."

The heartless tormentor seemed to have matured into a fine man, but she wanted to make sure Isaiah was prepared for the social frenzy. Amish folks tend to talk fast when they first get together—maybe because they have been saving up things to say. She looked up into Isaiah's face. He was grinning down at their linked arms. He pulled his arm loose only to snake it around her waist.

The gesture stopped her fluttering heart for several seconds, especially when he brushed a kiss across the top of her *kapp.*

"No," she said, shaking her head. How could she explain that such displays of affection weren't appropriate between courting couples unless an engagement had been announced? She repeated the word "no" and shrugged away from him. "Let's eat." She angled her head toward the canopy.

He nodded, with disappointment and confusion evident on his face. They walked to the rapidly filling picnic tables. She hoped they could get in line, fill their plates from the dessert selections, and find a quiet spot to enjoy the treats.

But her fond hopes were not to be. As soon as they reached the tent, young people surrounded them…and every one of them wanted to talk to Isaiah.

"You were great in that game. Next time I want you on my team."

"Where has Catherine Yost been hiding you all these years? Welcome back."

"Isaiah, I'm Becka Morgan, Sam's fiancée. I'm glad you joined us tonight and hope you and Catherine will come back soon."

"Do you remember me? I was in your class at school. I sat two rows behind."

"Isaiah, my *grossdawdi* is hard of hearing too. I'm getting pretty good communicating with him," said a well-intentioned girl, speaking loud enough to rattle wind chimes.

All people under the tent canopy were well intentioned that night, but the end result was still disastrous. Some folks talked loudly, thinking that would make a difference, while many tried to illustrate their words with unrecognizable pantomimes. So many vied for the attention of the man who had spent his days in the company of deer, chipmunks, and his faithful dog. Catherine watched the goings-on with increasing alarm, helpless to intervene.

Isaiah valiantly tried to follow their gestures and read lips, but the situation turned bizarre—too many people, talking too fast, using words he didn't know. After several minutes, red blotches appeared on his face and neck, while beads of perspiration formed across his forehead and upper lip. Still he tried to figure out what they were saying, balancing a plate of brownies in one hand.

"Please excuse us," said Catherine. "Give us a chance to eat our desserts. There's too many of you talking at once." She grasped his arm and broke through the crowd, her own plate precariously angled.

"Sorry, Catherine," called Becka Morgan. "We're just a little excited because we haven't seen Isaiah in a long time."

She nodded in response but didn't turn around. They kept moving toward the bonfire. Catherine would have thought he would be grateful she had rescued him from the throng, but his response was quite the opposite. He not so subtly tugged his arm back from hers as they walked. Once they reached the campfire, he perched on an upended log instead of taking a bench made for two. He concentrated on eating his plate of snacks while she nibbled on a dry Rice Krispie bar.

Fortunately, no one else arrived to roast marshmallows. Catherine stared into the dancing flames of the bonfire, trying to determine her next course of action. Her appetite had vanished. After a few bites, she set her plate in the grass for foraging skunks and raccoons to find later. When Isaiah finished eating, he threw his paper plate into the blaze. She reached for his hand.

He shook his head, fixed her with a dark look on par with poison, and said succinctly, "Home, Cat. Home."

Eighteen

Nathan strapped his son in his car seat and then attached the seat inside his buggy with taut bungee cords. It would be a long drive to Carol Baker's home, but the time would be well spent. He had plenty to think about as the buggy clip-clopped down the road toward Wooster.

What would he say to the men and women of Mrs. Daly's therapy meeting?

How would he explain why he had lashed out at another man who had been floundering in grief without his wife?

How would the *Englischers* receive his explanations and apologies, when most had no contact with the Amish other than passing them on the road or buying a dozen eggs at a roadside stand?

The social worker had been surprised when he had called her from a pay phone—surprised but pleased. Patricia had told him apologies weren't necessary because the others understood his pain. But an act of humble contrition was necessary for *his* sake. And so he left his house by four o'clock to arrive by six-thirty, thanking God that Mrs. Baker had again invited the group to her home. He refused Patricia's offer of a ride for the same reasons he had walked home on that fateful night. She shouldn't leave the others to take him home. And because Abraham would be with him, he doubted he'd stay until the session ended. Although Iris had volunteered to watch him, Nathan wanted the group members to meet his son…Ruth's son…firsthand.

After parking on the side of the driveway next to Patricia's low-slung red car, he lifted the sleeping child from the car seat and transferred him to the carrier. Abraham barely stirred, the heat and humidity lulling him into deep slumber. Nathan strode toward the house with renewed energy. The purple pansies and red geraniums still beckoned visitors along the walkway. The giant sunflower nodded its plastic head from the garden. The tidy ranch house with lace curtains and brightly colored front door had remained exactly the same. But he had changed. He wasn't the same man who had lashed out with bitterness.

He knocked twice and waited. "Welcome, Nathan," said Patricia, sweeping open the door. "Come on in. Everyone's already here. Oh, my. You brought your baby. Look at that sweet face. Don't they resemble angels while they are asleep?" She rattled on while he stepped inside Mrs. Baker's kitchen, smelling sweetly of vanilla and cinnamon.

Nathan smiled and relaxed. Leave it to Patricia Daly to talk her way through any uncomfortable moments. "I brought him along so you could check his bottom for diaper rash," he said, biting the inside of his cheek.

She stared at him, wide eyed, and then she burst out laughing. "Good one. You had me going for a moment there, Nathan. Let's join the others."

In the front room, the people he'd met before were sitting in their same chairs, as if they had assigned seats. Their heads turned in his direction and all chatter ceased.

"Hello, everyone," he said, while everyone simultaneously called out greetings. "I wanted to show you my son, Abraham." He held up the plastic infant carrier for them to see as though his son were a prize-winning beefsteak tomato at the county fair.

The women jumped up and quickly surrounded him, oohhing and ahhhing as they peered at the sleeping baby.

"A fine-looking boy," declared the woman who had lost her sister.

"How can he sleep through all this racket?" asked Bob, who had yearned to celebrate his fiftieth wedding anniversary.

"I can't believe they make Amish clothes *so small*," said the young mother with two surviving daughters.

"My aunt Iris sewed his outfit," said Nathan.

"Oh, right." The woman's face blushed a bright pink. "It's not like you folks shop at Walmart."

"Actually, we do shop at Walmart. Just not for our clothes."

Everyone laughed at this, and he felt the last of his nervousness drain away. He placed the baby carrier on a table by the window and sat on the same folding chair he'd occupied weeks ago. "I didn't come here tonight solely to show off my son. I owe you all an apology for my behavior—"

His sentence was cut short as several people interrupted. They began talking at once, denying the need for apologies.

Nathan held up a hand. "Hold on there. I came here critical and judgmental of your ways. That's inexcusable, whether this is a grief therapy session or not." He crossed his legs at the ankles and leaned back in his chair. "Truth is, I was angry—mostly with God, because He chose to call home my wife, who hadn't had a chance to live yet. I was also mad at myself for being so fired up about having kids. And I was mad at the world. With so many nasty people out there, many of them delivering healthy babies every day, why should my sweet Ruth be the one to die?"

He didn't meet anyone's gaze, but he noticed several heads nodding in agreement. "But dwelling on all that wasn't helping me become a good father. I was raised better than to take out my anger on folks just trying to help. Lots of you are on the right track, and I've been giving things you said some thought. Anyway, I'm sorry to have stormed out like I had a bee up my pant leg."

Everyone laughed again, while Bob boomed out a loud, "Apology accepted."

Patricia stood up. "Because Nathan came in his buggy, he can't stay for the entire session. Why don't we go around the circle so each of us can bring him up to date on the progress we've made."

"I'll serve coffee and dessert now so Nathan doesn't miss my new recipe for pineapple upside down cake," said Carol, bustling into the kitchen.

Nathan relaxed, listening to his fellow mourners describe recent triumphs in their daily lives. Bob had decided to take his children and grandchildren to see the Great Wall of China.

The third male participant had made a contribution to Alcoholics Anonymous in his late brother's name.

The abused sister took a bouquet of flowers and a lawn chair to the cemetery. She enjoyed a long chat with her sibling to clear away past anger and bitterness.

And the young mother and her husband were attending family counseling to become better parents.

Nathan offered encouragement to each one. When it was his turn to speak, he said simply, "I asked God for forgiveness, and I believe He has given it. I'm returning to church services this Sunday."

"Churches aren't just for the saints," said Bob. "They're for us sinners too or they would be mighty empty."

Nathan had never heard it put quite like that but couldn't disagree. He enjoyed the pineapple upside down cake along with the camaraderie of the *Englischers*. Mrs. Baker packed up an extra piece of cake for him to take home. When he and his son were leaving, everyone encouraged him to stay in touch and return to meetings whenever he could. He said he would try, but in his heart he knew he wouldn't be back. Talking therapy worked fine for some people, but for others, quiet time on the back porch with the Good Book worked even better. He prayed for each of the people he'd come to know that they would fine peace and solace.

He had one more task to complete on his own road to healing. After he rubbed down and turned his horse out to pasture and put his sleeping son to bed, he turned up the kerosene lamp on the kitchen table. Taking paper and pen from the drawer, along with the address he'd received from Mrs. Daly weeks ago, he began to write one long overdue letter.

Abby sat at the kitchen table, savoring her third cup of coffee. In the several days since she'd been home, this was her first time alone. Either Jake or Laura tagged behind asking her endless questions, or Daniel hovered nearby trying to get her to eat more, or Catherine filled her in on everything that had happened on the farm or in their district while she'd been away.

Finally, their lives were returning to normal. Because the new school year had started, she had walked Laura to school that morning and then left Jake at the neighbors' for a few hours so he could play with their boys. Daniel and Isaiah were cutting firewood in the hills to get a head start on winter. And Catherine was sewing up in her room by the window. Abby worried about her sister. Her effervescent personality had turned melancholy. If she felt reluctant to move back home, Abby intended to insist that she stay longer. She enjoyed having another woman in the house. Two pairs of hands accomplished chores such as canning, herb drying, or fall cleaning faster. And she was curious about the progress Catherine had made with Isaiah. But with everyone hovering nearby, she'd had no opportunity to ask.

Besides, lately the man in question had been scarcer than a robin in winter. He'd welcomed her home with a bouquet of flowers and then practically disappeared.

The sudden jangle of her cell phone pulled her from contemplation. "Hello," she said.

"Abby? It's me, Rachelle. I got a message that I should call you." Her former cellmate sounded as though she were a thousand miles away.

"It's so good to hear from you!" Abby was delighted. The main reason she'd kept her cell phone charged was on the other end at last. "I wanted to apologize for leaving so abruptly and not saying goodbye."

Rachelle laughed with abandon. "Not to worry. Time served is the same as a get-out-of-jail-now card. You did what anybody would do… beat feet straight for home."

Her giggle sounded wonderful, even though her analogies were hard to decipher. "That may be, but I would have liked to give you my phone number and address for whenever you get out."

"That's real sweet, but you're Amish and all. Your husband probably wouldn't like me dropping in on you."

Abby considered how best to proceed, so it wouldn't sound as though she were telling Rachelle what to do. "That's not true. I talked to Daniel about you and he feels the same as me. If you need a place to stay temporarily when you're released, we want you to come here." *And not back to that boyfriend.* "We don't have cable TV—or any TV at all, for that matter—but we have plenty of good food and an extra bedroom. Plus we have horses for you to ride. You did say you loved horses. And don't forget you wanted to learn to knit too."

The other end was so silent Abby thought they might have been disconnected. Then Rachelle spoke in a soft voice. "Wow, I sure didn't see this coming. Thanks, Abby, because that's about the nicest thing anybody's ever wanted to do for me. But don't worry. I'm not going back to bad-news Al. I have lots of friends I can crash with."

"All right, but please save my number and also write down my address. You never know, Rachelle. You might change your mind someday."

"Thanks, I will keep it. Maybe someday I'll write a letter to let you know how I'm doing if that's okay."

"I'd like nothing better. Do you think you'll continue with Bible study?" Abby hoped she wasn't stepping into none-of-your-business territory.

"Are you kidding? I went yesterday and I'll be there each week until I get out. Mrs. Jarvis bought me my own Bible, and it's easy to read—not with all those big, old-fashioned words. Is that what yours is like?" she asked.

Abby thought of the family's German Bible and smiled. "My English Bible is easy to understand, yes."

"I plan to start going to church when I get out too. I don't know which one yet. Depends on where I live. But there's *some* kind of church in every town in America. I don't intend to be picky."

"Sounds like a good idea." Abby breathed a sigh of relief.

"How do you like being home?"

Abby glanced around her tidy kitchen and through the window toward the rolling hills. Splashes of gold and crimson dotted the forest to herald autumn, just around the corner. "It's better than I remember. I don't even want to leave to go to the Dollar Store, and that's saying a lot." She leaned back in her chair and closed her eyes. "But I do rather miss beef stew out of a can. If you don't look in the bowl, you don't know which vegetable you're eating. They all taste the same."

Rachelle snorted with laughter. "And I miss *you,* Abby. My new roommate wants to babble all night. A girl needs her beauty sleep. Well, I'd better hang up. There's a line to use the pay phone. I'll write whenever I get to where I'm going."

"Don't forget my offer. It's always open." Before they hung up, Abby recited her address and also the neighbors' phone number, and then she whispered a silent prayer. *Let Rachelle draw close to You, Lord, and find a safe place in this world.*

She heard the screen door open and bang shut as she hung up the phone. Daniel marched into the kitchen, his cheeks bright pink. He tossed the Amish newspaper and a stack of mail onto the counter. "What's this, *fraa*? You're sitting around, sipping coffee while a hardworking man needs his lunch?" He buzzed a kiss across her cheek.

"You're home early. Even when you're working in the fields you never come to the house before noon." She rose to her feet and headed toward the fridge.

"I missed you." He lifted her up and swung her around the kitchen. "I don't ever want to be separated again." He nibbled at her neck.

"Put me down. You're acting like a teenager," she demanded, but only halfheartedly.

"I think they must have spoiled you in that place," he teased while washing his hands. "Bringing you gourmet meals on a tray without your having to lift a finger. Now you are back to the grind, Mrs. Graber, if I must chain you to that stove." He snapped the hand towel toward her skirt hem.

Abby jumped back in time, and then she carried bread, lunchmeat, cheese, and a tomato to the counter to make sandwiches. "No chain will be necessary. I'll stay willingly." Her gaze flickered over the sprawled pile of mail, landing on one handwritten envelope. She didn't recognize the return address of any regular correspondent. Abby set down her paring knife, tore open the envelope, and extracted the single sheet.

She looked first at the signature. "I got a letter from Nathan Fisher," she said with a ripple of unease.

Daniel sat down at the table with a glass of milk. "Read it aloud, Abby."

She glanced at him and then back at the small, cramped handwriting. "Dear Mrs. Graber," she read. "I saw in the papers that they let you out of jail. I would like to talk to you, face-to-face. If you'll be home, I'll stop over this Sunday after church. Expect me sometime in the late afternoon."

Her gaze met his. "That's it?" he asked.

"*Jah,* just his signature—Nathan Fisher. No 'very truly yours' or 'best regards' or anything else." She returned to making sandwiches, cleaving the tomato into uniform slices even as apprehension took away her appetite.

"Men aren't very good with letter-writing. You can give him some pointers when you see him."

"True, but I wonder what Mr. Fisher wants with me." She placed Daniel's first sandwich in front of him.

"I guess you'll find out Sunday." He took a large bite, ending up with mustard on his lips.

"You sound very casual about this, while I'm…a little nervous." *Which is a bit of an understatement.*

"There's nothing to be nervous about, Abigail. Come and sit down. Tell me what you have planned for the afternoon. I thought maybe we could—"

"How do you know that, Daniel?"

"What could you possibly be afraid of?"

Abby crossed her arms. "Well, let's see…it was in the papers that I administered a 'dangerous' drug to his wife and that I'm out after only a few months' jail time. Oh, and that I'm allowed to resume delivering babies. In fact, I'm *expected* to midwife or I must pay five thousand dollars."

He sat quietly looking at her while holding his sandwich in midair.

"He's had plenty of time to think…and miss his wife. Maybe he's changed his mind about not holding me responsible. Maybe Nathan wishes the judge would have thrown the book at me." Even as she said that she realized she'd picked up more than one English expression from Rachelle.

"And maybe you're making a mountain out of one little letter." Daniel got up and walked to the counter where she stood and wrapped his arms around her. "Maybe you should let God be in charge of this one. Put it out of your mind."

She nodded, inhaling a deep breath. "Okay, I'll not think about Mr. Fisher until he drives into our yard this weekend." She picked up her lunch and carried it to the table.

But following through with actions proved to be a whole lot harder than saying the words.

Catherine rocked in the porch swing, staring at a yellow moon breaking the horizon in the east—a harvest moon, because at no other time of the year did the moon look so large or glow so brightly. Supper was finished, the dishes dried and put away, and yet Isaiah's meal still remained on the picnic table. Probably the moment she went inside for a bath, the plate would mysteriously disappear. She hadn't seen him since the volleyball party. The man avoided crossing paths with her better than the slyest coyote.

During the ride home from the Millers', he'd focused on the road ahead, ignoring any effort at conversation or her attempts to apologize. She understood he'd been embarrassed and uncomfortable when so many had crowded around, all talking at once. *But was that my doing? Who could have known people would be so friendly and eager to make up for lost years? It's not my fault. I meant well.*

Yet the truth remained no matter how hard she tried to ignore it. She had forced Isaiah into a situation he neither wanted nor was prepared for, and in so doing had resurrected old pain from the past. Abby's delicious pot roast churned in her stomach. *She* was to blame… not Sam Miller this time.

If she had some socks to darn, bread to bake, or a story to read to the *kinner,* it wouldn't be so bad. But with her *schwester* back in her role as wife and mother, Catherine found less and less to occupy her time.

Suddenly a shout rang out in the yard. "Abigail!" called Daniel. "Come quick."

Although the kitchen had been empty a minute ago, Abby emerged from the house by the time Daniel reached the porch. "What is it, *ehemann*? Is someone hurt?" Her thin face paled with fear.

"Not *someone,*" he said breathlessly. "It's Boots. That fool pup stuck her head down a hole in the ground to figure out what was making all the noise. Turned out to be a nest of ground hornets, and she got stung at least a dozen times on her face and paws, everywhere the fur was sparse."

Catherine jumped to her feet. Abby's hand grasped her throat. "How is she? Will the dog be all right?"

"I don't know. Call Doc Longo on your cell phone. His home number is in the book. Tell him we're on our way to his place in the buggy. Ask him if he could meet us on the road with whatever he gives for allergic reactions. Boots is unconscious and not breathing right."

Catherine's eyes filled with tears while Abby flew into the house to find her phone. When Daniel turned to leave, Catherine followed him down the steps. "Please wait a moment, Daniel. I'm awfully fond of that dog too. May I ride with you to the vet's?" She felt her heart thumping against her ribcage.

He leveled her a patient gaze. "No, Catherine. We're taking the dog in the back of the two-seater so it'll be faster." He hurried down the walkway toward the barn.

She ran after him, grabbing a hold of his shirt. "Please, Daniel. Truth be told, I'm fond of Isaiah too. I'd like to lend moral support, to be there for him in case Boots…"

The word hung unspoken in the air while Daniel's expression turned pitiful. "I'm aware of that. And I suggested that you ride along after he carried the dog up to the buggy. But he said no and was quite adamant about it." He made a sideways chopping motion with his hand. "I'm sorry." He sprinted toward the buggy shed, leaving her rigid on the path.

She knew the meaning of Isaiah's gesture. *He hates me. He despises me for the trouble I have caused.* She covered her face with her hands in an attempt to hold back her emotions. Once she regained her composure, she walked inside the house.

Abby was sitting at the table, a cup of coffee in hand. "Dr. Longo was home. He'll meet Daniel and Isaiah with an anaphylactic injection along Route 514. I explained the way they would take." It was then that Abby noticed Catherine's face. "What's wrong? You look as though you are on the verge of tears. Did Boots die before they had a chance hitch up the team?"

Abby's question tipped Catherine over the edge. Tears coursed down her cheeks. "Not as far as I know. I heard the buggy leave just before I came inside."

"Whew," breathed Abby with palpable relief. "Then what's wrong? Dr. Longo is the best vet around. If they can reach him in time, he'll save the dog."

Catherine slumped into a chair, awash with despair. "I hope that's true, but my tears aren't for Boots. I'm afraid they're purely selfish." Shame rose up her throat like acid indigestion. She stared at the wall, sniveling like a child.

"Tell me what's wrong. It must have something to do with Isaiah. You've been moping around the house since I got home, yet I know you're happy to see *me.*" She winked at Catherine. "And if I had a dollar for each time you checked the back porch or scanned the cornfield looking for him, I'd have the five thousand dollars to pay Judge O'Neil and never have to midwife again."

Catherine laughed, despite herself. "Apparently, I'm as subtle as a herd of elephants marching to town."

Abby set a cold glass of water in front of her. "You have stewed enough. It's time to tell me what's happened. You never know, Catherine. I might be able to help."

And so Catherine began more or less at the beginning and told the story of her short-lived romance with Isaiah. Abby's eyes grew wide hearing that her sister had entered his remote cabin alone, she blinked several times upon learning about the bountiful berry patch, and she shook her head with disbelief when again Catherine described how she had mounted a horse to ride the pasture on a moonlit night. During the narration, Abby remained quiet until Catherine reached the part at the snack table after the volleyball game. Then she clucked her tongue with disapproval. "Oh, no. Poor Isaiah. He *hates* not being able to communicate with other people."

"I know. That's why I tried to help. But instead I only made things worse." Catherine took a long drink, feeling the water ease her parched mouth.

"Not on purpose. Your intentions were noble." Abby patted her arm.

"A candle left to light the way can burn down a house, same as an arsonist."

Abby shook her head to remove the mental picture. "Let's not speak of such things. Besides, this conclusion is nowhere near as foregone. Isaiah might simply need time to collect himself."

"That's what I hoped, but he refused to let me to ride with them to the vet's."

Abby's expression revealed more than her words. "He might not want you to see Boots die."

"Please, sister. This isn't helping. You weren't there when we came home from the party. I grabbed his hand and tried to talk to him. He yanked it away like I was a rattlesnake. He motioned for me to go the house and glared with his arms crossed until I did. Then he took the horse to the barn and I haven't seen him since." Catherine's eyes smarted with unshed tears. "He hates me."

"I doubt that. Hate is not an emotion Isaiah knows."

"Well, he sure doesn't want me near him." Her voice cracked.

"Not right now. His ego has been bruised. He is a man, after all." Abby attempted half a smile.

"I want to make it easier for him to come get his meals. I'll return home as soon as Daniel can take me or I can get word to our *bruder*."

"Oh, Catherine. Let's not be hasty. Why don't you—"

"It's been well over a week. That's hardly being hasty. Besides, you're home. This is your family. Your *kinner* don't need a nanny anymore."

"Maybe not, but I still need my *schwester*."

"Please, Abby, let me go home," she pleaded. "I can't stay here any longer, torturing myself because…I love him. And each day would only remind me of what I cannot have."

Nineteen

Sunday dawned clear and mild—a good day for new beginnings. Nathan shaved his upper lip and then combed and trimmed his beard. It had been a long time since he'd worn his Sunday best clothes, including his *mutza,* the Amish vest, and polished black shoes. Iris had used so much starch on his white shirt that it would stand up on its own. The collar chafed his sunburned neck, but he'd be able to tolerate that minor discomfort and a whole lot worse. After all, it was the Lord's Day. And he was returning to preaching services.

He could hear Iris humming a tune in the kitchen while she fed Abraham his breakfast. The horse, already hitched to the buggy, stood in the shade swishing flies with his tail. With a final tug of the comb through his thick hair, Nathan walked downstairs with a spring in his step. He feared nothing. The decision he'd made after prayers last night had allowed him to sleep soundly for a change.

"*Guder mariye,*" said Iris. "Ready to go, I see. Sit down and eat some oatmeal. Otherwise your grumbling stomach will keep the rest of us from concentrating on the sermon."

He grinned while pouring coffee. He would miss Aunt Iris. He'd grown as fond of her as his own *mamm*. She certainly had a better sense of humor than his *mamm*. "All right, I'll have a bowl." He carried his cup to the table where Abraham tried to capture dust motes in the streaming sunshine. "Good morning, son. How goes your day so far?" He spoke to the child in *Deutsch* because children didn't usually learn English until they started school. The boy giggled.

"Strawberries or bananas?" asked Iris. When he indicated the latter, she added a heaping pile to his oats.

"What do you think about the church service at your own home?"

Iris sat down to finish her own breakfast. "All I have to say is my daughters-in-law had better be wearing running shoes if that house isn't spick-and-span."

He glanced up to find her eyes twinkling. "You would chase after them with your broom?"

"If need be, but I'm not too worried. They are good girls."

"Are you anxious to get back to your family?" When the question caught in his throat, he gulped down some coffee.

"You're my family too, Nathan, you and Abraham. Don't you forget that." She wiped her mouth and then pulled her apron over her head.

"I don't think I will ever stop being grateful." He scraped the sides of his bowl with his spoon.

"For what? For taking care of this little angel?" She lifted the baby from the highchair, making all the appropriate noises, and hugged him to her chest. "This child is a gift from God." Abraham gurgled while reaching for a *kapp* ribbon.

"That he is, but we'd better be off. I don't want to be late." He carried his bowl to the sink and carefully positioned his black hat on his head.

"Are you nervous?" she asked, wrapping a lightweight quilt around the boy's legs. "These are just Plain folk, nephew, and no different than you or me."

"They might wonder why I've stayed away after everybody was so nice at the funeral." He picked up the hamper of pies she had baked yesterday for the lunch table.

She emitted a dismissive snort. "Nonsense. Many of those folks have walked in your shoes. You're not the only one to suffer sorrow."

So like Iris to put things in perspective. "In that case I'm as ready as I ever will be." He opened the door for her and they walked into glorious sunshine, perfect for a day to give thanks.

Neither spoke much during the drive to the service except for the requisite comments about the weather. Once at Iris' home, they had to park quite a distance from the house. Nathan hefted the heavy hamper while she carried the infant. Because the bishop hadn't yet summoned people inside to worship yet, many milled around in the crisp fall air.

"Oh, my," called a voice. "Nathan has come with *mamm,* and they have brought the little one!" Iris' eldest daughter-in-law, Mary, ran toward them. "How he has grown and put on weight since I last saw him. *Mamm* Fisher is quite an expert with doing that." Mary slapped a hand on a well-rounded hip.

But Iris wasn't listening. She was studying the windows of her house, cocking her head to catch the reflection of sunlight on the glass. "Did you wash the windows this past week? You had plenty of notice about this service."

Mary exchanged a sly look with Nathan. "*Jah,* with vinegar and old newspapers, just how you taught me. Let me take that *boppli* to show around. People will be itchin' to see him." She pulled Abraham from Iris' arms and began bouncing him on her hip.

Iris was itching to see the inside of her home. "You go on ahead. I'm going in for a moment."

Mary chuckled under her breath. "Welcome back, Nathan. I'll show off your son while I hide from my mother-in-law, just until she finishes her inspection. Her other sons' wives are inside in case something needs last-minute polishing." Mary strode off toward the knot of women, while Nathan walked to the menfolk. The bishop, minister, and deacon stood within the group.

"*Guder mariye,*" he said, sweeping off his hat.

Those who hadn't seen him approach pivoted, their expressions registering surprise. But in a moment they had surrounded him with warm welcomes, queries about his harvest, and complaints about the overly cool nights. He felt as though he'd been drawn into an Amish cocoon.

When the minister announced it was time to begin the service, the bishop placed a hand on his shoulder. "Hold up a moment," he ordered. Nathan peered into the elder's lined face and swallowed hard. The bishop waited until everyone else had filed into the house before speaking. "I've been wondering when you would return. If you didn't come back after the harvest, I was going to pay you a visit. Iris told me you needed some thinking time." He studied Nathan as though he were a peculiar bug on the windowsill. "You do your thinking, son?"

"*Jah,* sir, I did." He met the older man's gaze without blinking. "I'm sorry if—"

The bishop held up a palm. "You owe me no apology. You might owe Him some kind of explanation if you wandered too far from prayer." He turned his face skyward where clouds scuttled by on the high breeze.

"I've set things right in that department."

A slow smile pulled up one corner of his mouth. "*Wunderbaar!*" he boomed. "Then let's see what the minister has in store for the first sermon." His hand tightened on Nathan's shoulder as though he half expected him to bolt for the buggies.

But Nathan wasn't going anywhere. As the two men entered the front room, his heart swelled with hope as he heard voices lifted in the first hymn. He might still be in Ohio, but for now, it felt like home.

◻

When Catherine approached the kitchen that Sunday morning, the room was so quiet she thought it must surely be empty. Instead, all four Grabers were in various stages of breakfast. Jake and Laura were eating cereal and milk with heads propped up with their hands. Daniel sipped coffee, reading something in the German Bible, while Abby was filling another bowl with Cheerios. She didn't look up when Catherine entered the room.

"Hi, Aunt Catherine," said Laura. "*Mamm* says you're leaving soon. Is that true?" Her face expressed her opinion on the subject.

"What's your hurry?" asked Daniel. "Why not wait until the harvest is in and all the garden produce canned. We still need your help." He stared over his reading glasses.

"Maybe you can talk some sense into her. I've had no luck," muttered Abby, shutting the cupboard door with a clatter.

Catherine chose the child to answer. "*Jah,* little one. Your *grossmammi* might need me for a while. But maybe I can return for a Saturday or two if your *mamm* can't manage without me."

"I want you to stay." Laura dropped her spoon into the bowl.

She patted the little girl's head. "*Danki,* I would if I could. I'll miss you too."

"You are being hasty and impetuous. Typical Catherine Yost behavior," declared Abby.

"I am not. I've thought the matter through." Catherine set down the coffeepot and narrowed her gaze across the room.

"Ladies, ladies," said Daniel. "It's the Lord's Day. At least postpone this discussion until after preaching."

Abby's face turned rosy pink. "Sorry," she murmured. "Daniel is right." She carried two bowls of cereal to the table, handed one to Catherine, and then bowed her head in silent prayer.

After a few minutes, Catherine spoke. "There really isn't much to discuss. I've finished packing. My suitcase is in the hallway. If Daniel can take me home after the service, I'd be much obliged." She poured milk into her coffee.

Abby's head snapped up from her breakfast. "And miss his lunch? A man has to eat! It wouldn't hurt for *you* to eat a little something too, as you've lost your fondness for my cooking." She took a long gulp of coffee.

"That's not true, *schwester*. I've simply lost my appetite in general."

Daniel put his hand over his wife's and squeezed, but he focused on Catherine. "I'll take you home after we eat, but why don't you just ride home with your parents?"

"Because they will stay all day. I'd like to go home as soon as possible."

"All right, it's settled." He returned to reading the Bible passage.

Catherine ate a handful of dry cereal for something to do, but she couldn't contain her curiosity any longer. "How is Boots?" she blurted. "Does she continue to recover?"

"You know where Isaiah's cabin is," said Abby. "You should have walked down to check on the dog yourself."

Daniel rose from the table. "Why don't you help me carry the food out to the buggy? The team is already hitched. I'm afraid if you stay in here any longer, my wife might start pulling your hair, Sabbath or no."

Catherine put the box of cereal away, picked up a roaster full of sliced beef, and followed him outdoors. The September breeze felt good on her overheated skin. After they had stowed the food behind the seats, Daniel turned to face her. "Boots will make a full recovery. As I told you when I got home, Doc Longo injected her with medicine to counter the toxins in her system and then cleaned the stinger wounds. Her respiration had improved by the next morning. He put her on some pills to help her breathe easier, plus antibiotics twice a day to fight infection. The pills make her sleepy, and Doc says that's a good thing. She'll recover faster if she's not trying to run around. Isaiah has that big dog sleeping on the foot of his bed." He shook his head. "Big dog, big man—must make for cramped sleeping." He walked toward the house twenty paces.

"And how is Isaiah?" she asked, trailing one pace behind him.

"He's fine, Catherine. Just shook up by the ordeal." Daniel halted, put his hands around his mouth, and hollered, "Abby, time to go. Get the *kinner* loaded up."

"Thanks for telling me and for saving me from a hair-pulling." She stepped around him to help Abby carry anything else needed for the noon meal, and then she climbed into the backseat to ride to preaching.

Sitting between her niece and nephew, Catherine wouldn't see Abby pouting and could therefore concentrate on what to do with the rest of her life. Maybe she would look for another job watching other people's children because having her own had grown unlikely.

"The Lord said, come unto me all who are troubled and heavy laden, and I shall give you peace," the bishop said in German. His words eased Catherine's heart because she knew them to be true.

"He's talking to you, sister," whispered Abby over her daughter's head.

"*Jah,* peace at *mamm* and *daed*'s," Catherine whispered back.

Abby leaned over with another comment, but Catherine shook her head and stared at the doorway. A tardy man had entered the outbuilding and slipped into the last row on the men's side—a man who looked familiar. Tall, with a broad chest and shoulders, he had an exotic complexion the color of olive oil. His loose-limbed, catlike movements indicated he'd be more comfortable anywhere but on a hard bench for a three-hour church service.

She blinked twice. *This can't be. Isaiah doesn't come to preaching. He can't hear Scripture or the sermons, and he can't read the songbook to follow along with the hymns.*

Daniel had been correct about that. Isaiah could never get to know God in the traditional way. Nevertheless, while she watched, the man on his right elbowed the late-arrival in the ribs, motioning for him to remove his hat.

Catherine gasped as the room tilted to one side. There was no mistaking the silky long black hair, tucked behind his ears without the traditional Amish bangs. The man was definitely Isaiah Graber. Her face flushed as the temperature skyrocketed inside the barn. She pulled away from his hypnotic dark eyes and looked at her sister. Abby was staring with the same slack-jawed shock. Laura turned from her *mamm* to her *gefunden* and whispered, "It's Isaiah," in case they hadn't noticed.

After Catherine's heart rate slowed, she chanced a second peek. He was surreptitiously watching her while mimicking the other men's behavior. When their gazes met, he winked and smiled. She felt suddenly light-headed. Her palms had grown clammy, while her stomach complained about the meager handful of Cheerios. When it became hard to catch her breath, she feared she was suffering a heart attack. *What better place to die than in a church?*

For two sermons, much singing, many prayers, and plenty of Scripture, Catherine tried to keep her mind on worship, and at most times she succeeded. But during the three-hour service, something was growing deep in her gut—a seed of hope.

Why has he come? The only logical answer was hard for her to trust.

When church ended, people filed out into early fall sunshine to chat with friends and neighbors. Most of the women bustled to set the food on long tables for the noon meal. Catherine walked outdoors at her sister's side, while Laura scampered off to join the girls headed to the swings.

"We don't need your help with lunch, Catherine," said Abby. "We have plenty of ladies. Plus I think there's someone you need to talk to." She arched an eyebrow. "Time's awastin'. None of us is getting any younger."

Catherine's stomach twisted like a rope. "Okay, here goes nothing," she said. *Or everything,* she thought. Meandering toward the shade, she found a spot to assess the situation. Isaiah stood in the barnyard, surrounded by young men. One man slapped Isaiah on the back, while another stepped close to speak something she couldn't hear. At least they appeared to be taking turns and were not all talking at once. Isaiah glanced from one to the other, sometimes nodding in agreement, sometimes shrugging his shoulders in confusion. But he was smiling.

Catherine approached on legs barely capable of holding her weight. When she stood behind Isaiah, Sam Miller touched his arm and gestured for him to turn around. As he did, her heart attack symptoms ratcheted up a notch.

His expression grew into a full-blown grin. "Hullo, Cat." He winked without the least bit of shyness.

"Hello, Isaiah," she said. "Can I talk to you?" She used the sign language he had learned during their brief, happy times together.

He nodded to his compatriots and then took her arm. As they walked toward the pasture, away from hearing ears, her confidence drained away like water from a bathtub. *How can I explain? How can I say how sorry I am for shaming him?*

They stopped at the fence, overgrown with wild grapes. Plump purple berries still clung in bunches to the vines. Isaiah tipped up her chin with one finger.

She gasped from his touch and blurted, "How's Boots?" She used his gesture for calf-high footwear for the dog's name.

"*Gut,*" he answered and indicated the dog still slept most of the day.

"What do you think about today's weather?" She mimed that she thought it neither too hot nor too cold.

Isaiah laughed at her, agreeing that the temperature was just right.

In a soft voice she enunciated slowly, "Why did you come today?" Then Catherine gazed across the rolling fields, feeling like an idiot.

He took hold of her chin to turn her face. "For you, Cat. I came for you."

Then using verbal words and nonverbal articulations, he expressed that he wished to learn to read lips better and communicate more. In fact, his pantomimes were so concise and easily interpreted she knew he must have been practicing them...maybe since the evening of the volleyball party, or perhaps the night of the hornet emergency. But either way, Catherine clapped her hands as though a children's program had just concluded.

Isaiah didn't clap. He didn't even try to use words or gestures to make his heart's desire known. Instead he leaned down and kissed her as though he had all the time in the world and didn't care a fig if anyone saw them.

His meaning was crystal clear, in the age-old language of love.

Abby nibbled on a piece of corn on the cob and sampled some of the local fresh sausage. Delicious though it might be, she had little appetite once she sat down with her lunch. All around her, people were eating, visiting, and enjoying the Sabbath. Even her sister looked far different from the sullen woman who had stared blankly over Jake's head at scenery she'd viewed a hundred times before. And the reason for her change in attitude was sitting across from her at the long table reserved for single folks.

Isaiah worked on a plate of food that could have fed an average English family of four. Yet he ate without paying much attention to the meal. His eyes were glued on Catherine. He sat on the very end of the bench while she seemed to be talking for both of them. Seeing those two communicating was the only thing lifting Abby's spirits. Nathan Fisher's visit later that afternoon weighed heavily on her mind.

When Daniel pushed away his plate, he met her gaze with a grin. "Why did I eat so much, *fraa*? My stomach feels like it might explode."

"Because everything tastes better on a day as fine as this." Abby forced herself to finish her sausage and not be wasteful.

"Your sliced beef was a crowd-pleaser. There's barely enough left in the roaster for cold sandwiches tonight." He lowered his voice so no one would overhear him.

"Worry not, *ehemann*. I saved a bowlful at home so my dear one wouldn't go hungry."

"You are the best wife in the world!" he announced. Everyone around them laughed, while a few elderly matrons rolled their eyes.

"Enjoy the appreciation while you can get it, Abigail," called one woman midway down the table.

"True. Soon enough I'll return to my normal status—somewhere between peach pie à la mode and day-old white bread," answered Abby to the woman's delight.

Daniel clamped his hand over hers. "Never day-old. Always freshly baked in my book."

She smiled, wishing they could remain carefree with their friends for the rest of the day. "If you'll have nothing more to eat, please hitch up the buggy. I'll go look for Laura and Jake."

His brow furrowed. "What's the hurry? Evening milking is hours away."

"Have you forgotten? Nathan Fisher is coming by this afternoon."

Daniel stood, scratching his chin. "Slipped my mind. I'll hitch the horse and bring up the buggy." He tipped his hat to the district members and strode away.

Abby cleaned up their mess, packed her hamper, and thanked the hostess. She bid her parents goodbye, found her *kinner* and sent them to the buggy, and then she went looking for her sister. She wasn't hard to find. Catherine and Isaiah sat in the shade, where she was again trying to teach him sign language.

"Ready?" asked Abby as she approached their quilt. "It's time to go."

Both looked up in surprise. "What?" Catherine squawked. "It's barely one thirty."

"Don't you recall? Daniel is driving you home today after dropping me off at the farm. You're eager to return to *mamm* and *daed*'s." Abby perched a hand on her hip.

Every drop of blood in her body seemed to have rushed to Catherine's face. "Oh…*jah*. I almost forgot," she stammered.

Abby could practically see the wheels turning in her head.

"I hate to be selfish and demanding, because I'm sure Daniel enjoys talking to the other men." Catherine smoothed her skirt with her palms.

"You're not demanding at all," said Abby. "Daniel is bringing the buggy up to load at the barn. I need to leave anyway because I'm expecting a visitor this afternoon." She stretched out her hand. "Let me help you up."

Catherine glanced at Isaiah before accepting the hand. His head rotated from one woman to the other in confusion. "*Danki,*" she said. Once on her feet, she pulled Abby away from the quilt. "There's been a change of plans," she whispered. "I believe I will stay longer."

"But your packed bag is sitting in the back of the buggy."

"I know, but you're the one who accused me of being impetuous."

"You insisted you'd considered the matter carefully."

"Can't a woman change her mind?" Catherine's whisper was close to a hiss, while she stood so that Isaiah couldn't possibly read her lips.

"*Jah, schwester,* you certainly can. And a mind like yours should be changed…often." Abby stepped back before Catherine could pinch her. "I'll see you later. I trust you can persuade Isaiah to bring you home."

Catherine placed both hands on her hips. "You'd better hurry along so you don't keep Daniel waiting."

Abby did hurry toward the buggy, chuckling all the way…until she remembered Nathan Fisher, and then her good mood vanished.

Abigail had enough time to bake brownies and brew fresh iced tea before Nathan drove into their side yard. Her *kinner* were taking a nap after their busy day, while Daniel tended the livestock. Upon hearing the crunch of gravel, she dried her hands on a towel and walked outdoors to meet her fate.

Mr. Fisher was leaning into his buggy from the passenger side. Abby couldn't see what he was fussing with, but when he straightened up his arms were filled with a patchwork quilt.

"Oh, my," she whispered, starting down the steps. "*Guder nachmittag,* Mr. Fisher. What have you got there?"

"Good afternoon, Mrs. Graber," he called on his approach.

She felt apprehension ripple up her back. *Fear is the handiwork of the devil,* she thought and sucked in a deep, calming breath.

"I thought you might like to see little Abraham," said Nathan. With the bundle tucked into the crook of one arm, he used his free hand to draw back one corner of the cover. "What do you think? Has he changed much since the last time you saw him?"

Memories of the worst night of her life crept from the recesses of her mind. She batted them away like thirsty mosquitoes. Rubbing her hands down her skirt, she leaned forward for a better view. The *boppli* had fisted one hand by his rosebud mouth, while the other gripped a small stuffed bear. Dark thick eyelashes fluttered while he slept, as though he dreamed of future summer days playing in the sun. His round cheeks were pink with vitality and dusted with a smattering of tan freckles. Abraham was the prettiest baby boy she had ever seen— except for her own Jake. "A handsome son," she said. "Thank you for showing him to me." She stepped back as though pressing business awaited her in the house.

"Don't you want to hold him?" He didn't wait for her response but foisted the sleeping child toward her.

"But I—" Without an option, Abby accepted the bundle, hoping he wouldn't awaken and start to fuss. She shifted him to the crook of her arm as Nathan had done. She felt a swell of emotion gazing on the peaceful face in repose.

"He might not be here if not for you," said Nathan with conviction.

"I don't know about that." Abby focused on the child instead of the *daed*.

"I know it. Your actions saved my son. If you had stood around twiddling your thumbs like the authorities would have had you do, he could have died."

She wanted to argue, to deny his assumptions, but her throat had constricted. Finally after a long moment, she whispered. "God chooses who lives and who dies."

"That's true, but I'm grateful for what you did. I don't care much about English laws. I'm glad they released you to come home to your family."

"So you know about that drug I gave her?"

"Of course I know. I'm glad you tried to save my Ruth. You did no wrong in my book. This baby was Ruth's choice—there's no arguing that. And everything else that happened was God's choice." He gently took the baby back as Abraham began to stir. "I just thought you would like to hear that from me."

"*Danki,* Mr. Fisher. I'm grateful to hear your words and pleased to see him thriving." Abby smiled for the first time since their arrival. "I'll enjoy watching him grow up over the coming years. I'm sure we'll cross paths at barn raisings and the like." They walked toward Nathan's buggy, where his horse stood flicking his tail and pawing at the dirt.

"Maybe not. In six months, when my farm lease is up, I intend to move back to Indiana. My parents and sisters and brothers live there, so I'll have help tending the boy. And Abe will grow up surrounded by plenty of cousins. One of Iris' sons plans to lease my farm after I move out. Sounds like one of her boys wants a home away from the rest of the clan." He laughed a rich, throaty sound. This made Abraham laugh too, while he kicked his legs within the confining quilt.

Nathan strapped the boy into the car seat. "*Danki,* Mrs. Graber. I will remember you each night in my prayers for the rest of my life. And when I tell my son about his *mamm,* I'll also tell him about you someday when he's old enough to understand." Then he climbed up, tipped his hat, and drove away.

Once the buggy turned the corner, Abby exhaled a sigh of relief. "Thank You, Lord, for Your gift of peace at long last."

Twenty

Early October

Boots lifted her head from the porch boards to stare at a fat brown squirrel. The audacious rodent had the effrontery to gather acorns within twenty feet of the steps. If the dog weren't tied up, that squirrel would be running for his life instead of gathering food for a long winter.

Isaiah smiled and patted Boots' head. The new red collar and chain were for her benefit. Otherwise, the dog would romp and play and then end up gasping for breath. Within a few weeks, Boots would be good as new again. Isaiah's readjustment period would take much longer, maybe even a full year. But when he returned to Shreve, Ohio, he would come back a different man.

And a beautiful, patient, kindhearted woman would be waiting for him—one who made the best banana nut bread in the county—only nobody had better tell his cousin Abby.

Catherine—*his Cat*. Each time he thought about her or saw her sweet face, he knew it would be worth any embarrassment, any discomfort he faced during the weeks ahead. He loved her and she loved him. Without means to express his heart or fully understand hers, they both just knew.

Yet he longed to communicate with a woman who seemed to enjoy communicating more than anything else. Cat liked talking better than swimming in the pond, riding horses across moonlit fields, or eating vanilla ice cream topped with fresh berries and whipped cream. Isaiah grinned as he remembered her attempts to teach him to lip-read. Every time he watched her lips, he yearned to lean over and kiss her…despite the fact that she had whacked him on the arm all three times he'd tried.

He'd hoped she might love him when their gazes met at the preaching service.

He'd figured she must love him to cull him from the herd of men gabbing outside the barn.

Then he felt certain of her love when she cried during her apology for the volleyball party. Catherine owed him no apology. She had tried to bring him back into the Amish flock with a pure heart. And for that he would be eternally grateful. Shame passed, and prideful hurt feelings faded away. Pretty soon he found himself alone with only his thoughts. Boots might be his best friend, but she made poor company asleep by the fire on long winter nights. And no man wanted to grow old by himself.

Isaiah called the dog inside, combed his still-damp hair, and put on his hat. He'd been invited to supper at Daniel and Abby's. Together he and Cat would tell them of their plan, although he didn't understand all the details yet himself. Catherine had found a school for those like him—who could neither hear nor talk well—a school that accepted adults. His rare if not unique situation had generated interest with people who studied such things. He would live at the facility and work in exchange for his room and board. Whatever other expenses he encountered Catherine insisted they would find a way to pay. This wouldn't be easy. Figuring out what Cat was proposing hadn't been easy, but she would be here when he came home. And that was all he needed to know.

Isaiah arrived at the Graber kitchen promptly at five thirty. Catherine swept open the door looking pleased to see him. Abby joined her sister in the doorway. "Welcome," she said. "Come in." Abby pointed to a seat at the table, where Laura and Jake were already waiting. They waved their greeting, but Catherine's was the most enthusiastic by far. As soon as Abby turned her back, Cat pressed a kiss to his cheek and then began carrying bowls and platters of food. Isaiah sat down, anxious for the meal to be over and eager for some private time with Cat.

Maybe they would rock in the porch swing or ride across the newly harvested fields where corn had stood tall this past summer. Or maybe they would grab the flashlight and hike to their secret garden—one even the children hadn't discovered. Soon Daniel entered the kitchen carrying a parcel, and they all bowed their heads. Isaiah duplicated their behavior, but he didn't know whom they talked to with their eyes closed. Sometimes he saw their lips barely moving, or they would hold their breath for a moment. Who was this God Catherine talked about? Isaiah couldn't imagine a person no one could see or hear but could still feel His presence. And this person loved him even though he'd never met Him? How could anyone be everywhere at once and still know what goes on inside people's hearts?

This was far more confusing than anything that had happened in school all those years ago and more bewildering than this special school in a faraway state. Yet when he'd seen the way Cat's eyes shone every time she spoke of Him, he yearned to know more…about this God who could love even a backward man like him.

Catherine slipped into the chair next to Isaiah, grateful when Daniel came downstairs. He placed a wrapped package on the table but waited until after silent prayers to explain. "I bought something for

Isaiah," he announced, while Abby began passing the platter of meat-loaf and redskin potatoes.

When five pairs of eyes focused on him, Isaiah looked at Catherine with a perplexed shrug of his shoulders.

"It's a gift," she mouthed. "Open the package."

He looked nervous as he pulled off the ribbon and paper. Inside he found a brand-new Bible, which he held up for all to see. He studied the binding and cover and began leafing through it.

"It's in English, not German, because the only words he knows are English," declared Daniel. "I thought it was time he had his own Bible."

"That's a good idea, now that he'll be coming to preaching with us," added Abby. She placed a chicken leg on each of the *kinner*'s plates.

Catherine glanced at Isaiah. He had set the present aside, and seemed more interested in the bowl of buttered noodles. "*Jah,* that's *gut,*" she said to Daniel. "I'm in the process of explaining about the Good Book, but it'll take some time." She selected a small breast and scoop of yellow beans for her own plate. "But I do have some news to report." She waited until Isaiah looked over at her. "I told you that Isaiah agreed to attend school, even if it means being away from his cabin for many months. He understands that the other students will be deaf like him and with varying amounts of speech ability."

Abby and Daniel paused in their suppers to give Catherine their complete attention.

"I've found the perfect residential school in Kentucky. It's part of a teacher training facility connected to a large university. The program not only takes adult students, but they have accepted Isaiah into a work-study program. He can defray most of his boarding expenses by working on campus."

Abby appeared jubilant, but Daniel's expression turned skeptical. "I trust you have explained that Isaiah is Amish and therefore inexperienced with electric power tools and whatnot." He cocked his head to one side. "What kind of work can he do for them?"

"He can operate gas-powered lawn mowers, weed-whackers, and

rototillers," interjected Abby. "Will he work with the landscaping department?"

Catherine forked up some yellow beans and smiled with appreciation at her *schwester*. After she thoroughly chewed and wiped her mouth, she answered her brother-in-law. "Not to worry. They understand he's Amish. Plenty of Plain folk have moved to the state because of cheaper land prices than here in Ohio or in Pennsylvania. I think they are curious about us and want Isaiah in this federally funded program. Besides, the director said they could put him to work in the equine barns. The college is located near Lexington, in the heart of Kentucky thoroughbred country." She picked up her piece of chicken for a bite. "I wonder if their grass really looks blue."

"Blue grass?" Daniel looked from his wife back to her. "I suppose you told them about Isaiah's riding abilities in your letter of application."

"I might have mentioned it." Catherine laughed and winked at Isaiah. The man understood he was their topic of conversation, but he contented himself with the delicious meal.

"On behalf of Isaiah, I thank you for the Bible," Catherine said to Daniel. She placed her hand lovingly atop the book. "This is one reason why I want him to go to school. They have experts to teach the deaf lip-reading, sign language, and how to read. I'm not equipped to handle this on my own. I've made some progress, but I can't teach him to read. And I can't teach him about God until he learns to read." She glanced from one to the other.

"Isaiah's been away from formal education for a while," said Daniel after a moment. "This will be a long road for him."

"A long road for both of you if my assumptions are correct." Abby arched a brow above her sapphire blue eyes.

Catherine felt a blush rise up her neck to flood her face. "You are correct, sister. He cares for me and I care for him. We're officially courting, I suppose, even though he doesn't know the rules and customs that courting entails."

"Does he have any idea what he's getting himself into with one of the Yost gals?"

Abby slapped her *ehemann*'s arm playfully.

Catherine gazed at Isaiah, who had finished his supper and sat watching her. "I think he suspects but is willing to take a chance anyway."

"Aren't you glad you didn't rush home?" Abby popped a bean into her mouth.

"Truly, I am. He told me he actually liked the volleyball party despite everybody talking to him at once. So it's not just for my sake that he wishes to communicate better. I believe he wants to give the world another try. It must get lonely up in the woods with only wildlife, Cora, and Boots for company." Recognizing his dog's name, Isaiah reached over and took her hand. She savored his touch more than she would have thought possible.

"Does this mean you'll stay here with us?" asked Laura, turning her huge brown eyes toward her aunt.

"At least until Isaiah leaves for school."

"You had better stick around while he's in school too. The teachers might need to talk to his family from time to time, and I still have my cell phone." Abby winked with her smuggest smile.

"Besides," added Daniel. "Who'll take care of the *kinner* if my *fraa* stays at some farm all night, waiting for a *boppli* to arrive? You've grown on me, Catherine. The house won't be the same if you return to your *mamm* and *daed*'s." He leaned back while tightening his grip on Abby's hand.

"Have you decided to go back to work as a midwife?" Catherine asked Abby, straightening in her chair. "You told me you would never go back."

"I haven't made up my mind. Five thousand dollars is a lot of money, but I no longer feel confident in my abilities." Abby lifted her chin and set her jaw. "Let's not talk about this right now," she said with a wave of her hand.

Catherine nodded, exhaling as though a great weight had been lifted. "If *mamm* can spare me, maybe I'll stay through the winter, but I must talk to her first before I decide one way or the other."

"What will happen after Isaiah finishes school?" asked Abby. "Will you marry and live in his cabin in the woods? I think we could add on and make changes so you wouldn't have to take your shower in the barn." She fought back her grin.

"I don't believe the bishop would allow her to move into the cabin *without* marrying first," Daniel teased. Abby looked aghast and gave his arm a second slap.

Catherine rolled her eyes. "Will you two listen to yourselves? You'll be picking out the color of my rocking chair lap robe if I don't stop you now. Can't a woman see what plans God has in store for her?"

"Good idea, as long as you don't move away and take my cousin along. Isaiah is my right hand man until Jake gets a little older." Daniel ruffled his son's silky hair.

"You'll mess up your life if I don't butt my nose in," muttered Abby under her breath.

Catherine's hand shot out for a quick pinch. "How could I possibly go home? Life would be so dull because Meghan is no match for your sharp tongue." She rose to her feet and carried her and Isaiah's plates to the sink. "You know what? I think I might mess things up if I do the dishes. What if I break something? I'd better leave them to your capable hands." Catherine ran toward the door with Isaiah on her heels. The two fled into the cool night before Abby could protest.

Without need for discussion, Catherine and Isaiah headed down the path toward the orchard and dark looming woods. A chilly breeze blew from the north, bringing the scent of pine and tang of wood smoke from someone's fire miles away. Catherine had forgotten her sweater in her haste to escape the untidy Graber kitchen. Yet she knew she wouldn't get cold that night. She had a large calloused hand to hold and the sweet promise of new love to warm her from the inside out.

As the evening star rose in the west, she tried to see past Venus to catch a glimpse of God—the One who had made this and all good things possible.

When Abby glanced out the window, she spotted Daniel approaching from the pump house. He usually brought in the mail and newspaper on his way to lunch, but today his hands were empty. Lately the man had grown forgetful, content merely to spend his free time in her company. *I may as well enjoy it while it lasts,* she thought, heading out the front door on the errand herself.

Daniel was sitting at the table when she returned. He stretched out a hand for the paper. "*Ach, gut,* you fetched the *Budget.*"

Abby ignored his allusion to her being a dog and began opening the mail. One pink envelope had caught her attention. "Here's a letter from Rachelle, my former roommate at Hotel Wooster." She smiled, remembering Rachelle's moniker for the jail. "My goodness, it has a Soddy Daisy, Tennessee, return address—that's where her *grossmammi* lived." Abby tore open the envelope and read aloud.

Hi, Abby,

Check out the postmark—I'm in Tennessee. I was released early on probation and went to live at a women's group home that the Bible teacher told me about. Well, long story short, when I called my grandmother collect, she was not only happy to hear from me, but she also sent me three Greyhound bus tickets to come see her. I had to get permission from my probation officer to travel out of state, but when he agreed, I was on my way to the land of the Volunteers. That's what they call themselves. When Gram asked me to move into her spare room to help her take care of the place, I thought, "Why not?" I *love it here and my children do too. I got a part-time job as a salad girl at Appleby's that might become full-time next year if I work hard. It's good to make a fresh start. And, after all, Gram needs help in her yard too, because folks in a town called Soddy Daisy don't tolerate weedy flower beds. Write when you get a chance. I'll never forget you.*

Fondly, Rachelle

Abby swallowed down the large lump that had formed in her throat. *Watch over her, Lord, and keep her safe,* she whispered and then pawed through the rest of the mail.

"A letter from Dr. Weller," she announced, pulling it from the business envelope.

Daniel glanced up from the farm commodity prices. "What's he got to say? Is he begging you to come back to work? If you return to midwifery, we can use the five thousand in our savings account toward school tuition for Isaiah."

She studied him for a moment. They had had this particular discussion about her retirement several times. She wasn't comfortable placing herself in a precarious situation again—for the new mother or for herself. What if the doctor wasn't able to come when needed? Plain women had the habit of calling the midwife first and anybody else only when things went haywire. History could easily repeat itself if she went back because Dr. Weller was spread too thin to be counted on arriving anywhere on time.

Shaking off an uncomfortable feeling, Abby silently read the typed letter from her friend and former mentor, and then she stared at the sheet long after she finished.

Daniel scrambled to his feet and began pulling lunchmeat and cheese from the refrigerator drawer. "Looks like a man must fend for himself when his *fraa* receives so much urgent correspondence."

Abby scanned the letter's contents a second time before dropping it to the countertop. She reached for the bread and a tomato from the windowsill as hope and joy filled her heart. "Doc Weller has hired a new employee," she stated, slicing the tomato. "Apparently, a licensed midwife has moved to the area."

Silence spun out in the drowsy-warm room. Then Daniel asked, "To Shreve?"

"*Jah.* She's a registered nurse who worked in a Columbus hospital for twenty years in the ER. Her husband has retired, and they have bought a small farm outside town. He wishes to try his hand at raising alpacas." She wiggled her eyebrows at him.

Daniel snorted. "Dumb as sheep, those critters, but I guess you can get a decent price for their wool. I've heard some Plain folk have jumped on that bandwagon as well."

"But they have faces cute enough to kiss. Anyway, this nurse wants only to deliver babies in the Amish community, a sort of a semiretirement. She grew up Mennonite but left the faith during college." Abby chewed on her lower lip to steady her nerves.

"This nurse thinks attending expectant women in Wayne County would be akin to *retirement*? Does she have any idea what the birthrate is among the Amish?" His laughter filled the house and spilled out the open windows.

Abby chuckled too, remembering the time she had spent twenty-four hours waiting for a baby who refused to make a timely appearance. "If a person fully understood how perilous the journey is, no one would take that first step." She placed the bread and vegetables on the table and bowed her head to give thanks.

When she looked up she met her husband's gaze. "What else does Doc Weller say?" he asked.

"He wants me to assist the new midwife to lessen his workload. He doesn't want to be dragged out at all hours of the night to deliver

healthy babies to healthy women. He wants me to come back to work."
Abby lowered her voice to not betray her emotions.

"What do you plan to do, Abigail?" Daniel asked as he put his sandwich together.

"I thought you wanted me to stop working, to no longer be on call
all hours of the day and night. You said you wanted me home tending my family."

"That was before Judge O'Neil slapped you with a five-thousand-
dollar fine."

"Is it because of the amount of the fine? That's why you wish me to
go back?" Disappointment welled in her belly. Daniel had never been
overly motivated by money before.

"No. Using our savings to help Isaiah attend that school would be
an added benefit, that's all." He laid his sandwich on the plate. "What
I want is for you to be happy."

She was quick to defend herself. "I'm happy providing for my family and raising my *kinner.* I don't need to work to find contentment."

"I know that, but I also know you love bringing babies into the
world. And you were good at it. Not everyone has the patience or the
stomach to sit through long, drawn-out labors. Don't be in a hurry
to dismiss this, Abby. A licensed midwife moving to Shreve changes
everything, so don't doubt or second-guess yourself. If your heart leads
you back to work, then go with confidence. We will be fine. I've even
learned how to brew a pitcher of iced tea on my own." His grin was
downright prideful.

She clucked her tongue. "Wonders never cease while married to
you, Daniel Graber."

"Nor to you, Mrs. Graber." He winked and picked up his sandwich again.

Abby thought she might mull it over for a few days, spend some
time in prayer, or maybe even talk to her *daed* about the matter. Yet by
the time she finished her turkey and cheese, she'd made up her mind.
Some decisions needed no epiphanies of insight to understand what
she was meant to do. "I'll call Dr. Weller on my cell phone, once it's

charged up again. I'll tell him I'll come back on a trial basis. Maybe he has already hired someone else. Maybe the Columbus nurse and I won't see eye to eye. Maybe I'll get called out too often—Laura and Jake are still too young to be left alone should Catherine return to *mamm*'s while Isaiah's gone. A six-month trial period will allow things to sort out."

Daniel pulled on his beard. "Your time spent in the county 'hotel' did some good after all. You're thinking much more intelligently than in the old days."

He fled the kitchen so fast, the dishrag she hurled connected with only the pine panel of the back door. But Abby couldn't disagree with his assessment. Every one of life's trials or bumps in the road brought with it a better understanding of God's plan. *If I can just keep still and listen.*

That night being still wasn't difficult to do. As Jake and Laura chased around the yard, trying to capture the last of the season's fireflies, Abby and Daniel rocked on the porch content to enjoy the waning fair weather. Soon a heavy frost would put an end to the lightning bugs decorating the pasture with tiny points of light. Strong winds from the west would curtail porch sitting until next year.

But Abby had tonight to sit dreaming that her life would be long and fruitful, that her *kinner* would remain at this age forever, and the love she felt for Daniel would never ebb. Because if wealth could be measured by the number of life's joyous moments, Abigail Graber was a rich woman indeed.

Epilogue

Abby stepped onto a dew-damp porch and breathed in the frigid air. This wasn't a crisp fall evening or the usual weather of autumn. It was downright cold for the third week of November. Tightening her wool cape around her shoulders, she picked her way gingerly down the stone walk to the barn. A thin coating of frost made for slow progress.

"It's too early in the season for this nonsense," she muttered under her breath, even while her heart expanded with joyful anticipation. A baby was on the way. Another one of God's blessings was about to make his or her arrival. As usual, she sent up a short prayer for a safe, speedy delivery. The call from Isabel Taylor, the new midwife in the area, came ten minutes ago, just after she put on her soft flannel nightgown and slipped into bed, snug as a bug, as her *mamm* used to say. This would be her third assist on a home delivery since returning to work—once for Dr. Weller and twice for the licensed midwife. Isabel's business card read "Serving Wayne County," which she thought at the time would be no problem. After all, she owned a new four-wheel drive pickup capable of cutting through snowed-in driveways and traversing mud-rutted farm lanes. And it was appreciably faster than a horse and buggy. But true to Daniel's predictions, the Amish birthrate and requests for fill-ins at the modern birthing center in Baltic had Isabel hopping like a cricket.

Daniel was leading the mare by her bridle by the time Abby reached the barn. "Don't be driving her faster than a trot," he cautioned. "These roads will be slick tonight. Nobody has the salt trucks ready this early in the year." He smiled at her before turning his face up to study one low ominous cloud. "We'll be lucky not to get snowed in by morning."

As she looked too, a slice of moon peeked through an opening in the clouds. Beyond it, the starry sky looked infinitely, profoundly distant. She stepped up and took the reins for him. "Back to bed with you. Milking time will be here soon enough."

She was halfway down the drive before she heard him call, "Let's hope it's a girl or a boy this time."

And, as usual, she smiled.

About ninety minutes later, Abby turned up the lane of the expectant mother. Isabel's shiny black truck sat close to the porch steps. Abby hefted her tote bag from the buggy and walked into a warm, cheery kitchen. Every kerosene lamp had been lit, three stove burners held a pot of simmering water, and on the fourth a saucepan simmered. Chicken soup? Maybe a hearty broth for the new mother.

Abby washed up at the sink and then entered the large bedroom, equally well illuminated.

"Hi, Abby," sang Isabel. "You're right on time for the fun part. You already know Sarah, and this will be her sixth child, so things are moving along quickly. She barely had time to finish knitting the socks and sweaters she'd started."

"*Guder nachmittag,*" said Sarah in between panting breaths. "*Danki* for coming." The woman's contractions indicated the *boppli* would arrive within minutes, not hours, yet Sarah still managed a polite demeanor as though greeting a fellow district member at a quilting bee.

"Good evening to you. Looks like you and Isabel have this situation so well under control that I might as well sip tea in the kitchen and eat some of your cookies. Everyone raves about your snickerdoodles."

Sarah laughed so hard her next contraction caught her breathlessly gasping for air. "You go on in and make yourself comfortable. Me and my newest youngin will be joining you shortly."

And she wasn't too far off with her approximation. Within fifteen minutes, Elijah joined his Amish community with squalling, lively enthusiasm. He wouldn't remain their youngest district member for long, however. Three more arrivals were expected before Christmas. While Isabel delivered the afterbirth and tended to the mother, Abby washed the new baby at the sink and wrapped him snuggly in a receiving blanket. Sarah's husband held the infant close to the woodstove while Abby went outside to bury the placenta.

This was her least favorite part of the job, but as the assistant, the chore fell to her. Behind the house, she spotted several kerosene lanterns close to the fence line and a tall, thin girl standing with shovel in hand. Sarah's eldest daughter beckoned her with a wave. "I dug this earlier today, before the chill set in," the girl said proudly. "Is it deep enough?"

Abby glanced down at a hole large enough for a small cow. "*Danki,*" Abby said, "This is a big help to me."

"No trouble whatsoever." The girl stood ready to finish the job.

When they completed the task, Abby turned back toward the house as tears rushed expectedly to her eyes. "And *danki* to You, Lord," she whispered. She blinked them back as best she could as the first snow of the season drifted down on the peaceful, sleeping town of Shreve.

Catherine glanced at the steps once more as she gave the oatmeal a final stir. This was the third time she'd reheated it, and if Abby didn't come down soon it would harden into a block of cement. Daniel and Isaiah had gone to cut more firewood in the hills. Snow before

Christmas usually foretold a long, cold winter. Laura left to walk to school with a neighbor girl, while Jake had taken his building blocks to the front room after breakfast.

"Good morning," Abby crowed, slipping her apron over her head.

"Finally! I thought you'd never get out of bed." Catherine reached for a cup. "I'll bet you can use some of this." She filled it to the rim with strong hot coffee.

"*Danki*," said Abby. "I didn't get home until two o'clock this morning. Mrs. Yoder chose the middle of the night to deliver. I'm glad Isabel picked me up and brought me home. I certainly don't like driving the buggy at night when it's snowing." She sipped her coffee and peered into the saucepan. "What's that—wallpaper paste? You know *daed* will never let us have anything other than plain painted walls."

"Ha-ha. Very funny." Catherine tried to scoop some into a bowl, but it refused to come off the serving spoon. "It wouldn't be half as sticky if you hadn't slept so late. I reheated it three times." She whacked the spoon on the side of the bowl, yet still the oats wouldn't dislodge.

Abby leaned over and kissed Catherine's cheek. "I don't mean to hurt your feelings, but I think I'll have a bowl of cornflakes."

Catherine nodded and set the pot aside to deal with later. "Maybe the sow won't be so picky," she said. "I received some news from home. A letter from *mamm* arrived yesterday while you were at the Yoders'."

Abby settled into a chair with her cold cereal. "Is everyone well? You look upset."

Catherine hadn't wished to reveal her feelings. "Everyone is fine—no worries there, but I had wanted to stay here while Isaiah attends school in Kentucky." She slumped into a chair.

"And you know we want you to stay. Does *mamm* need your help?"

"No, Meghan does."

"Really? She is a nanny for some nice *Englischers* down the road. What could our little sister possibly need help with?"

"She has quit her nanny job. Apparently, the schoolteacher is in a family way and will not be returning to the classroom after Christmas."

Abby's brows lifted. "Oh, no."

"Oh, yes. Meghan begged *daed* to appoint her as the replacement teacher, at least for the remainder of the school year."

"That might not be a good idea."

"She's been working as the teacher's assistant for a month to learn the job. Unfortunately, there are far more rambunctious boys in school than quiet, docile little girls, and it doesn't look like Meghan will be able to handle them once she's there alone."

"And that's where you come in?" Abby's question was filled with compassion.

"*Jah.* Because I'm twenty-three and Meghan is only nineteen, *daed* wants me to be the head teacher. Meghan will be my assistant for the term in hopes of assuming the position next fall."

Abby reached for Catherine's hand. "This will be a trial by fire. Do you remember what Meghan was like as a student?"

"I'm trying to forget the time she locked her teacher in the outhouse."

Abby bit her lower lip. "Hopefully, none of the current students have heard that story."

"I had hoped to remain here, planning the addition and changes to the cabin during the year Isaiah is gone." Catherine rose to her feet. "But because our sister needs me, home I will go. After all, with what I've learned about patience and forbearance, how much trouble can a room full of scholars be?" She walked to the stove for the pot of coffee, giving Abby a chance to stop laughing…and to start praying.

Being a mother, she knew *exactly* how much trouble a room full of *kinner* could be.

Discussion Questions

1. Well aware of her doctor's advice, why would Ruth Fisher endanger her own life to give birth? Infertility is heartbreaking for all couples, but how is it uniquely tragic for an Amish woman?

2. What are some reasons why Nathan is initially reluctant to handle his newborn son?

3. Abby is stoic even while facing bail set at half a million dollars. What does she turn to during her incarceration?

4. Why is Daniel resentful of Catherine and reluctant to answer her questions regarding his cousin Isaiah?

5. Why is the Grabers' Amish district in such a quandary about raising Abby's bail?

6. Dr. Weller's visit is pivotal for Abby. What information does he convey that helps her to deal with separation from her family?

7. Aunt Iris at times seems impatient with her nephew. Why does she demand so much from a young man trying to come to terms with loss?

8. What gifts has God given Isaiah that more than make up for his lack of hearing and speech?

9. Frightening news from her public defender sends Abby deep into the Old Testament. What stories and biblical heroes help her to keep her faith?

10. Daniel gets a firsthand look at Catherine and Isaiah during the swimming outing. Why is he softening his attitude toward his sister-in-law?

11. Why does Nathan finally reach out to the English social worker?

12. When the judge has a change of heart, Abby has an opportunity to go home. Why does she choose to return to her jail cell instead?

13. Although the Amish rarely display temper, what causes Nathan to lash out at the other grief therapy participants?

14. What sours Abby's poignant visit with Daniel and her beloved children during their jail visitation?

15. What happened in Isaiah's past that makes outings among other people, both Amish and English, difficult for him?

16. Why does Abigail change her mind about revealing the person who had supplied the anti-hemorrhage drug?

17. When Isaiah takes Catherine to his "secret garden," why does he relent and agree to go to the volleyball party?

18. Abby makes an unlikely friend while incarcerated. How does this friendship benefit both women?

19. Why had Nathan stayed away from church services for so long?

20. What is Isaiah missing in his life that makes Catherine bound and determined to teach him to speak, and especially to read?

About the Author

Mary Ellis grew up close to the eastern Ohio Amish Community, Geauga County, where her parents often took her to farmers' markets and woodworking fairs. She and her husband now live in Medina County, close to the largest population of Amish families, and enjoy the simple way of life.

Abigail's New Hope is the first book in The Wayne County Series. Discover Mary's other books, especially the bestselling Miller Family Series, at

maryeellis@yahoo.com

or

www.harvesthousepublishers.com